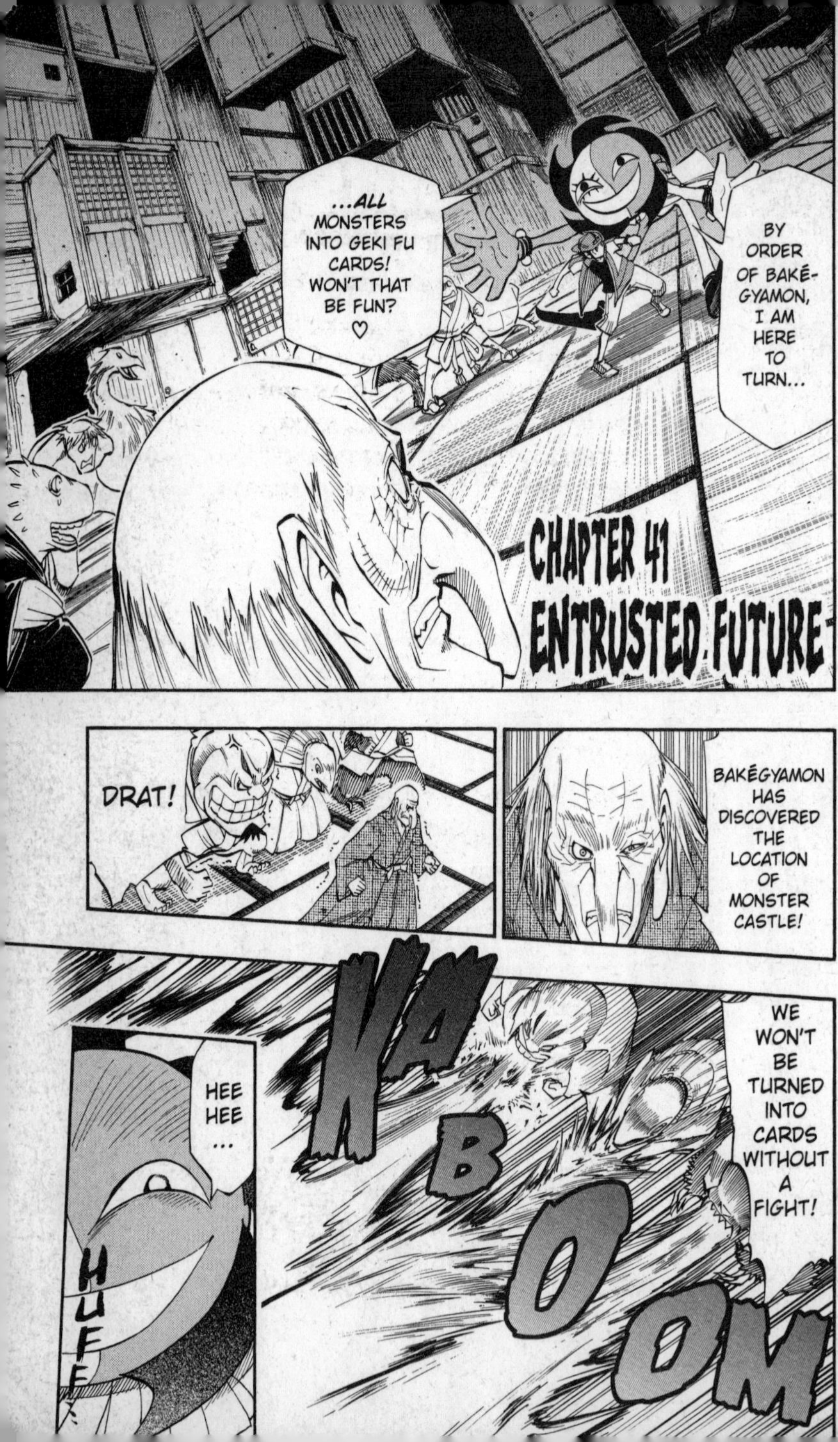
BY ORDER OF BAKÉ-GYAMON, I AM HERE TO TURN...
...ALL MONSTERS INTO GEKI FU CARDS! WON'T THAT BE FUN? ♡
CHAPTER 41
ENTRUSTED FUTURE
BAKÉGYAMON HAS DISCOVERED THE LOCATION OF MONSTER CASTLE!
DRAT!
WE WON'T BE TURNED INTO CARDS WITHOUT A FIGHT!
KABOOM
HEE HEE ...
HUFF

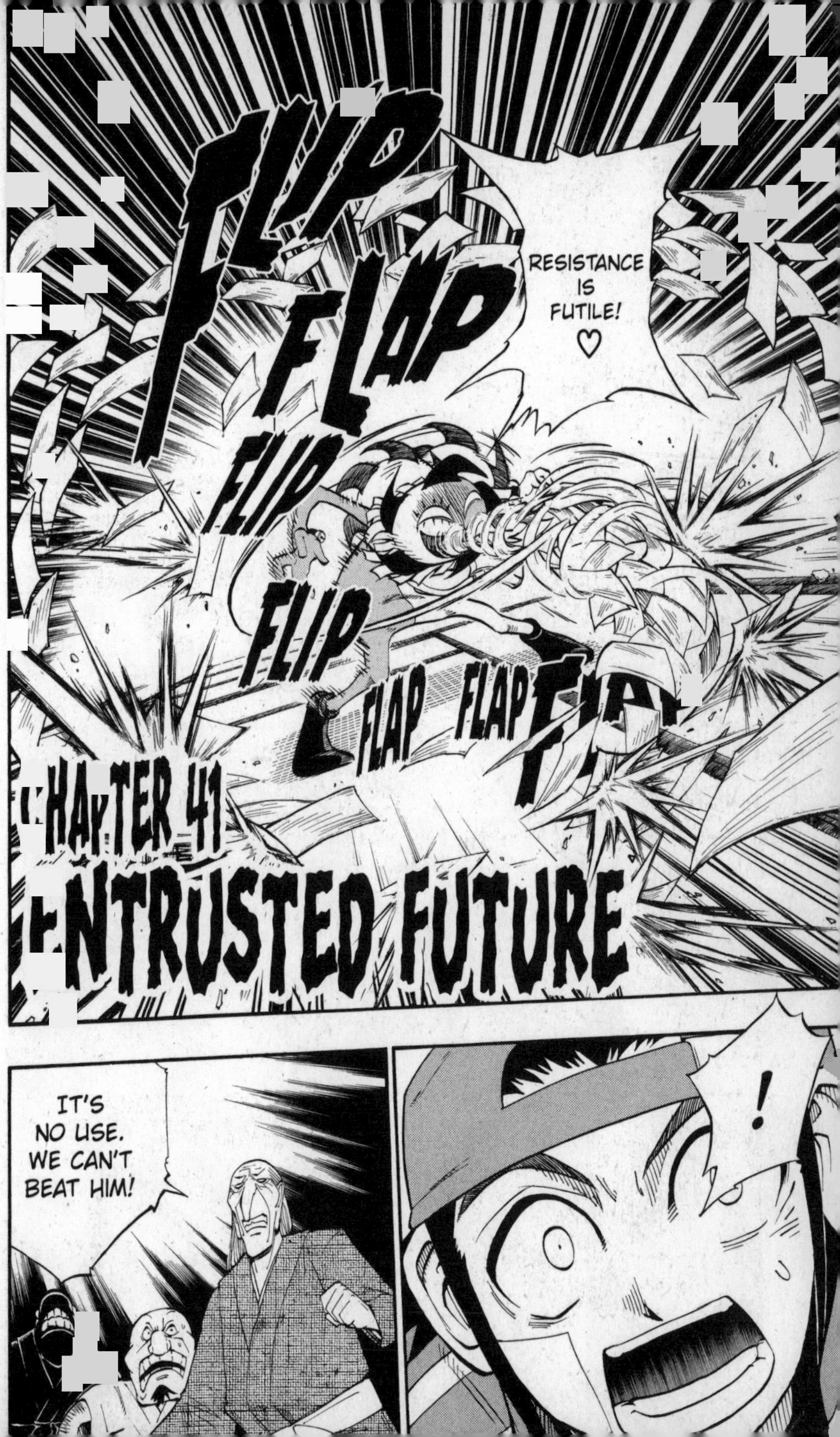
FLIP
FLAP
RESISTANCE IS FUTILE! ♡
FLIP
FLIP
FLAP FLAP
CHAPTER 41
ENTRUSTED FUTURE
!
IT'S NO USE. WE CAN'T BEAT HIM!

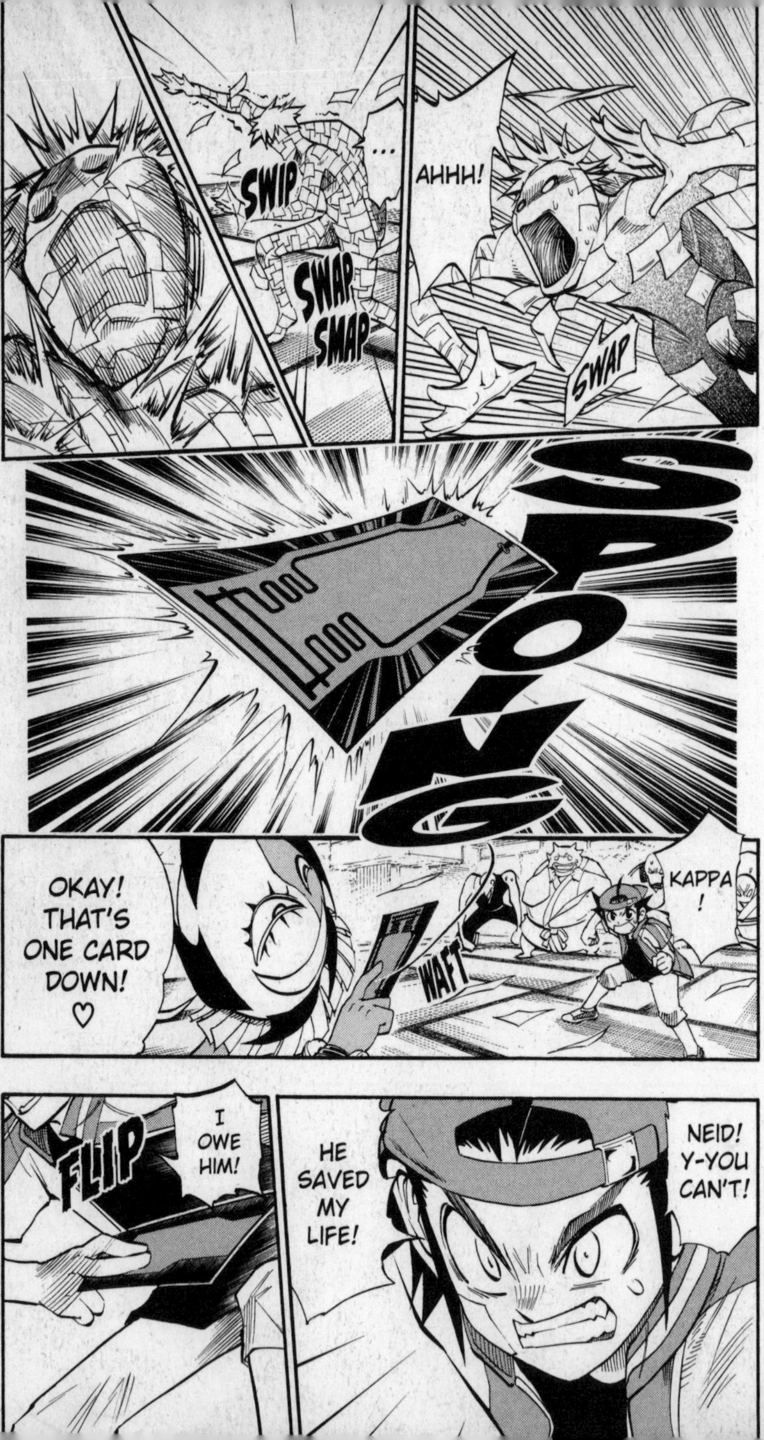
AHHH!
SWAP
...
SWIP
SWAP
SMAP
SPOING
KAPPA!
WAFT
OKAY! THAT'S ONE CARD DOWN! ♡
NEID! Y-YOU CAN'T!
HE SAVED MY LIFE!
I OWE HIM!
FLIP

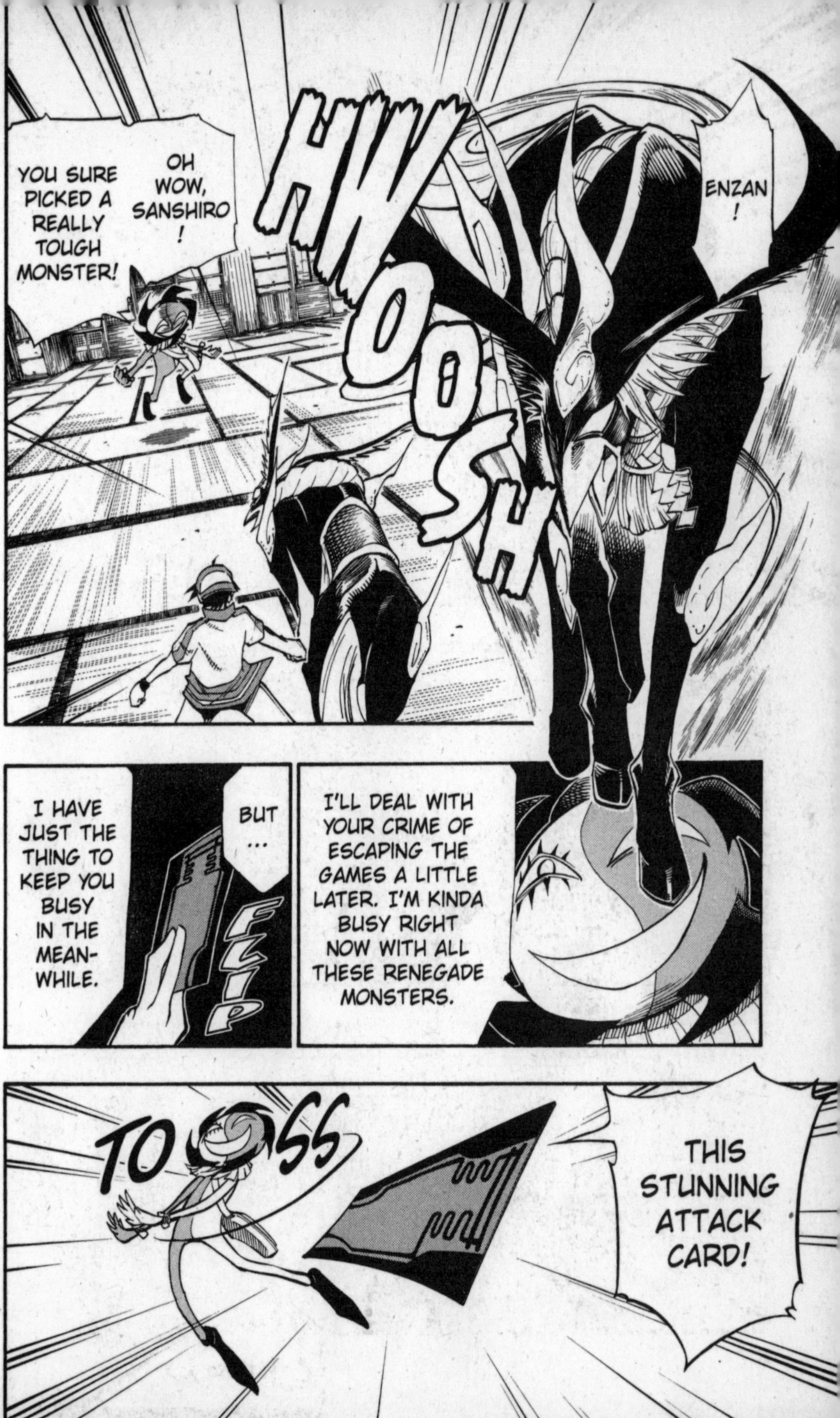
ENZAN!
OH WOW, SANSHIRO!
YOU SURE PICKED A REALLY TOUGH MONSTER!
HWOOOSH
I'LL DEAL WITH YOUR CRIME OF ESCAPING THE GAMES A LITTLE LATER. I'M KINDA BUSY RIGHT NOW WITH ALL THESE RENEGADE MONSTERS.
BUT...
I HAVE JUST THE THING TO KEEP YOU BUSY IN THE MEAN-WHILE.
FLIP
THIS STUNNING ATTACK CARD!
TOSS

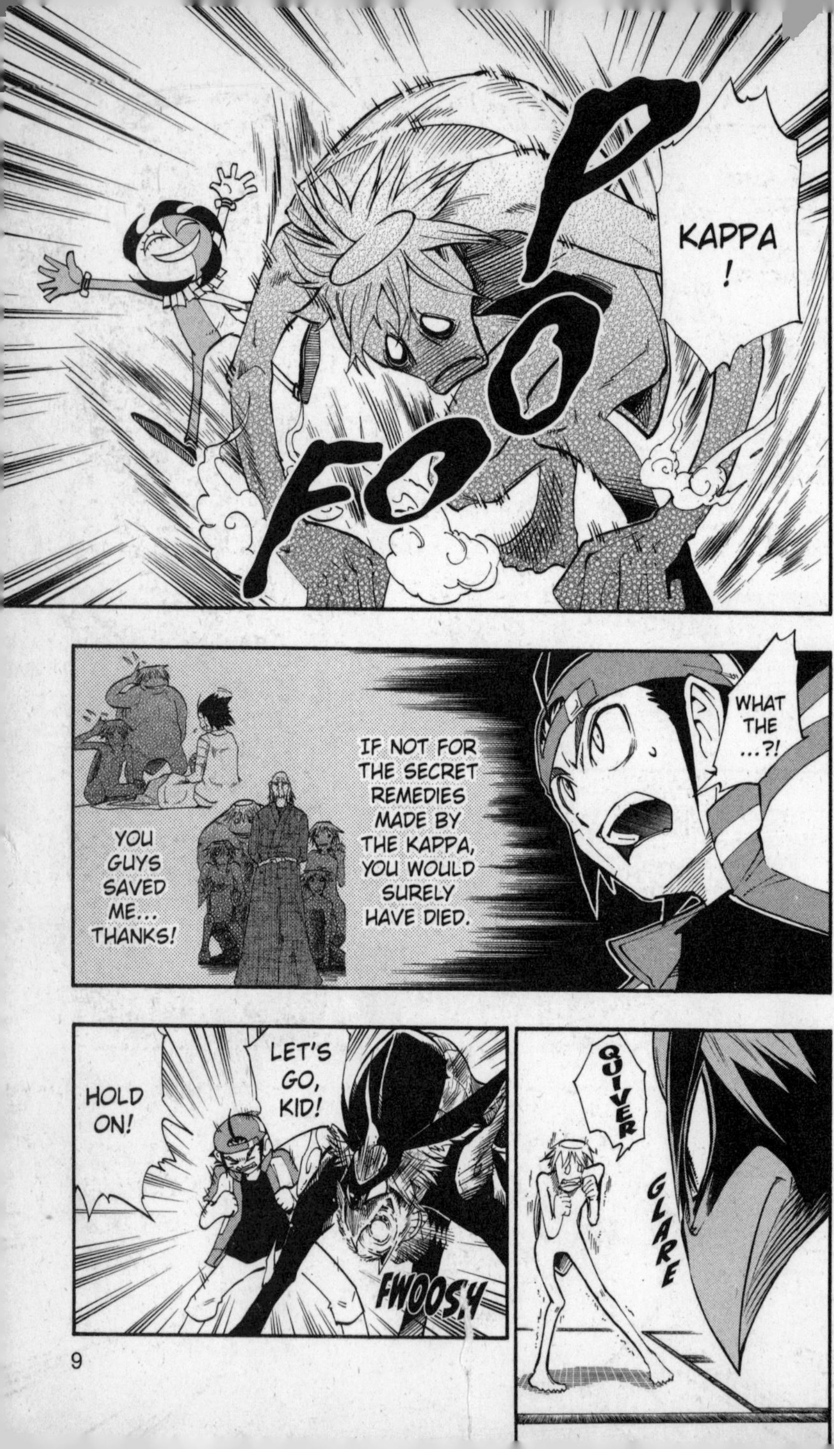
POOF
KAPPA!
WHAT THE ...?!
IF NOT FOR THE SECRET REMEDIES MADE BY THE KAPPA, YOU WOULD SURELY HAVE DIED.
YOU GUYS SAVED ME... THANKS!
QUIVER
GLARE
LET'S GO, KID!
HOLD ON!
FWOOSH

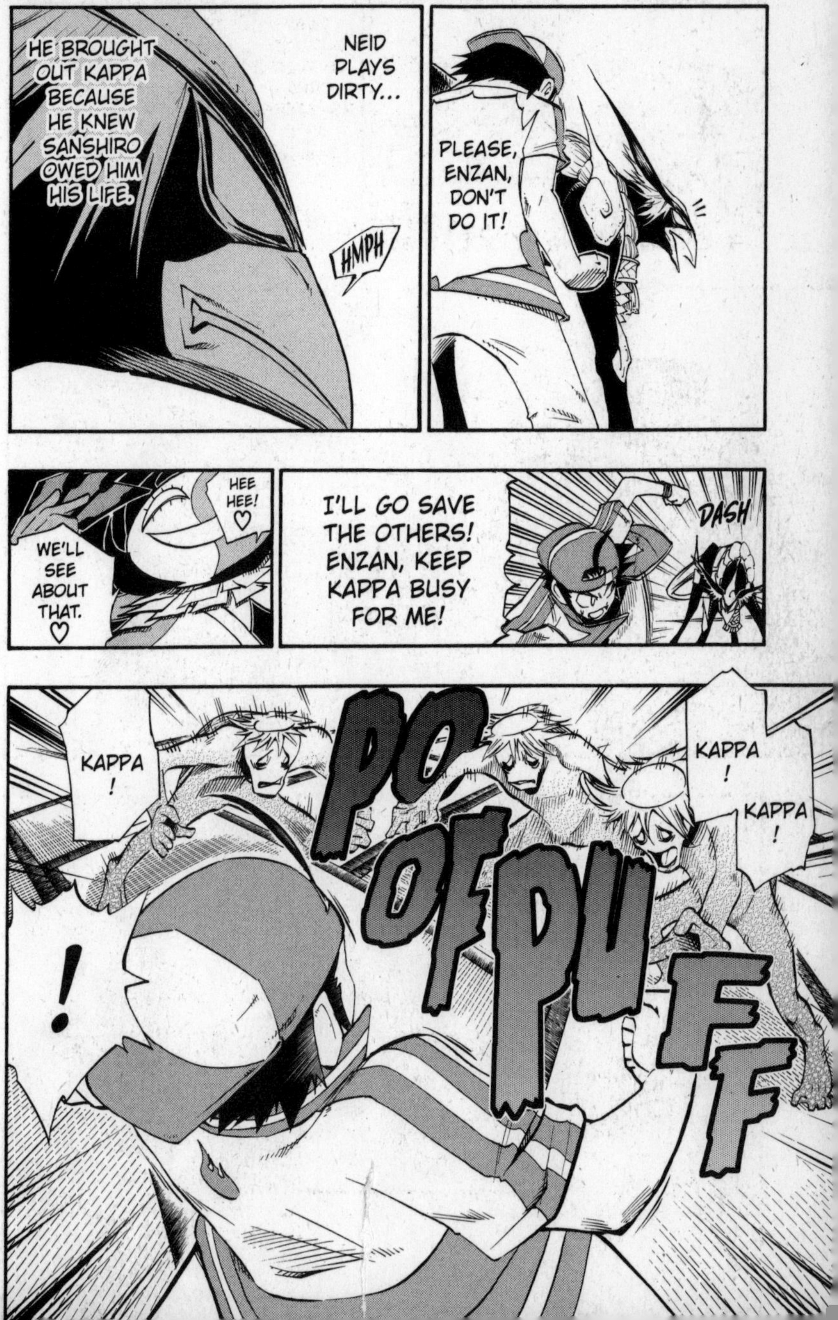
PLEASE, ENZAN, DON'T DO IT!
NEID PLAYS DIRTY...
HE BROUGHT OUT KAPPA BECAUSE HE KNEW SANSHIRO OWED HIM HIS LIFE.
HMPH
I'LL GO SAVE THE OTHERS! ENZAN, KEEP KAPPA BUSY FOR ME!
DASH
HEE HEE! ♡
WE'LL SEE ABOUT THAT. ♡
KAPPA!
KAPPA!
POOF
PUFF
KAPPA!
!

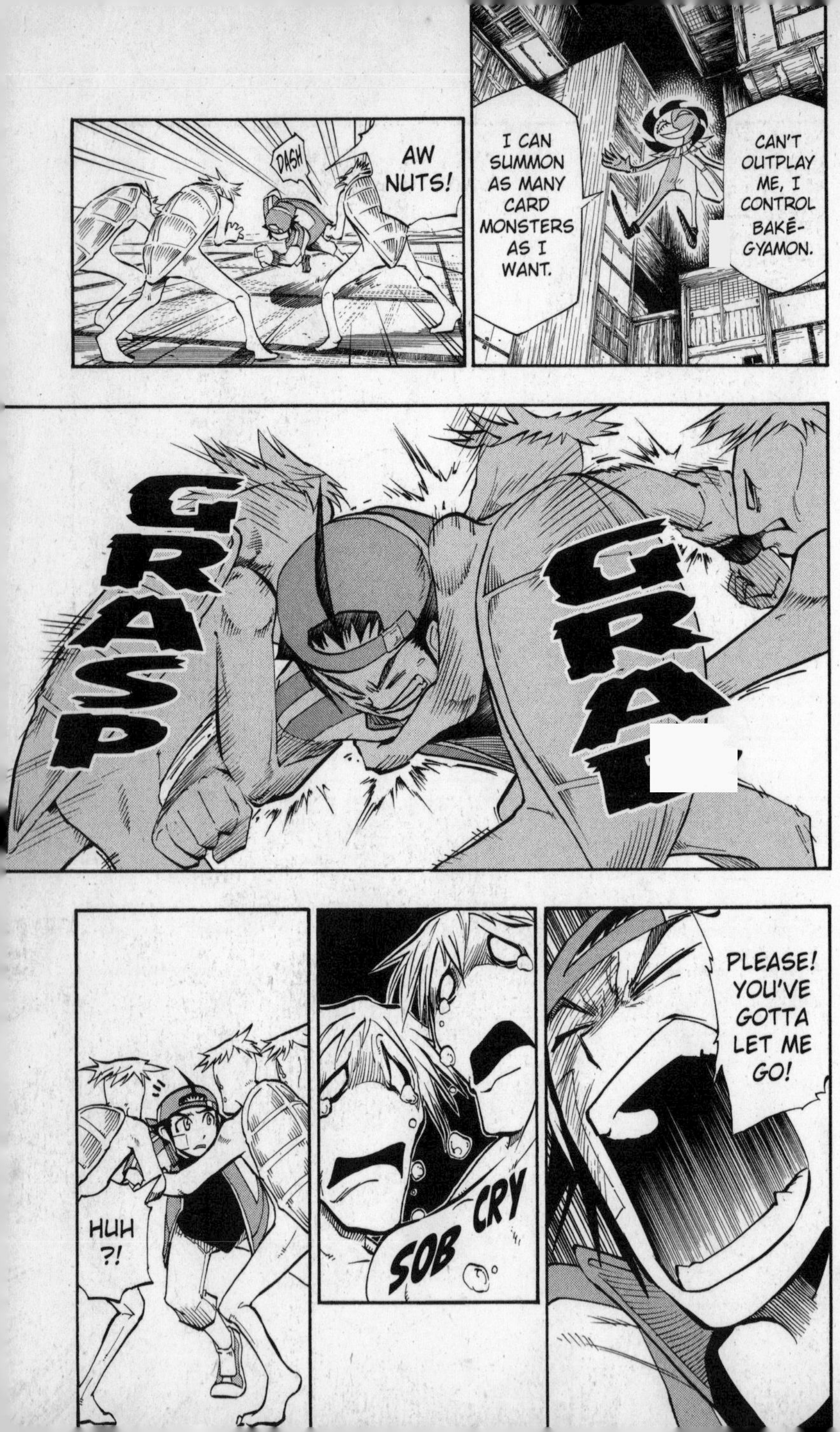
CAN'T OUTPLAY ME, I CONTROL BAKÉ-GYAMON.
I CAN SUMMON AS MANY CARD MONSTERS AS I WANT.
AW NUTS!
DASH
GRAB
GRASP
PLEASE! YOU'VE GOTTA LET ME GO!
CRY
SOB
HUH ?!

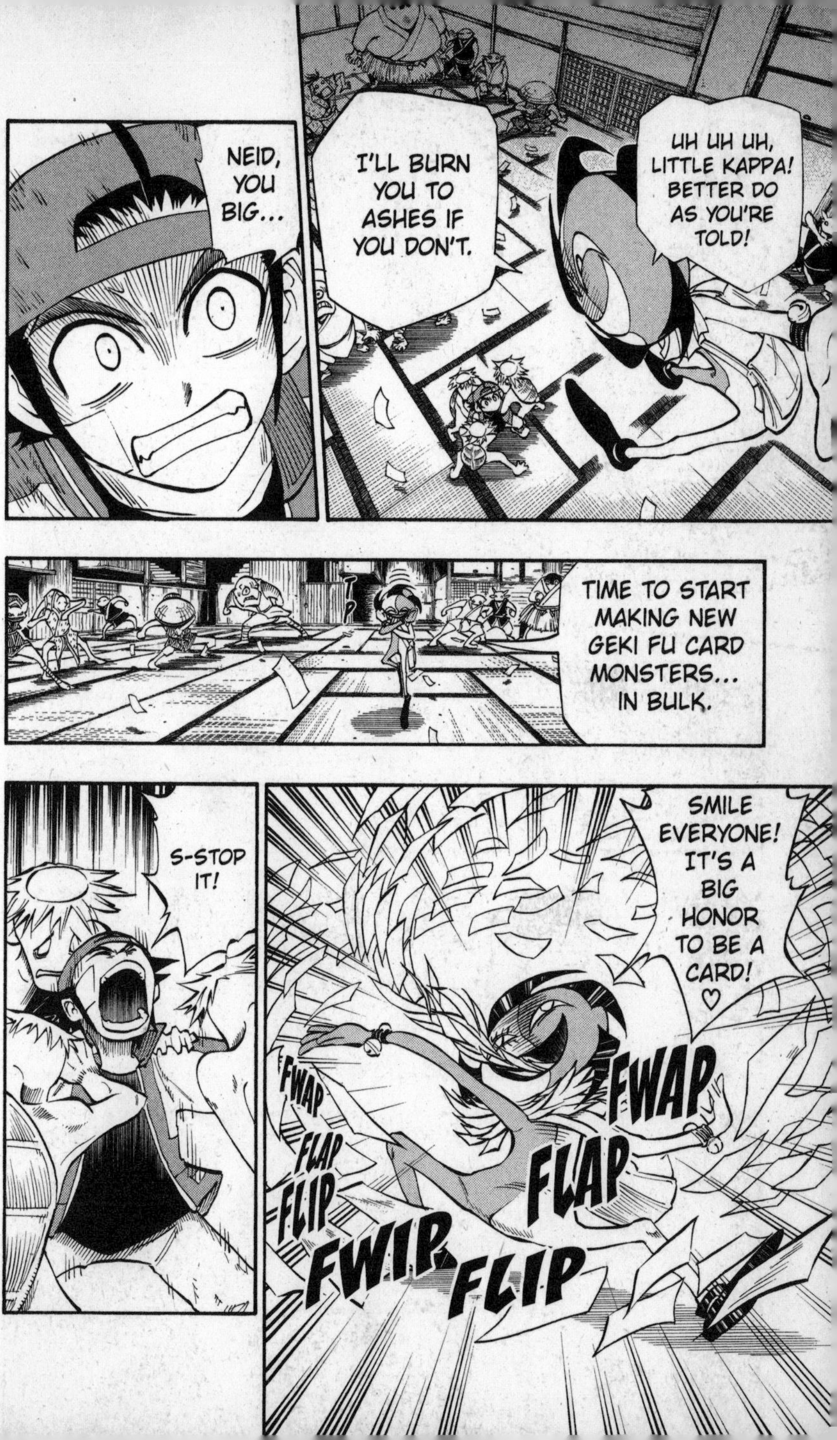
UH UH UH, LITTLE KAPPA! BETTER DO AS YOU'RE TOLD!
I'LL BURN YOU TO ASHES IF YOU DON'T.
NEID, YOU BIG...
TP
TIME TO START MAKING NEW GEKI FU CARD MONSTERS... IN BULK.
SMILE EVERYONE! IT'S A BIG HONOR TO BE A CARD! ♡
FWAP
FLAP
FWAP
FLAP
FLIP
FWIP
FLIP
S-STOP IT!

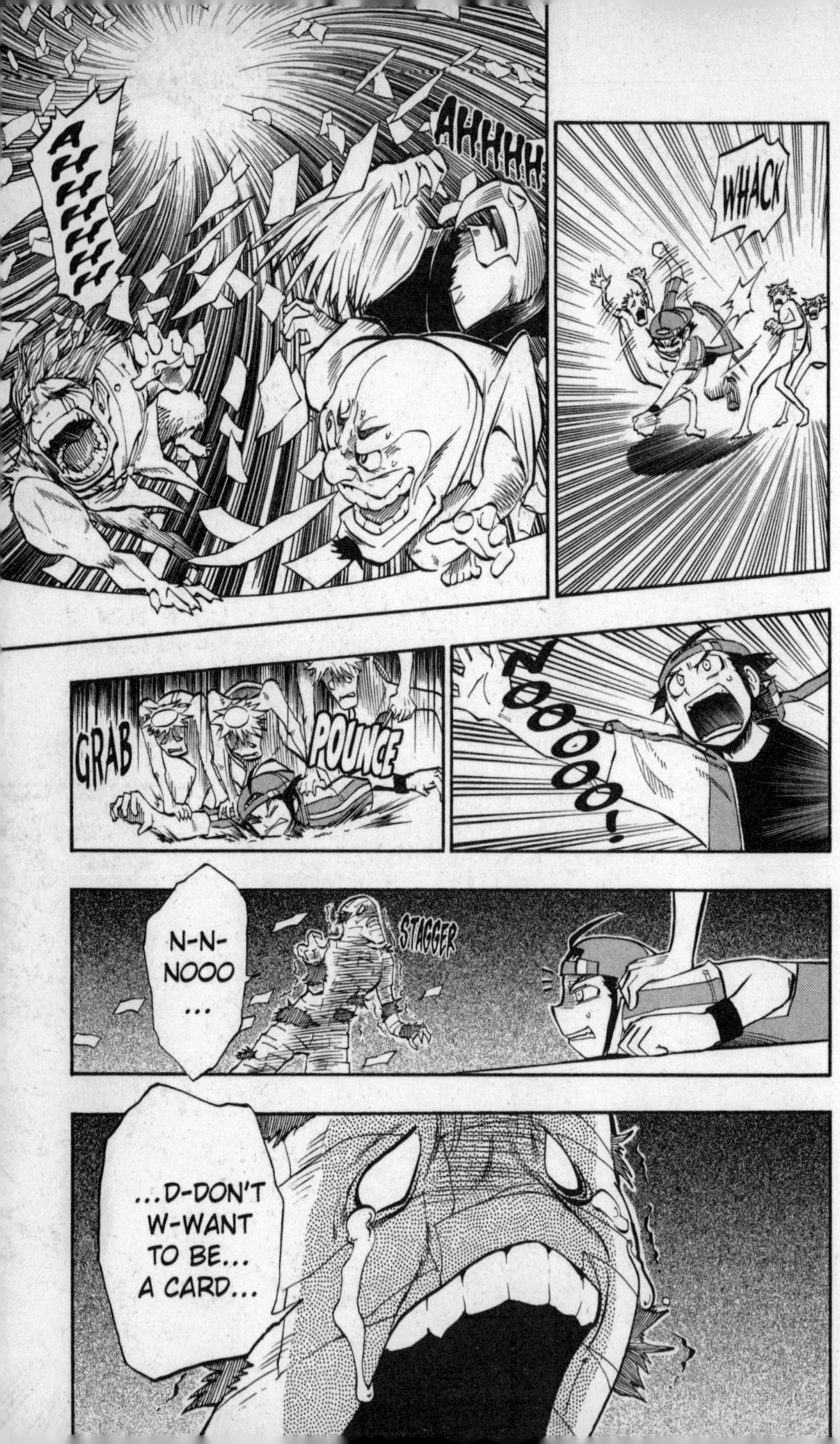
WHACK
AHHHHH
AHHHHHHH
NOOOOOO!
POUNCE
GRAB
STAGGER
N-N-NOOO...
...D-DON'T W-WANT TO BE... A CARD...

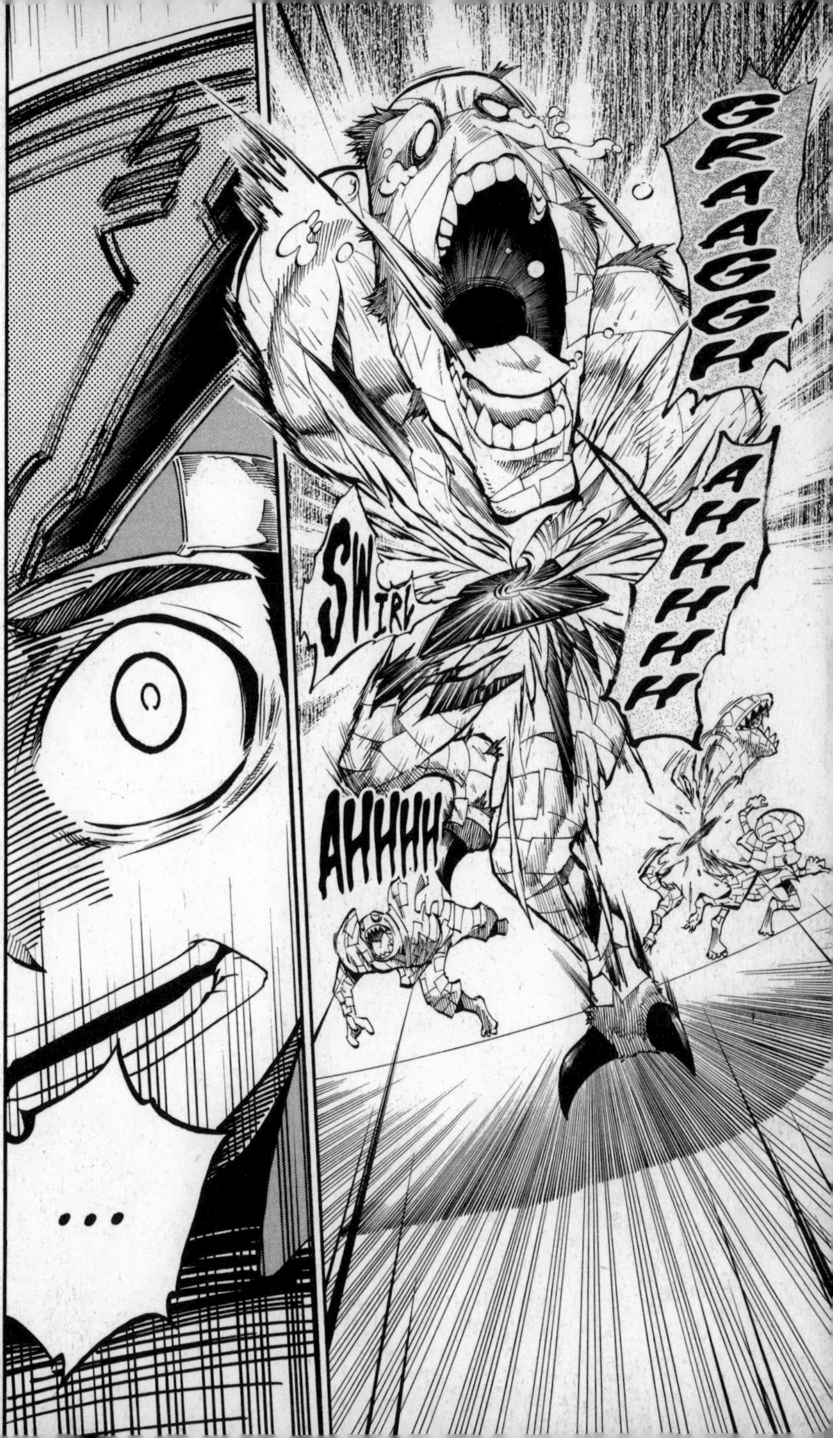
GRAAGGH
AHHHHHH
SWIRL
AHHHH
...

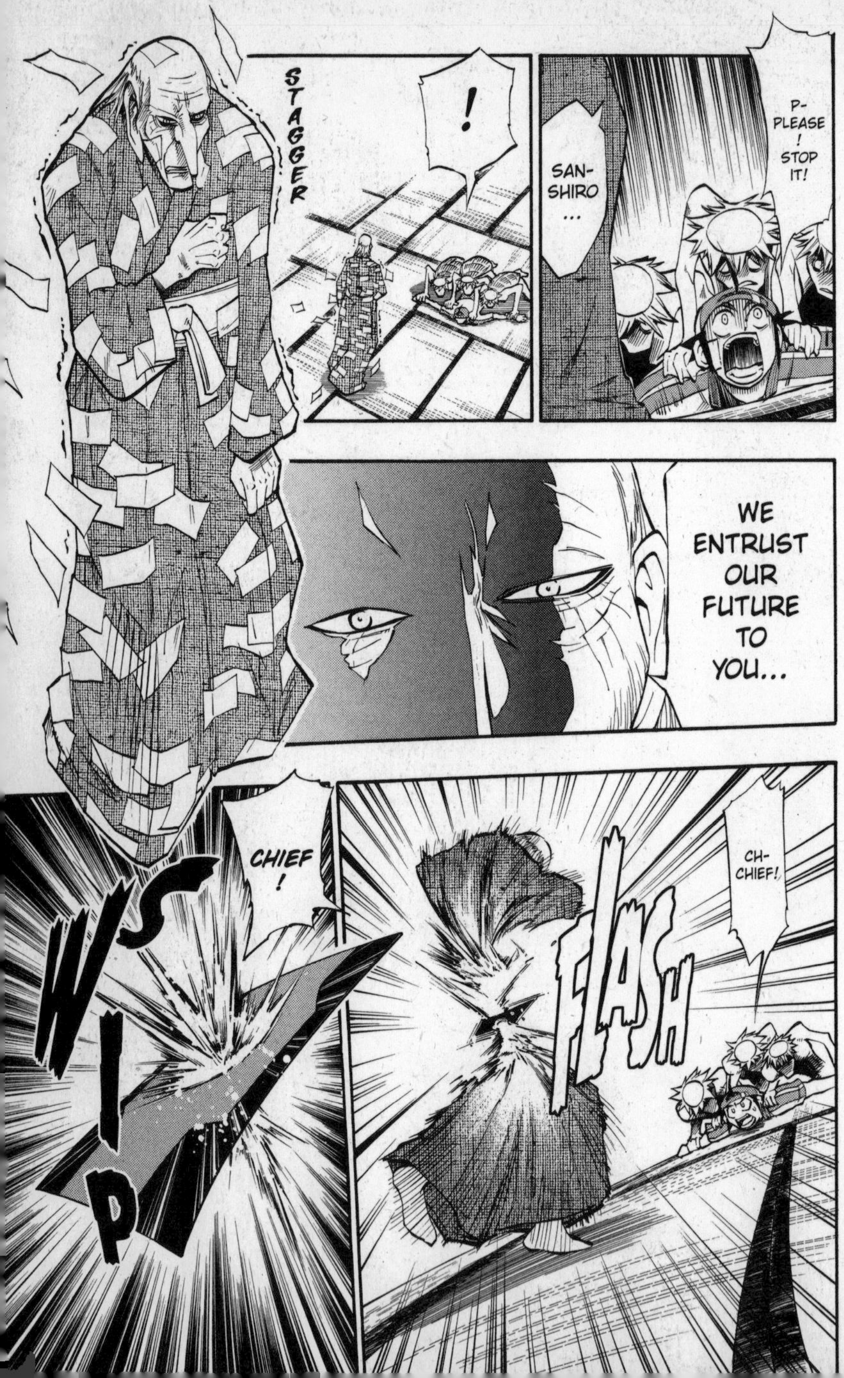
P-PLEASE! STOP IT!
SAN-SHIRO...
!
STAGGER
WE ENTRUST OUR FUTURE TO YOU...
CH-CHIEF!
FLASH
CHIEF!
WHSIP

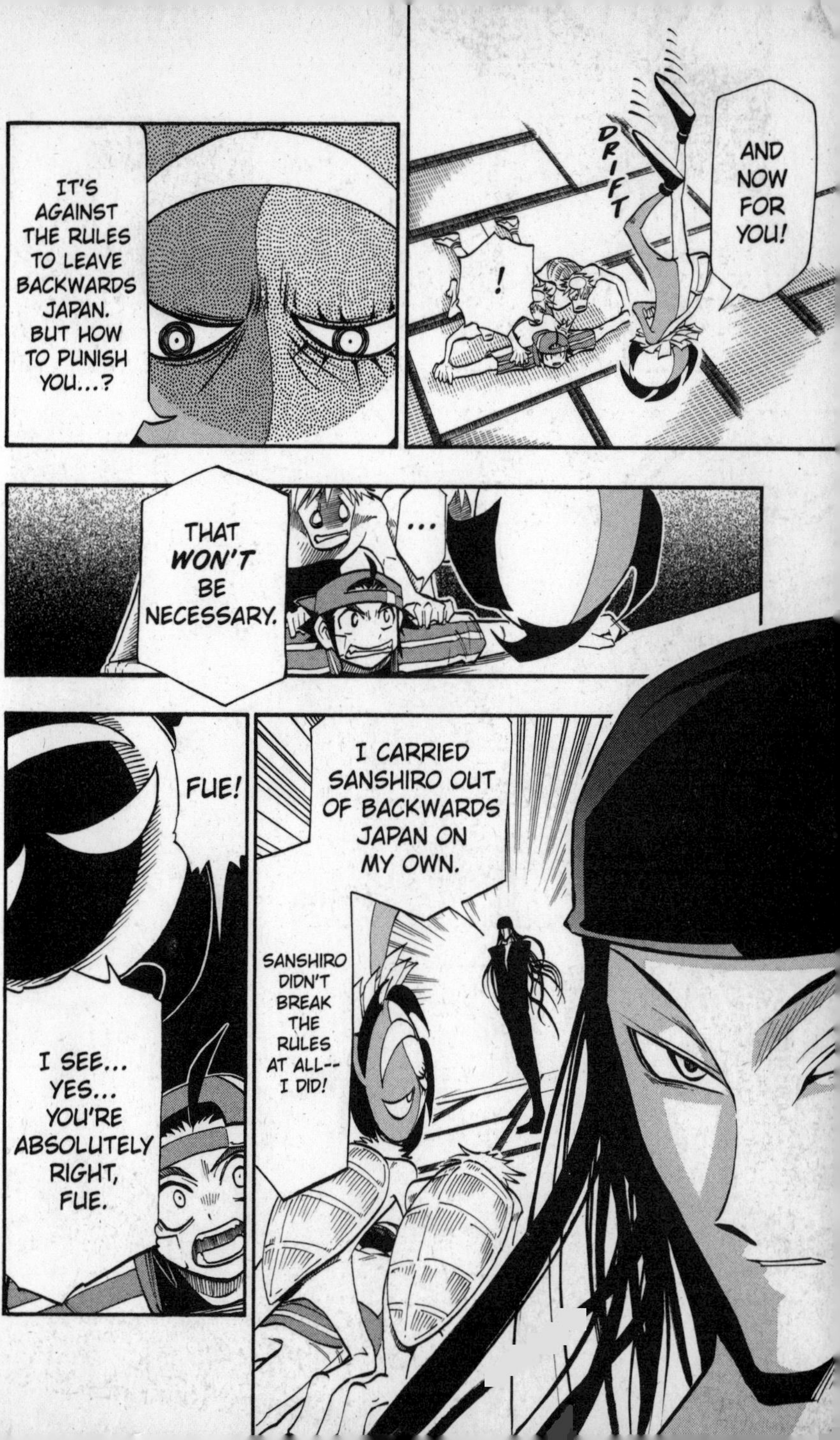
AND NOW FOR YOU!
DRIFT
!
IT'S AGAINST THE RULES TO LEAVE BACKWARDS JAPAN. BUT HOW TO PUNISH YOU...?
...
THAT *WON'T* BE NECESSARY.
I CARRIED SANSHIRO OUT OF BACKWARDS JAPAN ON MY OWN.
SANSHIRO DIDN'T BREAK THE RULES AT ALL-- I DID!
FUE!
I SEE... YES... YOU'RE ABSOLUTELY RIGHT, FUE.

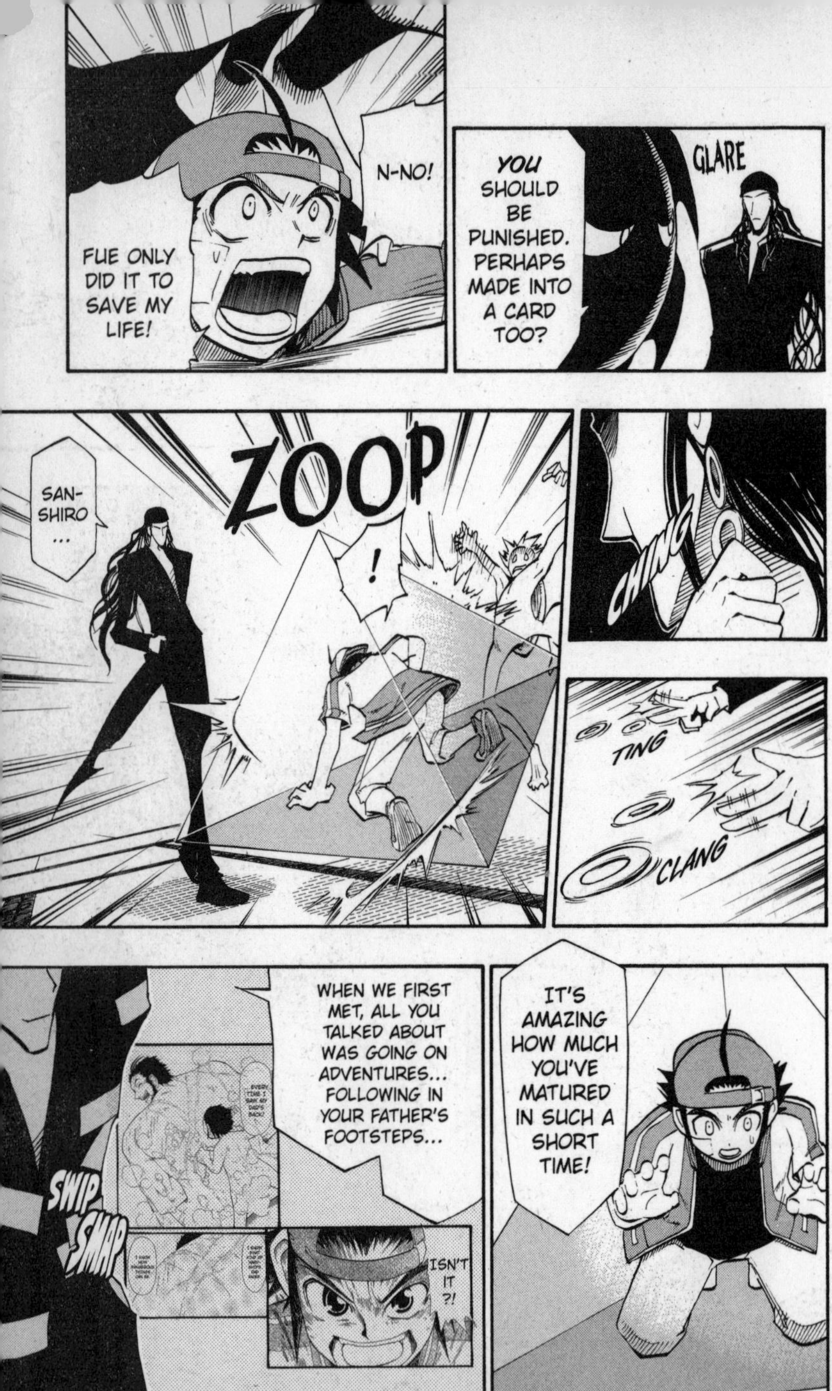
GLARE
YOU SHOULD BE PUNISHED. PERHAPS MADE INTO A CARD TOO?
N-NO!
FUE ONLY DID IT TO SAVE MY LIFE!
CHING
TING
CLANG
ZOOP
!
SAN-SHIRO ...
IT'S AMAZING HOW MUCH YOU'VE MATURED IN SUCH A SHORT TIME!
WHEN WE FIRST MET, ALL YOU TALKED ABOUT WAS GOING ON ADVENTURES... FOLLOWING IN YOUR FATHER'S FOOTSTEPS...
SWIP
SMAP
ISN'T IT ?!

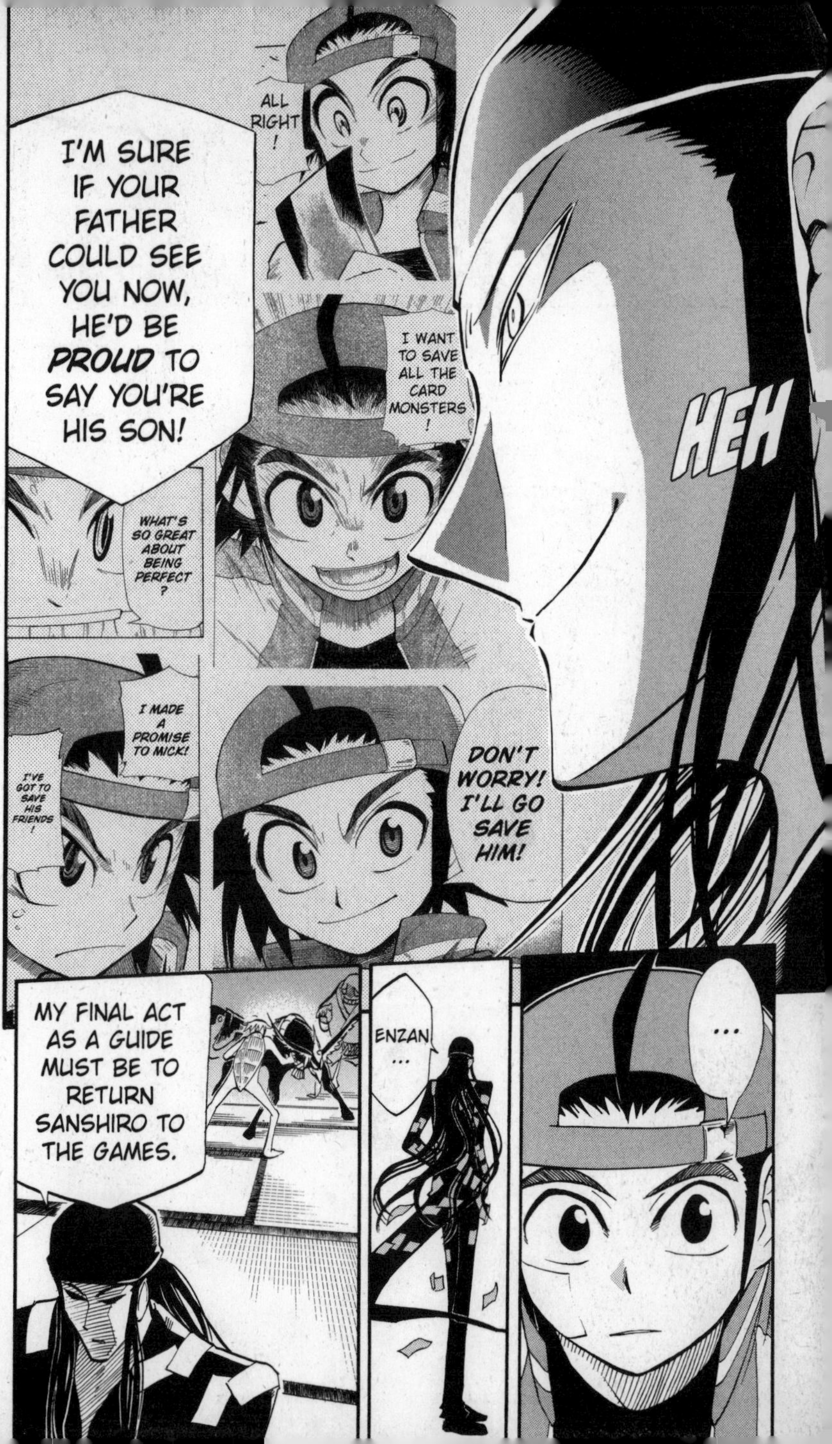
HEH
I'M SURE IF YOUR FATHER COULD SEE YOU NOW, HE'D BE PROUD TO SAY YOU'RE HIS SON!
ALL RIGHT!
I WANT TO SAVE ALL THE CARD MONSTERS!
WHAT'S SO GREAT ABOUT BEING PERFECT?
DON'T WORRY! I'LL GO SAVE HIM!
I MADE A PROMISE TO MICK!
I'VE GOT TO SAVE HIS FRIENDS!
...
ENZAN...
MY FINAL ACT AS A GUIDE MUST BE TO RETURN SANSHIRO TO THE GAMES.

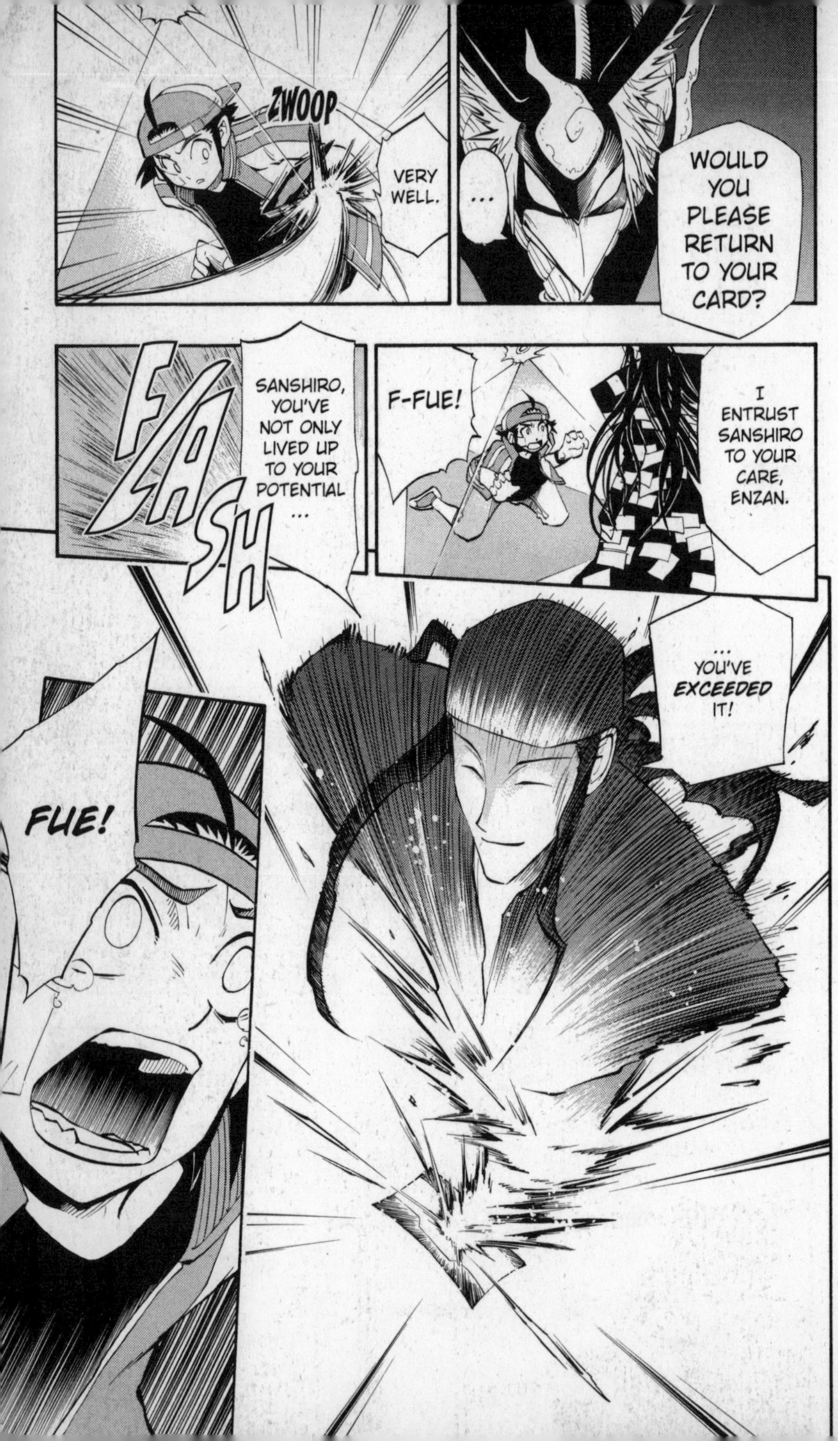
WOULD YOU PLEASE RETURN TO YOUR CARD?
...
VERY WELL.
ZWOOP
I ENTRUST SANSHIRO TO YOUR CARE, ENZAN.
F-FUE!
SANSHIRO, YOU'VE NOT ONLY LIVED UP TO YOUR POTENTIAL ...
FLASH
... YOU'VE *EXCEEDED* IT!
FUE!

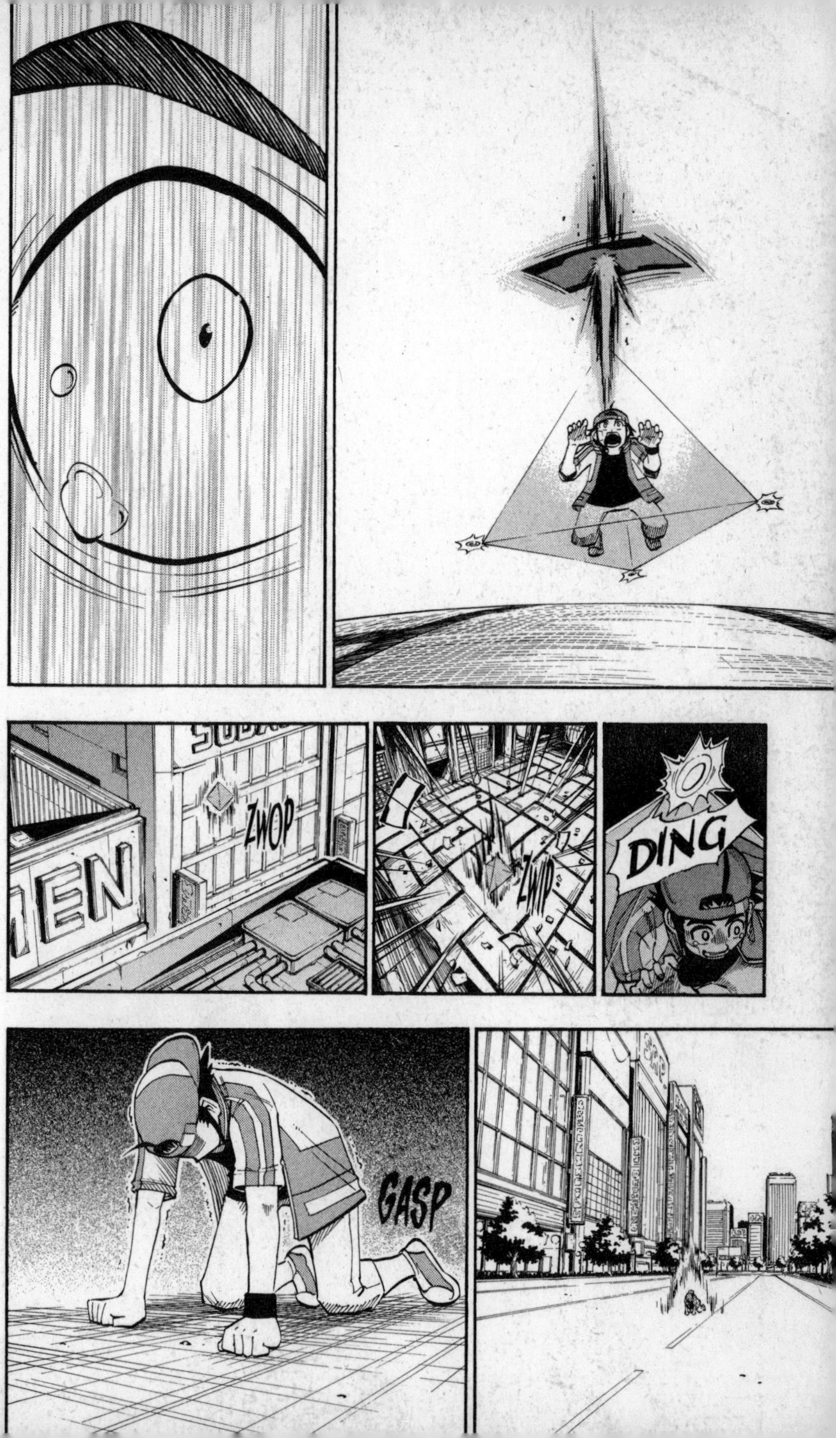
DING
ZWIP
ZWOP
GASP

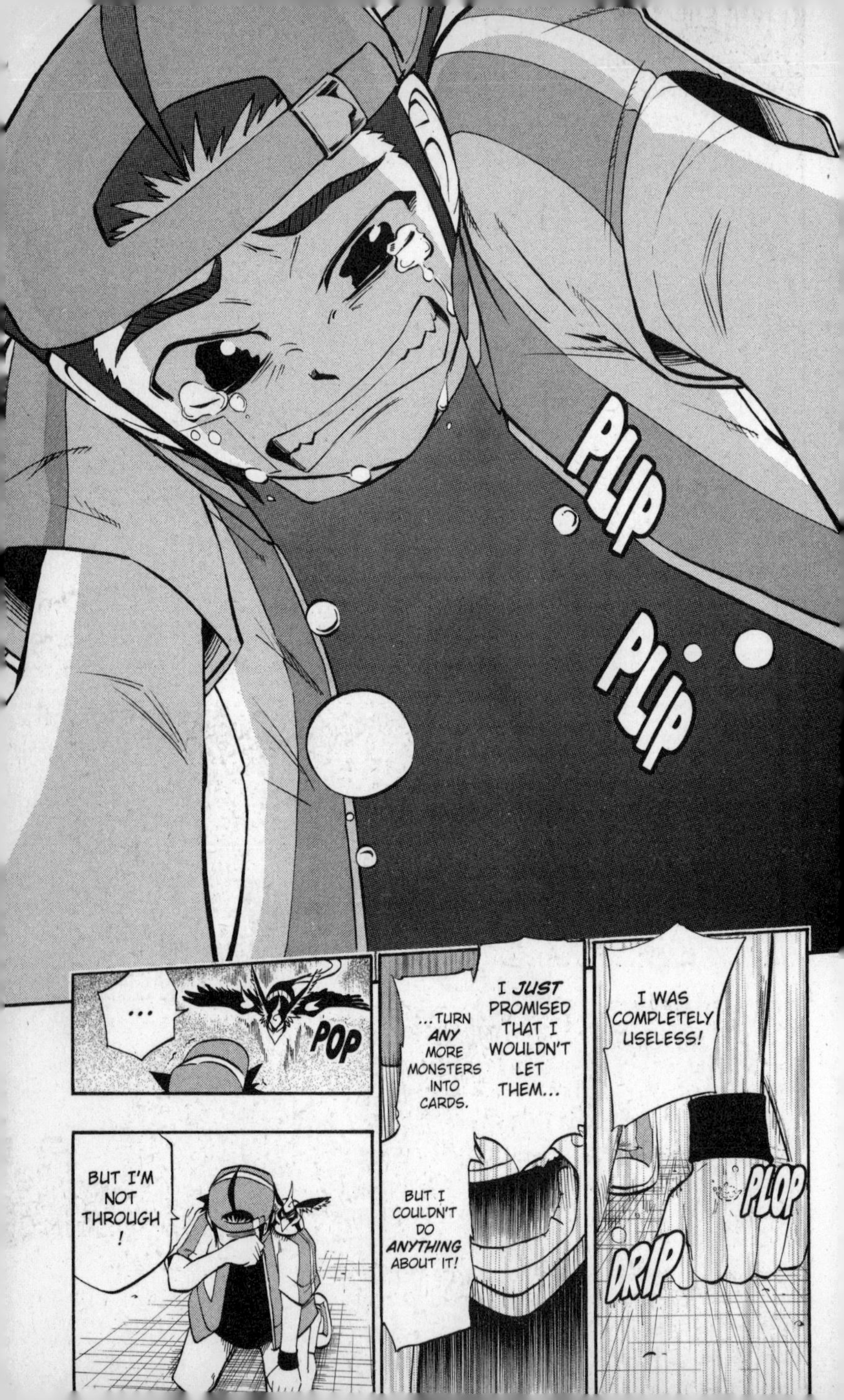
PLIP
PLIP
I WAS COMPLETELY USELESS!
PLOP
DRIP
I JUST PROMISED THAT I WOULDN'T LET THEM...
...TURN ANY MORE MONSTERS INTO CARDS.
BUT I COULDN'T DO ANYTHING ABOUT IT!
...
POP
BUT I'M NOT THROUGH!

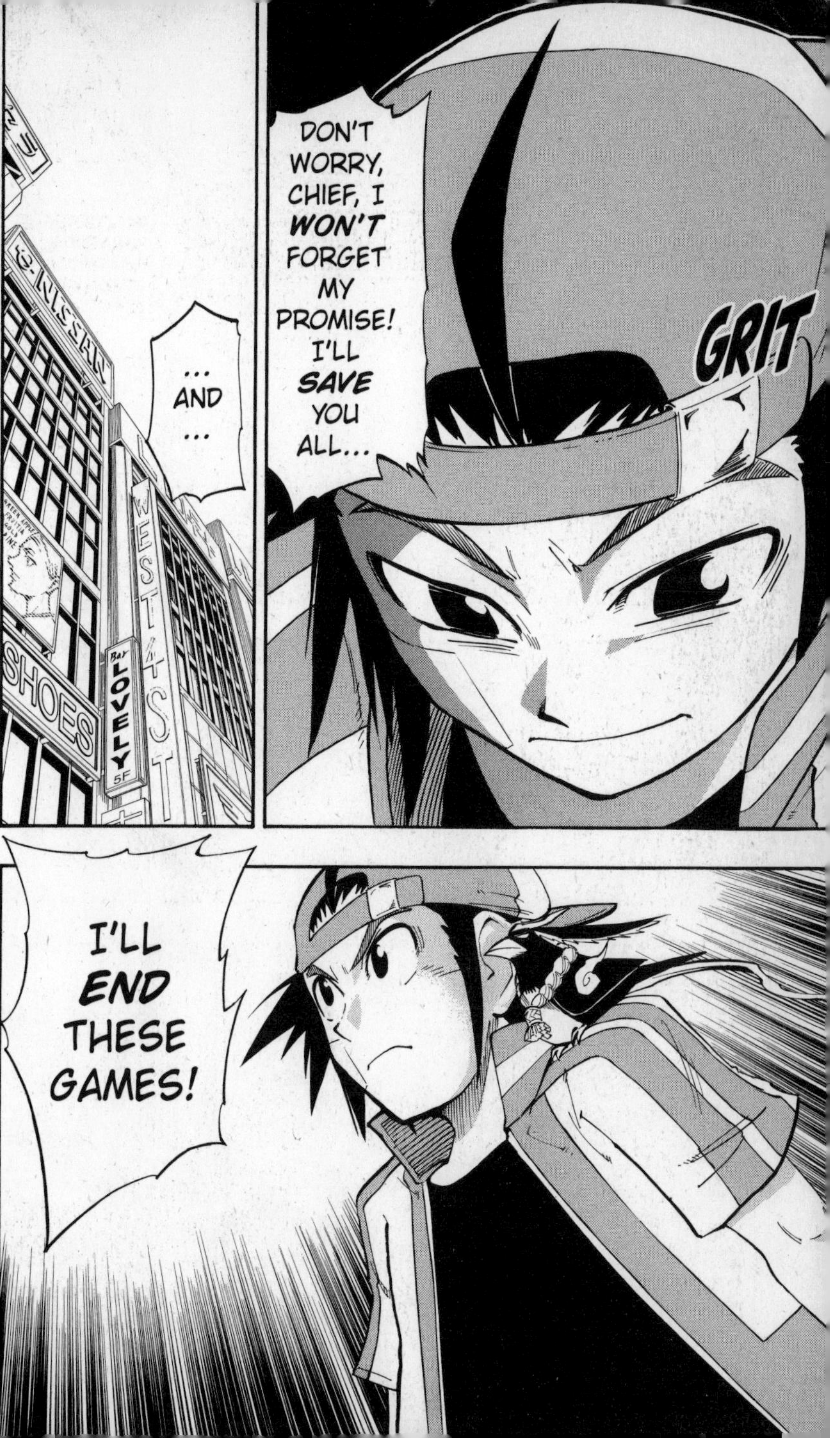
DON'T WORRY, CHIEF, I WON'T FORGET MY PROMISE! I'LL SAVE YOU ALL...
GRIT
... AND ...
NISSAN
WEST 4 ST
BAY LOVELY 5F
SHOES
I'LL END THESE GAMES!

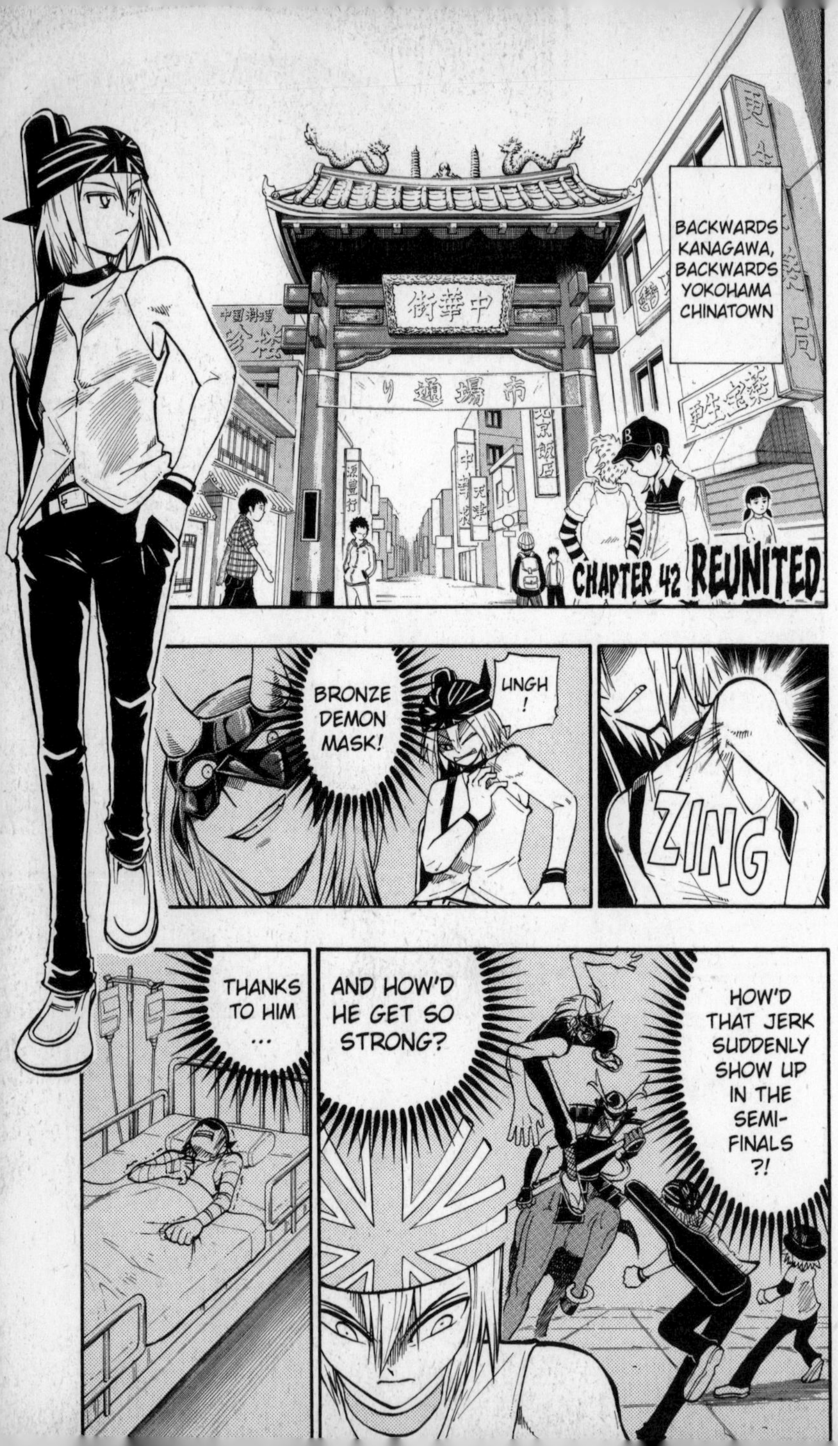
BACKWARDS KANAGAWA, BACKWARDS YOKOHAMA CHINATOWN
中華街
市場通り
CHAPTER 42 REUNITED
ZING
UNGH!
BRONZE DEMON MASK!
HOW'D THAT JERK SUDDENLY SHOW UP IN THE SEMI-FINALS?!
AND HOW'D HE GET SO STRONG?
THANKS TO HIM...

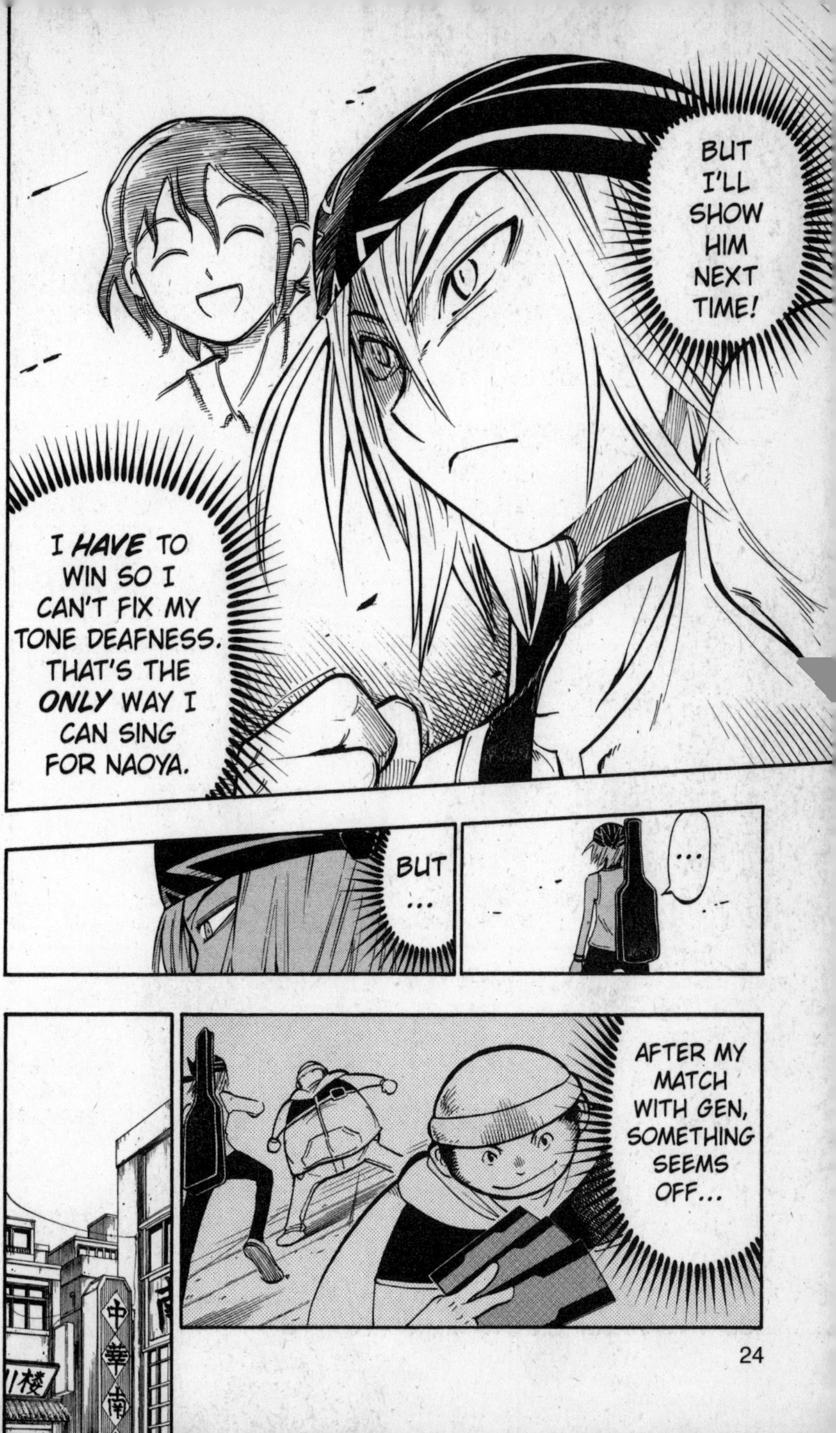
BUT I'LL SHOW HIM NEXT TIME!
I *HAVE* TO WIN SO I CAN'T FIX MY TONE DEAFNESS. THAT'S THE *ONLY* WAY I CAN SING FOR NAOYA.
...
BUT ...
AFTER MY MATCH WITH GEN, SOMETHING SEEMS OFF...
中華南

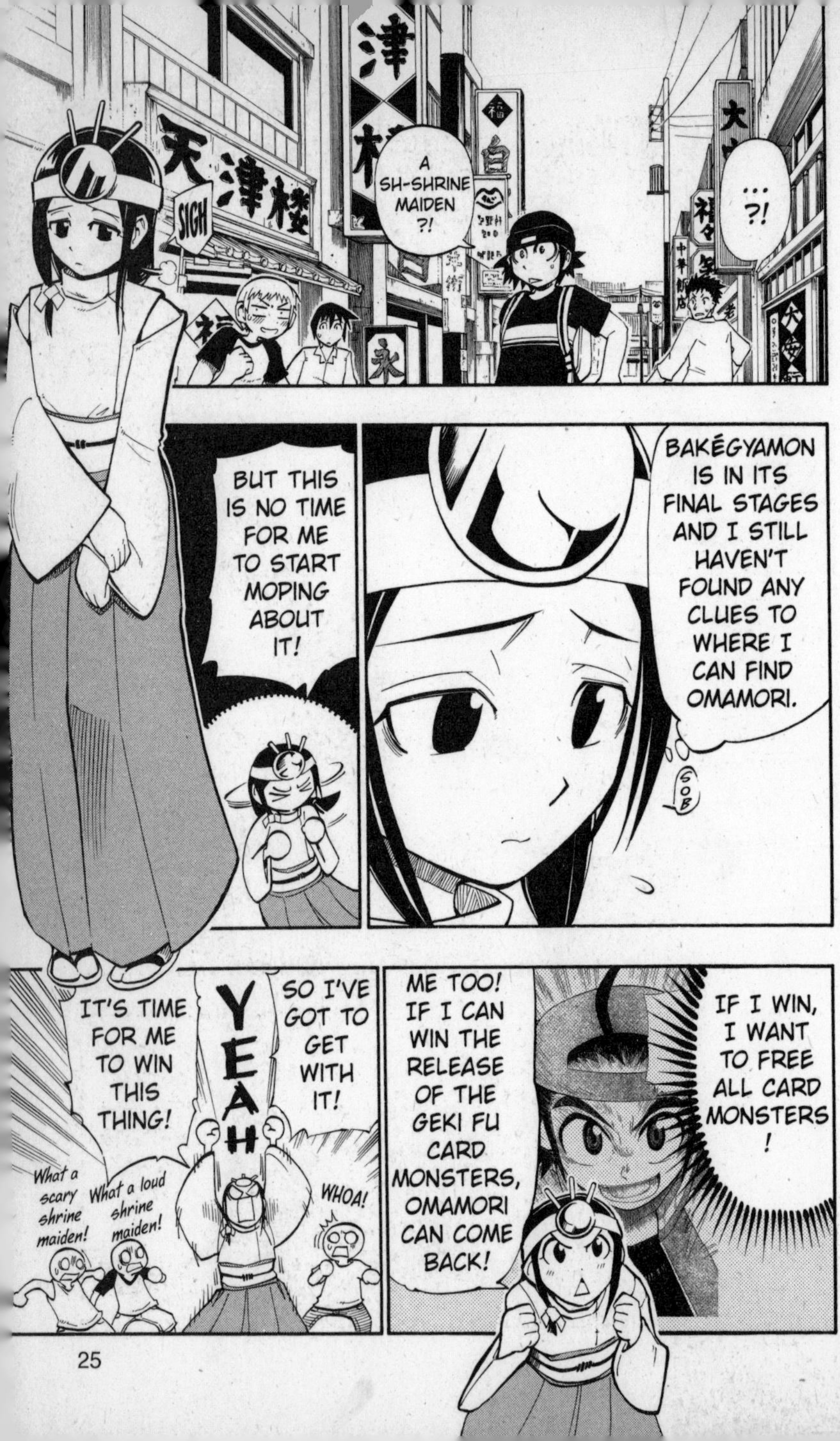
...?!
A SH-SHRINE MAIDEN ?!
SIGH
BAKÉGYAMON IS IN ITS FINAL STAGES AND I STILL HAVEN'T FOUND ANY CLUES TO WHERE I CAN FIND OMAMORI.
SOB
BUT THIS IS NO TIME FOR ME TO START MOPING ABOUT IT!
IF I WIN, I WANT TO FREE ALL CARD MONSTERS!
ME TOO! IF I CAN WIN THE RELEASE OF THE GEKI FU CARD MONSTERS, OMAMORI CAN COME BACK!
SO I'VE GOT TO GET WITH IT!
YEAH
IT'S TIME FOR ME TO WIN THIS THING!
WHOA!
What a loud shrine maiden!
What a scary shrine maiden!

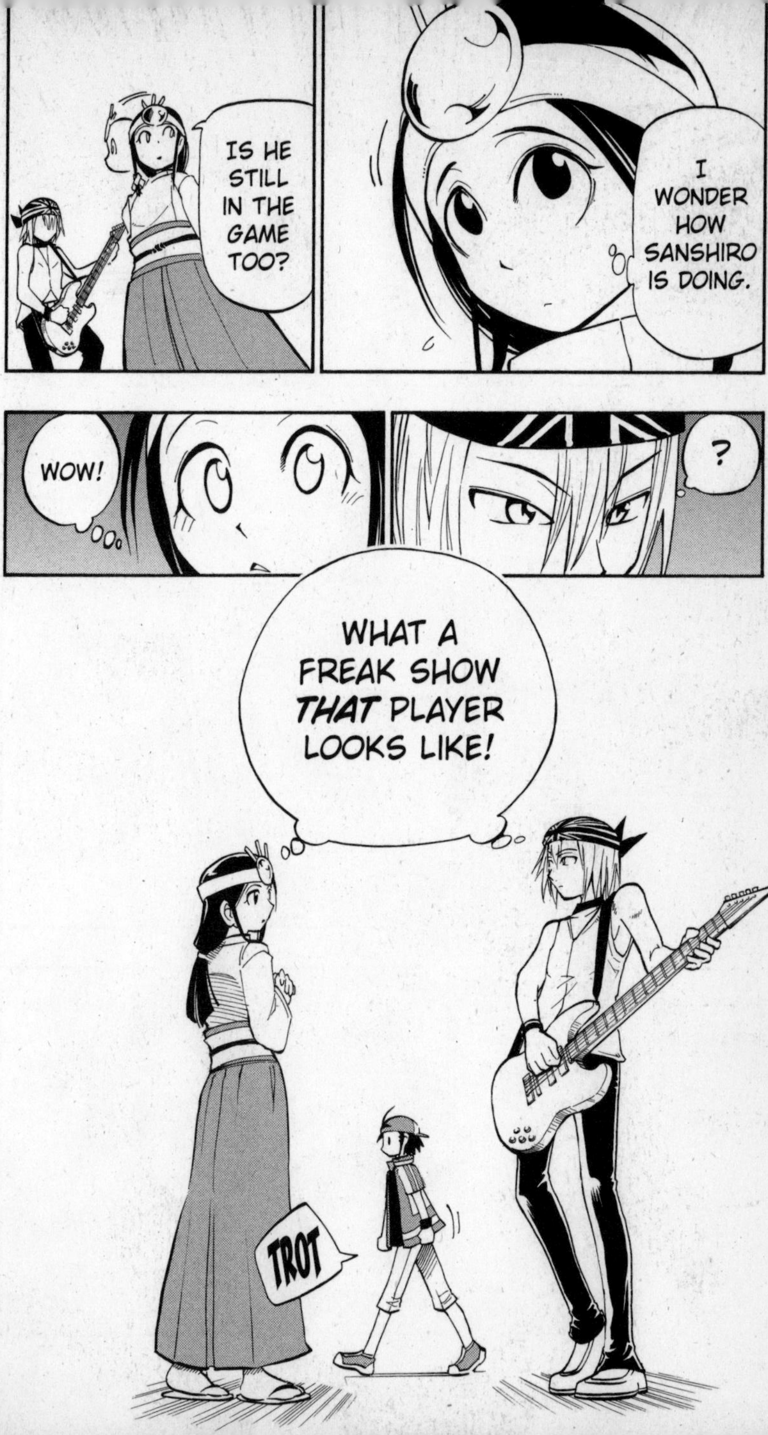
I WONDER HOW SANSHIRO IS DOING.
IS HE STILL IN THE GAME TOO?
?
WOW!
WHAT A FREAK SHOW *THAT* PLAYER LOOKS LIKE!
TROT

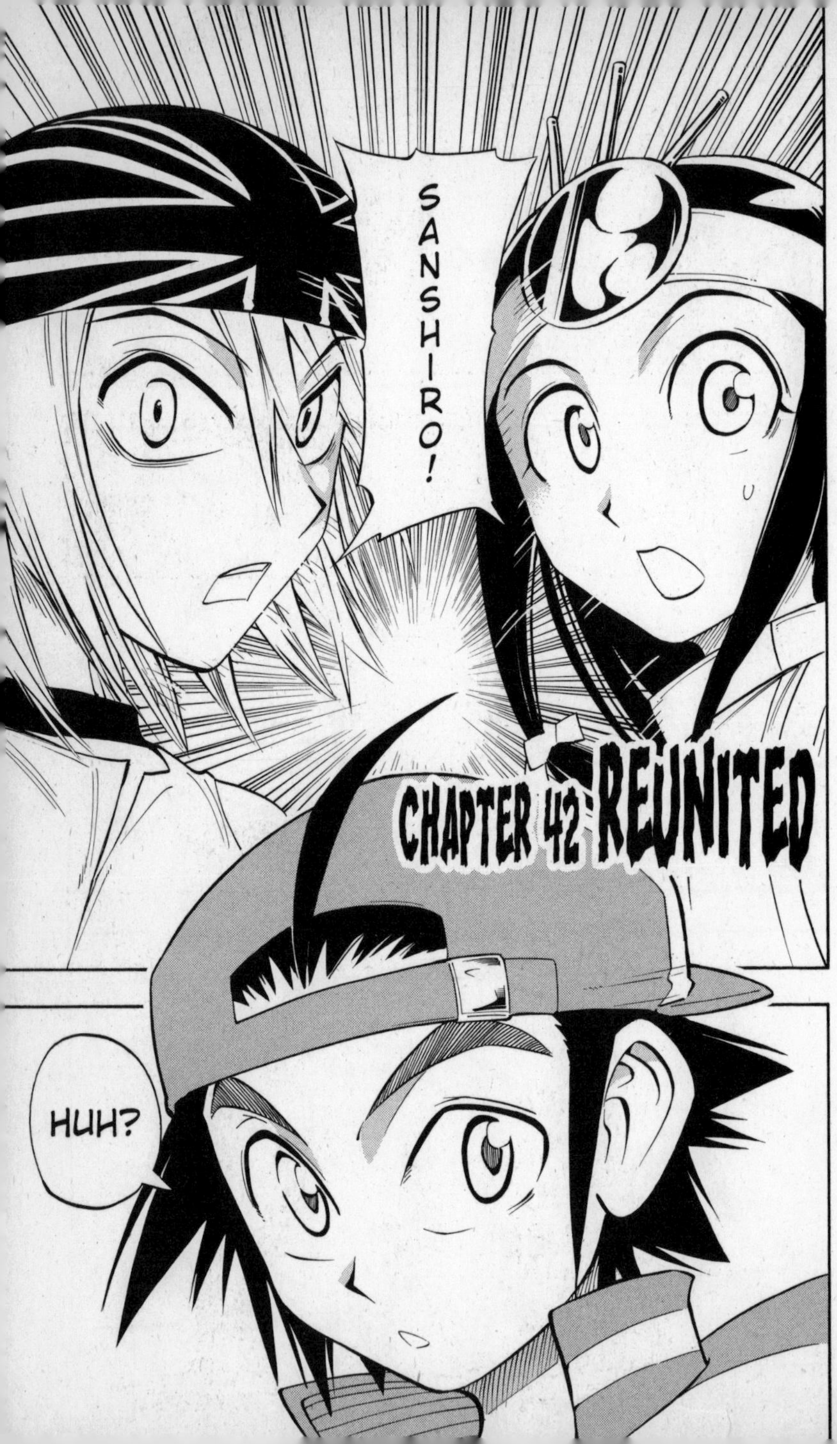
SANSHIRO!
CHAPTER 42 REUNITED
HUH?

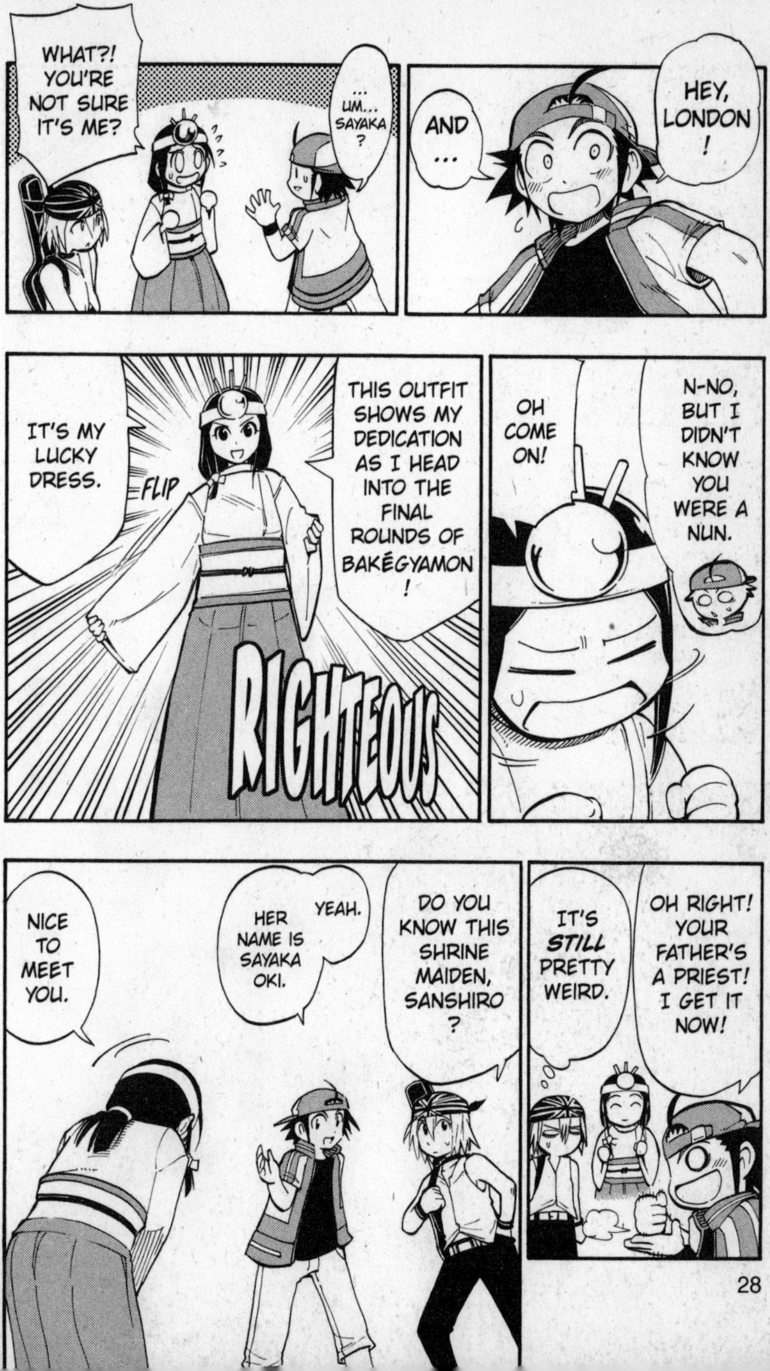
HEY, LONDON!
AND ...
... UM... SAYAKA?
WHAT?! YOU'RE NOT SURE IT'S ME?
N-NO, BUT I DIDN'T KNOW YOU WERE A NUN.
OH COME ON!
THIS OUTFIT SHOWS MY DEDICATION AS I HEAD INTO THE FINAL ROUNDS OF BAKÉGYAMON!
IT'S MY LUCKY DRESS.
FLIP
RIGHTEOUS
OH RIGHT! YOUR FATHER'S A PRIEST! I GET IT NOW!
IT'S *STILL* PRETTY WEIRD.
DO YOU KNOW THIS SHRINE MAIDEN, SANSHIRO?
YEAH.
HER NAME IS SAYAKA OKI.
NICE TO MEET YOU.

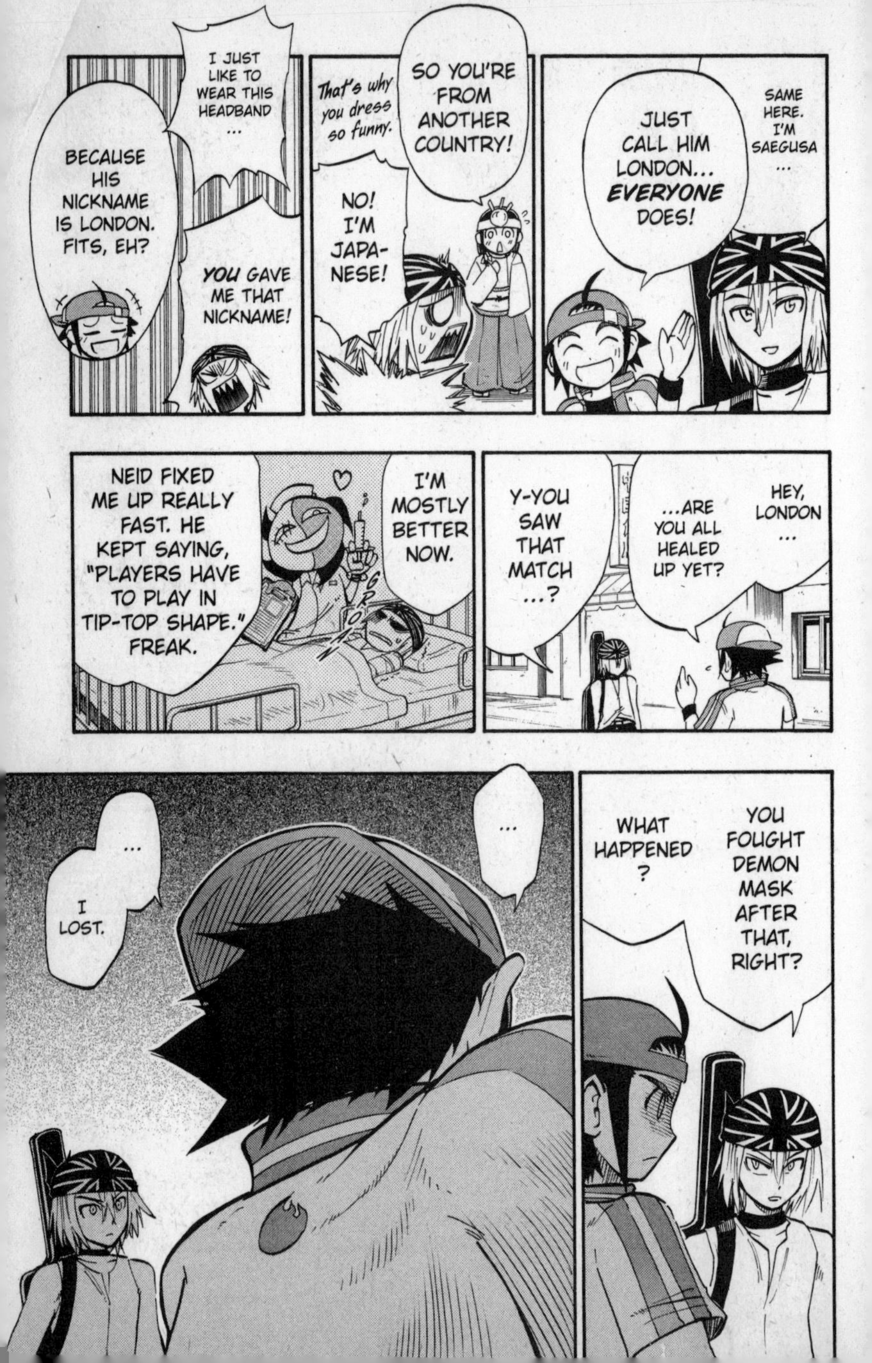
SAME HERE. I'M SAEGUSA ...
JUST CALL HIM LONDON... ***EVERYONE*** DOES!
SO YOU'RE FROM ANOTHER COUNTRY!
That's why you dress so funny.
NO! I'M JAPANESE!
I JUST LIKE TO WEAR THIS HEADBAND ...
BECAUSE HIS NICKNAME IS LONDON. FITS, EH?
YOU GAVE ME THAT NICKNAME!
HEY, LONDON ...
...ARE YOU ALL HEALED UP YET?
Y-YOU SAW THAT MATCH ...?
I'M MOSTLY BETTER NOW.
NEID FIXED ME UP REALLY FAST. HE KEPT SAYING, "PLAYERS HAVE TO PLAY IN TIP-TOP SHAPE." FREAK.
YOU FOUGHT DEMON MASK AFTER THAT, RIGHT?
WHAT HAPPENED ?
...
...
I LOST.

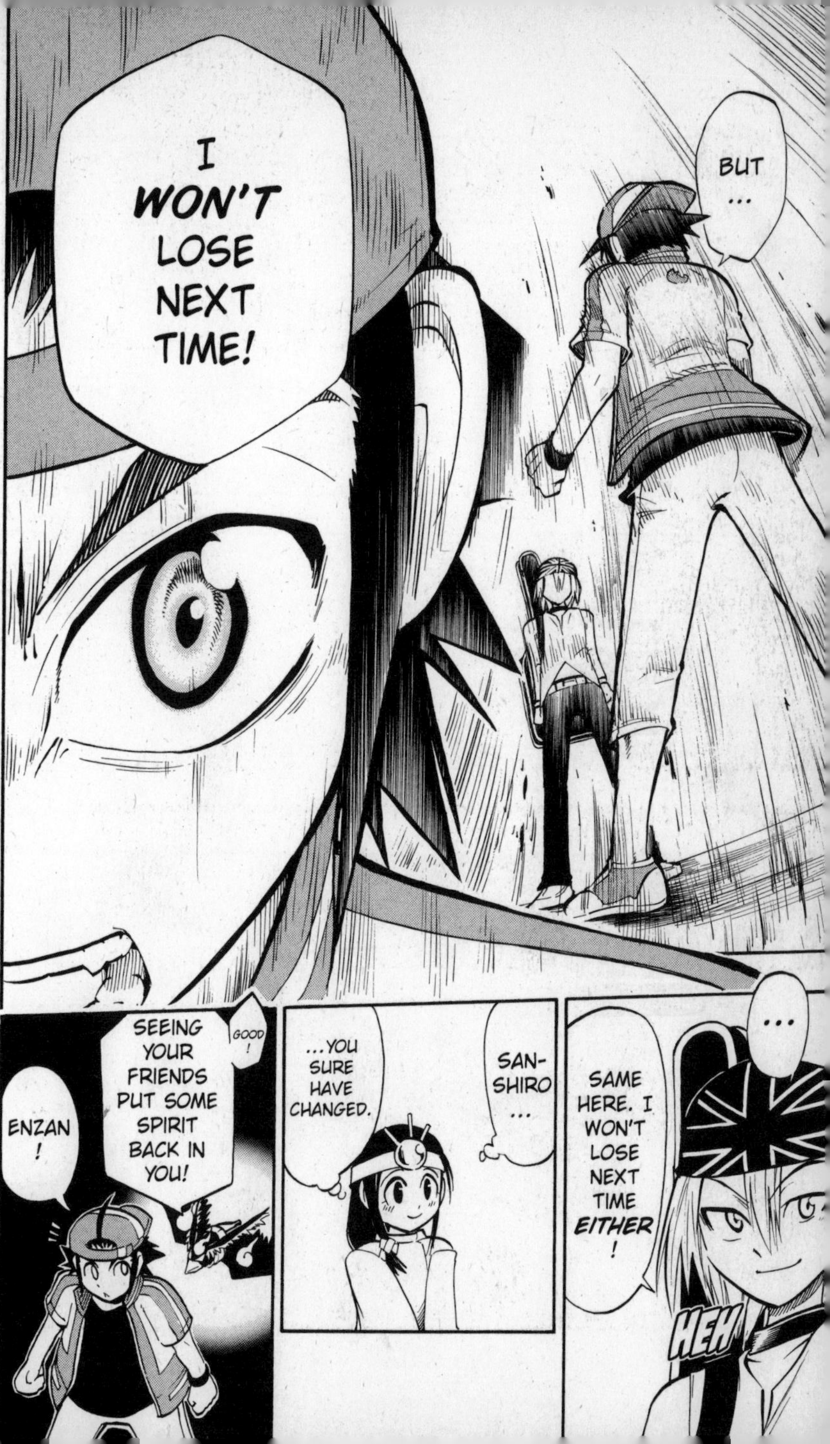
BUT ...
I WON'T LOSE NEXT TIME!
...
SAME HERE. I WON'T LOSE NEXT TIME EITHER!
HEH
SAN-SHIRO ...
...YOU SURE HAVE CHANGED.
GOOD!
SEEING YOUR FRIENDS PUT SOME SPIRIT BACK IN YOU!
ENZAN!

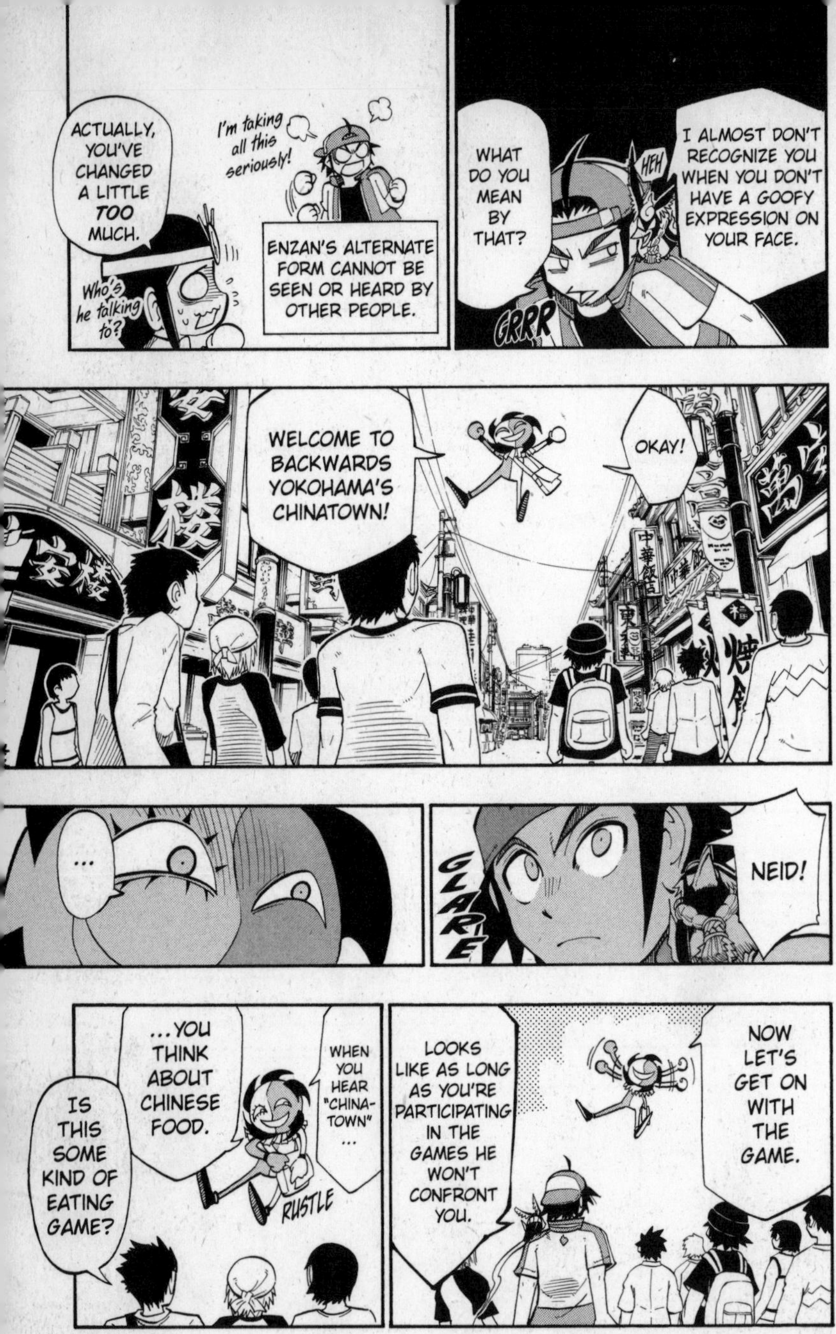
I ALMOST DON'T RECOGNIZE YOU WHEN YOU DON'T HAVE A GOOFY EXPRESSION ON YOUR FACE.
HEH
WHAT DO YOU MEAN BY THAT?
GRRR
I'm taking all this seriously!
ENZAN'S ALTERNATE FORM CANNOT BE SEEN OR HEARD BY OTHER PEOPLE.
ACTUALLY, YOU'VE CHANGED A LITTLE TOO MUCH.
Who's he talking to?
OKAY!
WELCOME TO BACKWARDS YOKOHAMA'S CHINATOWN!
GLARE
NEID!
...
NOW LET'S GET ON WITH THE GAME.
LOOKS LIKE AS LONG AS YOU'RE PARTICIPATING IN THE GAMES HE WON'T CONFRONT YOU.
WHEN YOU HEAR "CHINA-TOWN"...
...YOU THINK ABOUT CHINESE FOOD.
RUSTLE
IS THIS SOME KIND OF EATING GAME?

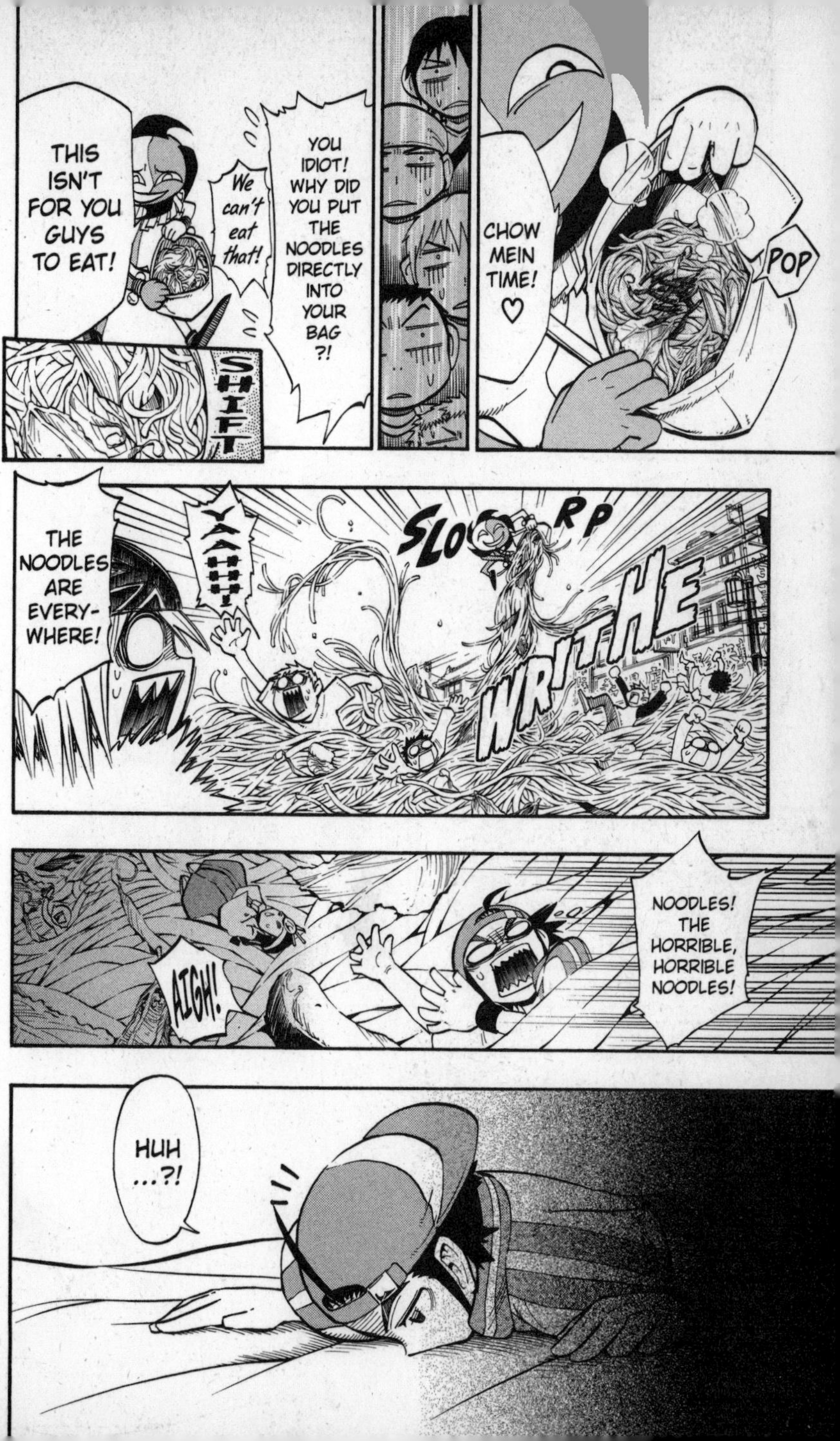
POP
CHOW MEIN TIME! ♡
YOU IDIOT! WHY DID YOU PUT THE NOODLES DIRECTLY INTO YOUR BAG ?!
We can't eat that!
THIS ISN'T FOR YOU GUYS TO EAT!
SHIFT
SLOORP
WRITHE
YAAHH!
THE NOODLES ARE EVERY-WHERE!
NOODLES! THE HORRIBLE, HORRIBLE NOODLES!
AIGH!
HUH ...?!

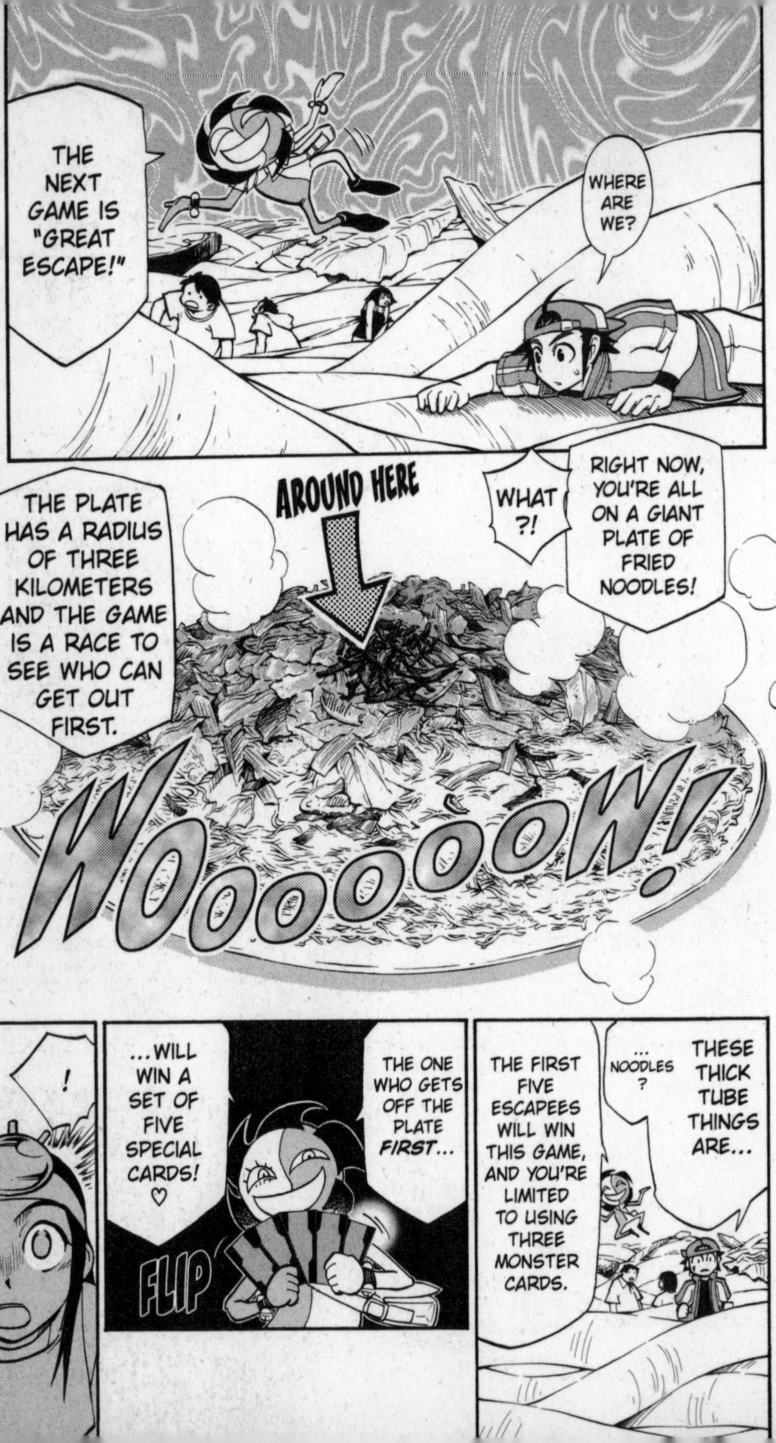
WHERE ARE WE?
THE NEXT GAME IS "GREAT ESCAPE!"
RIGHT NOW, YOU'RE ALL ON A GIANT PLATE OF FRIED NOODLES!
WHAT ?!
AROUND HERE
THE PLATE HAS A RADIUS OF THREE KILOMETERS AND THE GAME IS A RACE TO SEE WHO CAN GET OUT FIRST.
WOOOOOOW!
THESE THICK TUBE THINGS ARE...
... NOODLES ?
THE FIRST FIVE ESCAPEES WILL WIN THIS GAME, AND YOU'RE LIMITED TO USING THREE MONSTER CARDS.
THE ONE WHO GETS OFF THE PLATE *FIRST*...
...WILL WIN A SET OF FIVE SPECIAL CARDS! ♡
FLIP
!

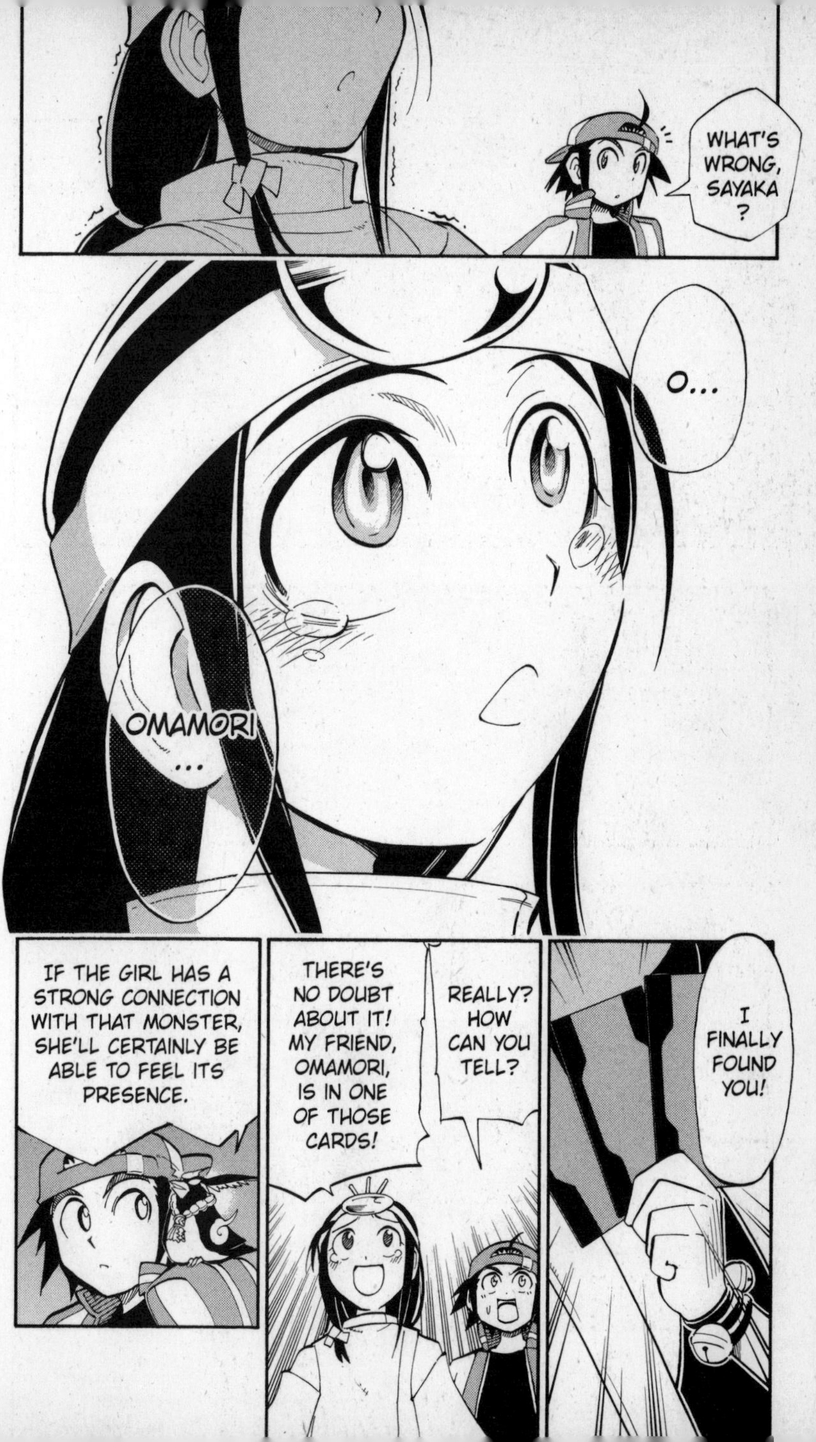
WHAT'S WRONG, SAYAKA?
O...
OMAMORI ...
I FINALLY FOUND YOU!
THERE'S NO DOUBT ABOUT IT! MY FRIEND, OMAMORI, IS IN ONE OF THOSE CARDS!
REALLY? HOW CAN YOU TELL?
IF THE GIRL HAS A STRONG CONNECTION WITH THAT MONSTER, SHE'LL CERTAINLY BE ABLE TO FEEL ITS PRESENCE.

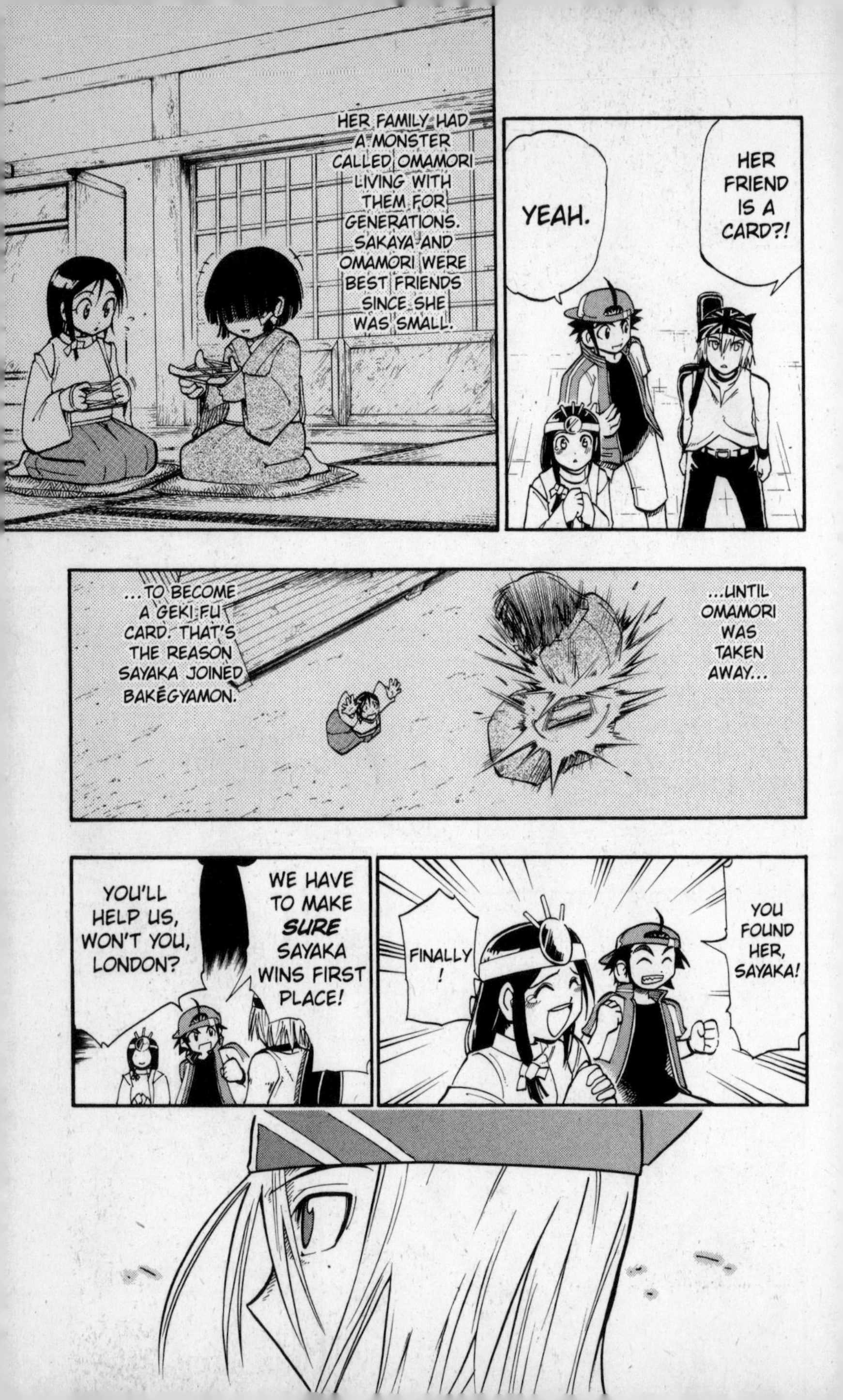
HER FRIEND IS A CARD?!
YEAH.
HER FAMILY HAD A MONSTER CALLED OMAMORI LIVING WITH THEM FOR GENERATIONS. SAKAYA AND OMAMORI WERE BEST FRIENDS SINCE SHE WAS SMALL.
...UNTIL OMAMORI WAS TAKEN AWAY...
...TO BECOME A GEKI FU CARD. THAT'S THE REASON SAYAKA JOINED BAKÉGYAMON.
YOU FOUND HER, SAYAKA!
FINALLY!
WE HAVE TO MAKE *SURE* SAYAKA WINS FIRST PLACE!
YOU'LL HELP US, WON'T YOU, LONDON?

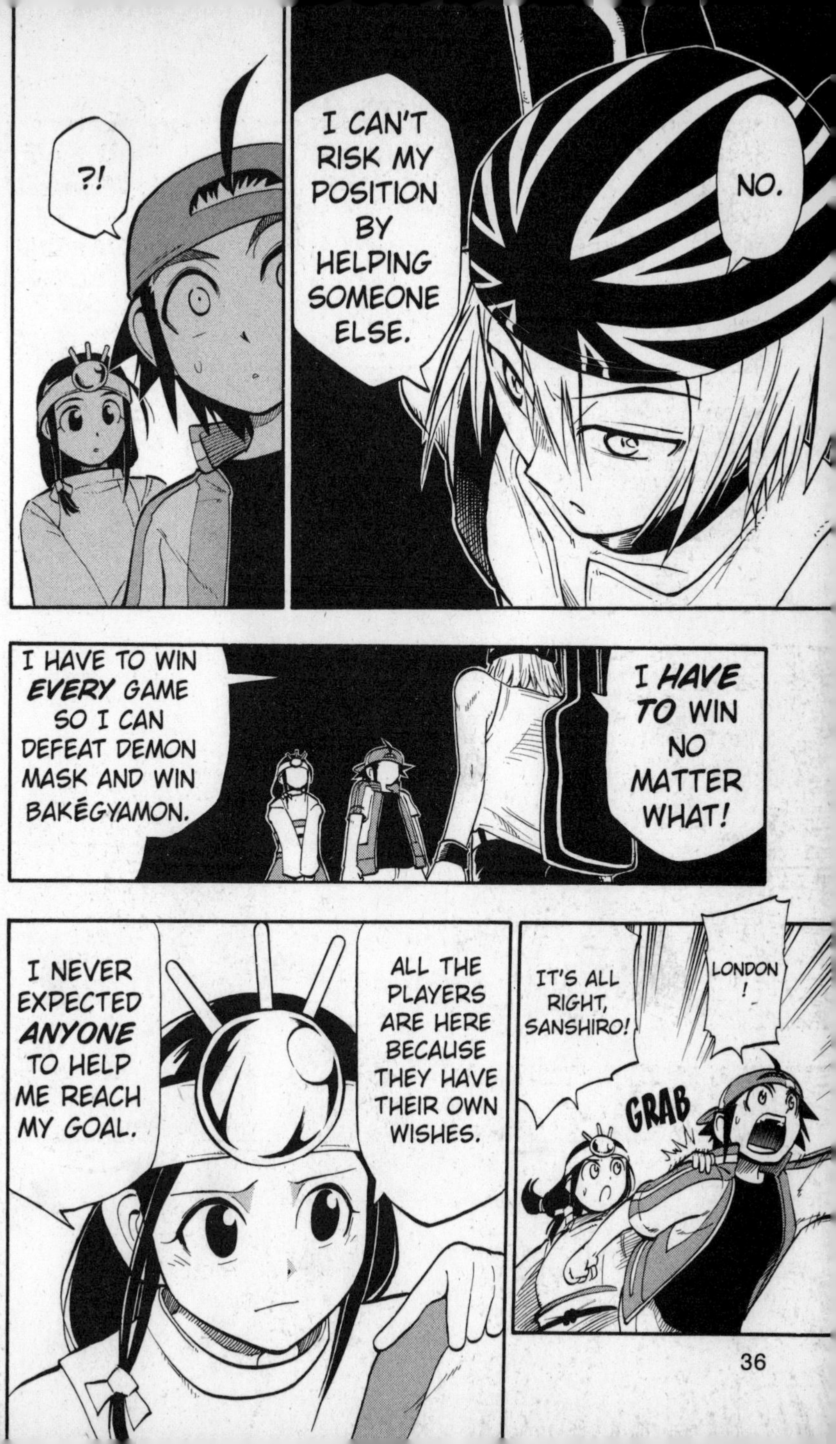
NO.
I CAN'T RISK MY POSITION BY HELPING SOMEONE ELSE.
?!
I *HAVE TO* WIN NO MATTER WHAT!
I HAVE TO WIN *EVERY* GAME SO I CAN DEFEAT DEMON MASK AND WIN BAKÉGYAMON.
LONDON!
IT'S ALL RIGHT, SANSHIRO!
GRAB
ALL THE PLAYERS ARE HERE BECAUSE THEY HAVE THEIR OWN WISHES.
I NEVER EXPECTED *ANYONE* TO HELP ME REACH MY GOAL.

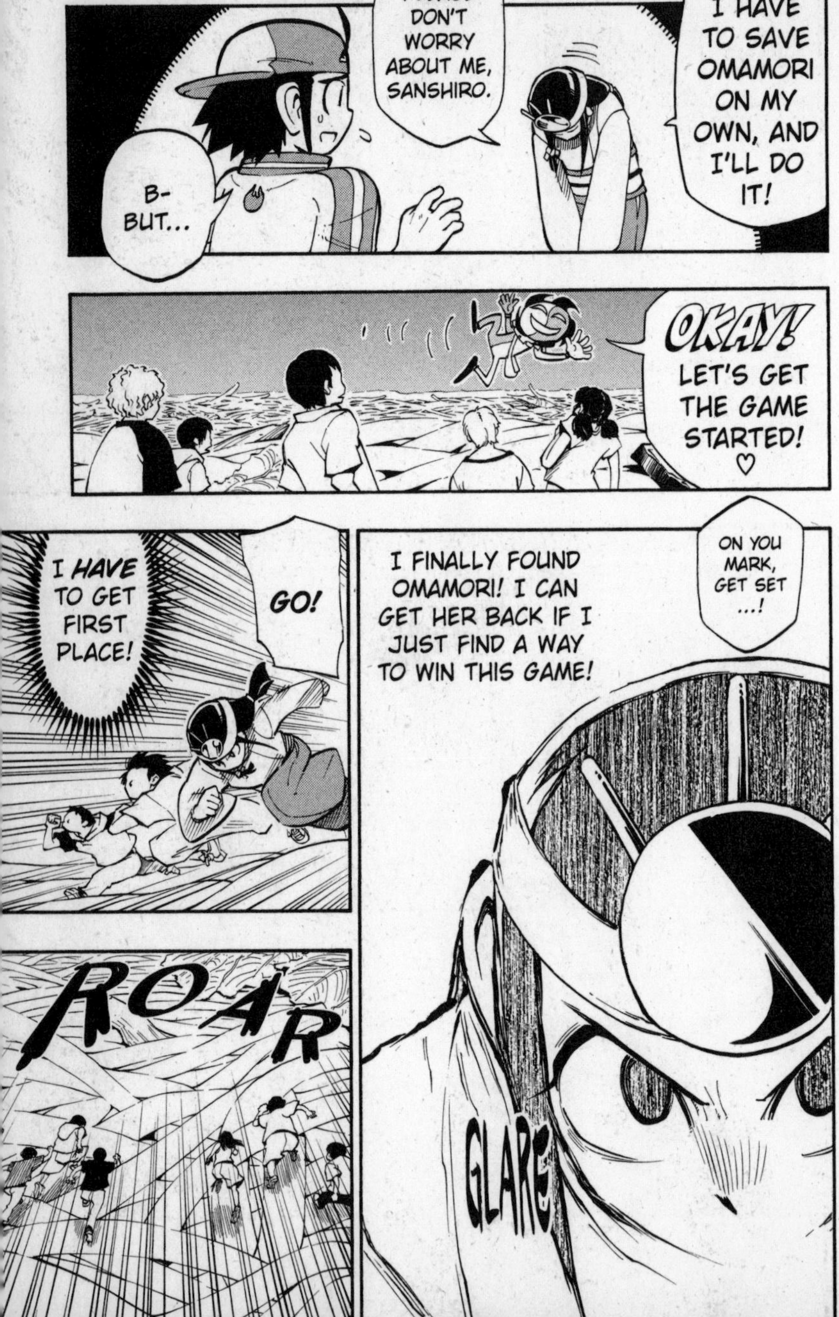
I HAVE TO SAVE OMAMORI ON MY OWN, AND I'LL DO IT!
PLEASE DON'T WORRY ABOUT ME, SANSHIRO.
B-BUT...
OKAY! LET'S GET THE GAME STARTED! ♡
ON YOU MARK, GET SET ...!
I FINALLY FOUND OMAMORI! I CAN GET HER BACK IF I JUST FIND A WAY TO WIN THIS GAME!
GLARE
GO!
I *HAVE* TO GET FIRST PLACE!
ROAR

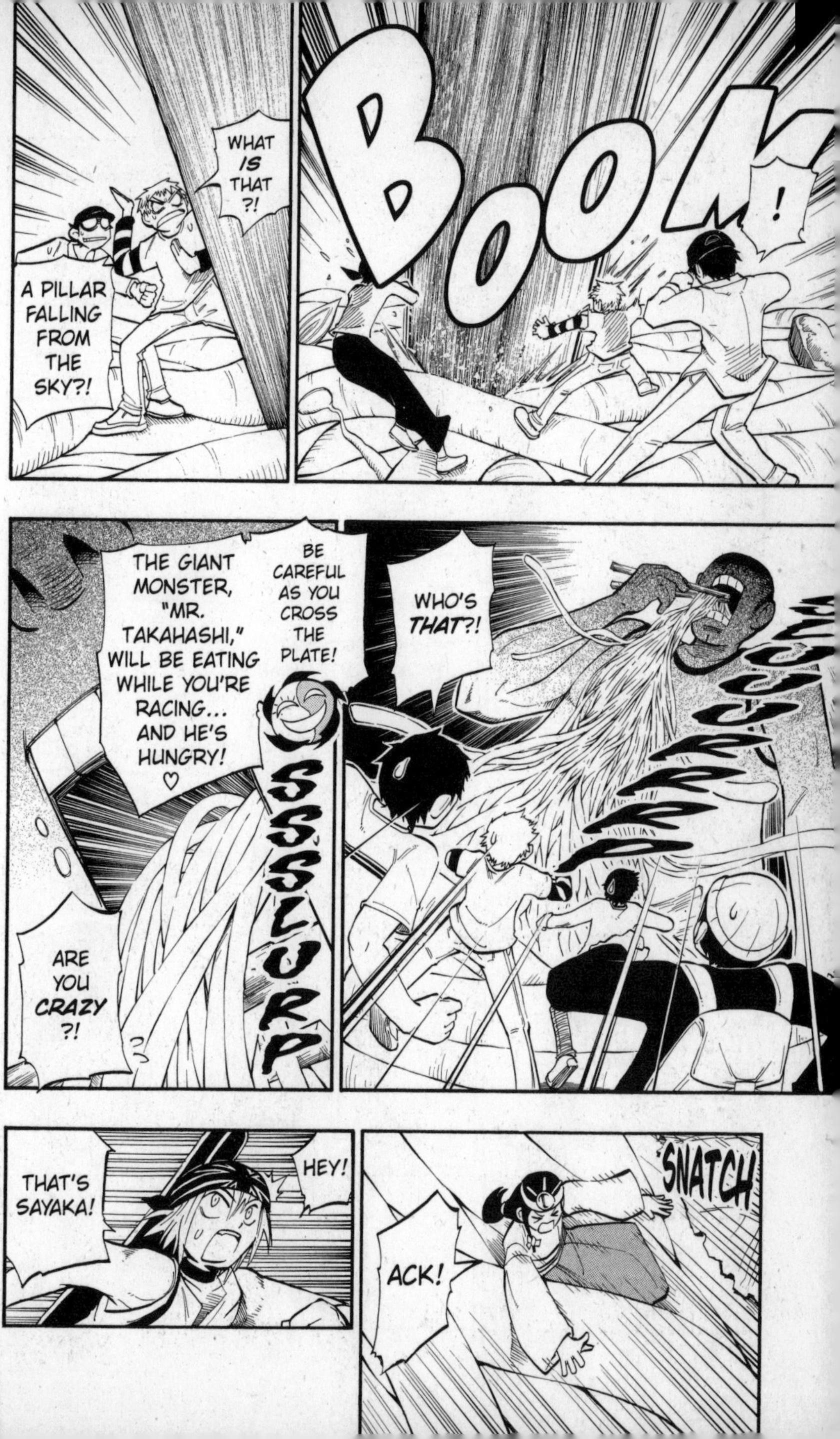
BOOM
!
WHAT *IS* THAT ?!
A PILLAR FALLING FROM THE SKY?!
WHO'S *THAT*?!
BE CAREFUL AS YOU CROSS THE PLATE!
THE GIANT MONSTER, "MR. TAKAHASHI," WILL BE EATING WHILE YOU'RE RACING... AND HE'S HUNGRY! ♡
SSSLURP
ARE YOU *CRAZY* ?!
SNATCH
ACK!
HEY!
THAT'S SAYAKA!

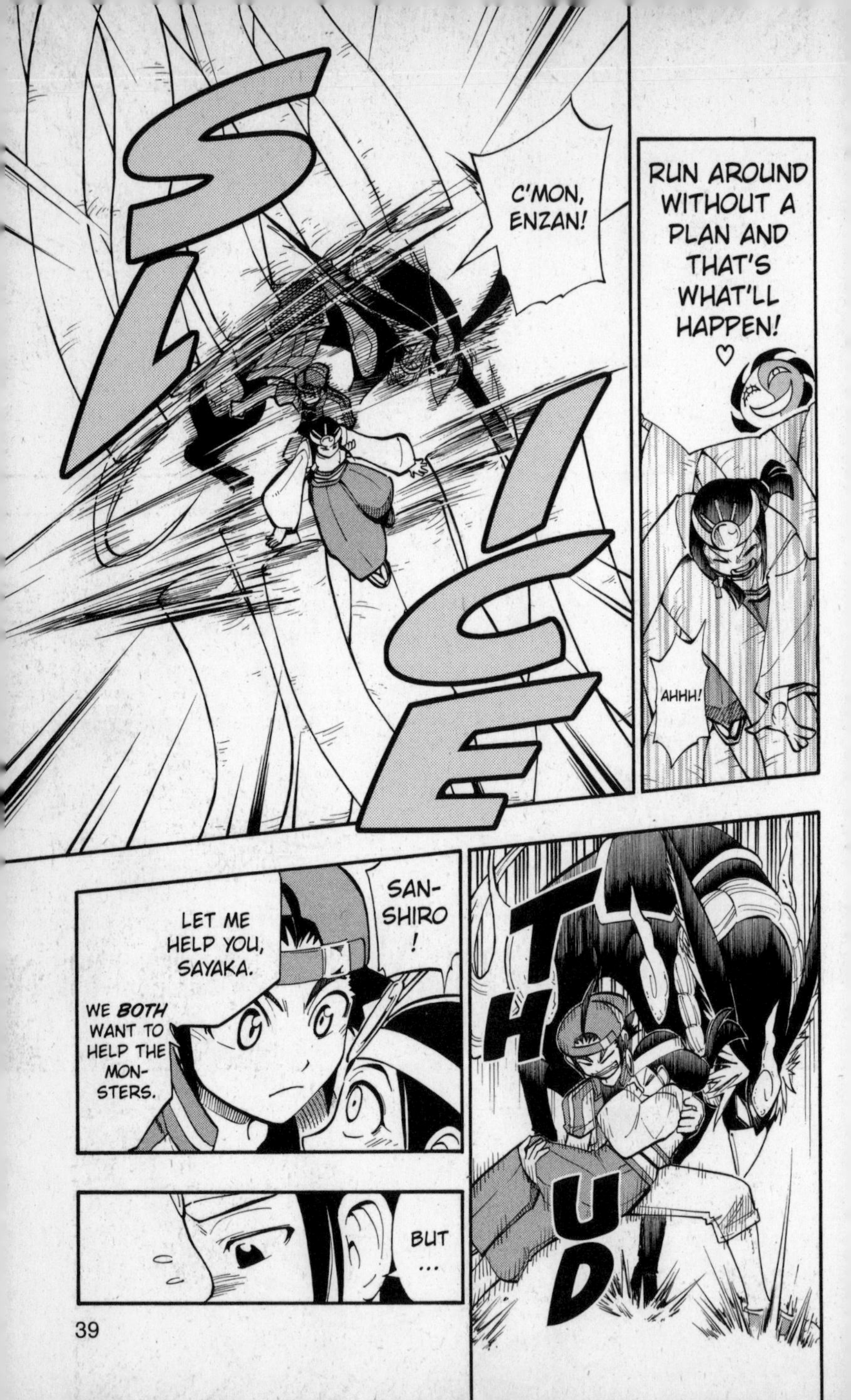
RUN AROUND WITHOUT A PLAN AND THAT'S WHAT'LL HAPPEN! ♡
AHHH!
C'MON, ENZAN!
SLICE
THUD
SAN-SHIRO!
LET ME HELP YOU, SAYAKA.
WE *BOTH* WANT TO HELP THE MON-STERS.
BUT ...

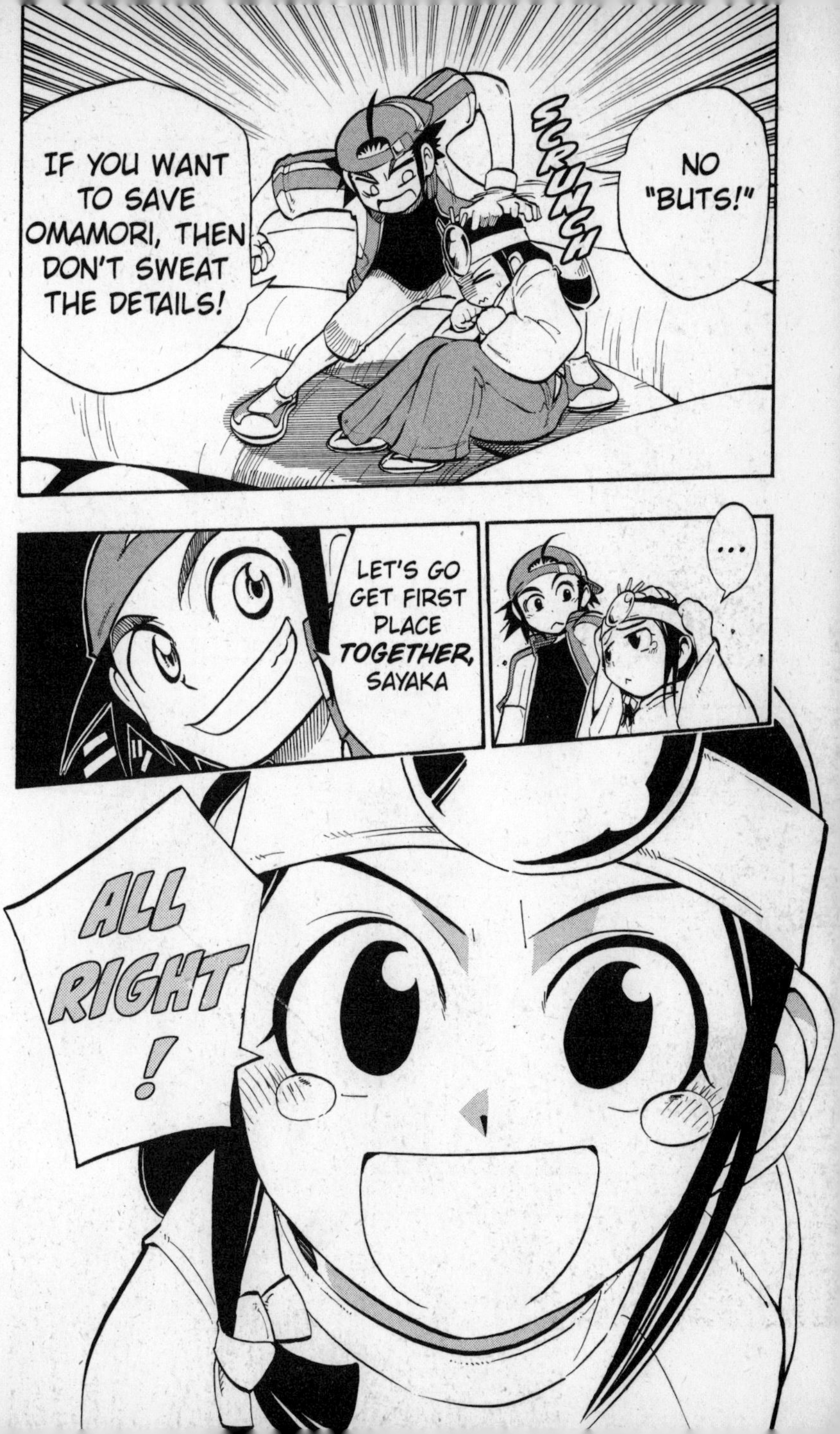
NO "BUTS!"
SCRUNCH
IF YOU WANT TO SAVE OMAMORI, THEN DON'T SWEAT THE DETAILS!
...
LET'S GO GET FIRST PLACE *TOGETHER*, SAYAKA
ALL RIGHT!

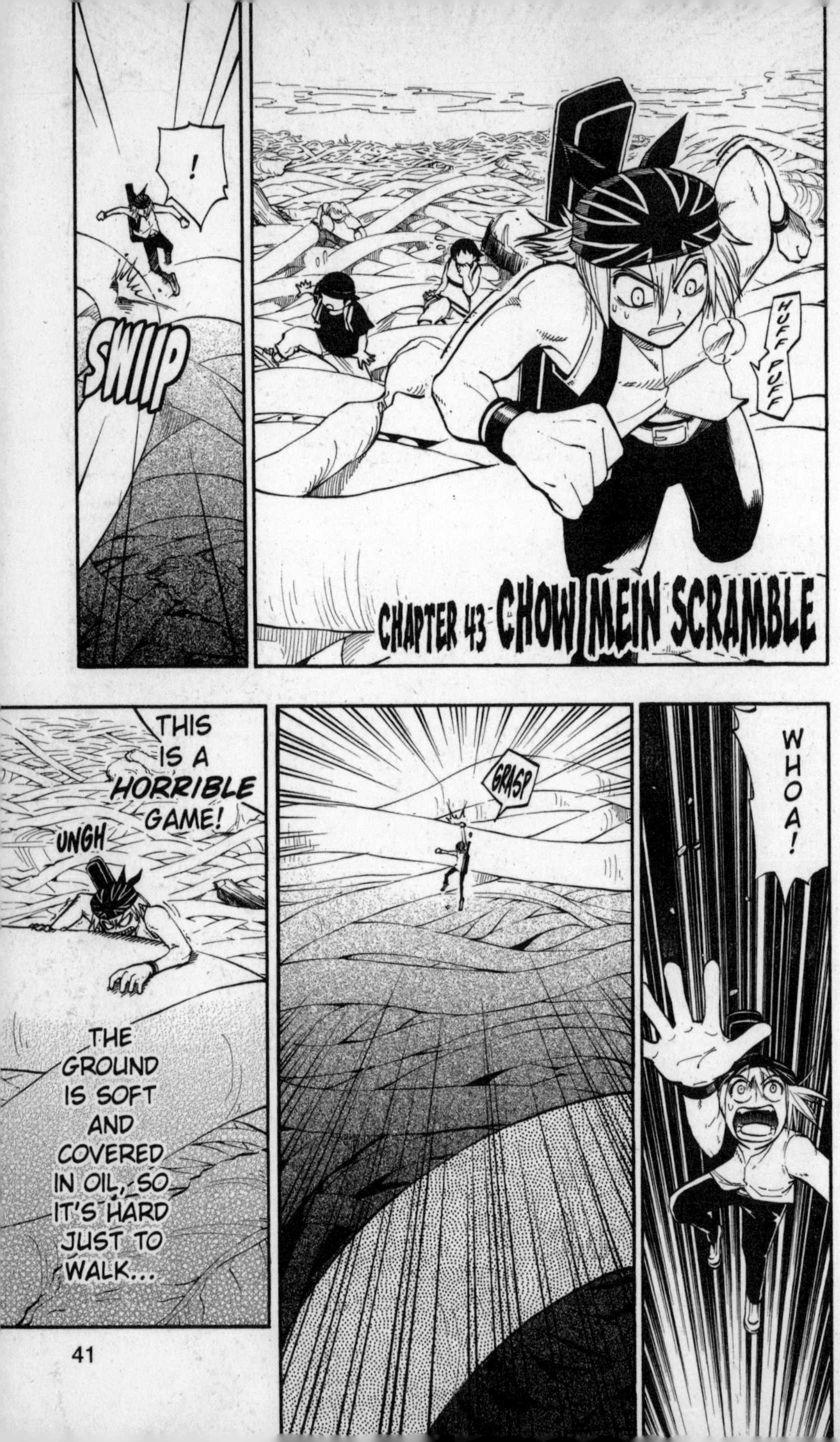
HUFF PUFF
CHAPTER 43 CHOW MEIN SCRAMBLE
!
SWIP
WHOA!
GRASP
THIS IS A HORRIBLE GAME!
UNGH
THE GROUND IS SOFT AND COVERED IN OIL, SO IT'S HARD JUST TO WALK...

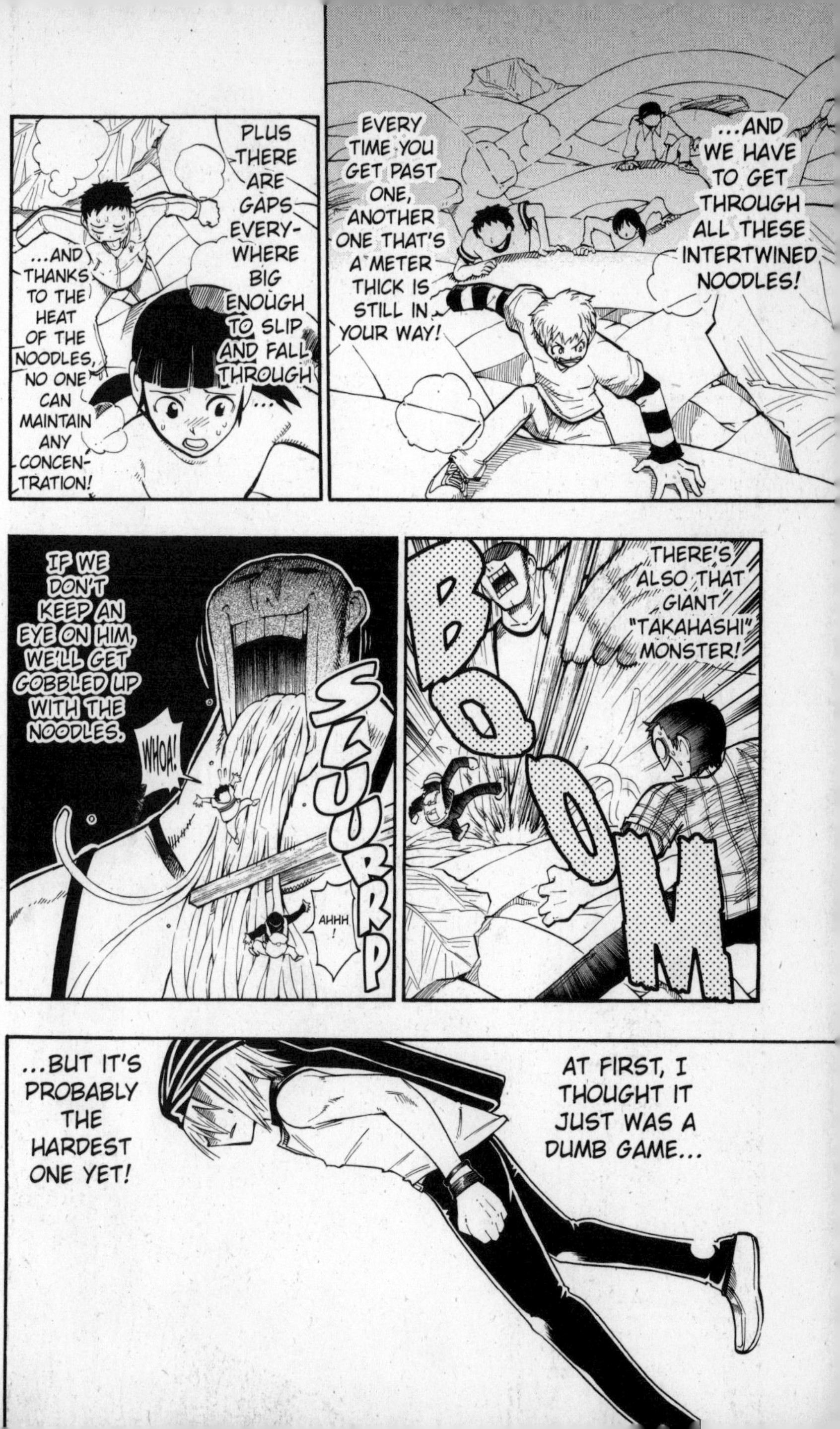
...AND WE HAVE TO GET THROUGH ALL THESE INTERTWINED NOODLES!
EVERY TIME YOU GET PAST ONE, ANOTHER ONE THAT'S A METER THICK IS STILL IN YOUR WAY!
PLUS THERE ARE GAPS EVERYWHERE BIG ENOUGH TO SLIP AND FALL THROUGH...
...AND THANKS TO THE HEAT OF THE NOODLES, NO ONE CAN MAINTAIN ANY CONCENTRATION!
THERE'S ALSO THAT GIANT "TAKAHASHI" MONSTER!
BOOOM
IF WE DON'T KEEP AN EYE ON HIM, WE'LL GET GOBBLED UP WITH THE NOODLES.
WHOA!
SLUUURRP
AHHH!
AT FIRST, I THOUGHT IT JUST WAS A DUMB GAME...
...BUT IT'S PROBABLY THE HARDEST ONE YET!

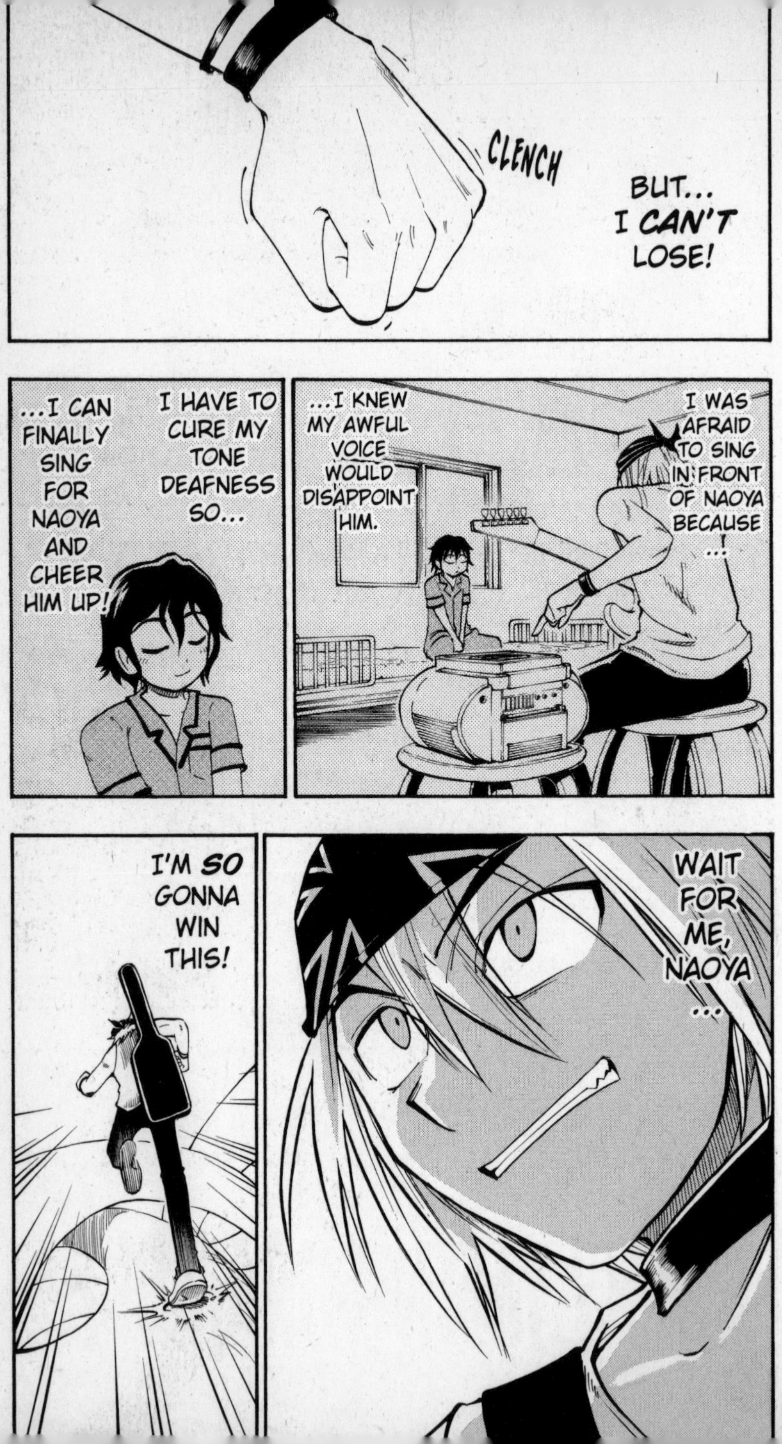
CLENCH
BUT... I CAN'T LOSE!
I WAS AFRAID TO SING IN FRONT OF NAOYA BECAUSE...
...I KNEW MY AWFUL VOICE WOULD DISAPPOINT HIM.
I HAVE TO CURE MY TONE DEAFNESS SO...
...I CAN FINALLY SING FOR NAOYA AND CHEER HIM UP!
WAIT FOR ME, NAOYA...
I'M SO GONNA WIN THIS!

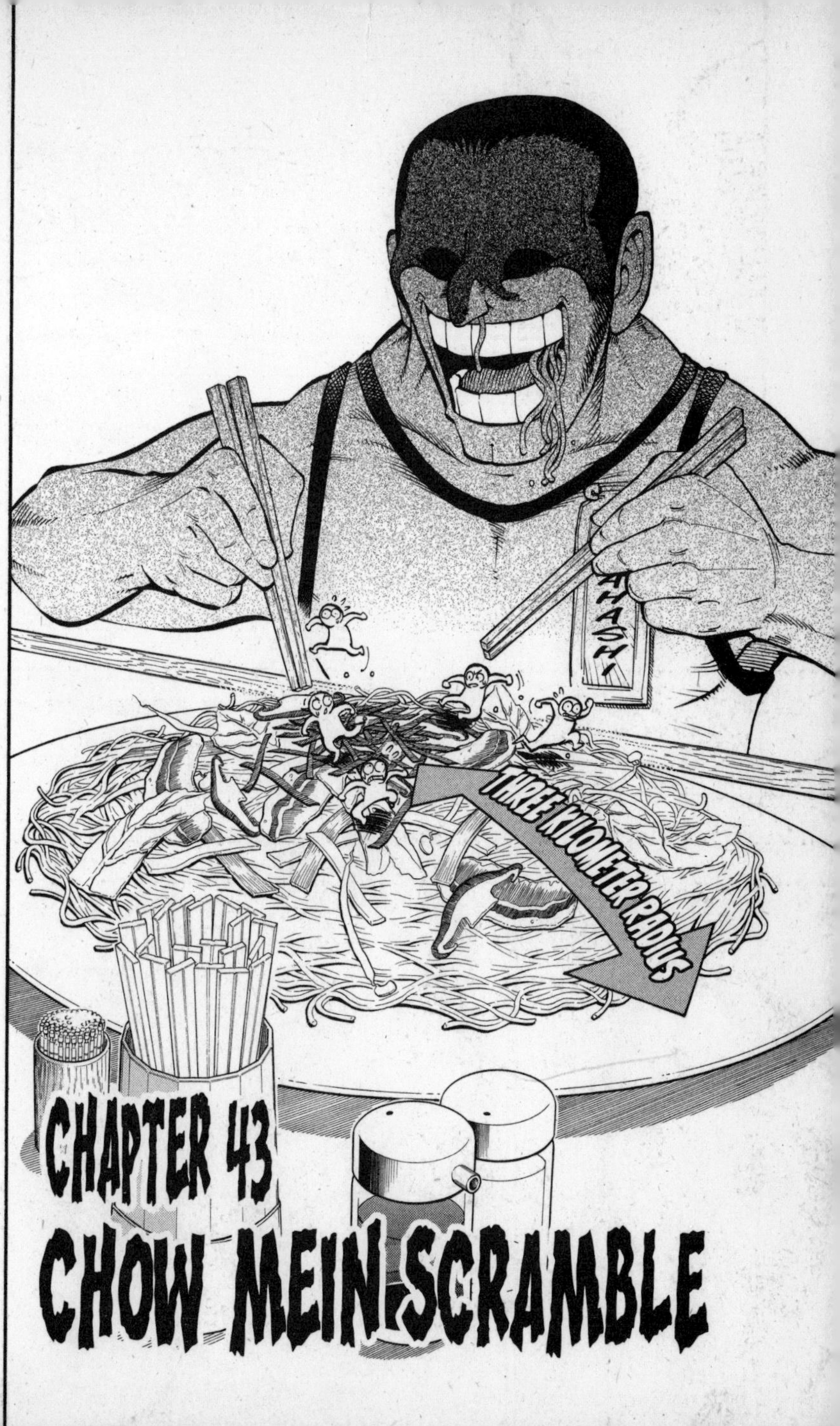
THREE KILOMETER RADIUS
CHAPTER 43
CHOW MEIN SCRAMBLE

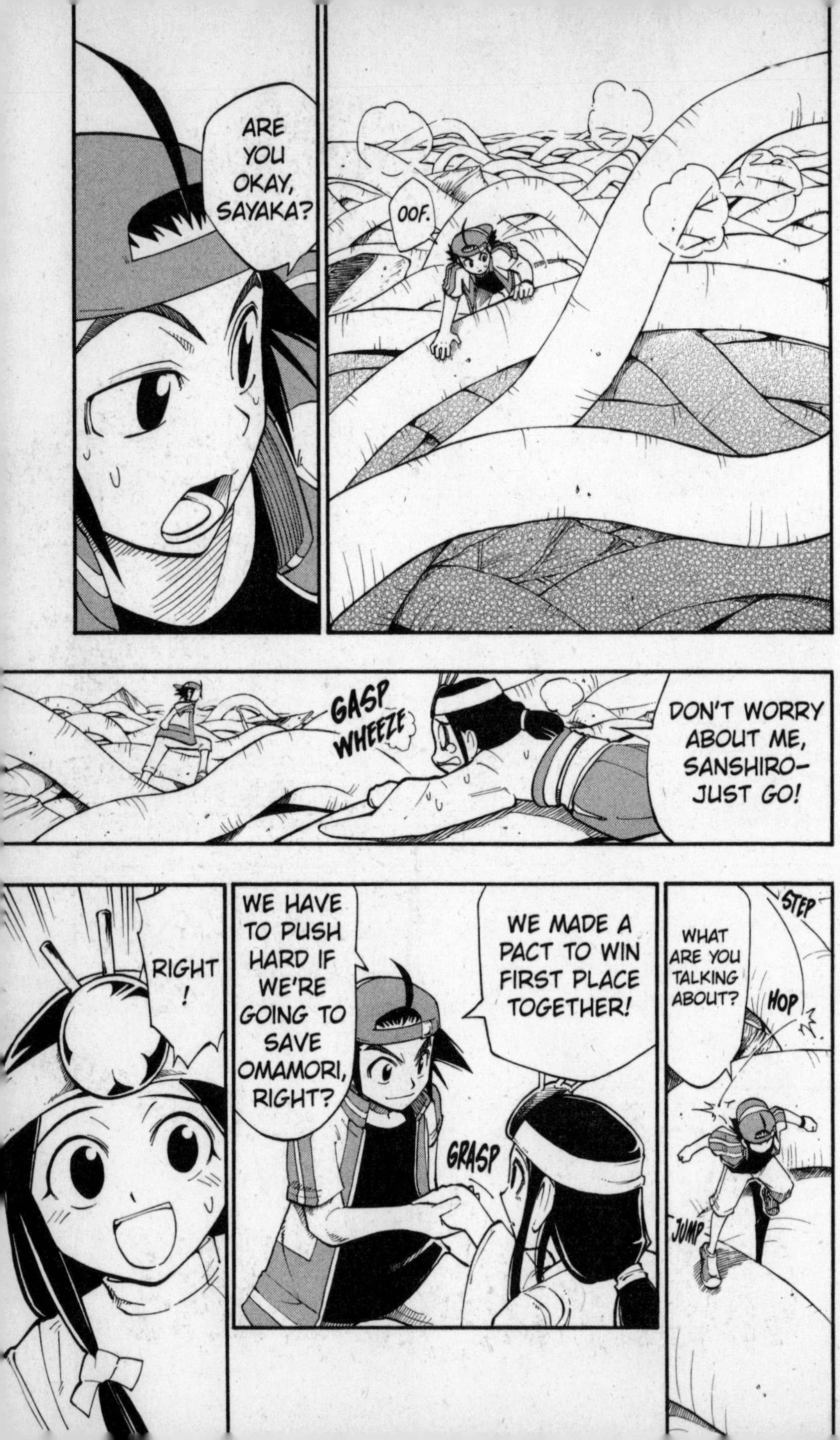
OOF.
ARE YOU OKAY, SAYAKA?
DON'T WORRY ABOUT ME, SANSHIRO-JUST GO!
GASP
WHEEZE
STEP
WHAT ARE YOU TALKING ABOUT?
HOP
JUMP
WE MADE A PACT TO WIN FIRST PLACE TOGETHER!
WE HAVE TO PUSH HARD IF WE'RE GOING TO SAVE OMAMORI, RIGHT?
GRASP
RIGHT!

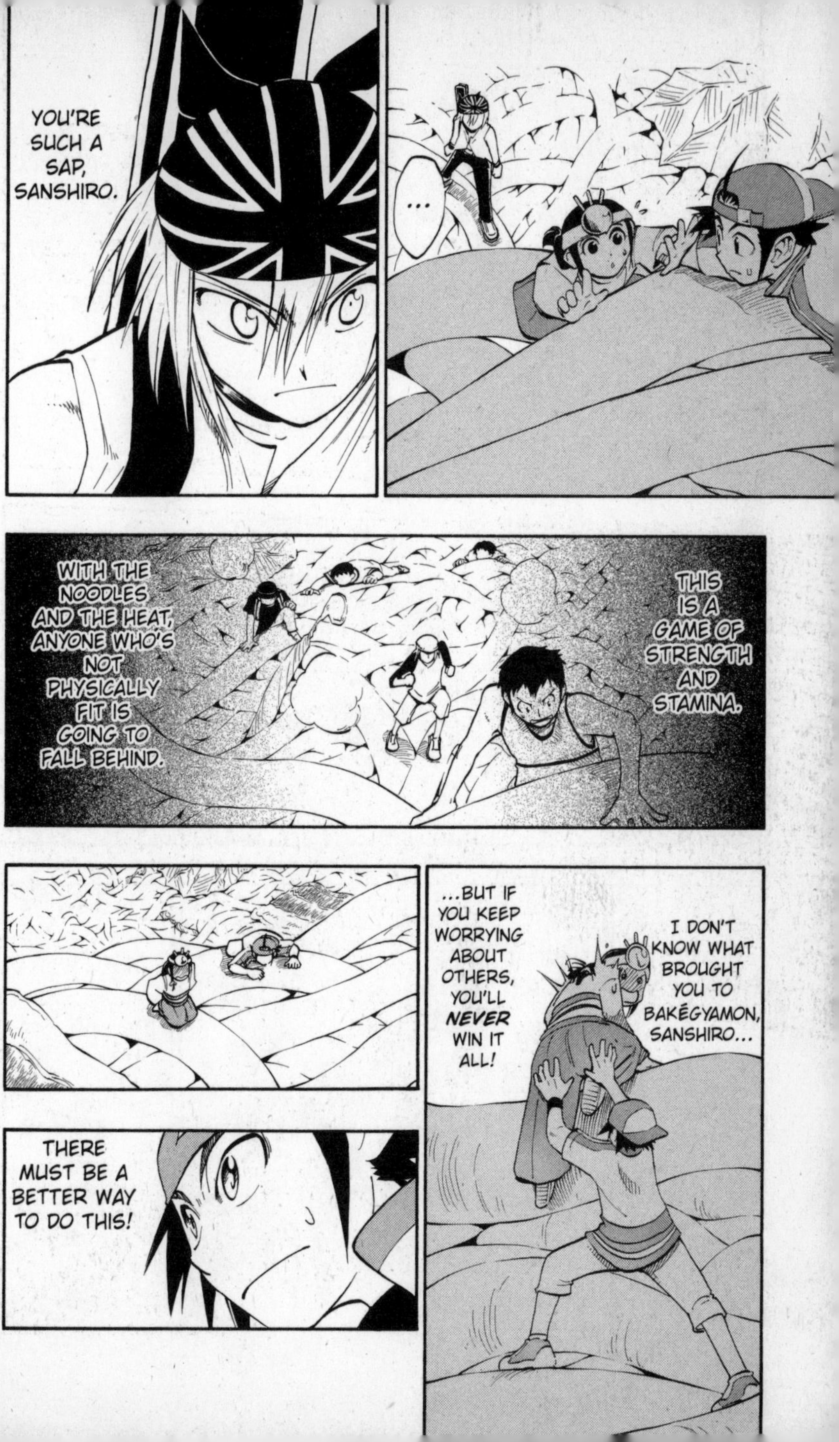
...
YOU'RE SUCH A SAP, SANSHIRO.
THIS IS A GAME OF STRENGTH AND STAMINA.
WITH THE NOODLES AND THE HEAT, ANYONE WHO'S NOT PHYSICALLY FIT IS GOING TO FALL BEHIND.
I DON'T KNOW WHAT BROUGHT YOU TO BAKÉGYAMON, SANSHIRO...
...BUT IF YOU KEEP WORRYING ABOUT OTHERS, YOU'LL NEVER WIN IT ALL!
THERE MUST BE A BETTER WAY TO DO THIS!

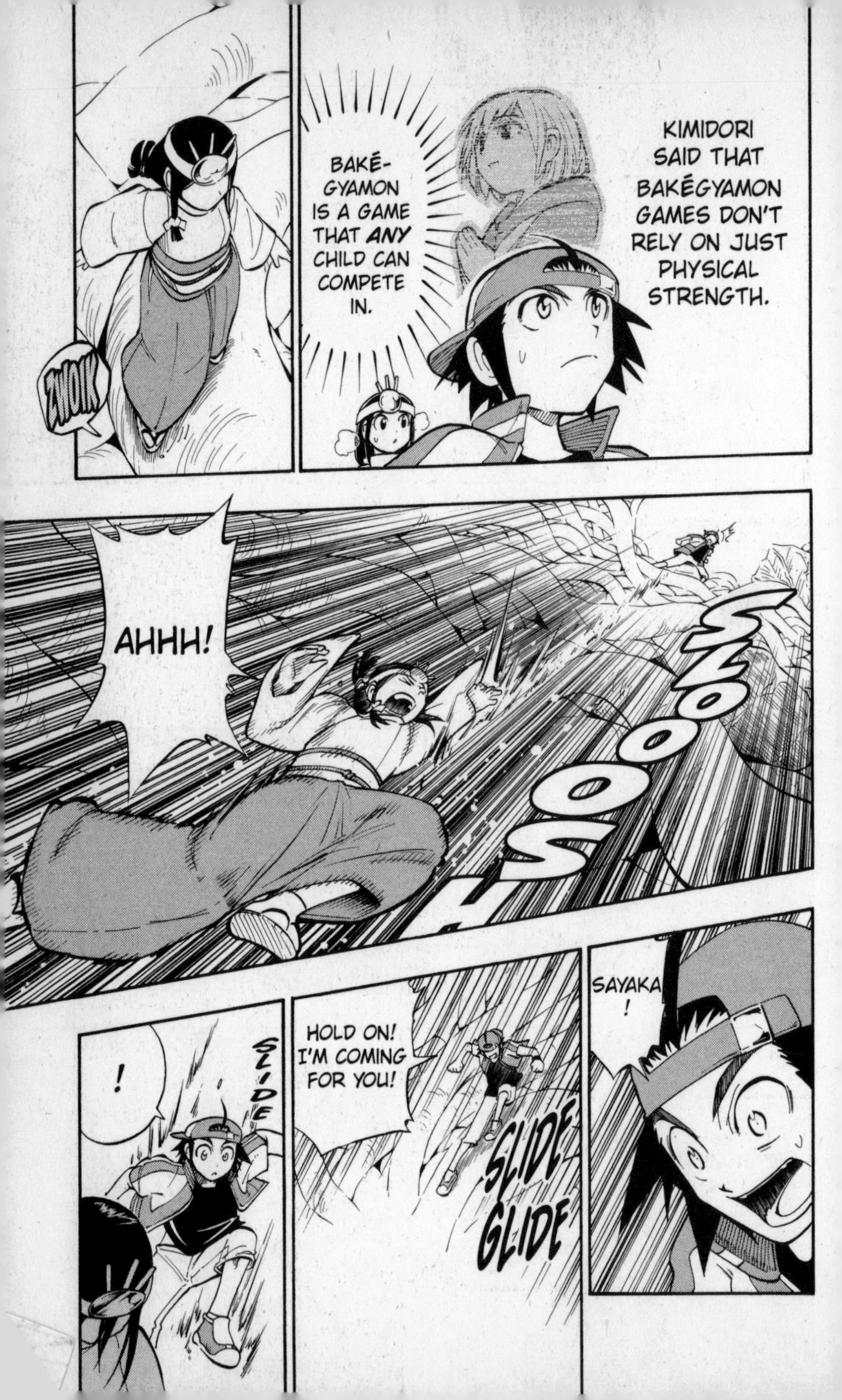

KIMIDORI SAID THAT BAKÉGYAMON GAMES DON'T RELY ON JUST PHYSICAL STRENGTH.
BAKÉ-GYAMON IS A GAME THAT ANY CHILD CAN COMPETE IN.
ZWOIK
SWOOOOSH
AHHH!
SAYAKA!
HOLD ON! I'M COMING FOR YOU!
SLIDE GLIDE
SLIDE
!

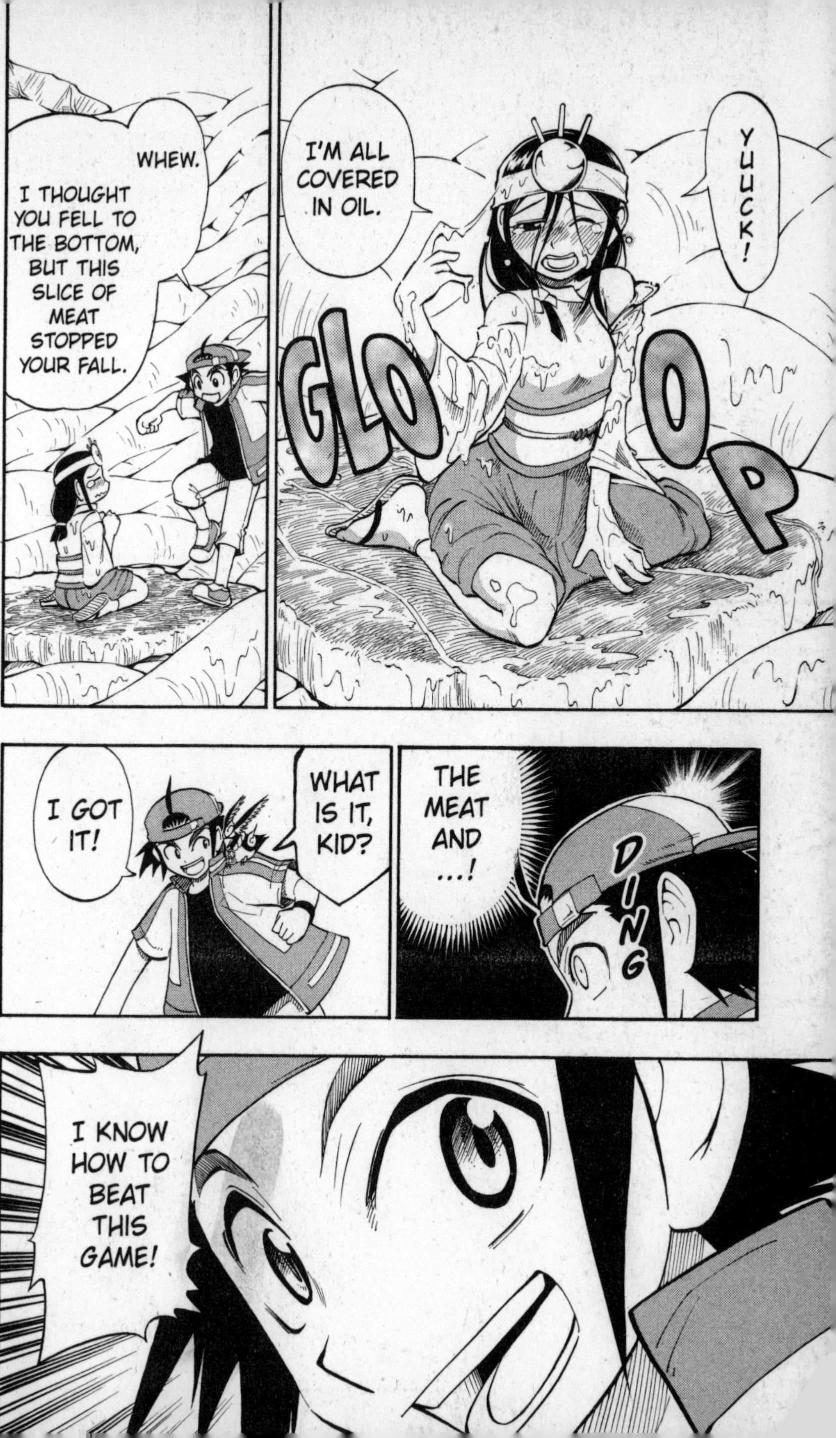
YUUCK!
I'M ALL COVERED IN OIL.
GLOOP
WHEW.
I THOUGHT YOU FELL TO THE BOTTOM, BUT THIS SLICE OF MEAT STOPPED YOUR FALL.
THE MEAT AND ...!
DING
I GOT IT!
WHAT IS IT, KID?
I KNOW HOW TO BEAT THIS GAME!

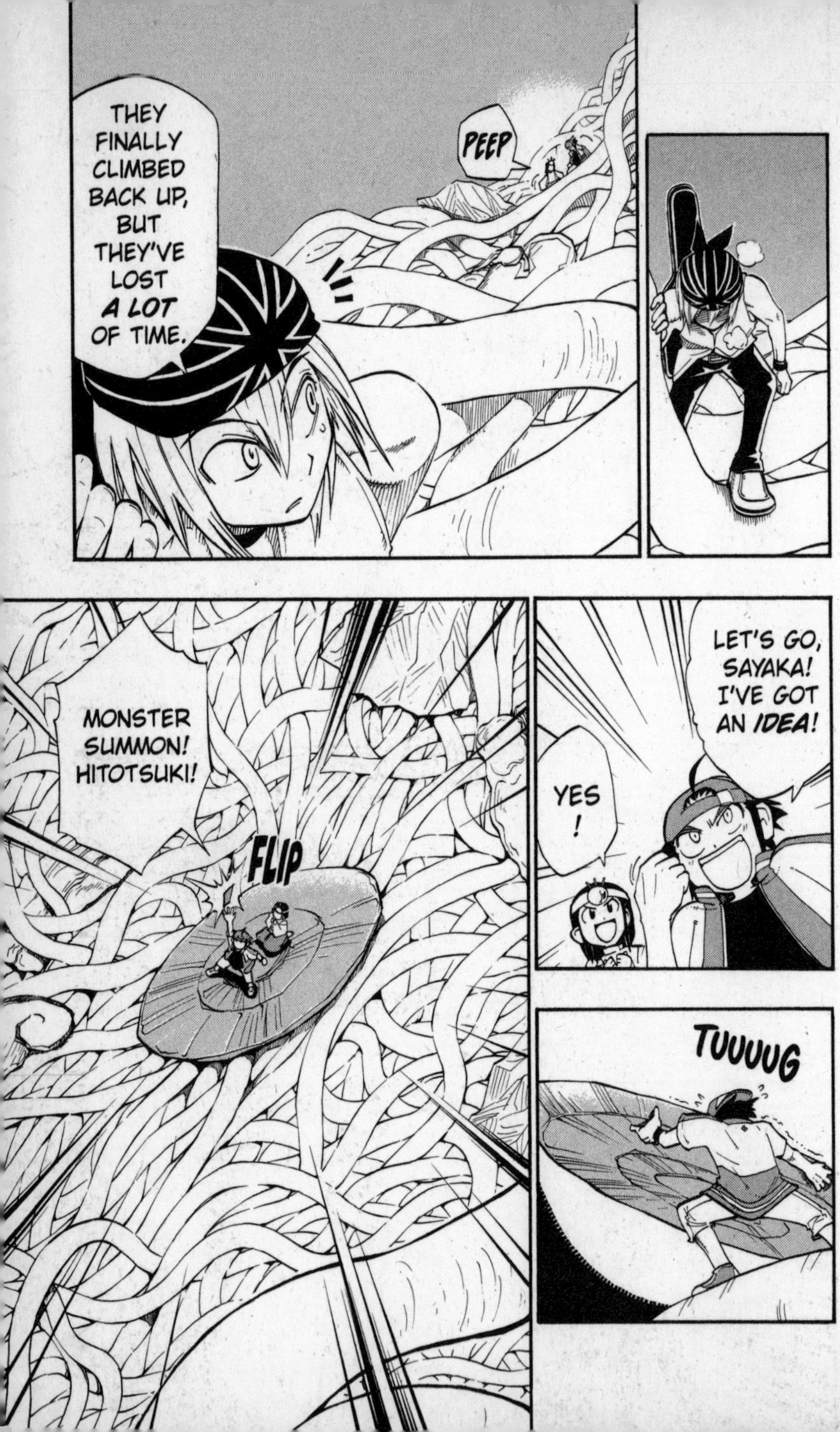
PEEP
THEY FINALLY CLIMBED BACK UP, BUT THEY'VE LOST A LOT OF TIME.
LET'S GO, SAYAKA! I'VE GOT AN IDEA!
YES!
TUUUUG
MONSTER SUMMON! HITOTSUKI!
FLIP

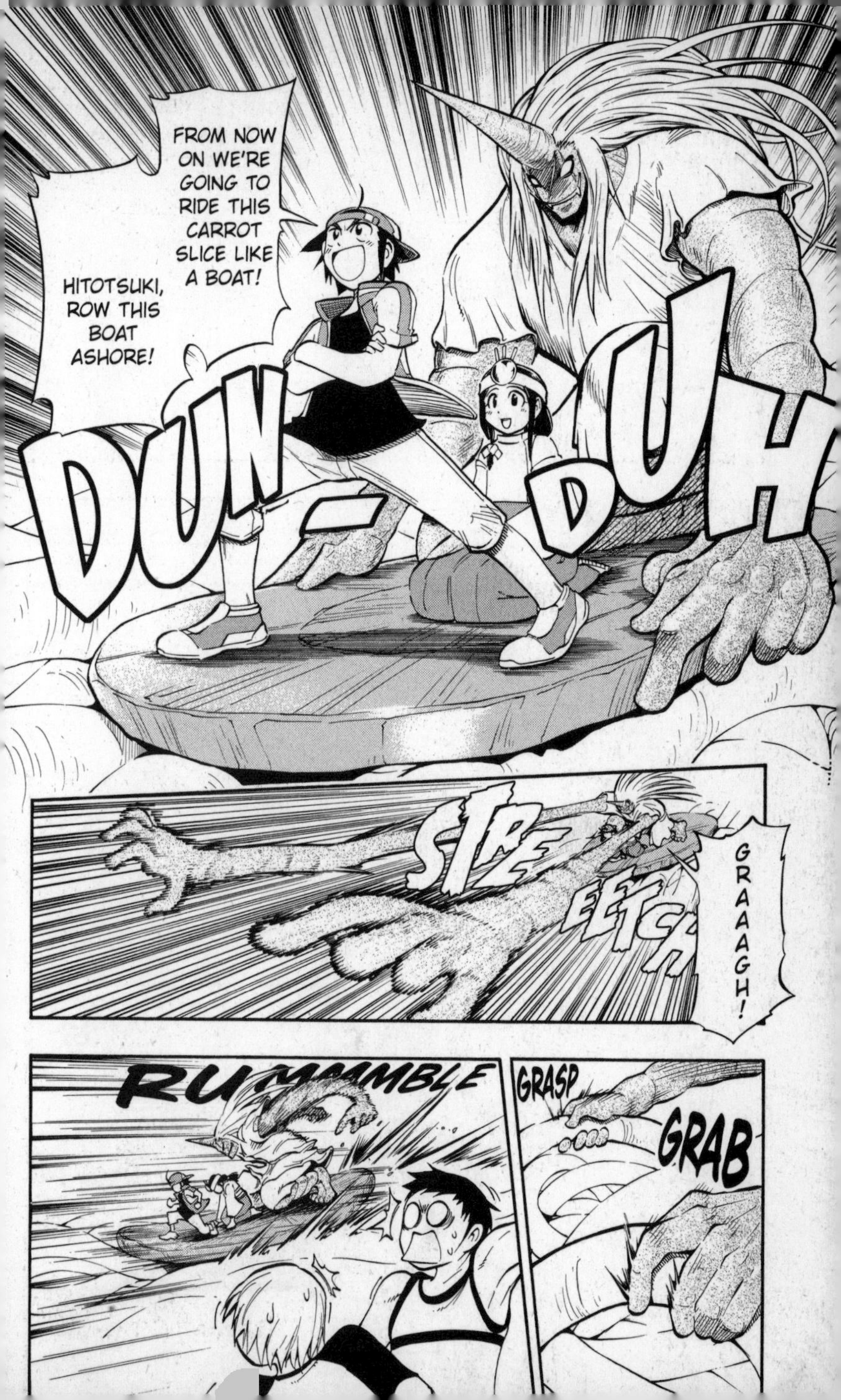
FROM NOW ON WE'RE GOING TO RIDE THIS CARROT SLICE LIKE A BOAT!
HITOTSUKI, ROW THIS BOAT ASHORE!
DUN-DUH
GRAAAAGH!
STREEETCH
GRASP
GRAB
RUMMMBLE

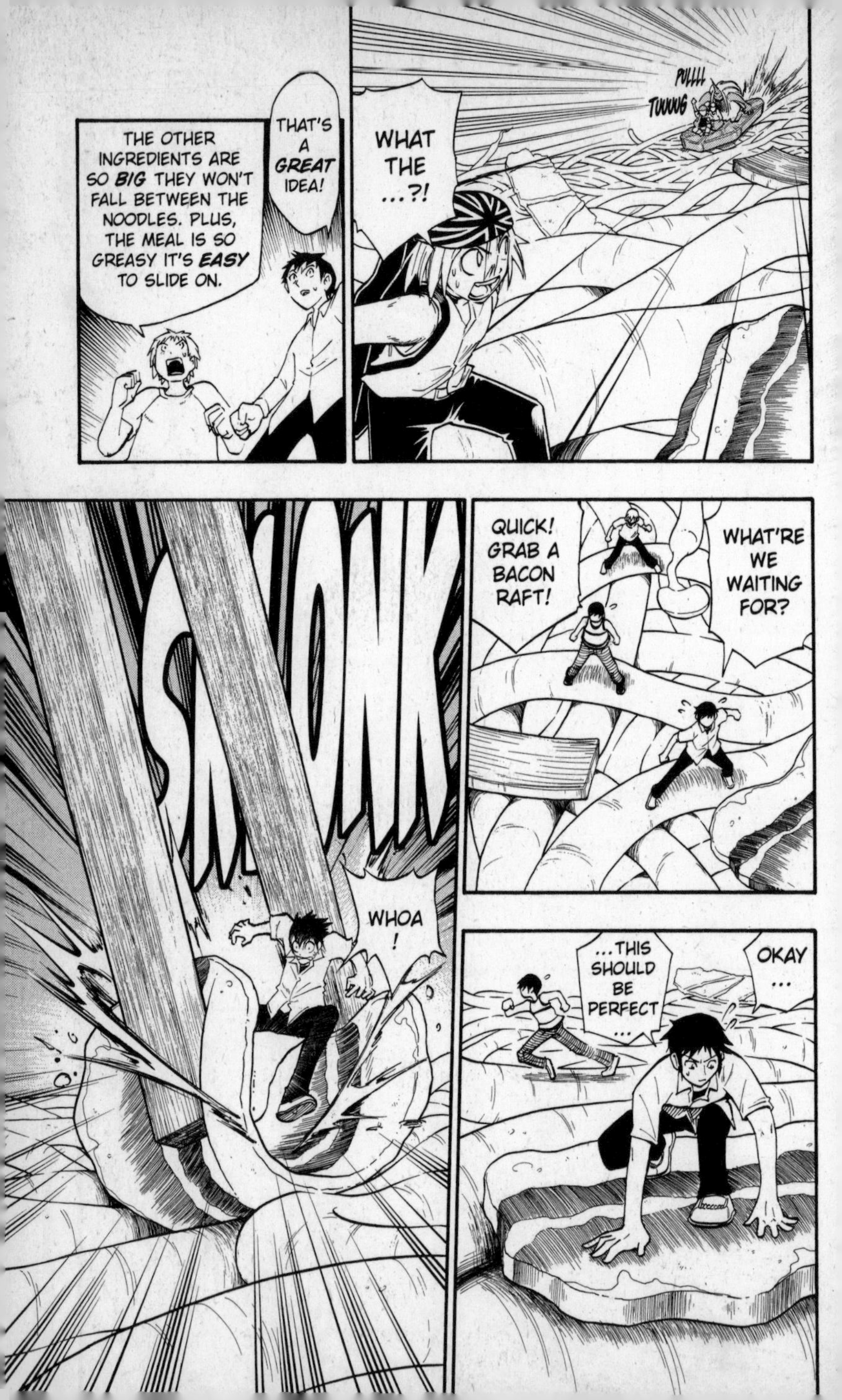
PULLLL
TUUUUG
WHAT THE ...?!
THAT'S A GREAT IDEA!
THE OTHER INGREDIENTS ARE SO BIG THEY WON'T FALL BETWEEN THE NOODLES. PLUS, THE MEAL IS SO GREASY IT'S EASY TO SLIDE ON.
WHAT'RE WE WAITING FOR?
QUICK! GRAB A BACON RAFT!
OKAY ...
...THIS SHOULD BE PERFECT ...
WHOA !

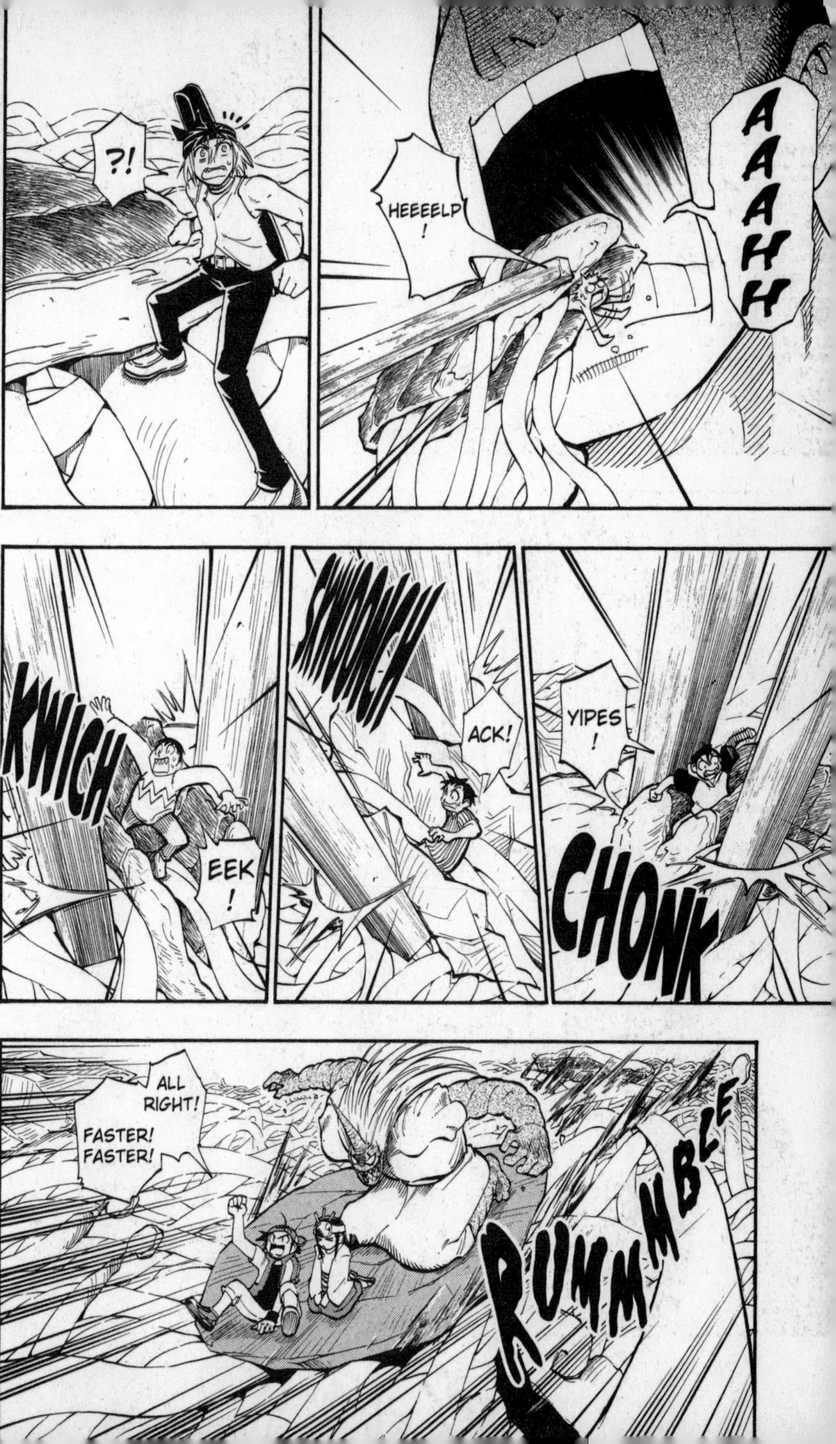
AAAAHH
HEEEELP!
?!
YIPES!
CHONK
ACK!
KNICH
EEK!
ALL RIGHT!
FASTER! FASTER!
RUMMMBLE

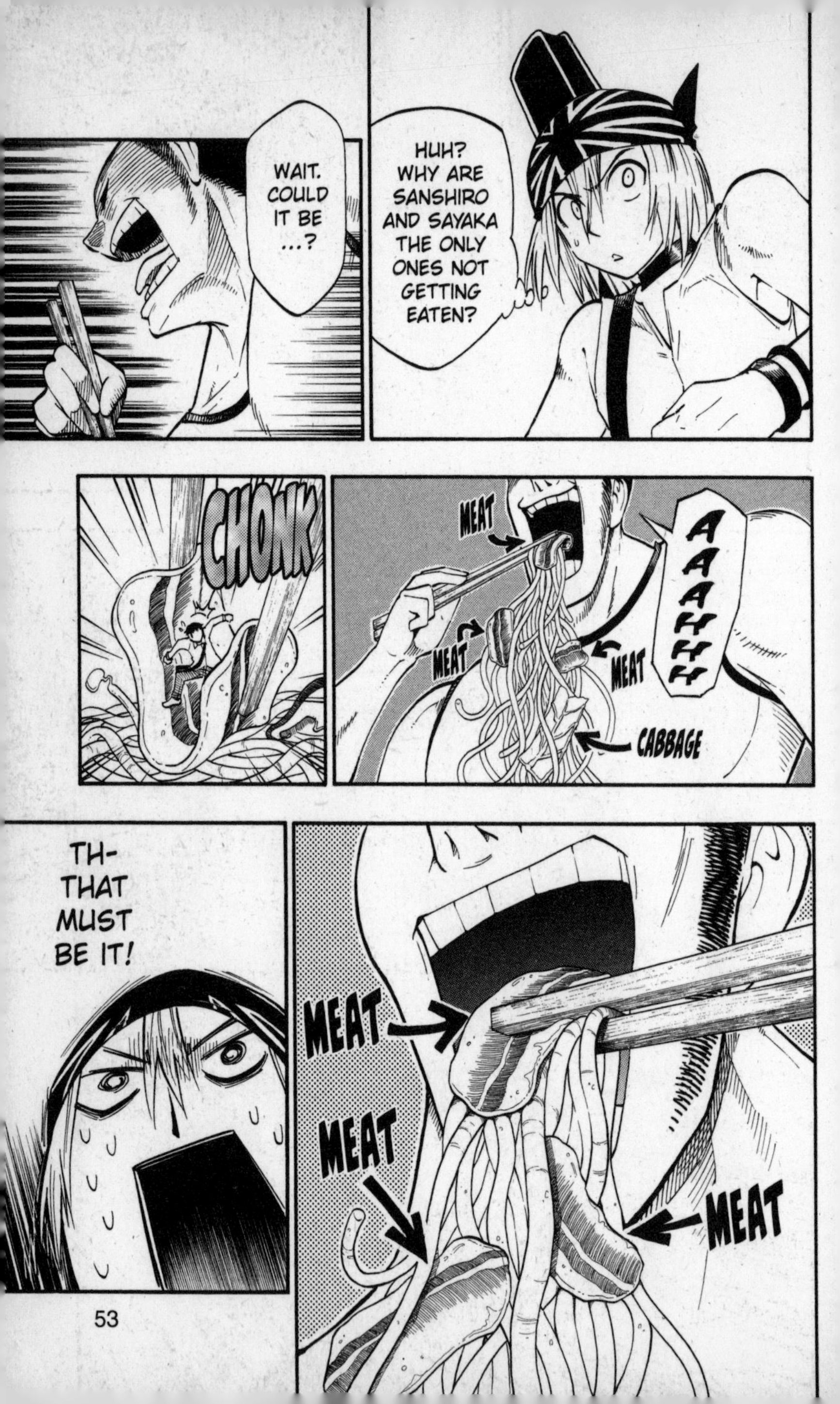
HUH? WHY ARE SANSHIRO AND SAYAKA THE ONLY ONES NOT GETTING EATEN?
WAIT. COULD IT BE ...?
AAAAHHH
MEAT
MEAT
MEAT
CABBAGE
CHONK
MEAT
MEAT
MEAT
TH-THAT MUST BE IT!

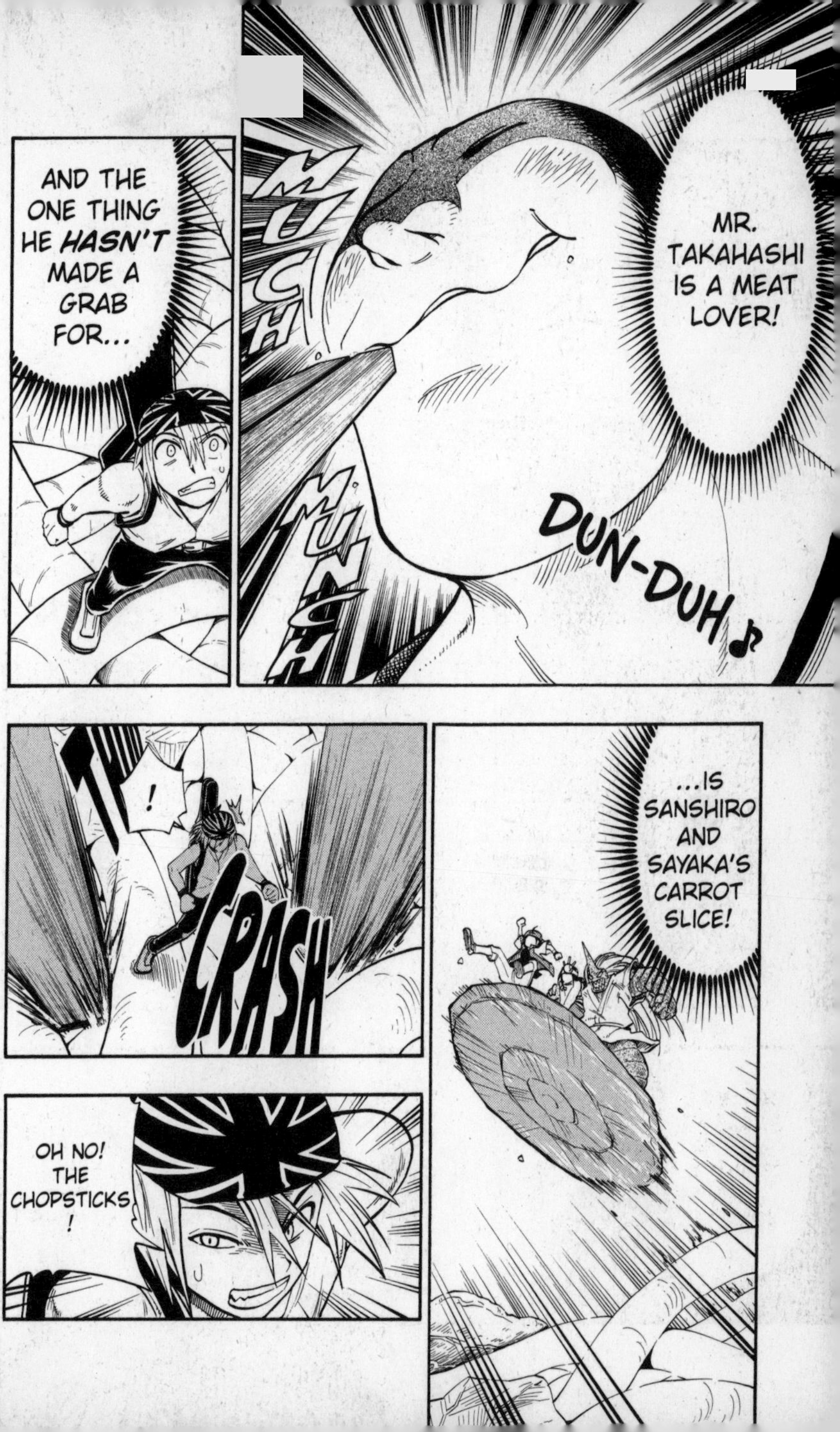
MR. TAKAHASHI IS A MEAT LOVER!
MUNCH
MUNCH
DUN-DUH ♪
AND THE ONE THING HE *HASN'T* MADE A GRAB FOR...
...IS SANSHIRO AND SAYAKA'S CARROT SLICE!
!
CRASH
OH NO! THE CHOPSTICKS!

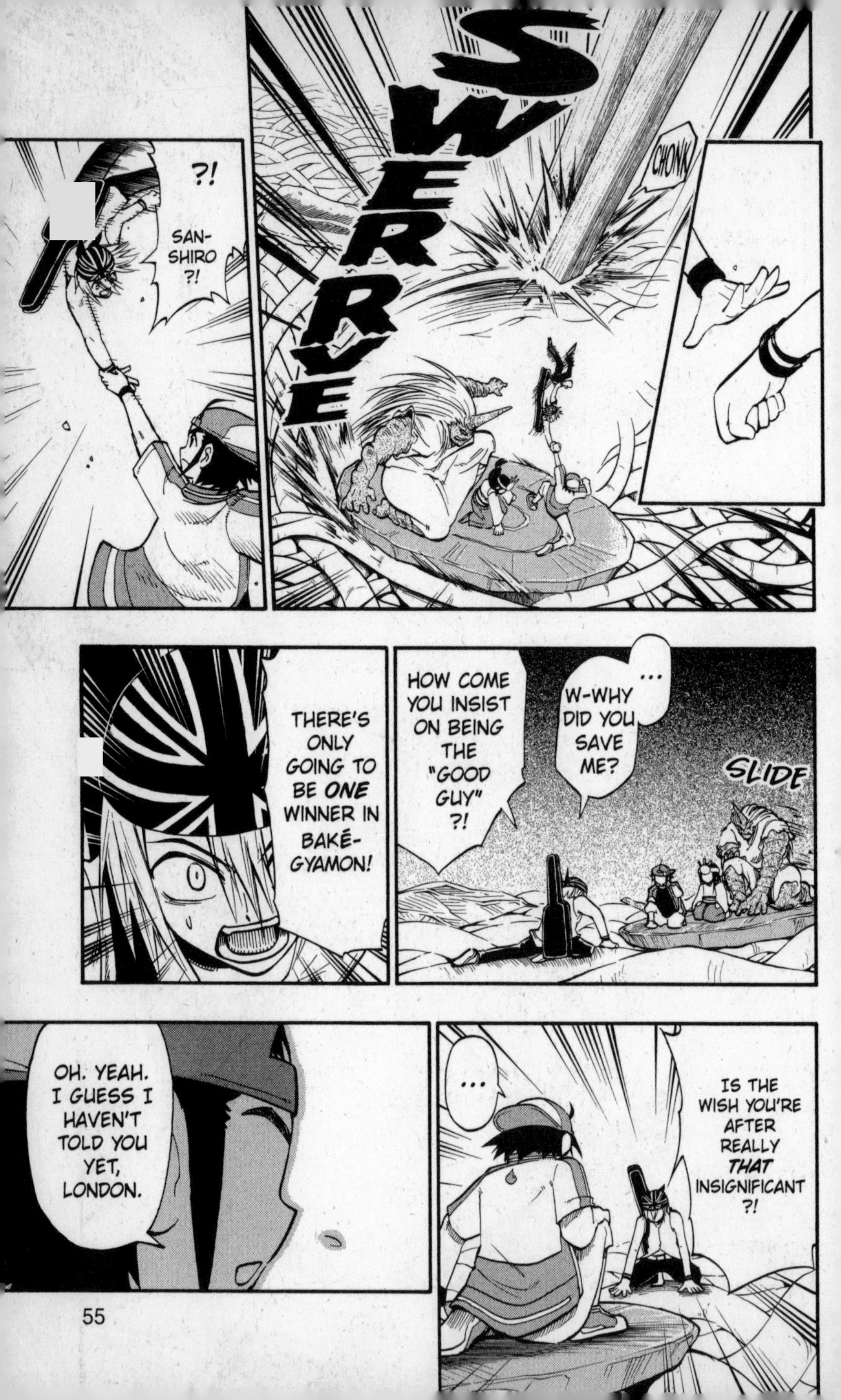
CHONK
SWERVE
?!
SAN-SHIRO ?!
...
W-WHY DID YOU SAVE ME?
HOW COME YOU INSIST ON BEING THE "GOOD GUY" ?!
SLIDE
THERE'S ONLY GOING TO BE ONE WINNER IN BAKÉ-GYAMON!
...
IS THE WISH YOU'RE AFTER REALLY THAT INSIGNIFICANT ?!
OH. YEAH. I GUESS I HAVEN'T TOLD YOU YET, LONDON.

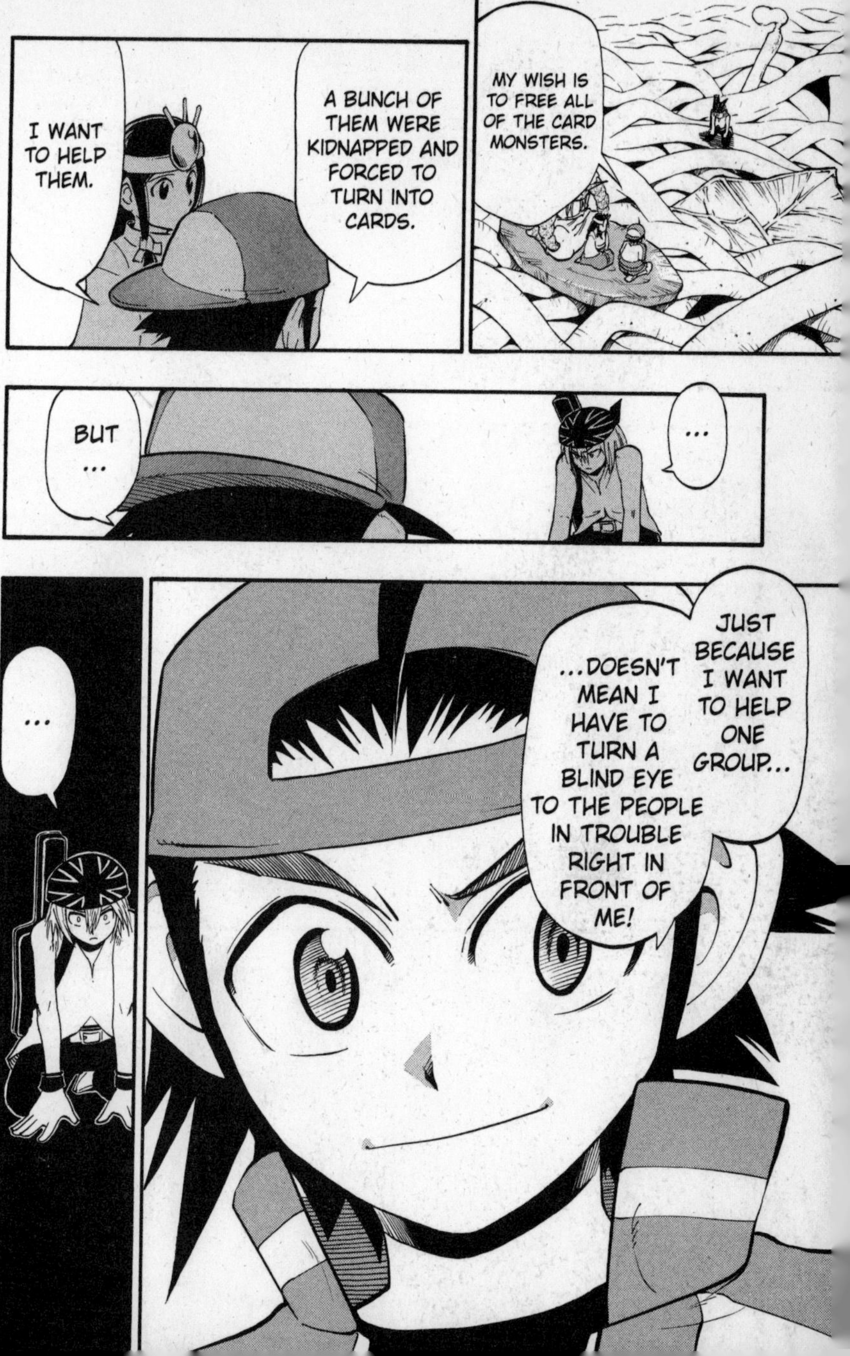
MY WISH IS TO FREE ALL OF THE CARD MONSTERS.
A BUNCH OF THEM WERE KIDNAPPED AND FORCED TO TURN INTO CARDS.
I WANT TO HELP THEM.
...
BUT ...
JUST BECAUSE I WANT TO HELP ONE GROUP...
...DOESN'T MEAN I HAVE TO TURN A BLIND EYE TO THE PEOPLE IN TROUBLE RIGHT IN FRONT OF ME!
...

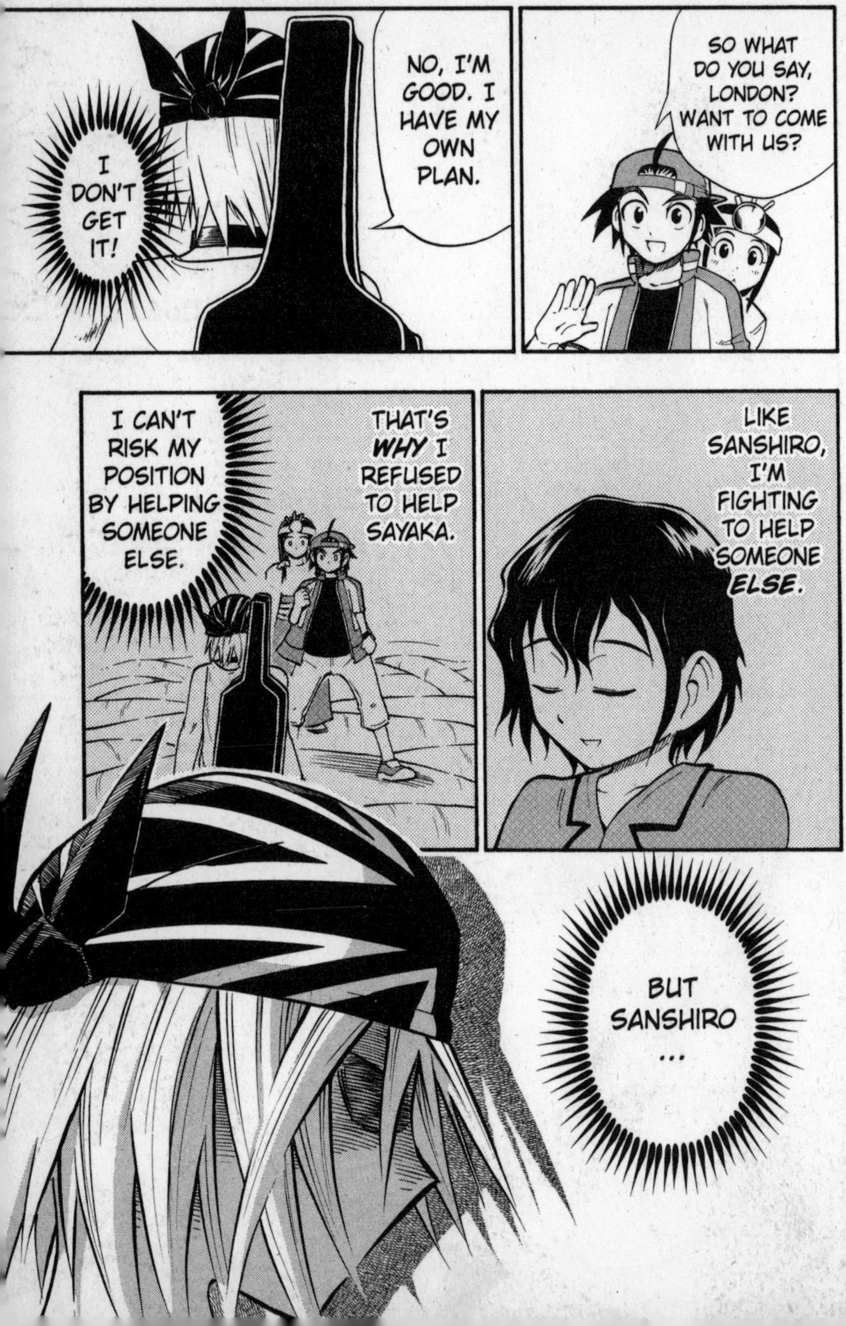
SO WHAT DO YOU SAY, LONDON? WANT TO COME WITH US?
NO, I'M GOOD. I HAVE MY OWN PLAN.
I DON'T GET IT!
LIKE SANSHIRO, I'M FIGHTING TO HELP SOMEONE ELSE.
THAT'S WHY I REFUSED TO HELP SAYAKA.
I CAN'T RISK MY POSITION BY HELPING SOMEONE ELSE.
BUT SANSHIRO...

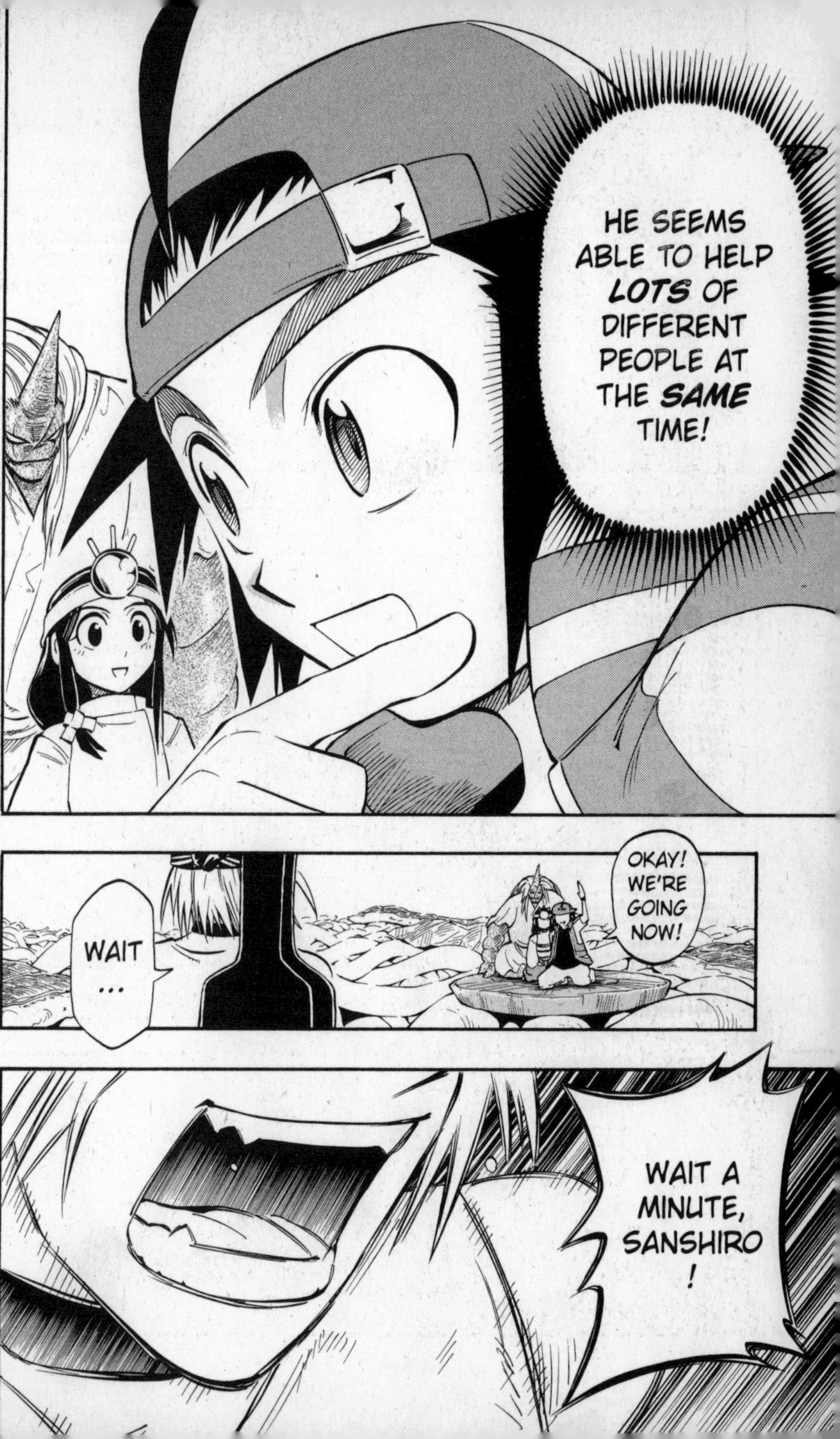
HE SEEMS ABLE TO HELP LOTS OF DIFFERENT PEOPLE AT THE SAME TIME!
OKAY! WE'RE GOING NOW!
WAIT ...
WAIT A MINUTE, SANSHIRO!

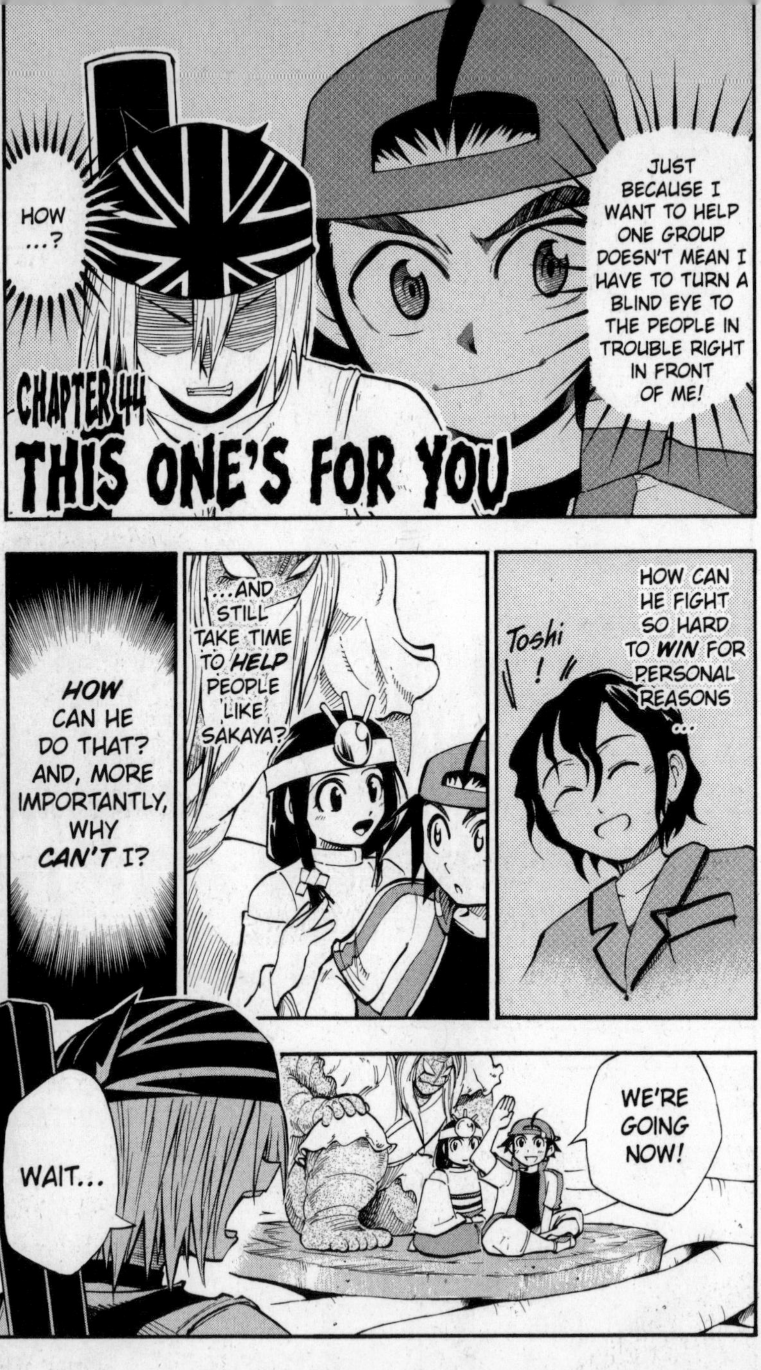
JUST BECAUSE I WANT TO HELP ONE GROUP DOESN'T MEAN I HAVE TO TURN A BLIND EYE TO THE PEOPLE IN TROUBLE RIGHT IN FRONT OF ME!
HOW ...?
CHAPTER 44
THIS ONE'S FOR YOU
HOW CAN HE FIGHT SO HARD TO WIN FOR PERSONAL REASONS ...
Toshi !
...AND STILL TAKE TIME TO HELP PEOPLE LIKE SAKAYA?
HOW CAN HE DO THAT? AND, MORE IMPORTANTLY, WHY CAN'T I?
WE'RE GOING NOW!
WAIT...

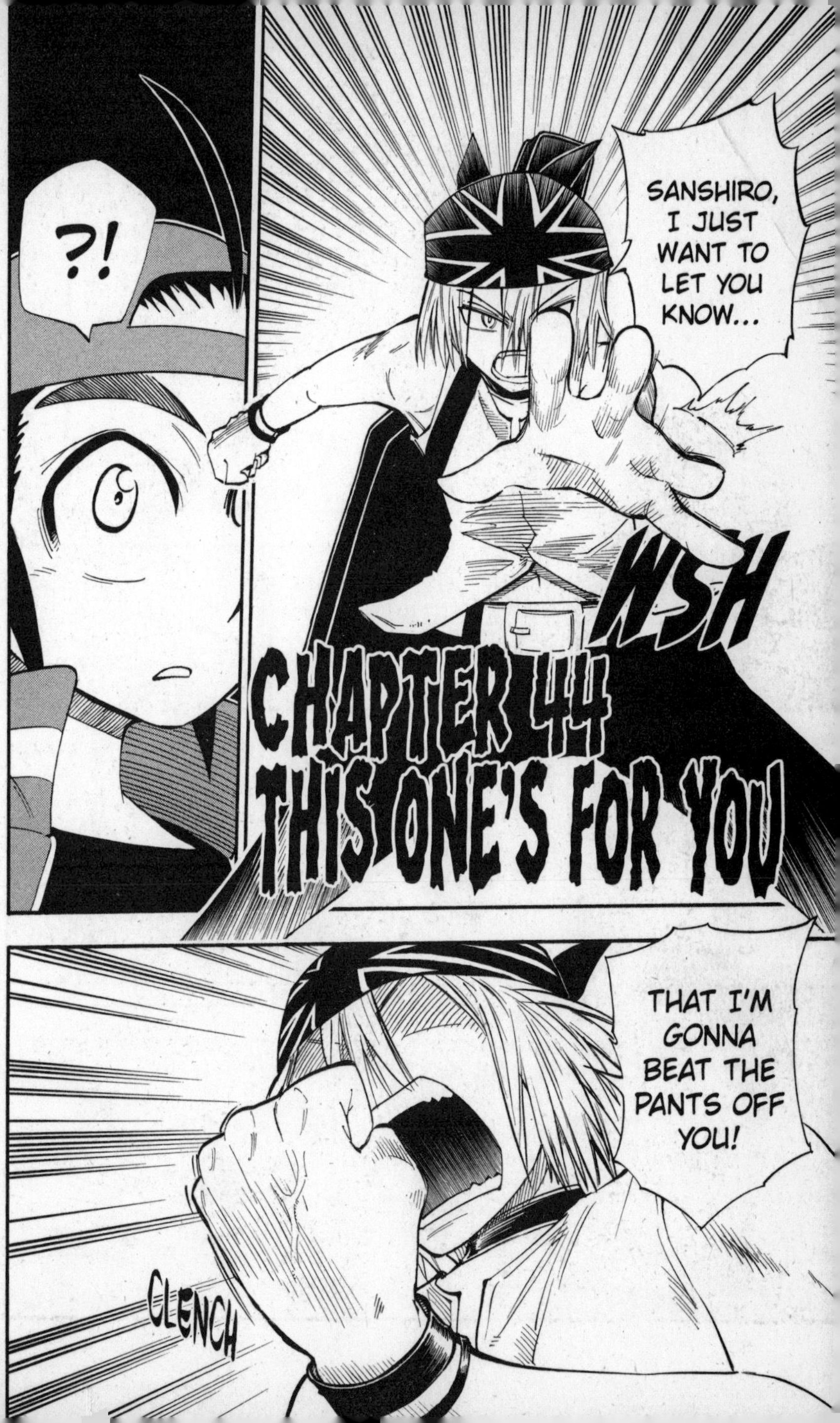
SANSHIRO, I JUST WANT TO LET YOU KNOW...
WSH
CHAPTER 44
THIS ONE'S FOR YOU
?!
THAT I'M GONNA BEAT THE PANTS OFF YOU!
CLENCH

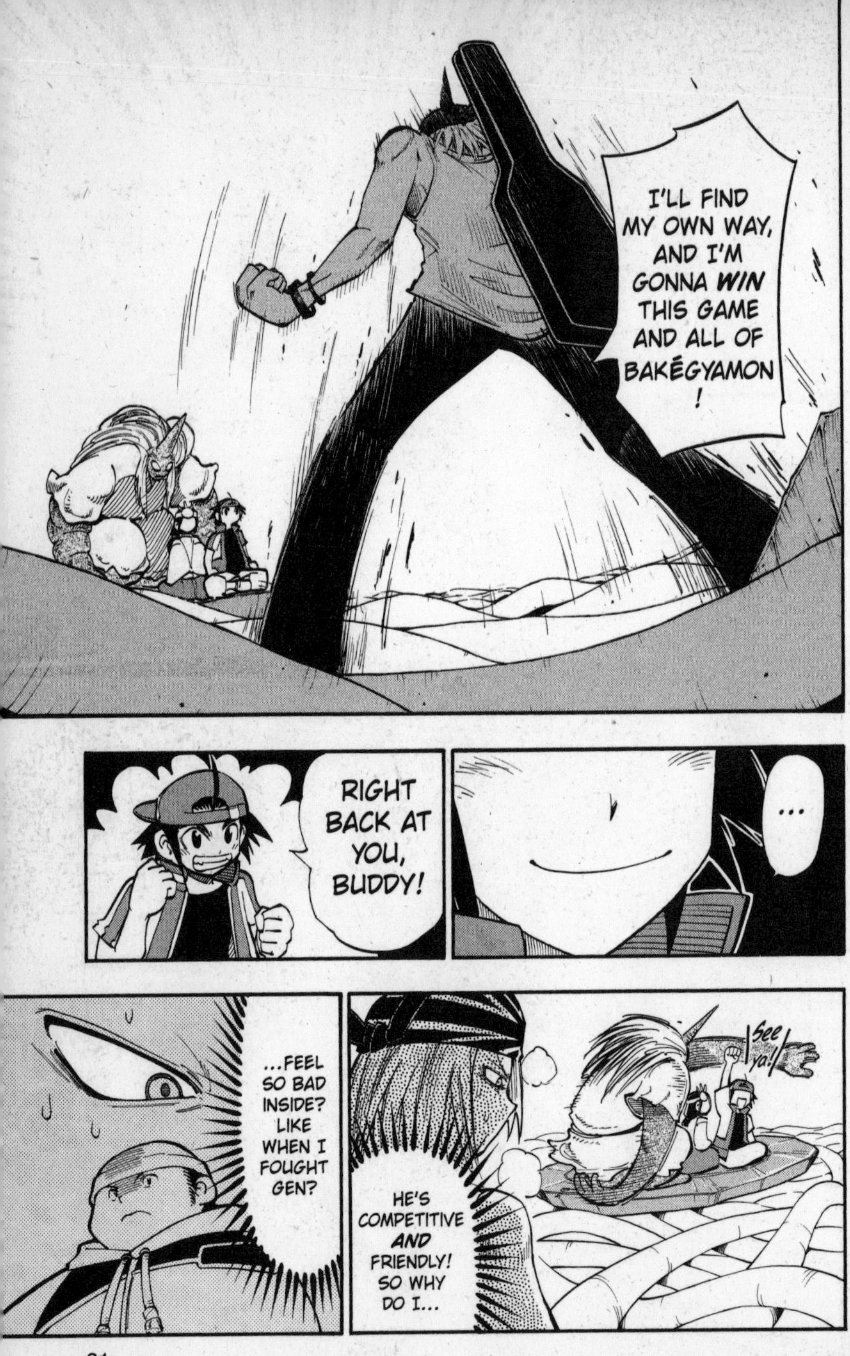
I'LL FIND MY OWN WAY, AND I'M GONNA WIN THIS GAME AND ALL OF BAKÉGYAMON!
...
RIGHT BACK AT YOU, BUDDY!
See ya!
HE'S COMPETITIVE AND FRIENDLY! SO WHY DO I...
...FEEL SO BAD INSIDE? LIKE WHEN I FOUGHT GEN?

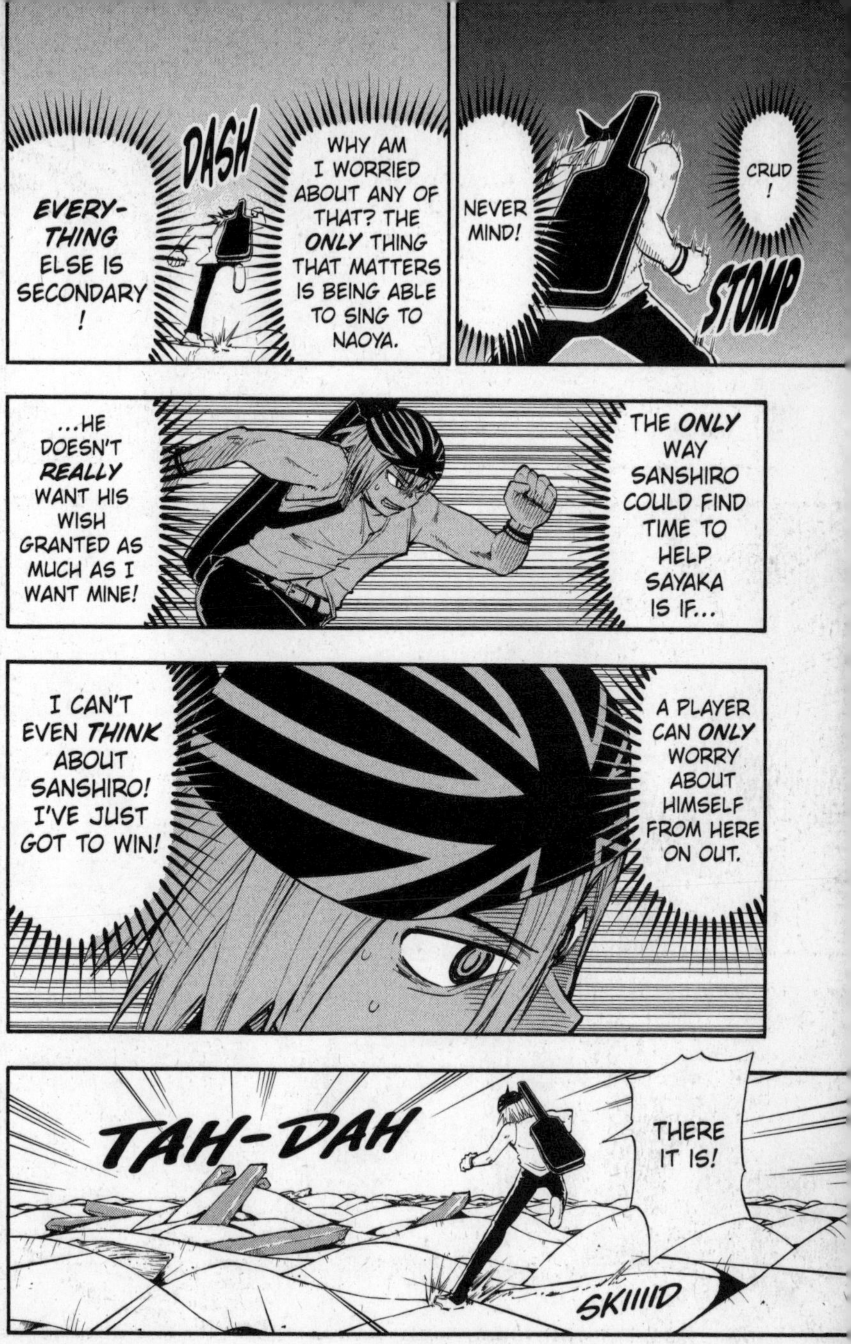
CRUD!
NEVER MIND!
STOMP
WHY AM I WORRIED ABOUT ANY OF THAT? THE ONLY THING THAT MATTERS IS BEING ABLE TO SING TO NAOYA.
DASH
EVERYTHING ELSE IS SECONDARY!
THE ONLY WAY SANSHIRO COULD FIND TIME TO HELP SAYAKA IS IF...
...HE DOESN'T REALLY WANT HIS WISH GRANTED AS MUCH AS I WANT MINE!
A PLAYER CAN ONLY WORRY ABOUT HIMSELF FROM HERE ON OUT.
I CAN'T EVEN THINK ABOUT SANSHIRO! I'VE JUST GOT TO WIN!
THERE IT IS!
TAH-DAH
SKIIIID

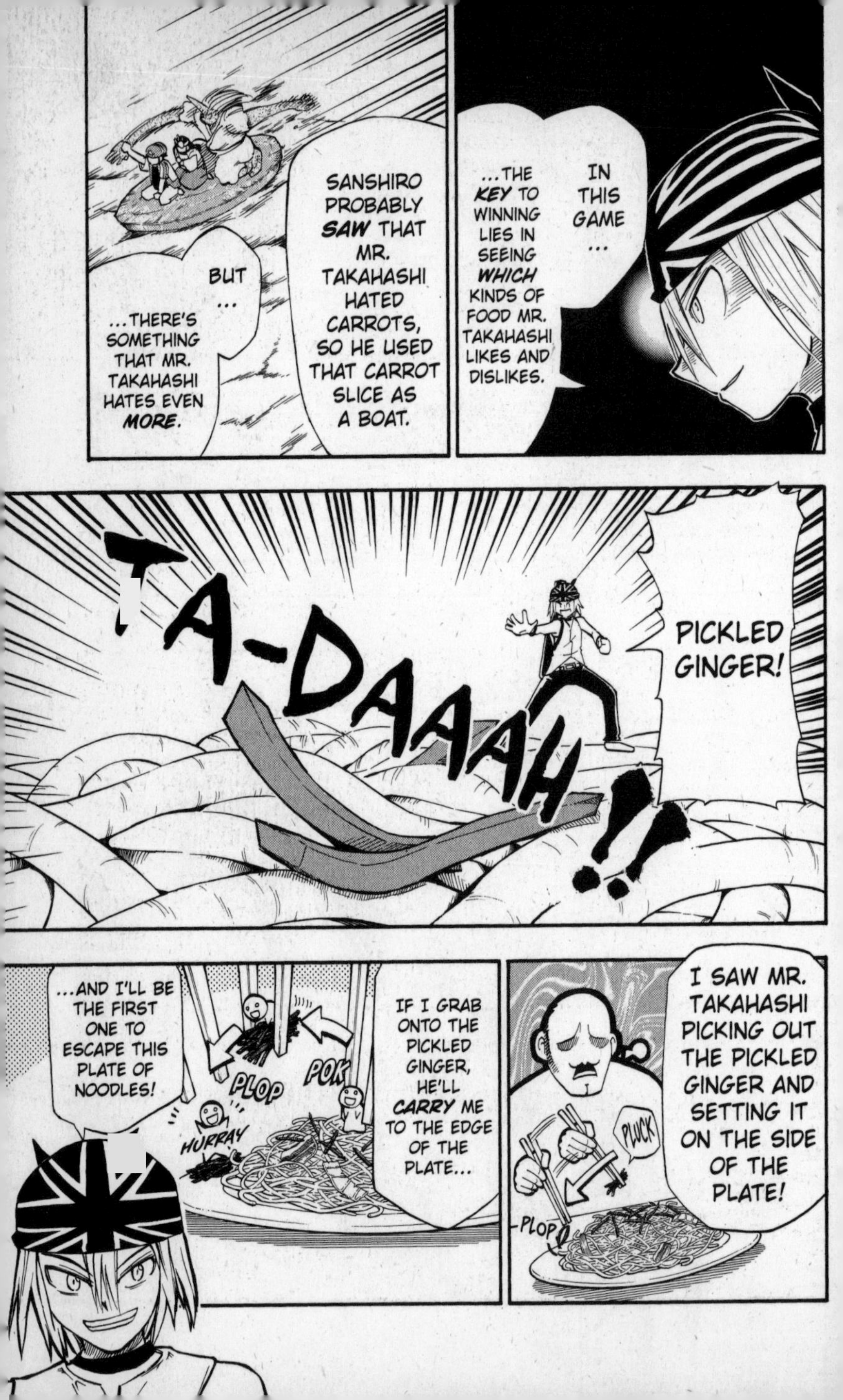
IN THIS GAME ...
...THE KEY TO WINNING LIES IN SEEING WHICH KINDS OF FOOD MR. TAKAHASHI LIKES AND DISLIKES.
SANSHIRO PROBABLY SAW THAT MR. TAKAHASHI HATED CARROTS, SO HE USED THAT CARROT SLICE AS A BOAT.
BUT ...
...THERE'S SOMETHING THAT MR. TAKAHASHI HATES EVEN MORE.
PICKLED GINGER!
TA-DAAAAH!!
I SAW MR. TAKAHASHI PICKING OUT THE PICKLED GINGER AND SETTING IT ON THE SIDE OF THE PLATE!
PLUCK
PLOP
IF I GRAB ONTO THE PICKLED GINGER, HE'LL CARRY ME TO THE EDGE OF THE PLATE...
POK
PLOP
HURRAY
...AND I'LL BE THE FIRST ONE TO ESCAPE THIS PLATE OF NOODLES!

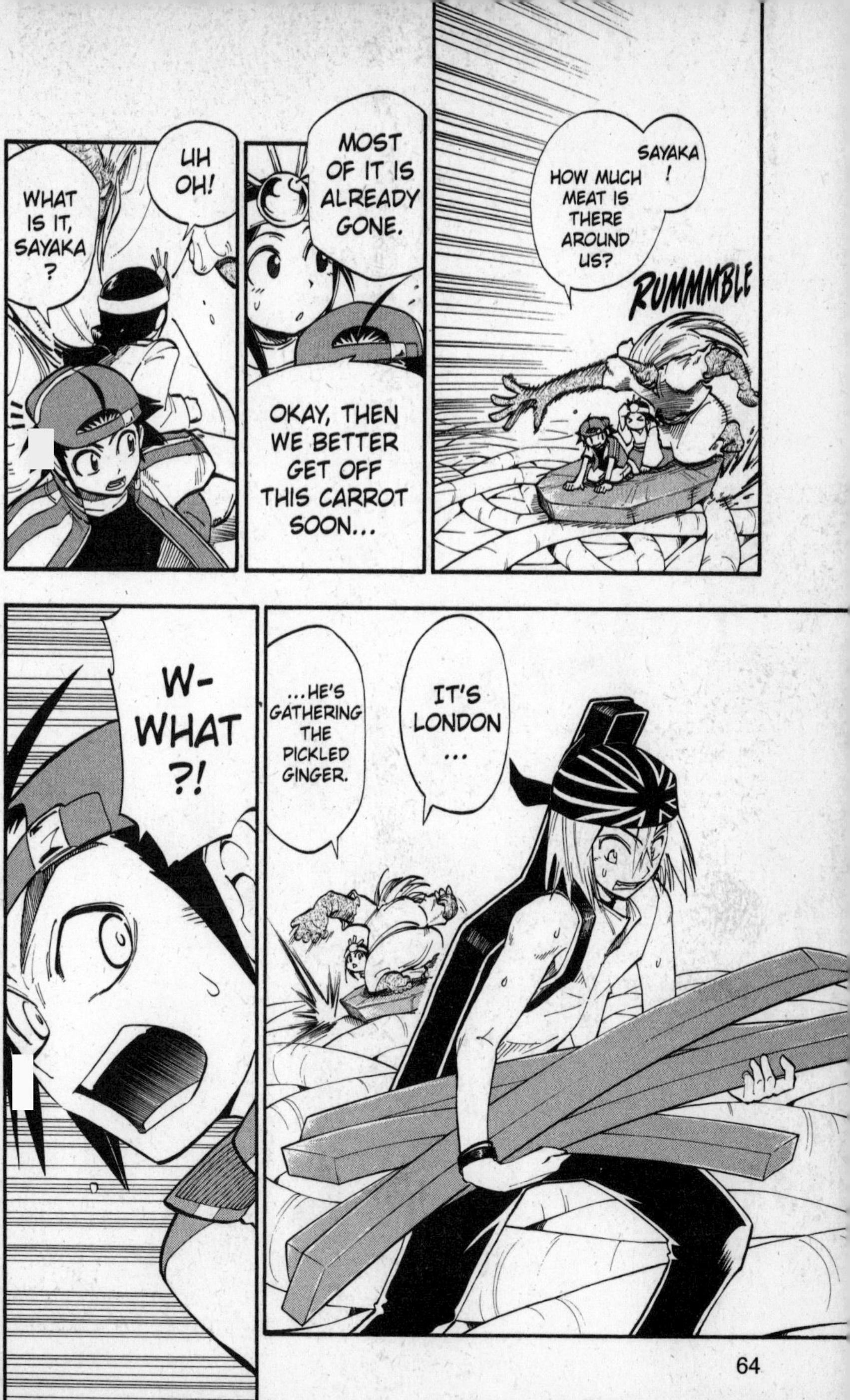
SAYAKA! HOW MUCH MEAT IS THERE AROUND US?
RUMMMBLE
MOST OF IT IS ALREADY GONE.
OKAY, THEN WE BETTER GET OFF THIS CARROT SOON...
UH OH!
WHAT IS IT, SAYAKA?
IT'S LONDON...
...HE'S GATHERING THE PICKLED GINGER.
W-WHAT?!

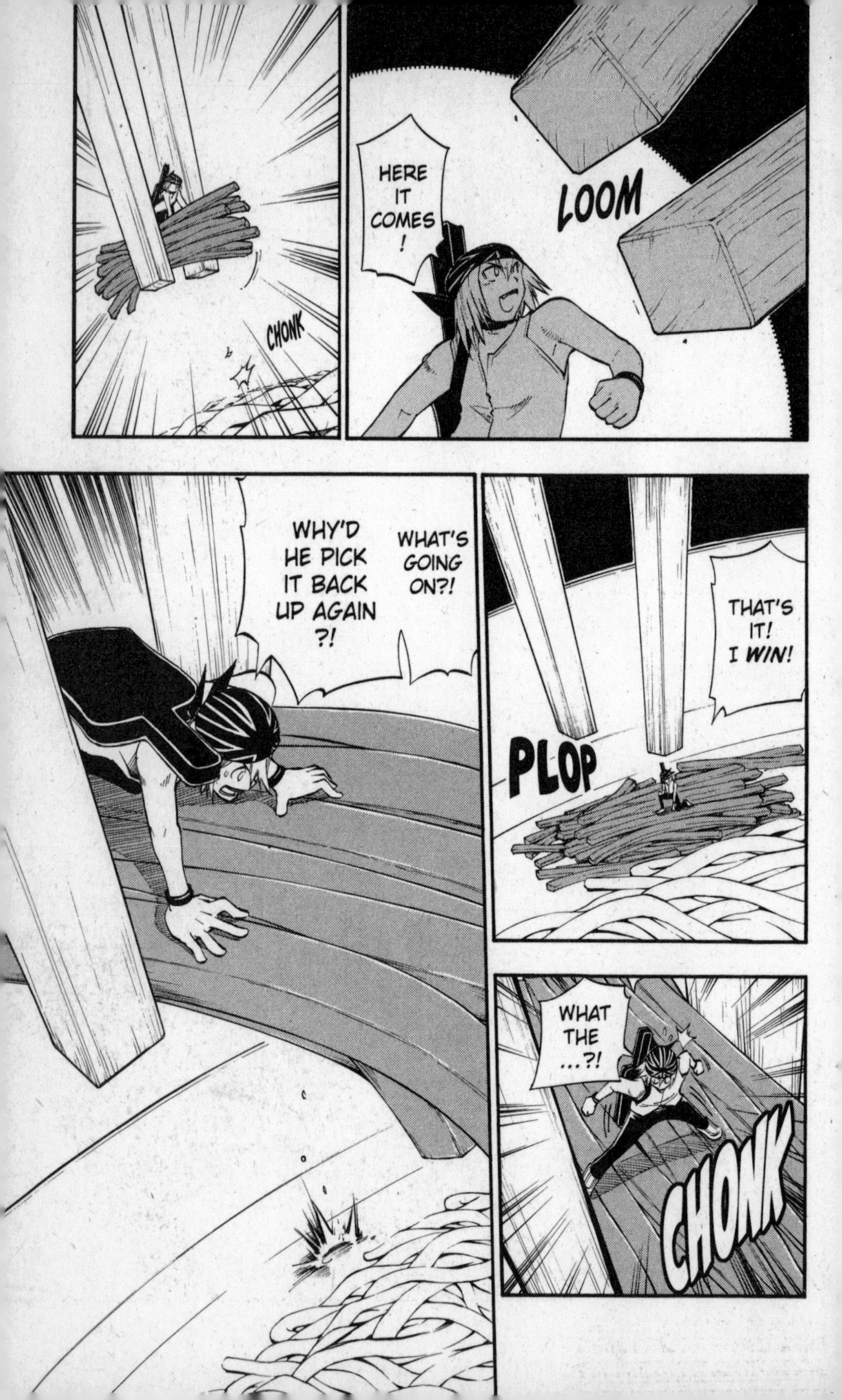
HERE IT COMES!
LOOM
CHONK
THAT'S IT! I *WIN*!
PLOP
WHAT THE ...?!
CHONK
WHAT'S GOING ON?!
WHY'D HE PICK IT BACK UP AGAIN?!

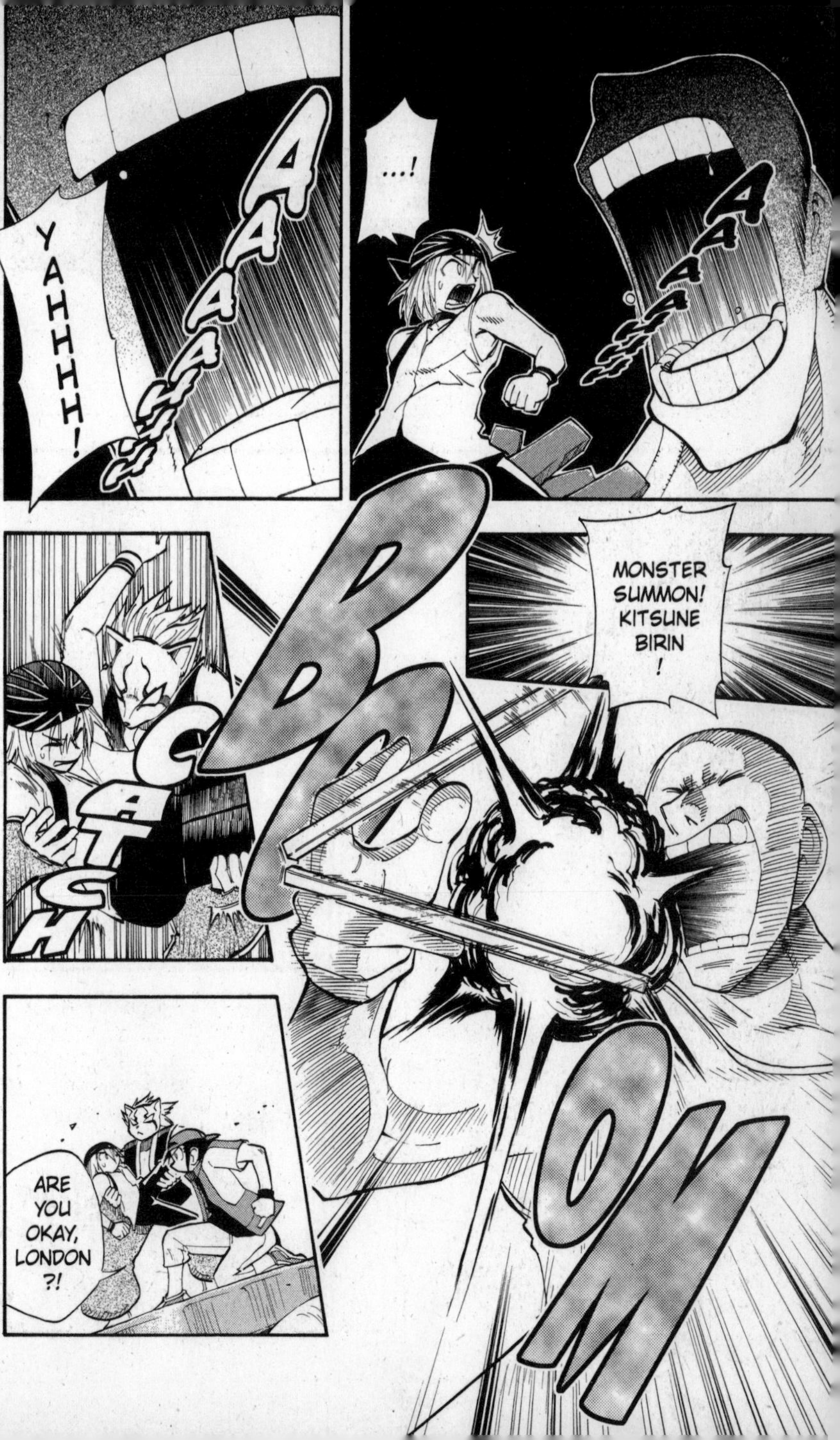
...!
YAHHHH!
MONSTER SUMMON! KITSUNE BIRIN!
BOOM
CATCH
ARE YOU OKAY, LONDON?!

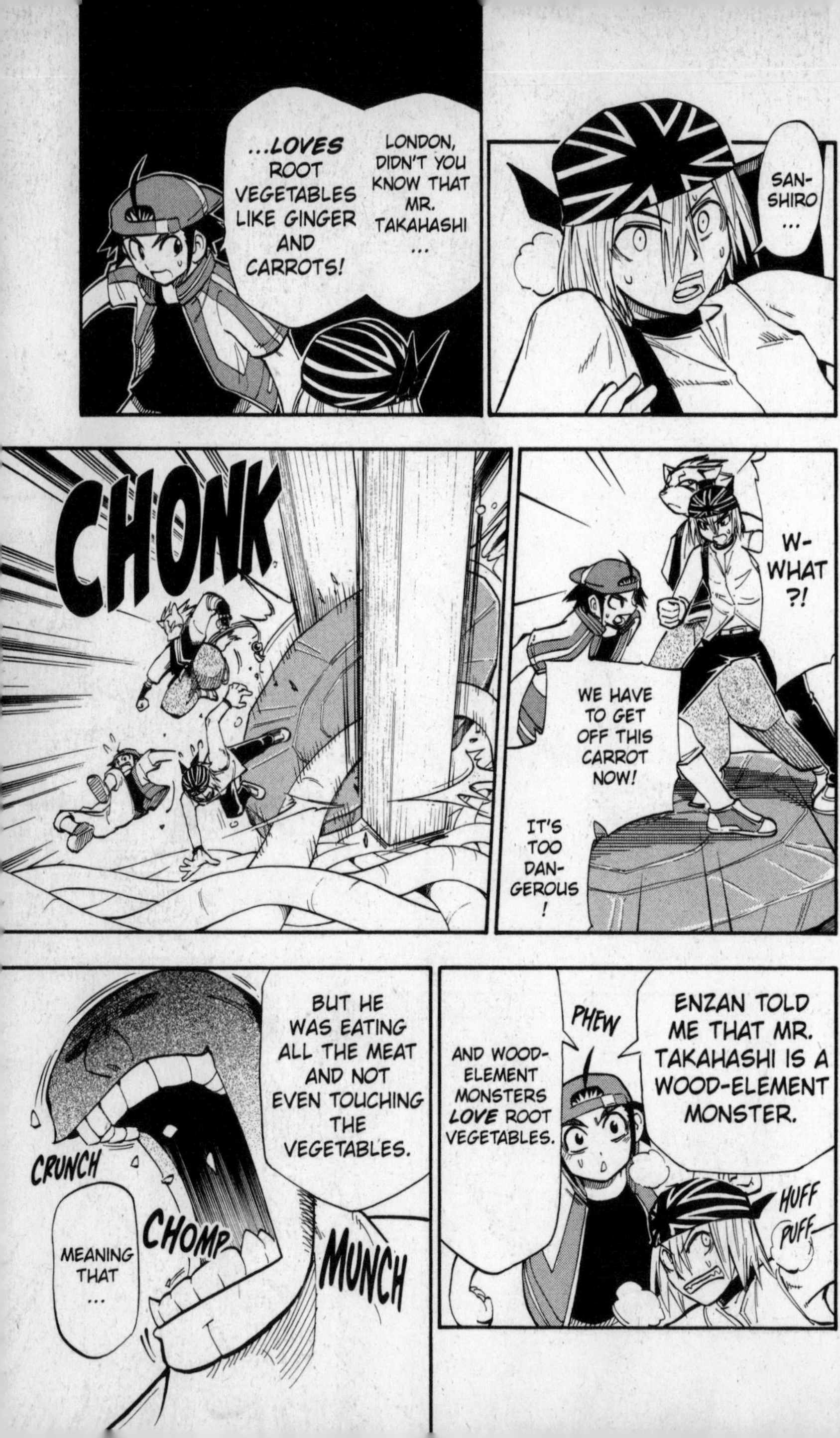
SAN-SHIRO...
LONDON, DIDN'T YOU KNOW THAT MR. TAKAHASHI...
...LOVES ROOT VEGETABLES LIKE GINGER AND CARROTS!
W-WHAT?!
WE HAVE TO GET OFF THIS CARROT NOW!
IT'S TOO DANGEROUS!
CHONK
PHEW
ENZAN TOLD ME THAT MR. TAKAHASHI IS A WOOD-ELEMENT MONSTER.
AND WOOD-ELEMENT MONSTERS LOVE ROOT VEGETABLES.
HUFF PUFF
BUT HE WAS EATING ALL THE MEAT AND NOT EVEN TOUCHING THE VEGETABLES.
CRUNCH
CHOMP
MUNCH
MEANING THAT...

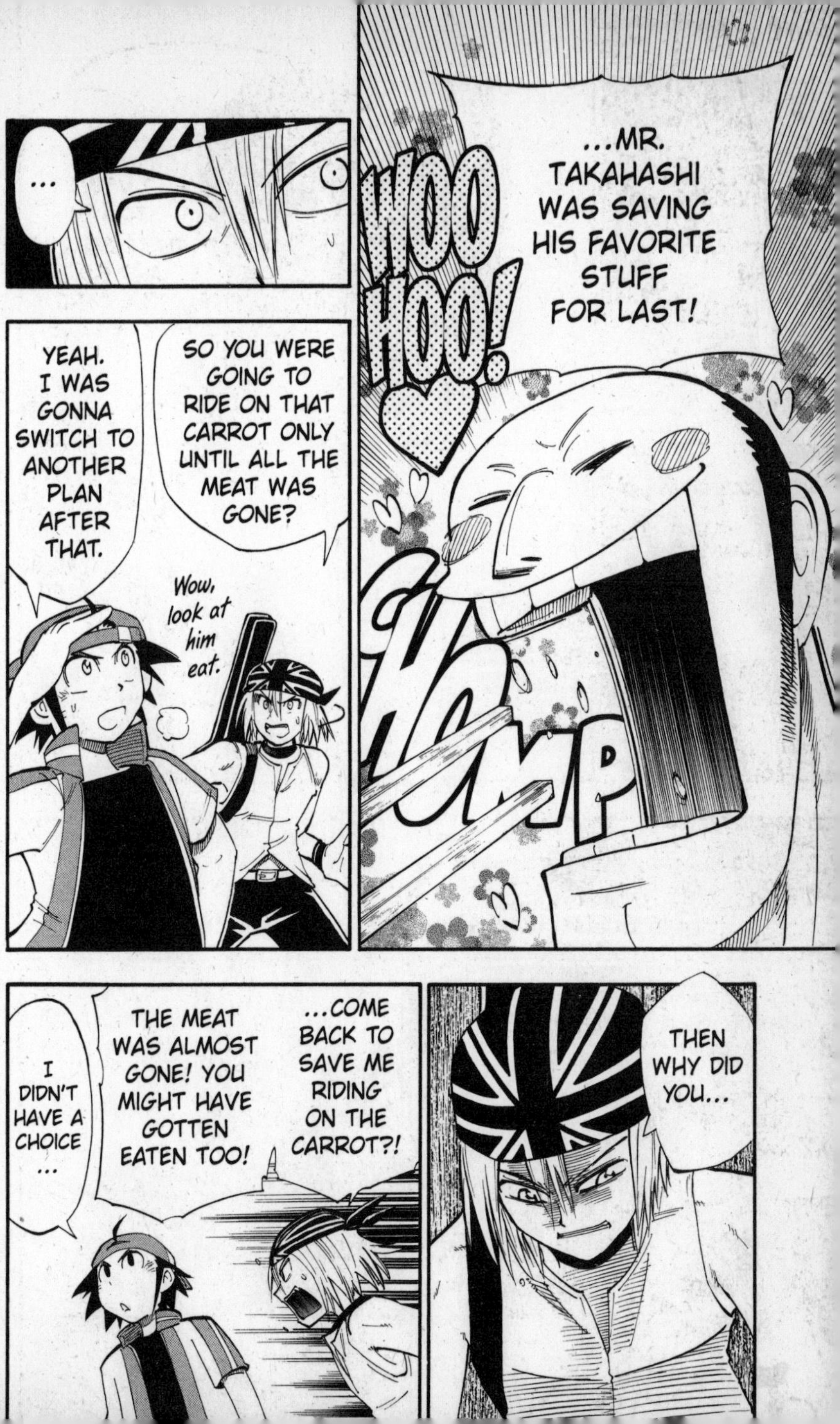
WOO HOO!
...MR. TAKAHASHI WAS SAVING HIS FAVORITE STUFF FOR LAST!
CHOMP
...
SO YOU WERE GOING TO RIDE ON THAT CARROT ONLY UNTIL ALL THE MEAT WAS GONE?
YEAH. I WAS GONNA SWITCH TO ANOTHER PLAN AFTER THAT.
Wow, look at him eat.
THEN WHY DID YOU...
...COME BACK TO SAVE ME RIDING ON THE CARROT?!
THE MEAT WAS ALMOST GONE! YOU MIGHT HAVE GOTTEN EATEN TOO!
I DIDN'T HAVE A CHOICE...

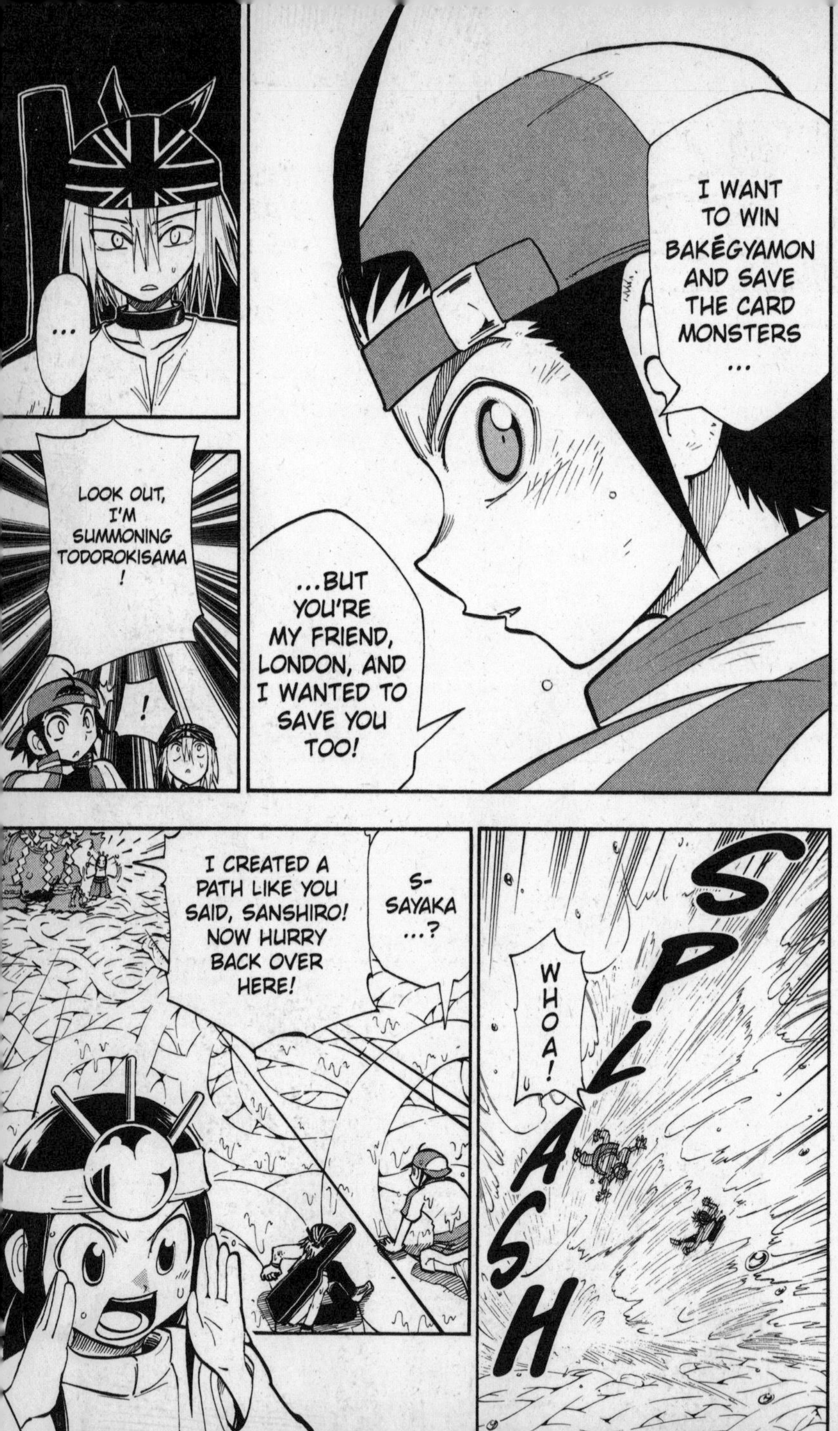
I WANT TO WIN BAKÉGYAMON AND SAVE THE CARD MONSTERS ...
...BUT YOU'RE MY FRIEND, LONDON, AND I WANTED TO SAVE YOU TOO!
...
LOOK OUT, I'M SUMMONING TODOROKISAMA !
!
SPLASH
WHOA!
S-SAYAKA ...?
I CREATED A PATH LIKE YOU SAID, SANSHIRO! NOW HURRY BACK OVER HERE!

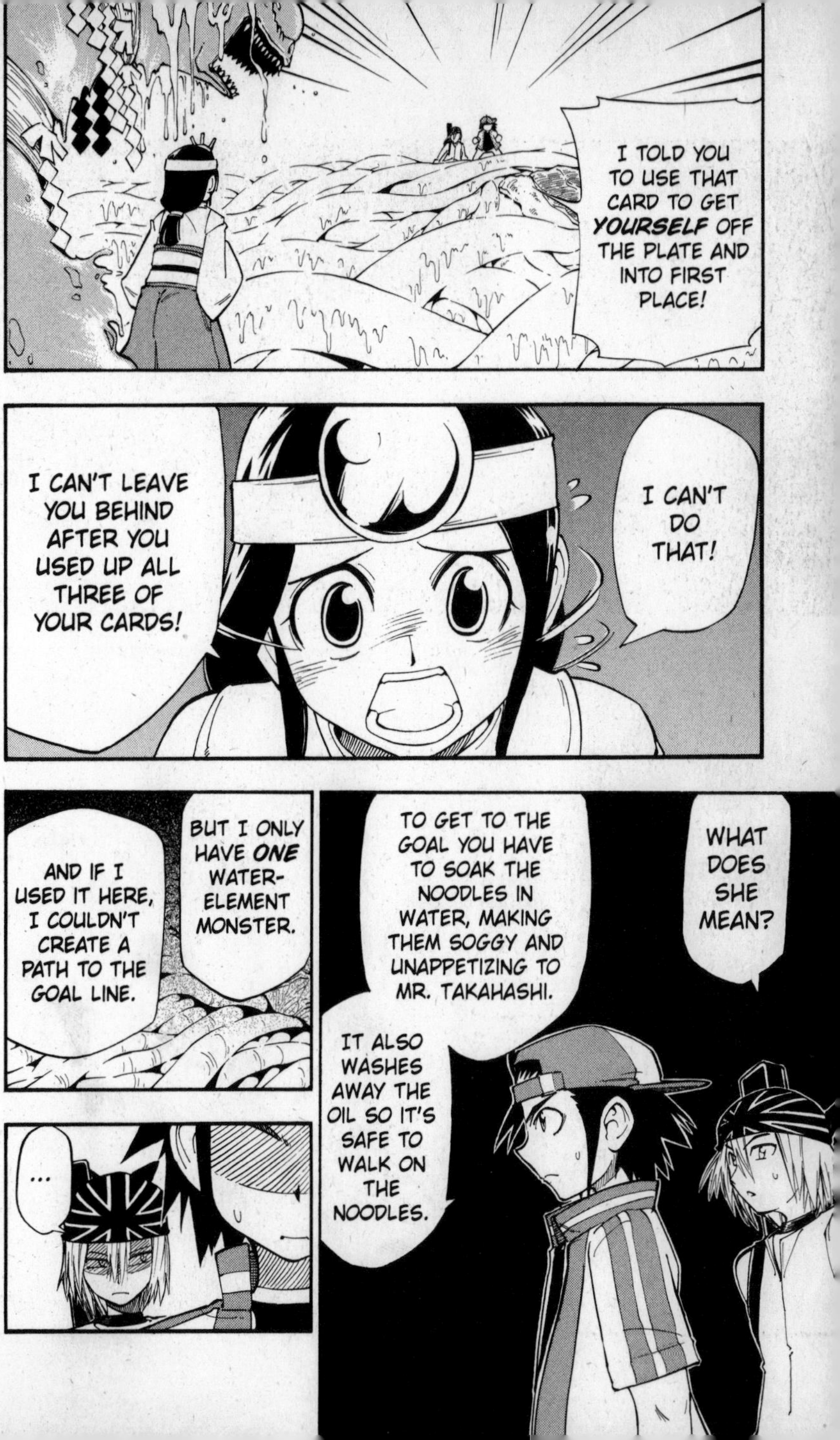

I TOLD YOU TO USE THAT CARD TO GET **YOURSELF** OFF THE PLATE AND INTO FIRST PLACE!
I CAN'T DO THAT!
I CAN'T LEAVE YOU BEHIND AFTER YOU USED UP ALL THREE OF YOUR CARDS!
WHAT DOES SHE MEAN?
TO GET TO THE GOAL YOU HAVE TO SOAK THE NOODLES IN WATER, MAKING THEM SOGGY AND UNAPPETIZING TO MR. TAKAHASHI.
IT ALSO WASHES AWAY THE OIL SO IT'S SAFE TO WALK ON THE NOODLES.
BUT I ONLY HAVE **ONE** WATER-ELEMENT MONSTER.
AND IF I USED IT HERE, I COULDN'T CREATE A PATH TO THE GOAL LINE.
...

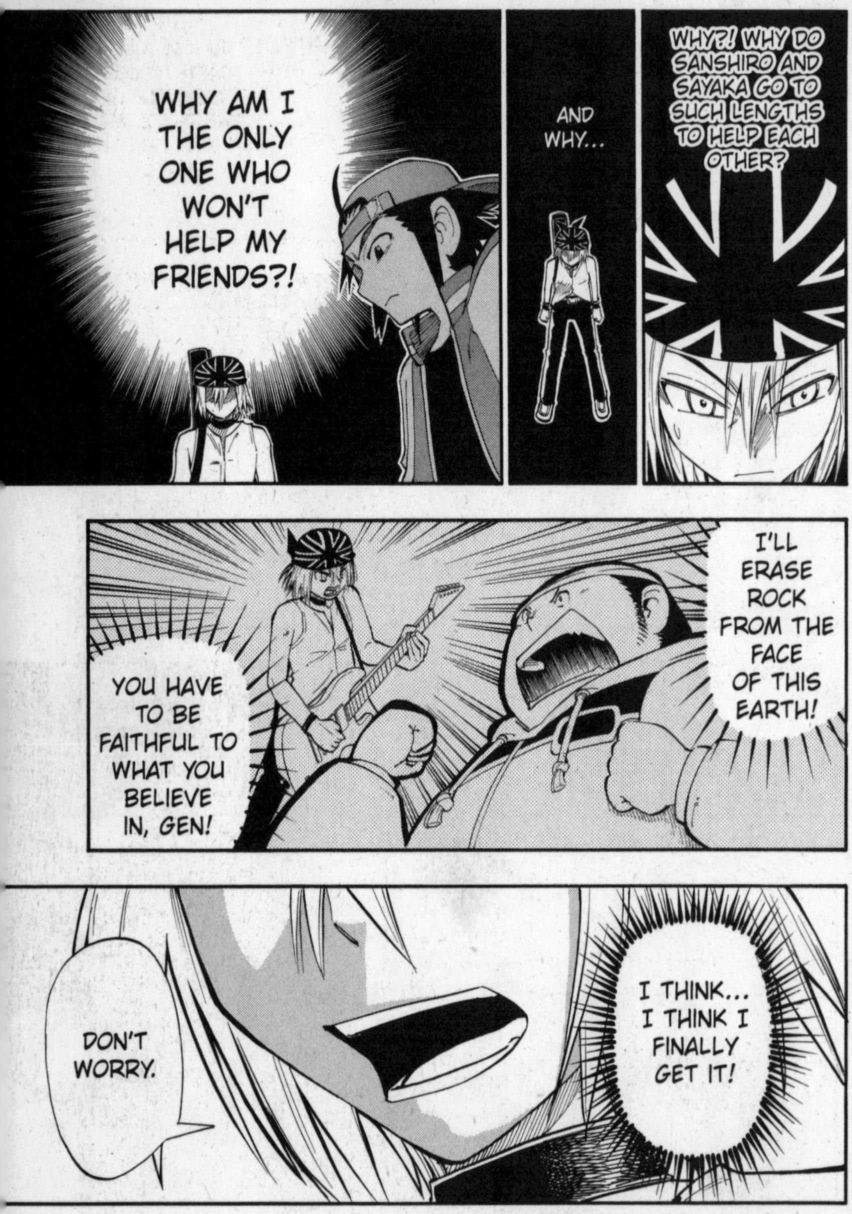
WHY?! WHY DO SANSHIRO AND SAYAKA GO TO SUCH LENGTHS TO HELP EACH OTHER?
AND WHY...
WHY AM I THE ONLY ONE WHO WON'T HELP MY FRIENDS?!
I'LL ERASE ROCK FROM THE FACE OF THIS EARTH!
YOU HAVE TO BE FAITHFUL TO WHAT YOU BELIEVE IN, GEN!
I THINK... I THINK I FINALLY GET IT!
DON'T WORRY.

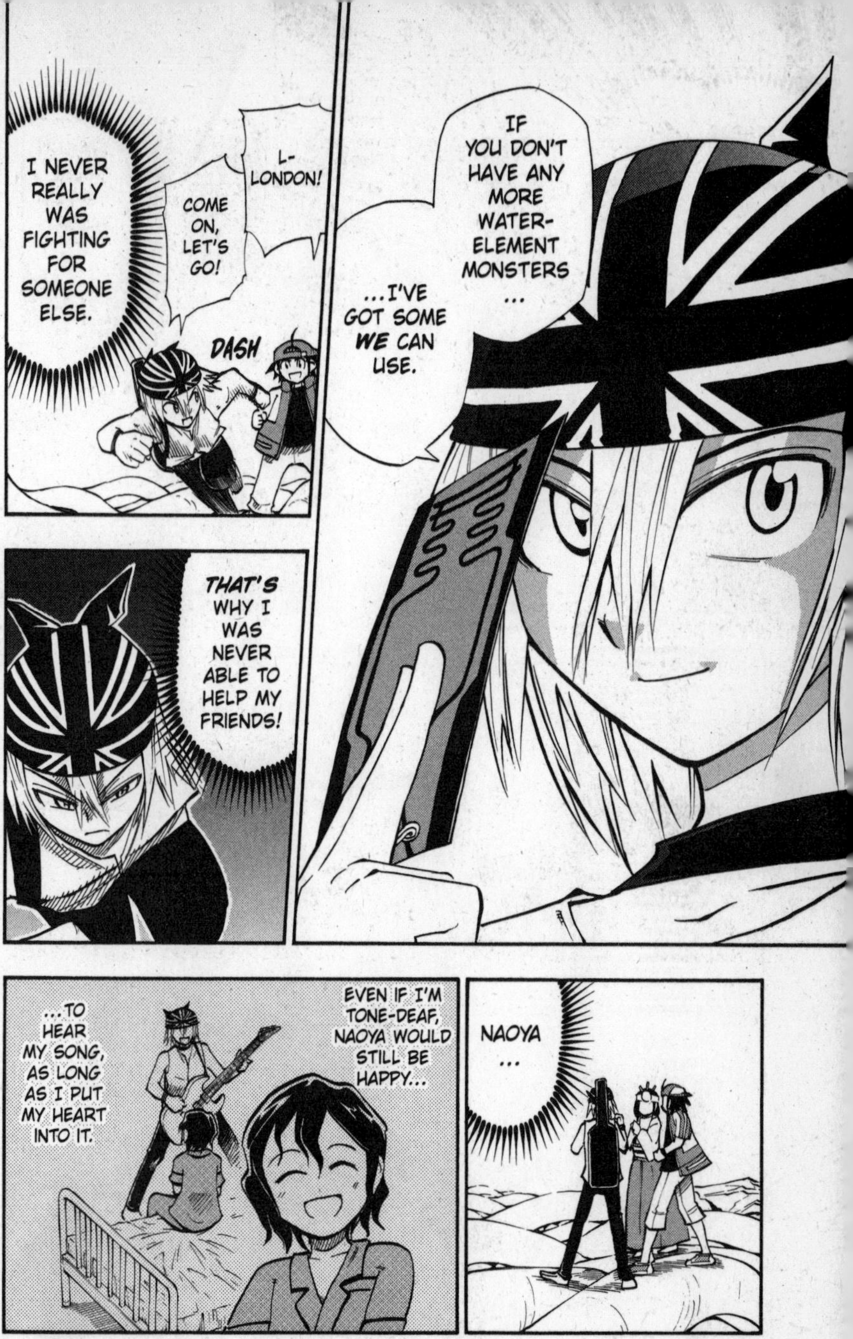
IF YOU DON'T HAVE ANY MORE WATER-ELEMENT MONSTERS...
...I'VE GOT SOME WE CAN USE.
L-LONDON!
COME ON, LET'S GO!
I NEVER REALLY WAS FIGHTING FOR SOMEONE ELSE.
DASH
THAT'S WHY I WAS NEVER ABLE TO HELP MY FRIENDS!
NAOYA...
EVEN IF I'M TONE-DEAF, NAOYA WOULD STILL BE HAPPY...
...TO HEAR MY SONG, AS LONG AS I PUT MY HEART INTO IT.

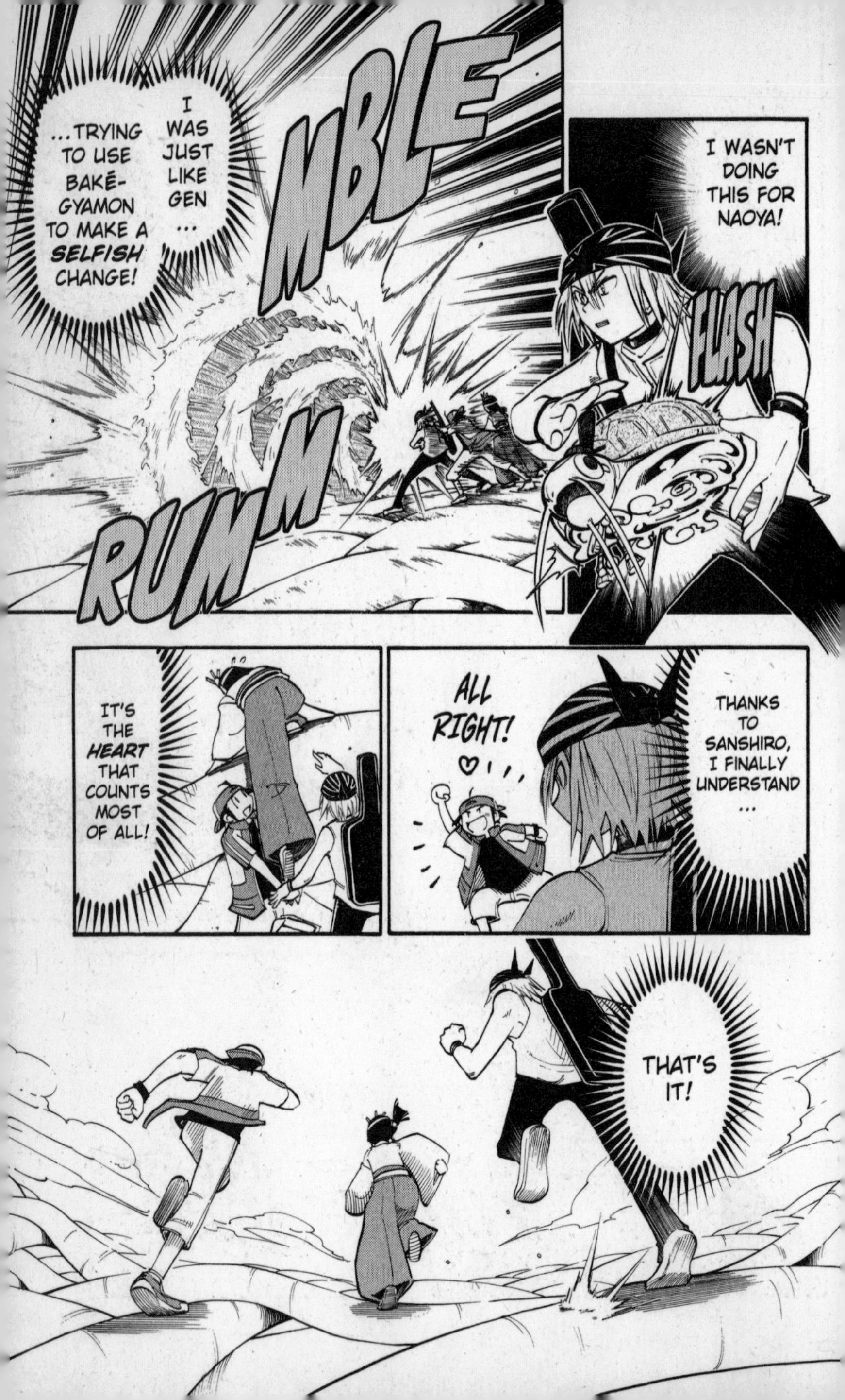
I WASN'T DOING THIS FOR NAOYA!
FLASH
I WAS JUST LIKE GEN...
...TRYING TO USE BAKÉ-GYAMON TO MAKE A SELFISH CHANGE!
RUMM
MBLE
THANKS TO SANSHIRO, I FINALLY UNDERSTAND...
ALL RIGHT!
IT'S THE HEART THAT COUNTS MOST OF ALL!
THAT'S IT!

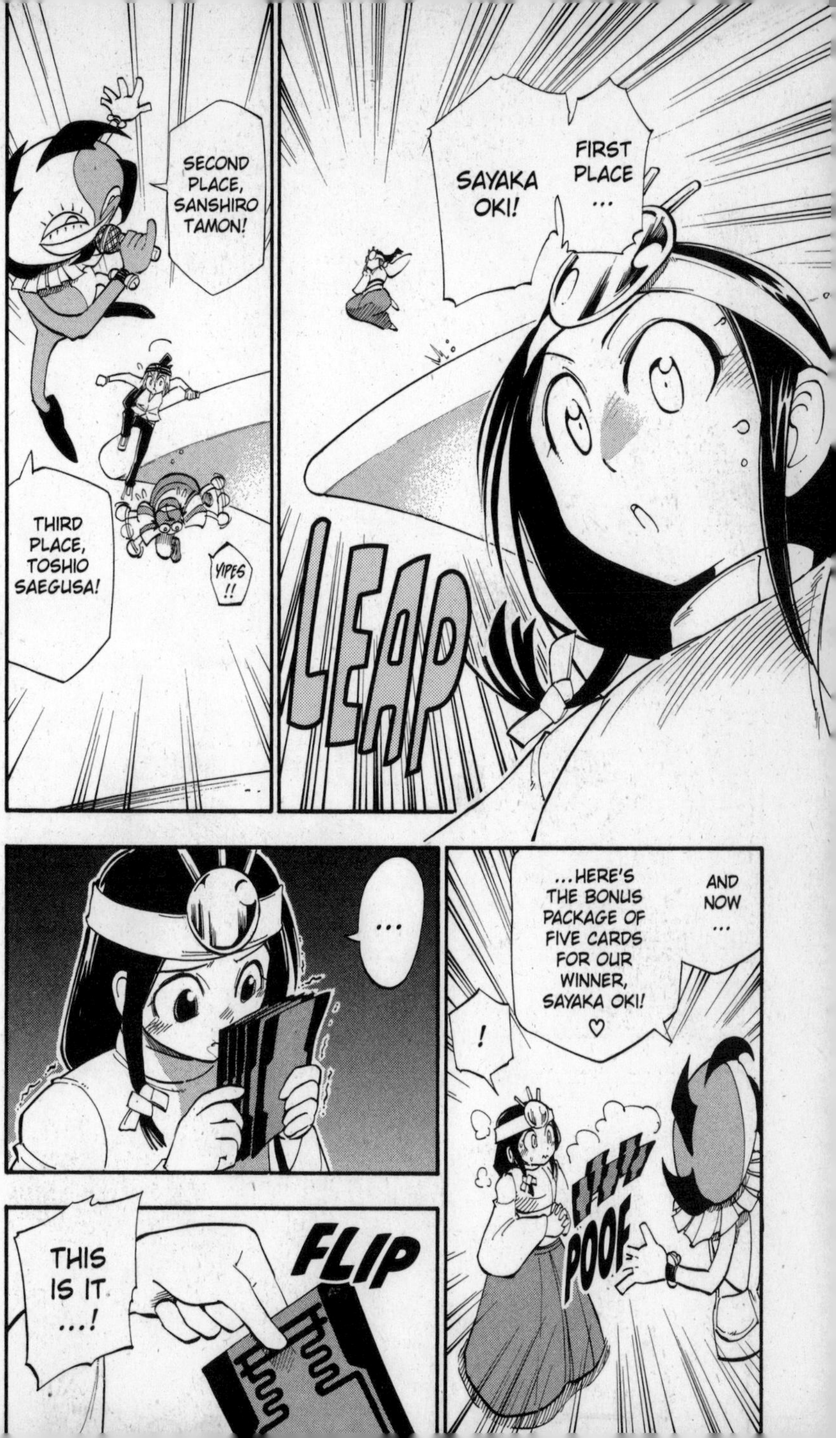
FIRST PLACE ...
SAYAKA OKI!
LEAP
SECOND PLACE, SANSHIRO TAMON!
THIRD PLACE, TOSHIO SAEGUSA!
YIPES !!
AND NOW ...
...HERE'S THE BONUS PACKAGE OF FIVE CARDS FOR OUR WINNER, SAYAKA OKI! ♡
!
POOF
...
THIS IS IT ...!
FLIP

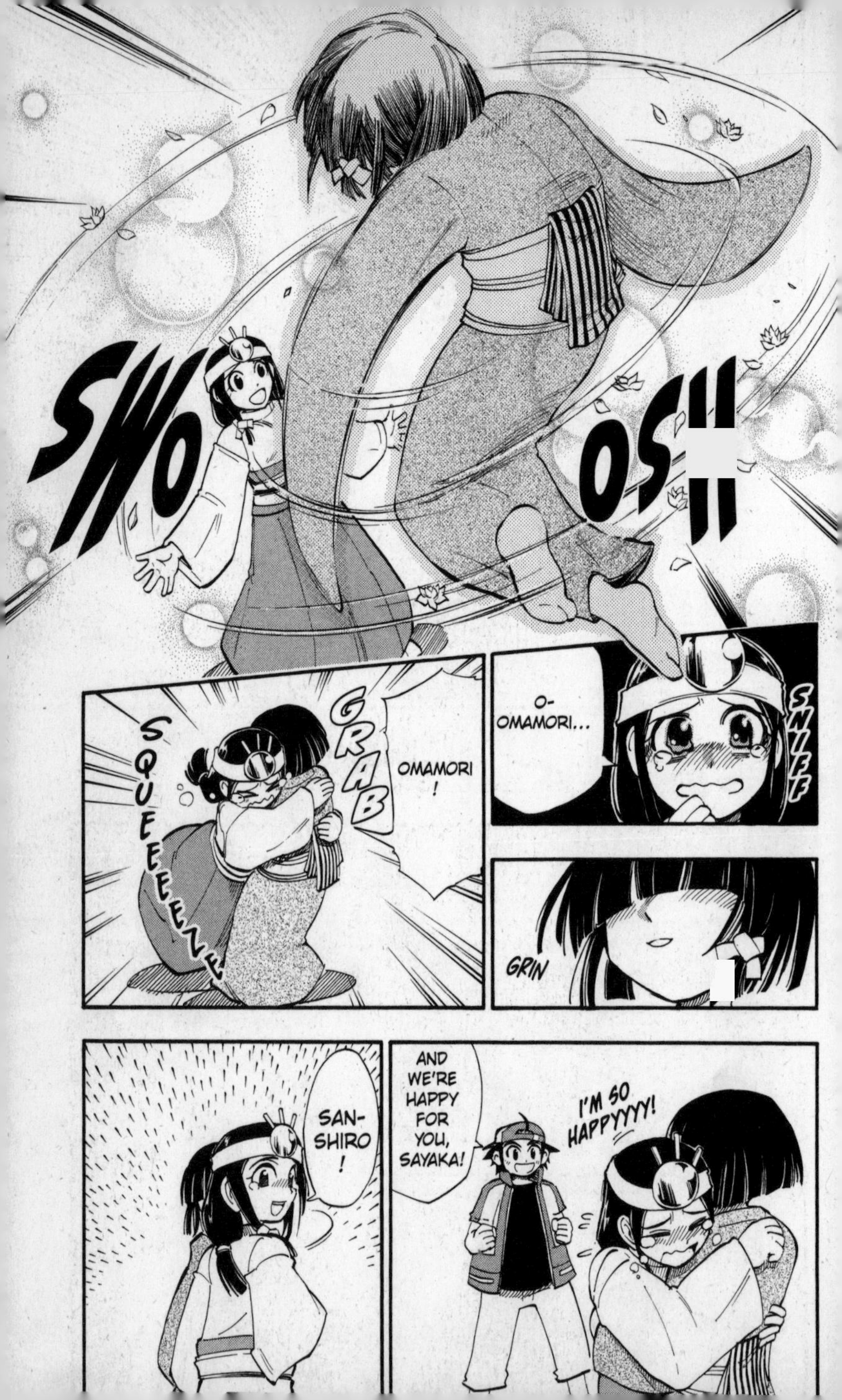
SWOOSH
O-OMAMORI...
SNIFF
GRIN
GRAB
OMAMORI!
SQUEEEEEEZE
I'M SO HAPPYYYY!
AND WE'RE HAPPY FOR YOU, SAYAKA!
SAN-SHIRO!

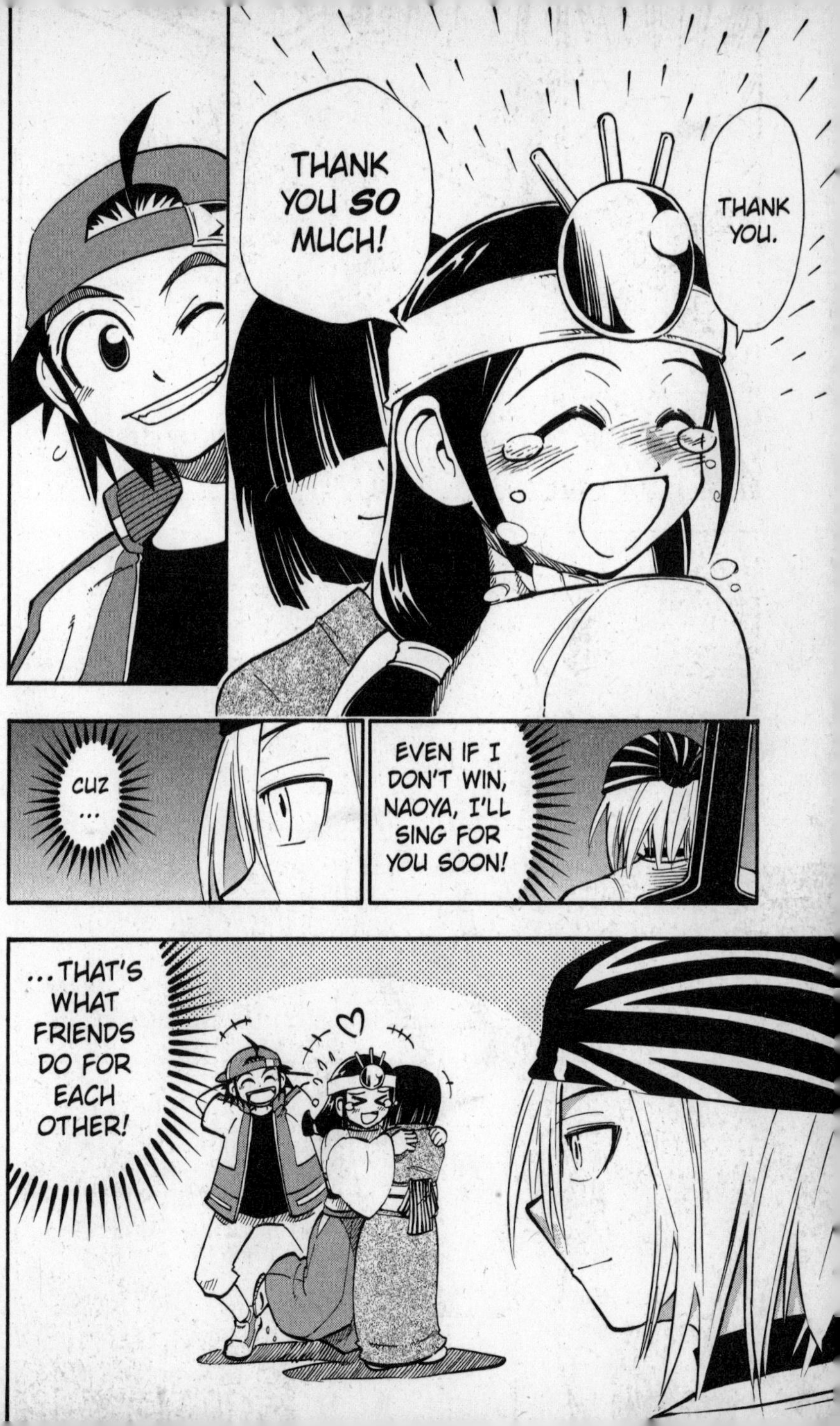
THANK YOU.
THANK YOU SO MUCH!
EVEN IF I DON'T WIN, NAOYA, I'LL SING FOR YOU SOON!
CUZ ...
...THAT'S WHAT FRIENDS DO FOR EACH OTHER!

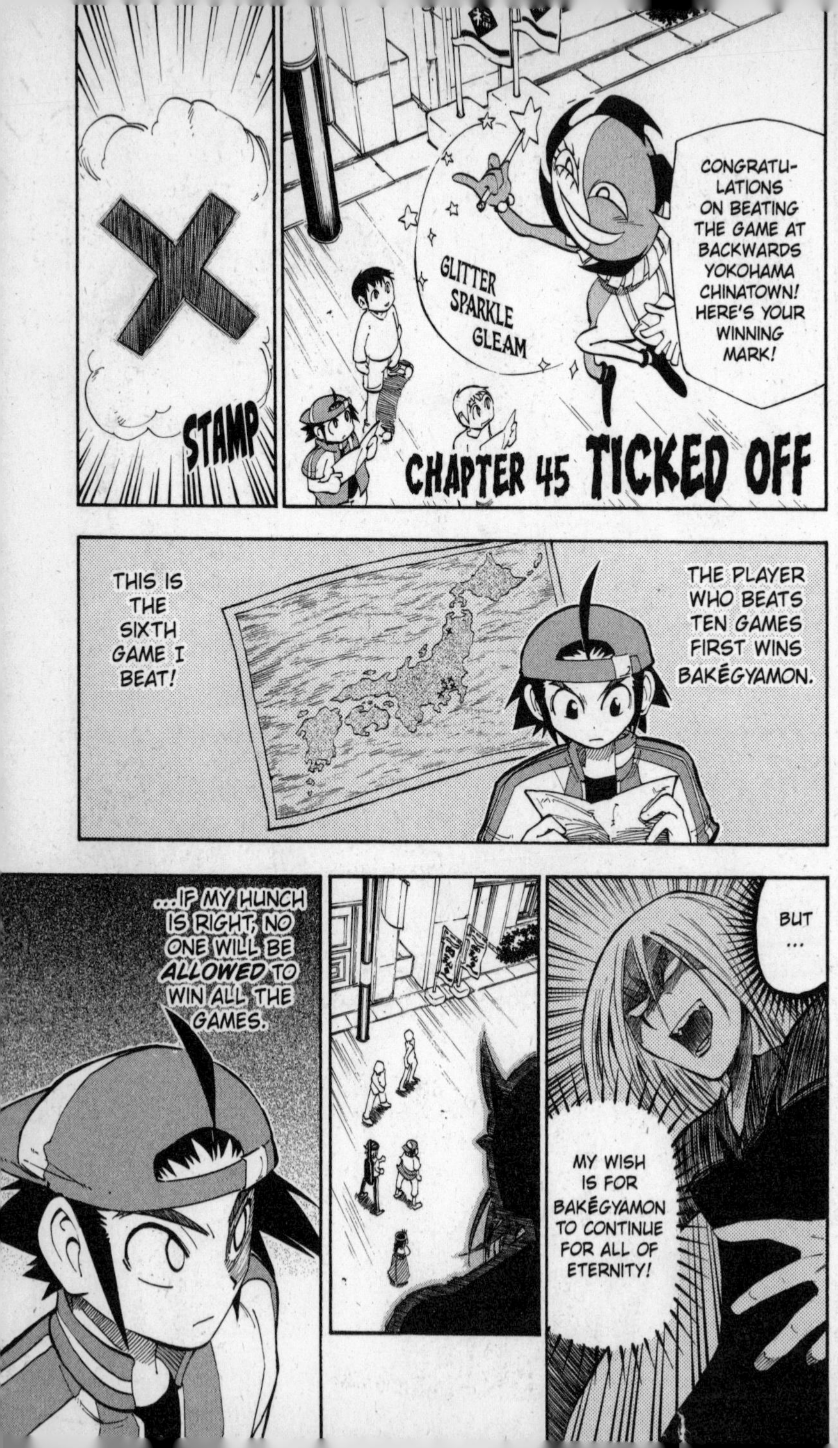
CONGRATULATIONS ON BEATING THE GAME AT BACKWARDS YOKOHAMA CHINATOWN! HERE'S YOUR WINNING MARK!
GLITTER SPARKLE GLEAM
STAMP
CHAPTER 45 TICKED OFF
THE PLAYER WHO BEATS TEN GAMES FIRST WINS BAKÉGYAMON.
THIS IS THE SIXTH GAME I BEAT!
BUT ...
MY WISH IS FOR BAKÉGYAMON TO CONTINUE FOR ALL OF ETERNITY!
...IF MY HUNCH IS RIGHT, NO ONE WILL BE ALLOWED TO WIN ALL THE GAMES.

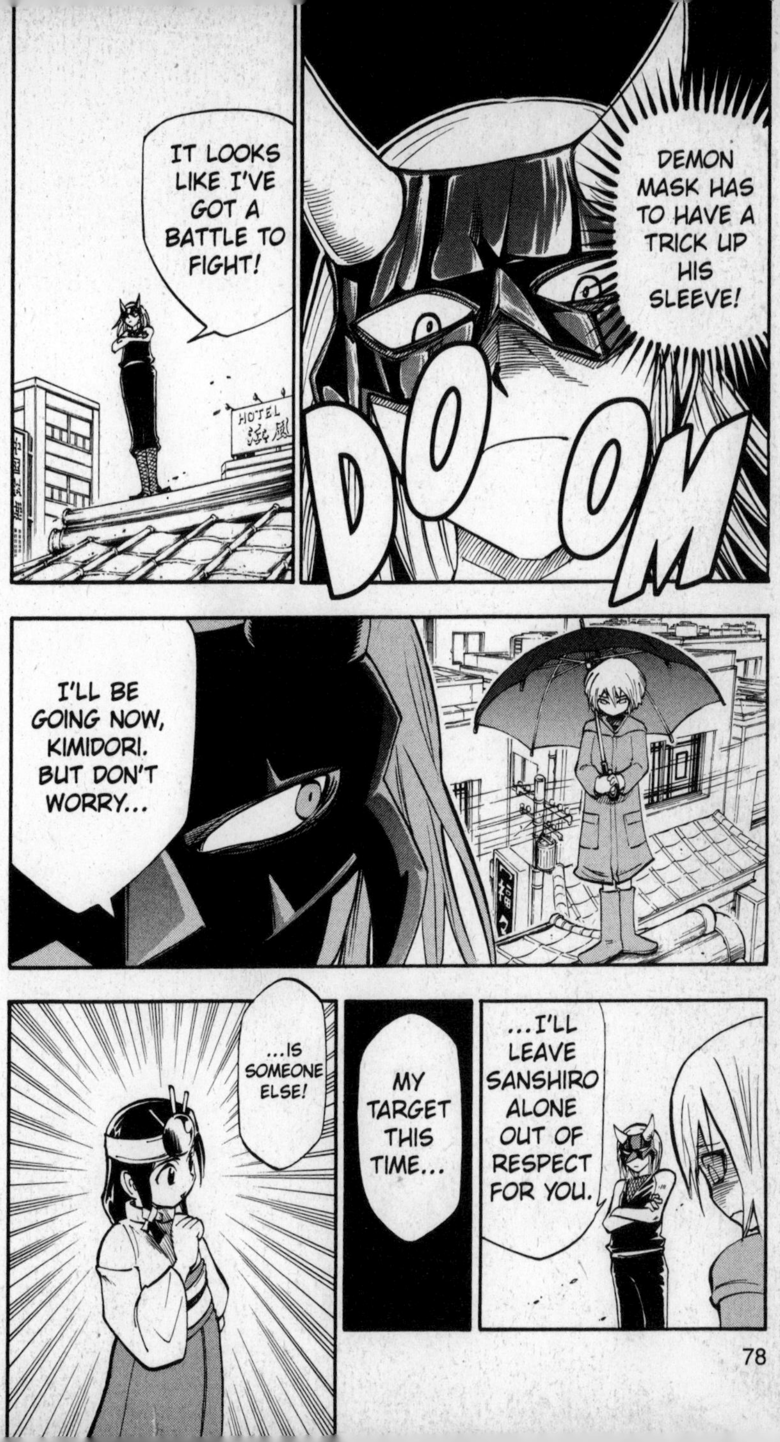
DEMON MASK HAS TO HAVE A TRICK UP HIS SLEEVE!
DOOM
IT LOOKS LIKE I'VE GOT A BATTLE TO FIGHT!
HOTEL
I'LL BE GOING NOW, KIMIDORI. BUT DON'T WORRY...
...I'LL LEAVE SANSHIRO ALONE OUT OF RESPECT FOR YOU.
MY TARGET THIS TIME...
...IS SOMEONE ELSE!

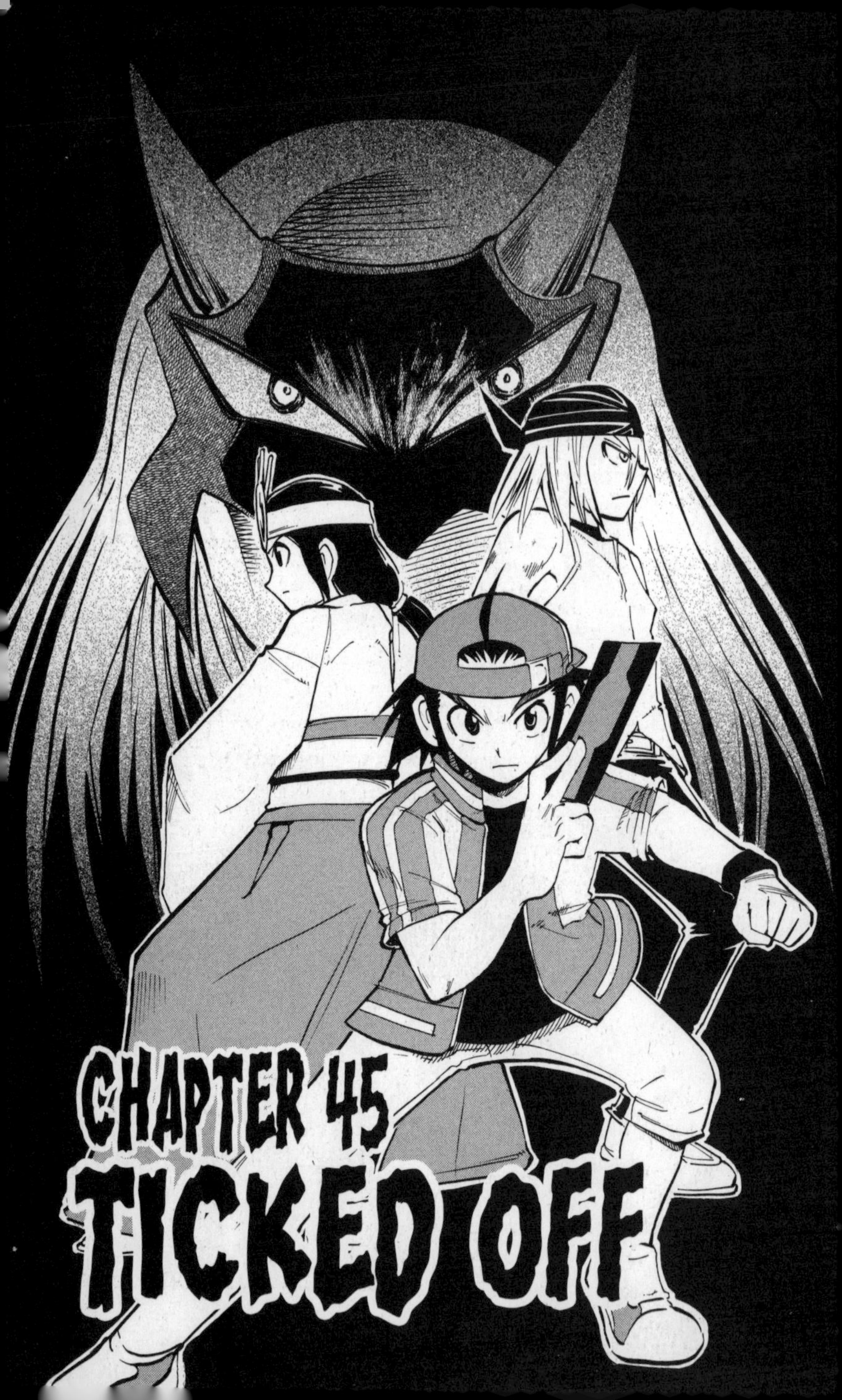
CHAPTER 45
TICKED OFF

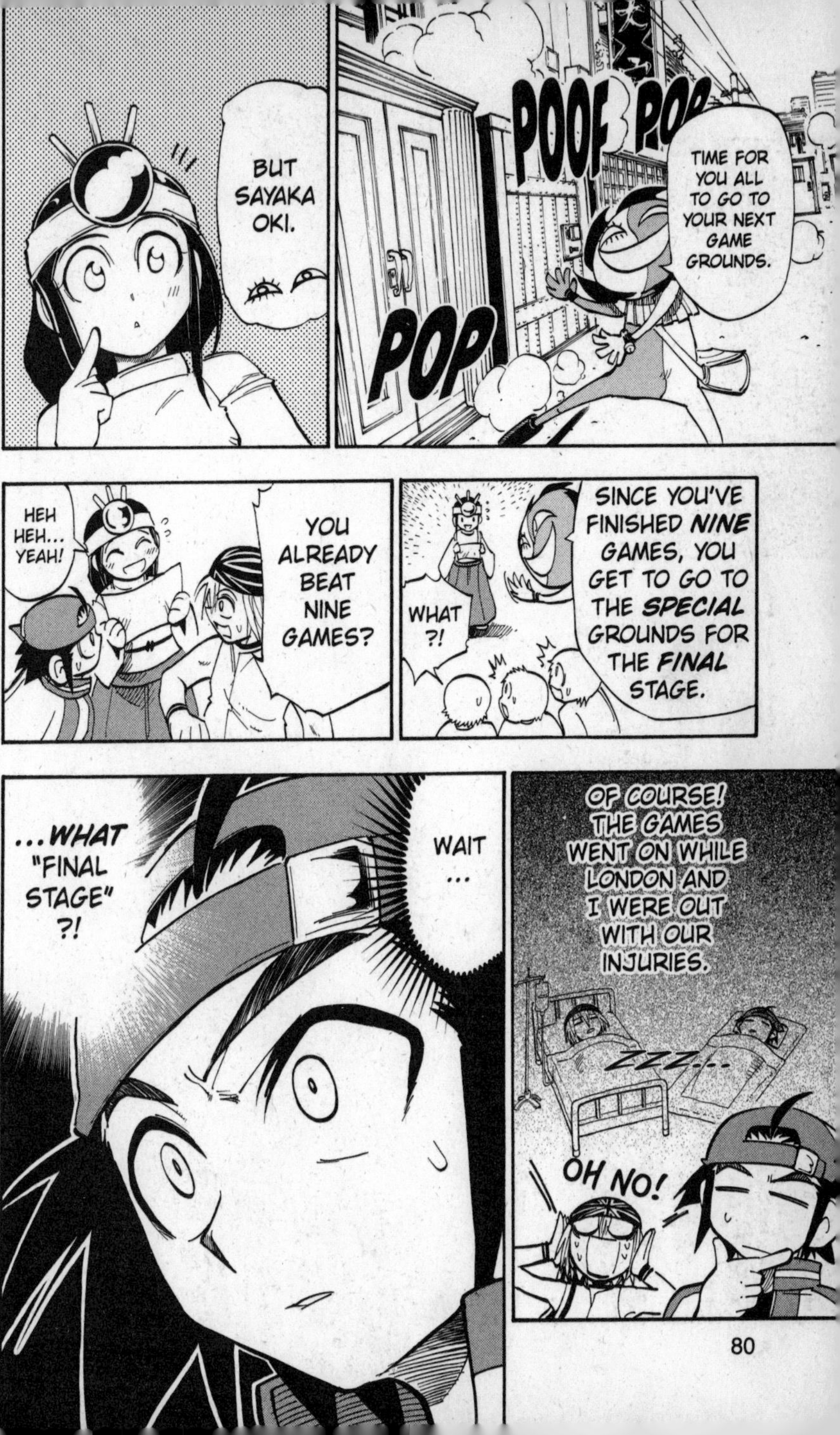
POOF PO
TIME FOR YOU ALL TO GO TO YOUR NEXT GAME GROUNDS.
POP
BUT SAYAKA OKI.
SINCE YOU'VE FINISHED NINE GAMES, YOU GET TO GO TO THE SPECIAL GROUNDS FOR THE FINAL STAGE.
WHAT ?!
YOU ALREADY BEAT NINE GAMES?
HEH HEH... YEAH!
OF COURSE! THE GAMES WENT ON WHILE LONDON AND I WERE OUT WITH OUR INJURIES.
ZZZ...
OH NO!
WAIT ...
...WHAT "FINAL STAGE" ?!

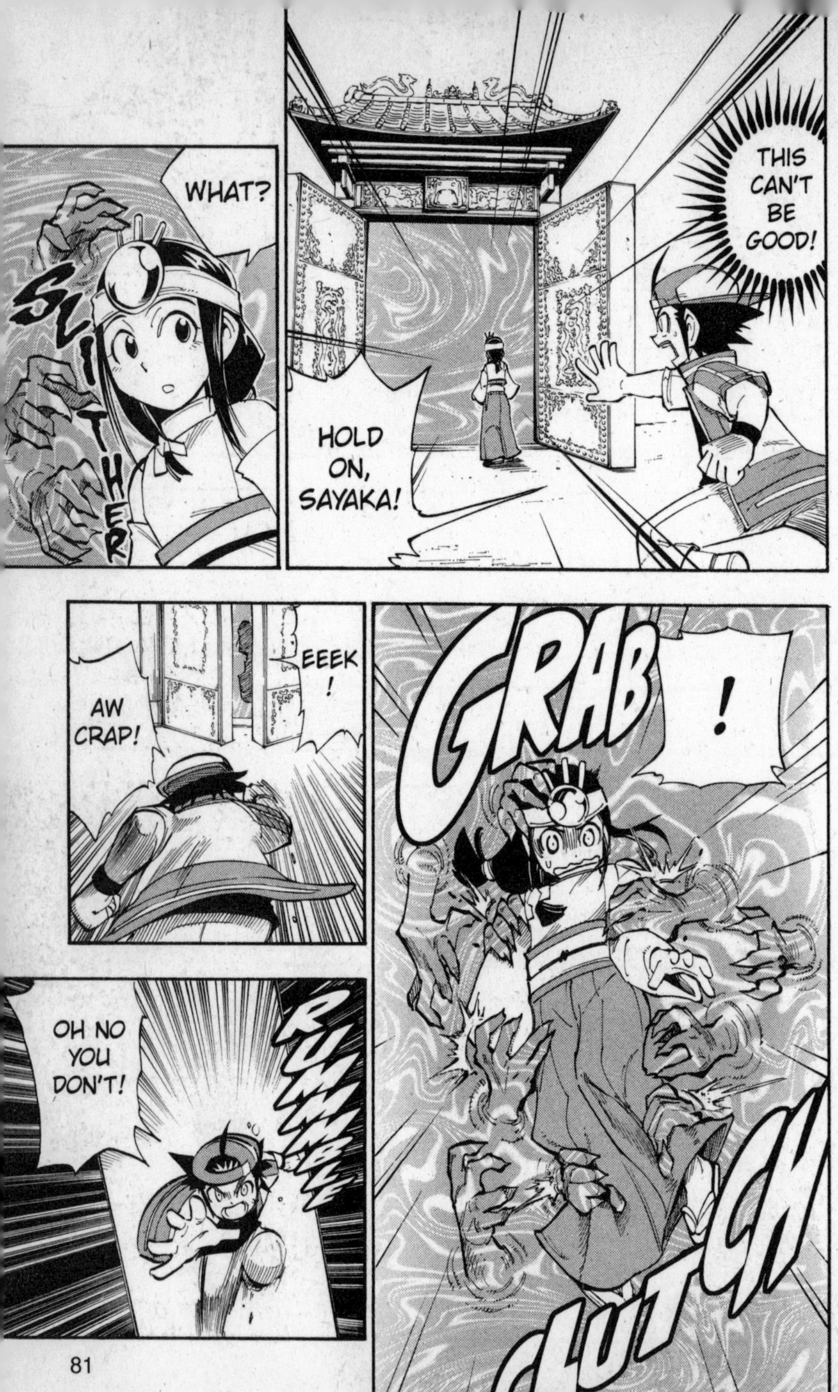
THIS CAN'T BE GOOD!
HOLD ON, SAYAKA!
WHAT?
SLITHER
GRAB
!
CLUTCH
EEEK !
AW CRAP!
OH NO YOU DON'T!
RUMMMBLE

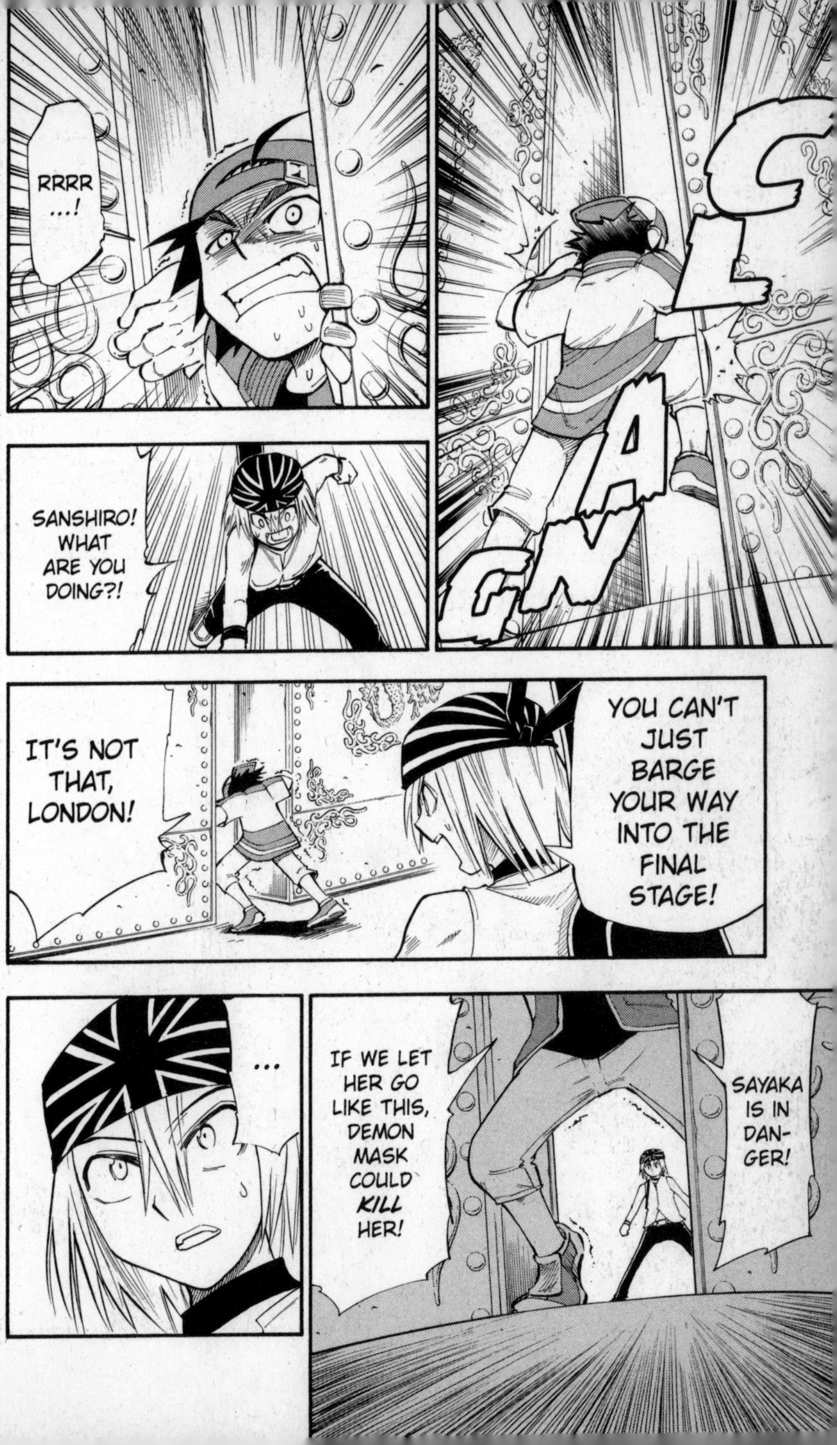
CLANG
RRRR ...!
SANSHIRO! WHAT ARE YOU DOING?!
YOU CAN'T JUST BARGE YOUR WAY INTO THE FINAL STAGE!
IT'S NOT THAT, LONDON!
SAYAKA IS IN DAN-GER!
IF WE LET HER GO LIKE THIS, DEMON MASK COULD *KILL* HER!
...

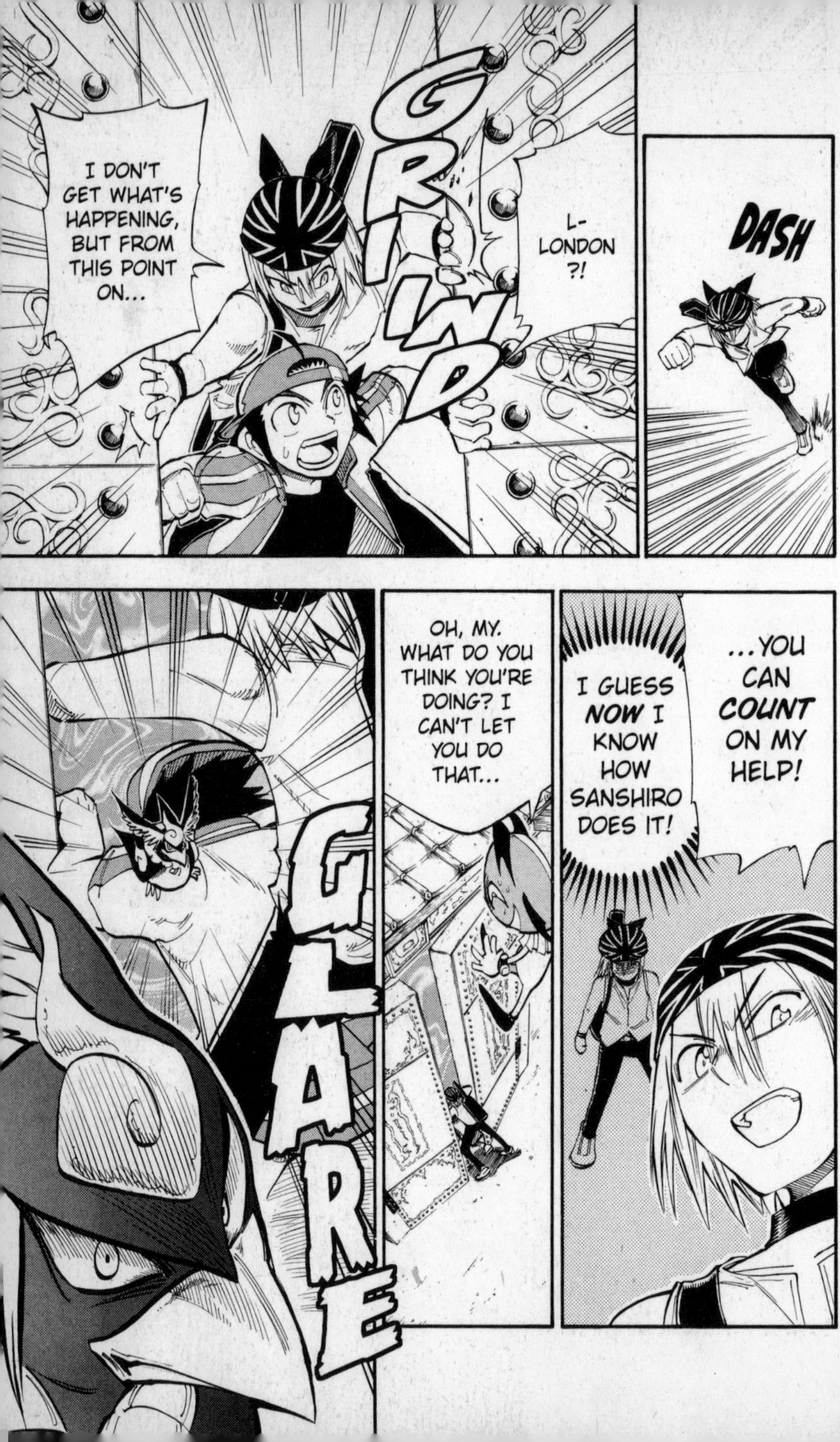
DASH
GRIND
L-LONDON ?!
I DON'T GET WHAT'S HAPPENING, BUT FROM THIS POINT ON...
...YOU CAN COUNT ON MY HELP!
I GUESS NOW I KNOW HOW SANSHIRO DOES IT!
OH, MY. WHAT DO YOU THINK YOU'RE DOING? I CAN'T LET YOU DO THAT...
GLARE

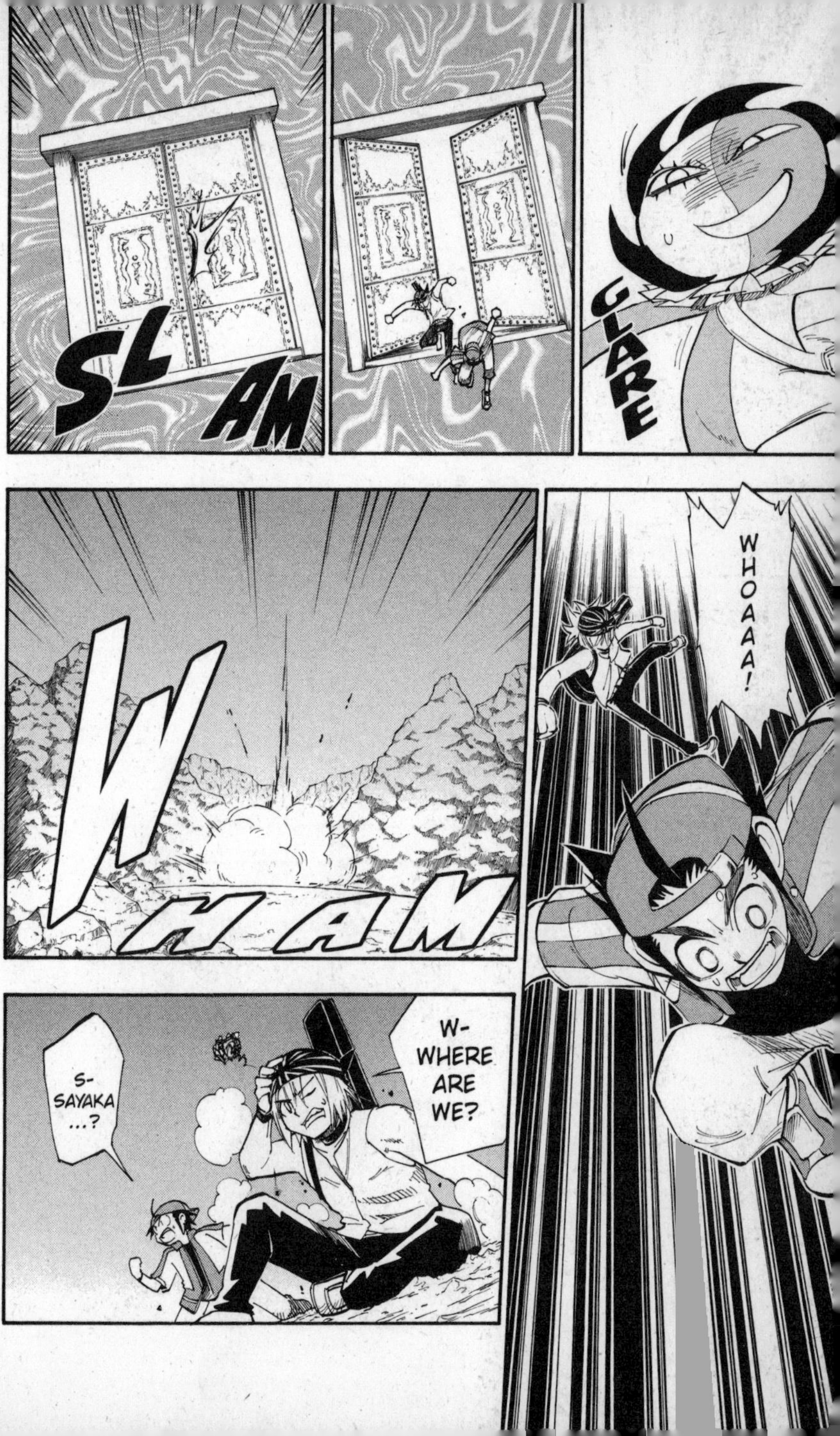
GLARE
SLAM
WHOAAAA!
WHAM
W- WHERE ARE WE?
S- SAYAKA ...?

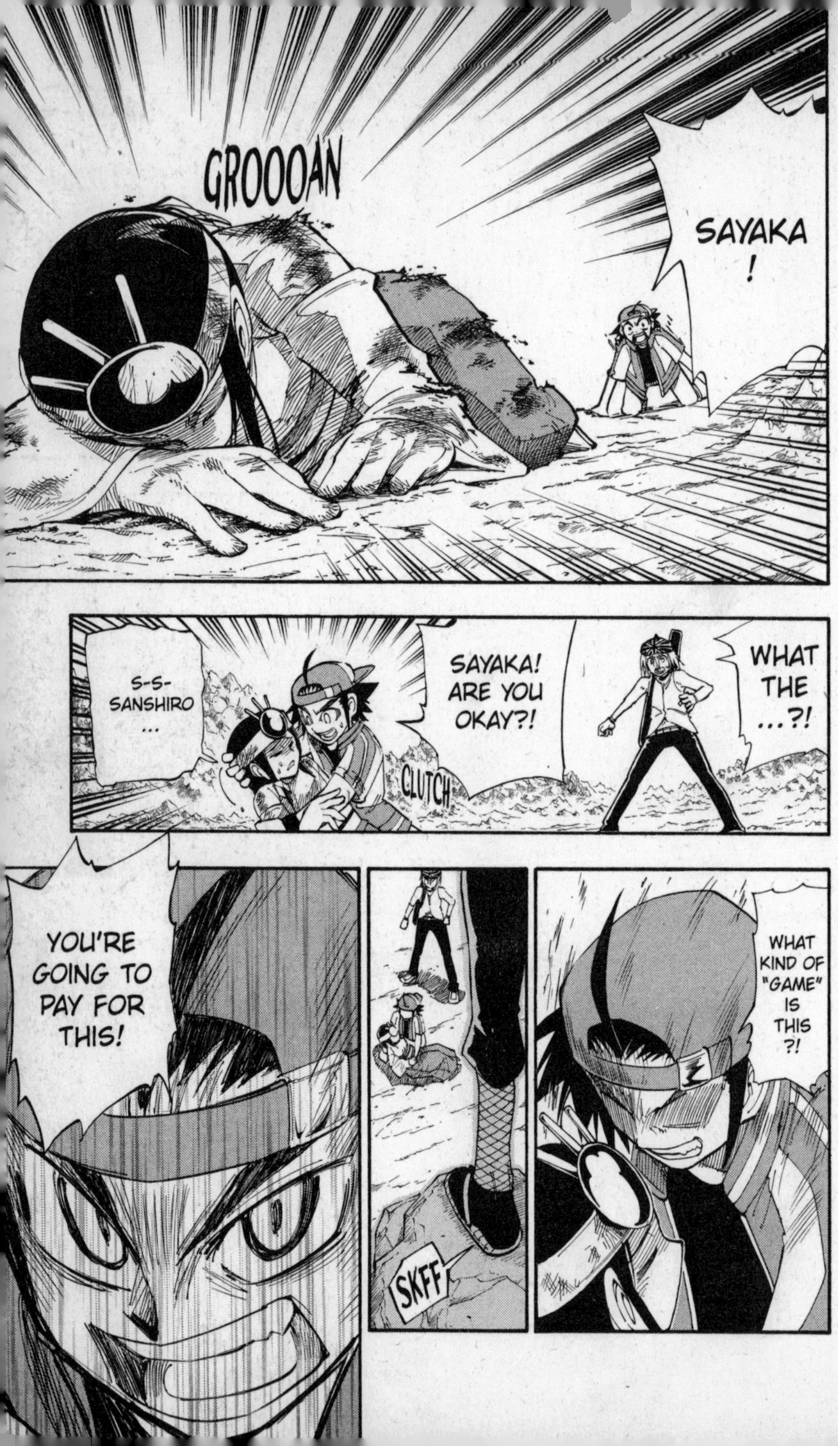
SAYAKA!
GROOOAN
WHAT THE ...?!
SAYAKA! ARE YOU OKAY?!
CLUTCH
S-S-SANSHIRO ...
WHAT KIND OF "GAME" IS THIS?!
SKFF
YOU'RE GOING TO PAY FOR THIS!

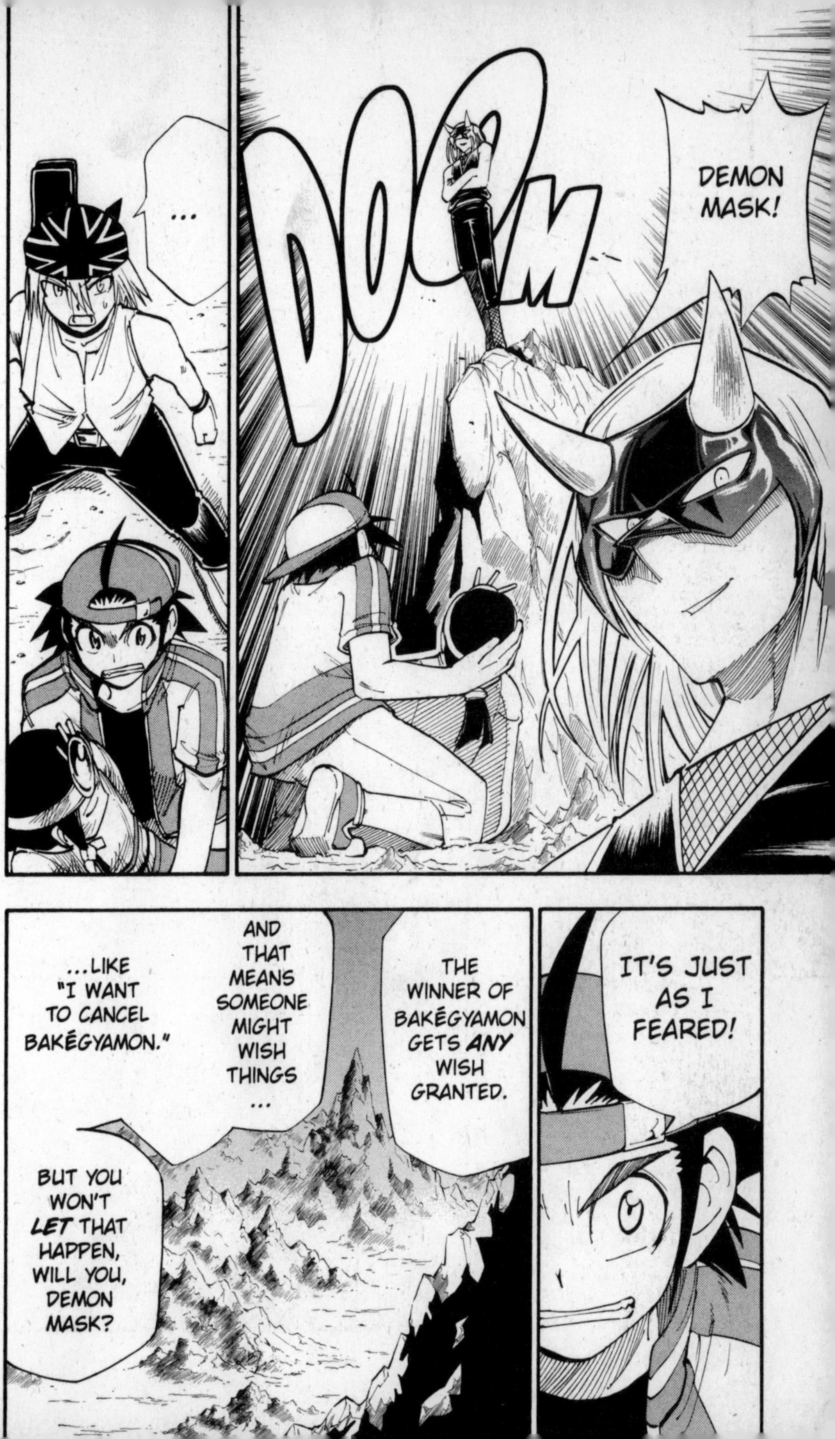
DEMON MASK!
DOOM
...
IT'S JUST AS I FEARED!
THE WINNER OF BAKÉGYAMON GETS *ANY* WISH GRANTED.
AND THAT MEANS SOMEONE MIGHT WISH THINGS ...
...LIKE "I WANT TO CANCEL BAKÉGYAMON."
BUT YOU WON'T *LET* THAT HAPPEN, WILL YOU, DEMON MASK?

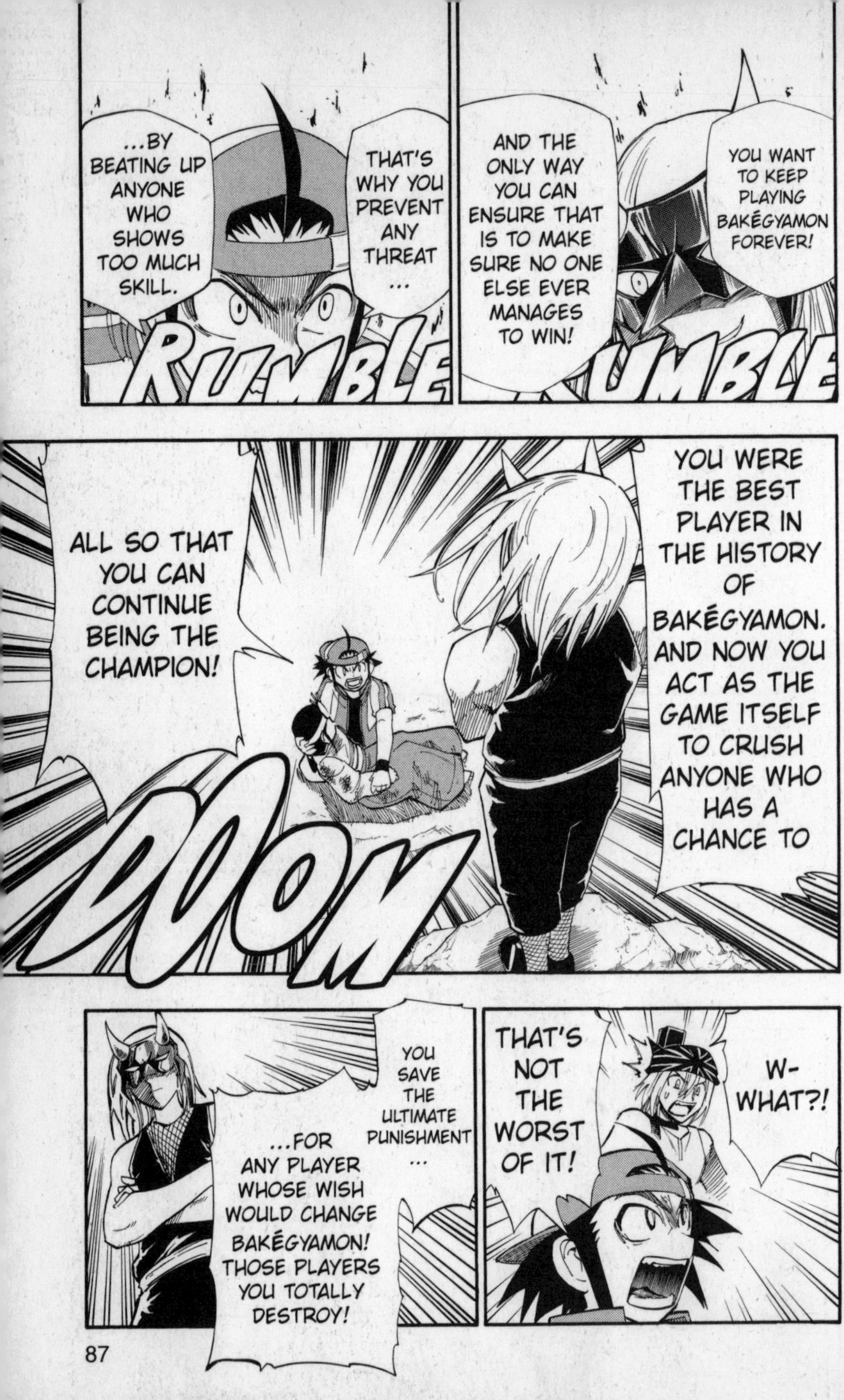
YOU WANT TO KEEP PLAYING BAKÉGYAMON FOREVER!
AND THE ONLY WAY YOU CAN ENSURE THAT IS TO MAKE SURE NO ONE ELSE EVER MANAGES TO WIN!
RUMBLE
THAT'S WHY YOU PREVENT ANY THREAT...
...BY BEATING UP ANYONE WHO SHOWS TOO MUCH SKILL.
RUMBLE
YOU WERE THE BEST PLAYER IN THE HISTORY OF BAKÉGYAMON. AND NOW YOU ACT AS THE GAME ITSELF TO CRUSH ANYONE WHO HAS A CHANCE TO
ALL SO THAT YOU CAN CONTINUE BEING THE CHAMPION!
W- WHAT?!
THAT'S NOT THE WORST OF IT!
YOU SAVE THE ULTIMATE PUNISHMENT...
...FOR ANY PLAYER WHOSE WISH WOULD CHANGE BAKÉGYAMON! THOSE PLAYERS YOU TOTALLY DESTROY!

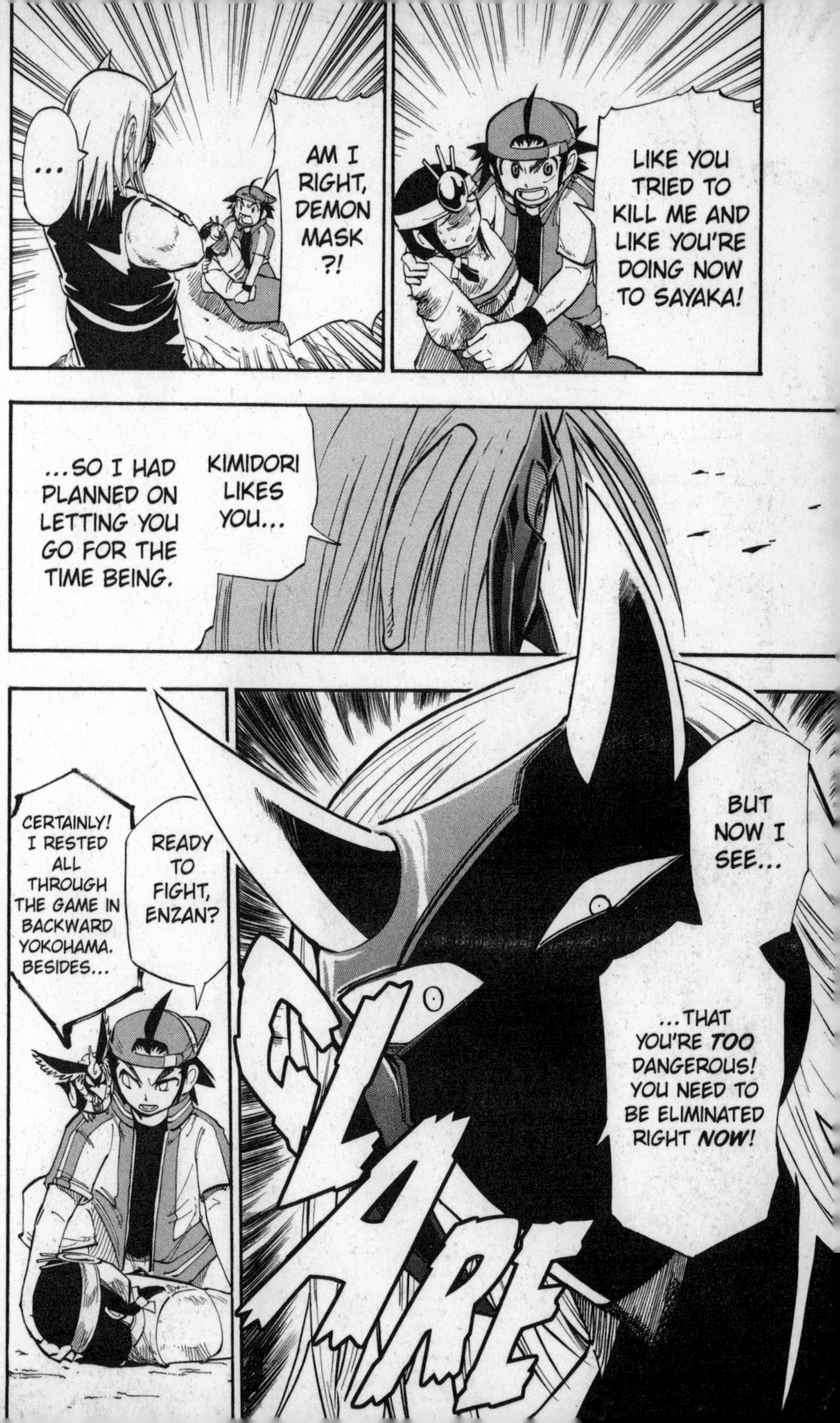
LIKE YOU TRIED TO KILL ME AND LIKE YOU'RE DOING NOW TO SAYAKA!
AM I RIGHT, DEMON MASK?!
...
KIMIDORI LIKES YOU...
...SO I HAD PLANNED ON LETTING YOU GO FOR THE TIME BEING.
BUT NOW I SEE...
...THAT YOU'RE *TOO* DANGEROUS! YOU NEED TO BE ELIMINATED RIGHT *NOW*!
READY TO FIGHT, ENZAN?
CERTAINLY! I RESTED ALL THROUGH THE GAME IN BACKWARD YOKOHAMA. BESIDES...

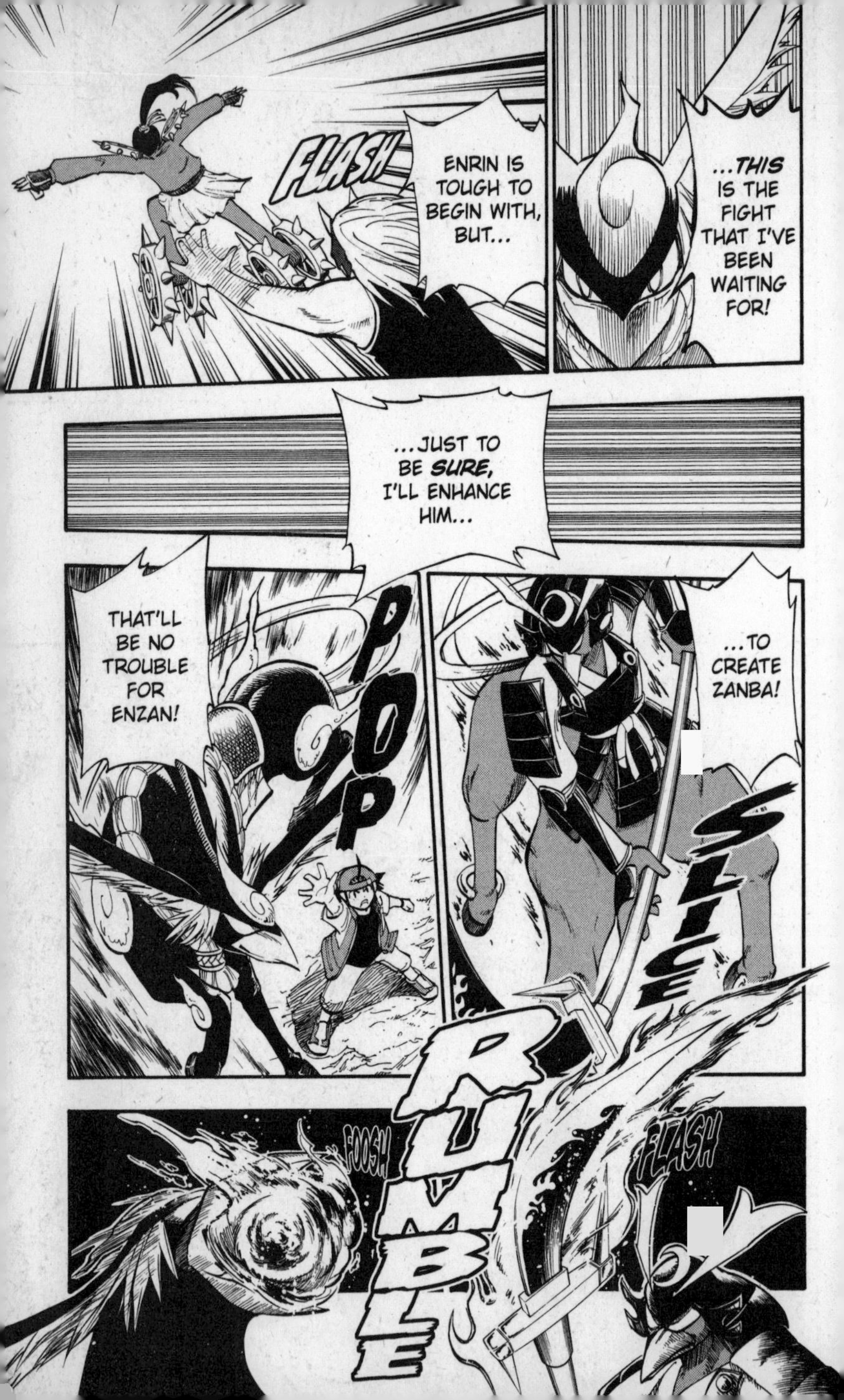
...THIS IS THE FIGHT THAT I'VE BEEN WAITING FOR!
ENRIN IS TOUGH TO BEGIN WITH, BUT...
FLASH
...JUST TO BE SURE, I'LL ENHANCE HIM...
...TO CREATE ZANBA!
SLICE
THAT'LL BE NO TROUBLE FOR ENZAN!
POOP
FLASH
RUMBLE
FOOSH

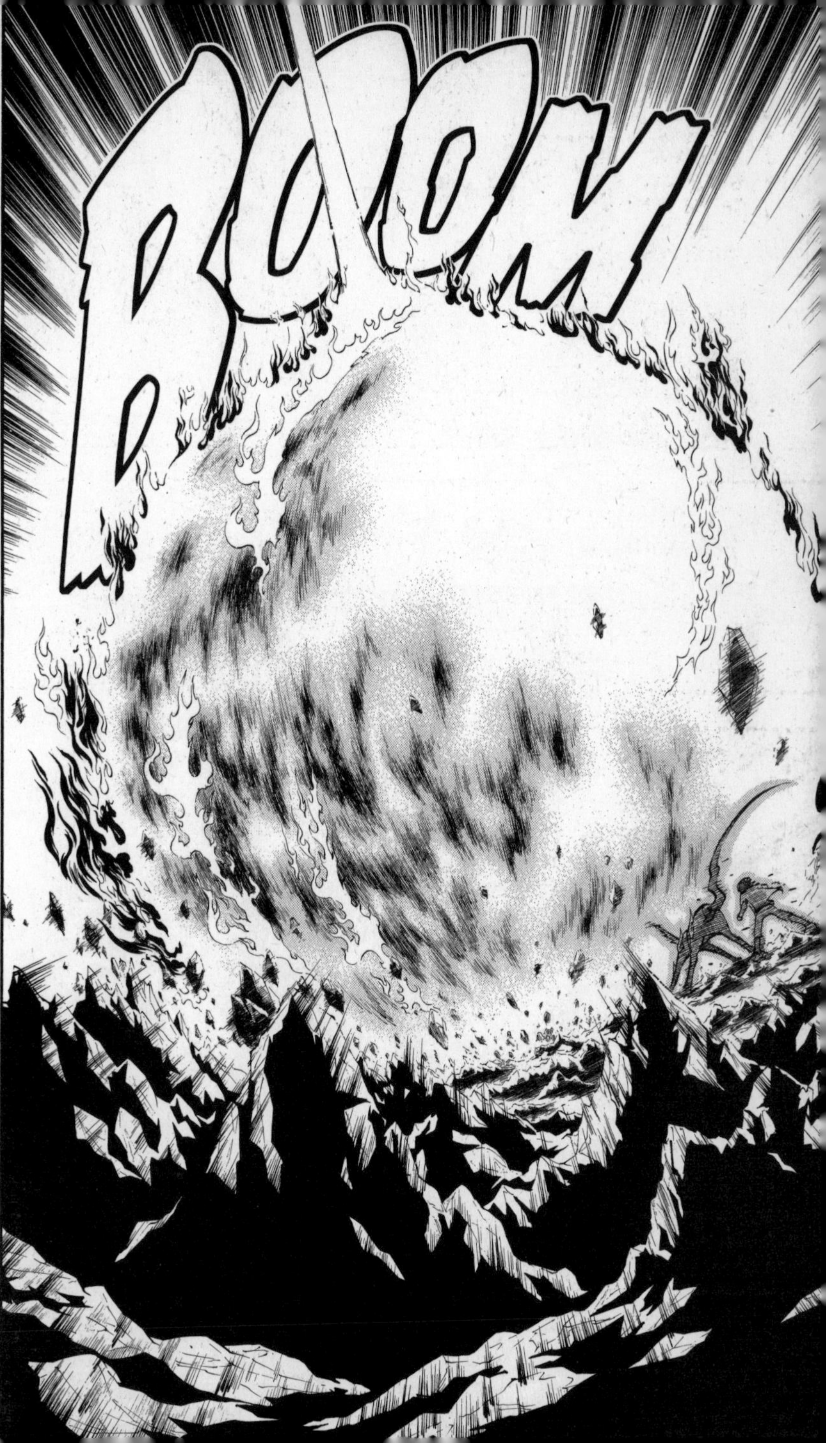
BOOM

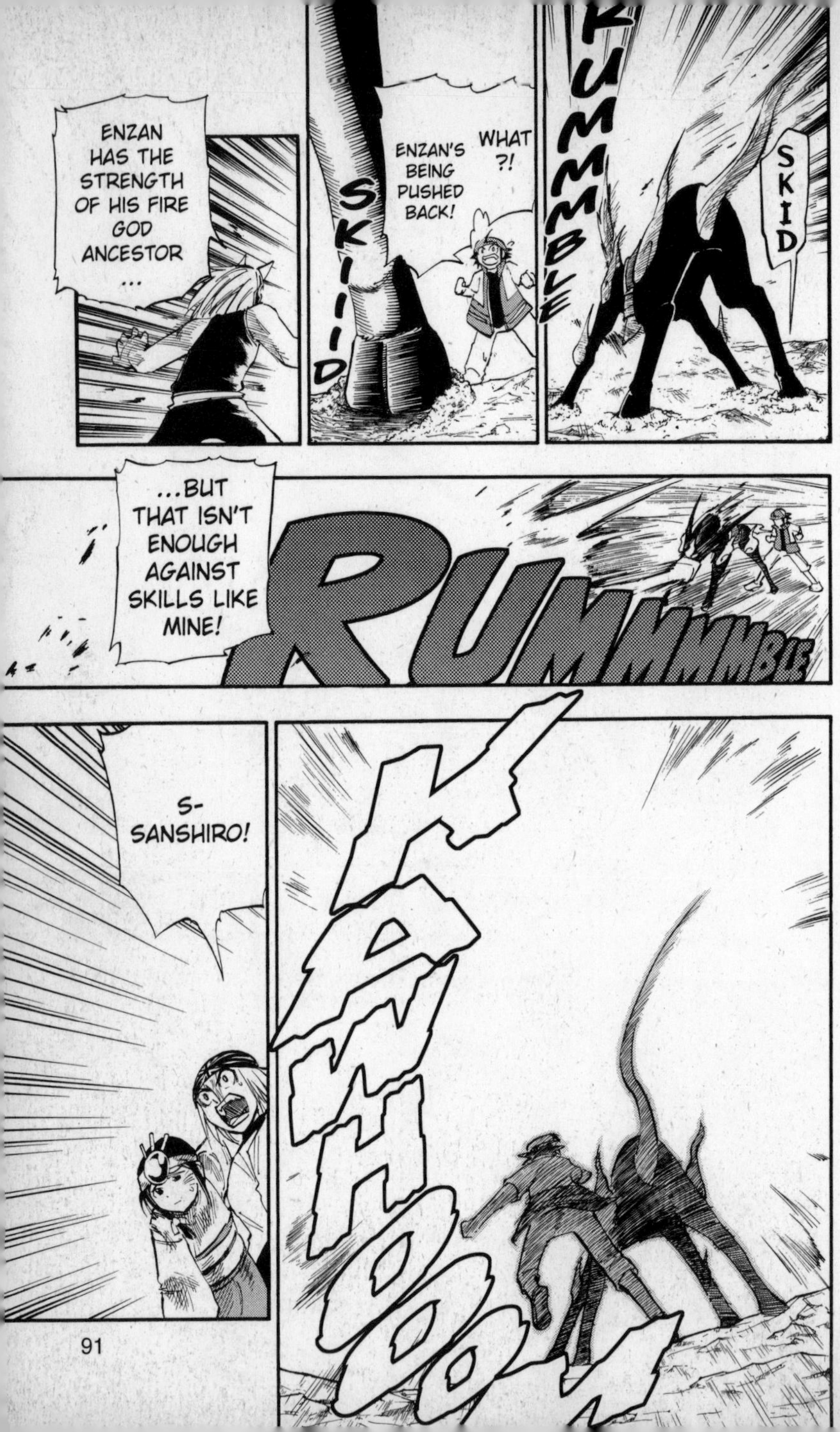
SKID
KUMMMBLE
WHAT ?!
ENZAN'S BEING PUSHED BACK!
SKIIID
ENZAN HAS THE STRENGTH OF HIS FIRE GOD ANCESTOR ...
...BUT THAT ISN'T ENOUGH AGAINST SKILLS LIKE MINE!
RUMMMMBLE
S- SANSHIRO!

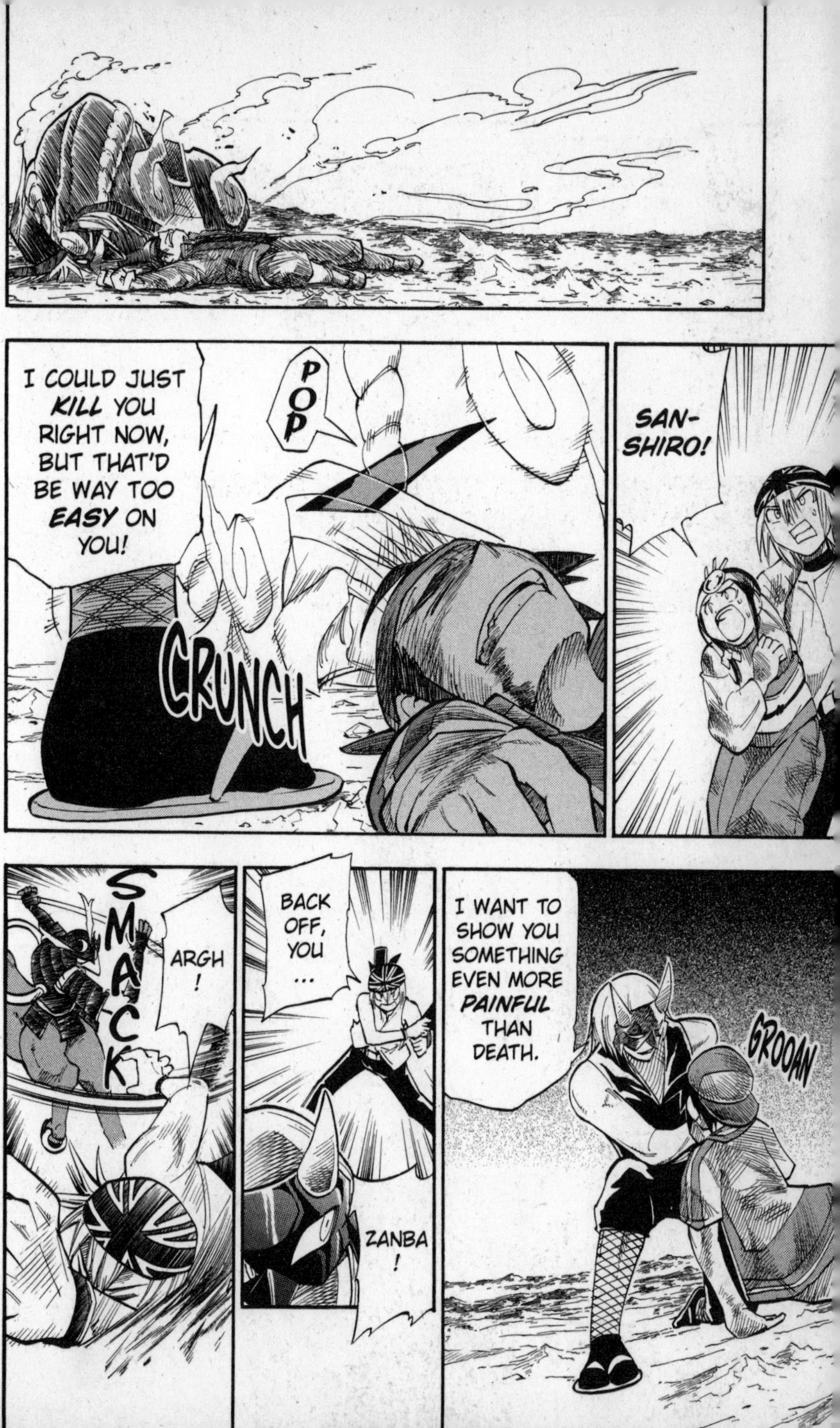
SAN-SHIRO!
POP
I COULD JUST KILL YOU RIGHT NOW, BUT THAT'D BE WAY TOO EASY ON YOU!
CRUNCH
I WANT TO SHOW YOU SOMETHING EVEN MORE PAINFUL THAN DEATH.
GROOAN
BACK OFF, YOU...
ZANBA!
SMACK
ARGH!

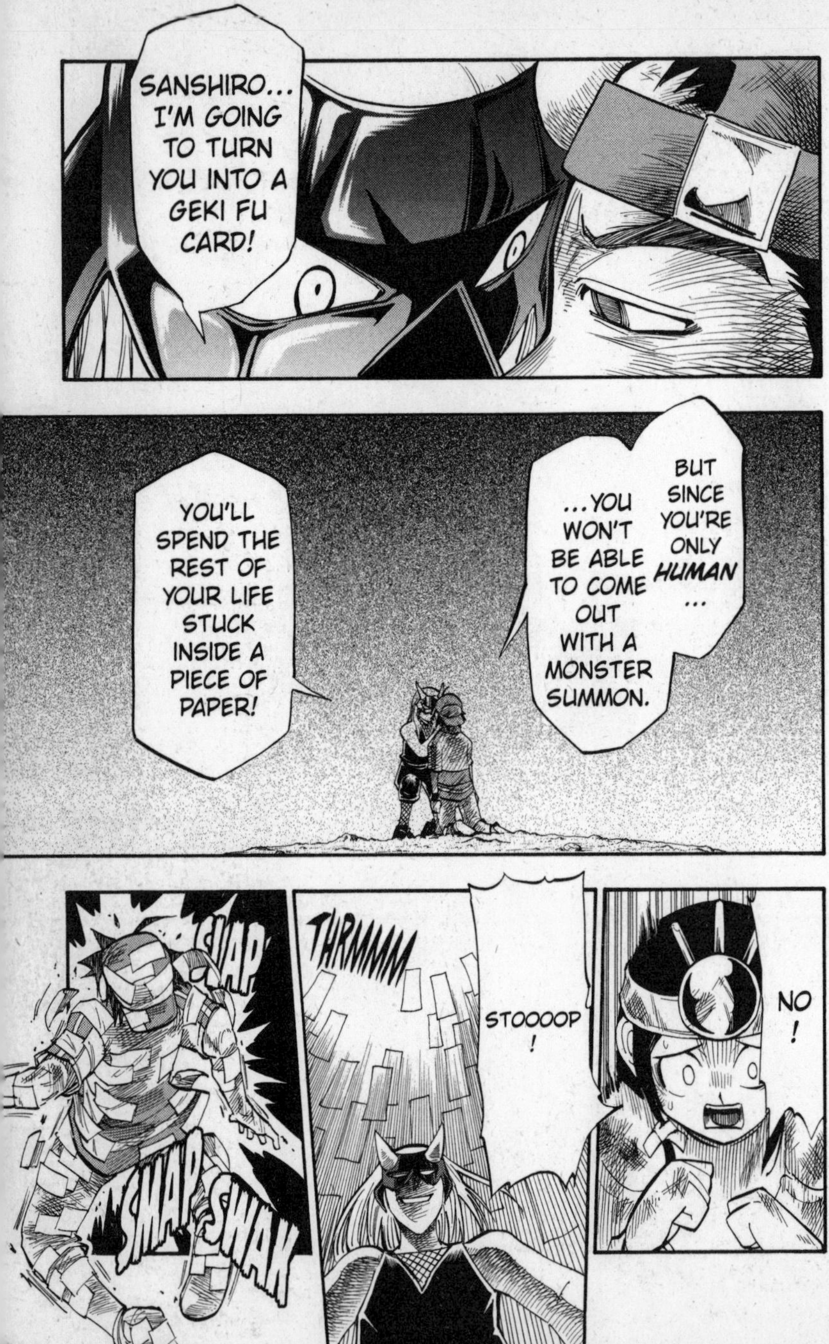
SANSHIRO... I'M GOING TO TURN YOU INTO A GEKI FU CARD!
BUT SINCE YOU'RE ONLY *HUMAN* ...
...YOU WON'T BE ABLE TO COME OUT WITH A MONSTER SUMMON.
YOU'LL SPEND THE REST OF YOUR LIFE STUCK INSIDE A PIECE OF PAPER!
NO!
STOOOOP!
THRMMMM
SNAP
SNAP SWAK

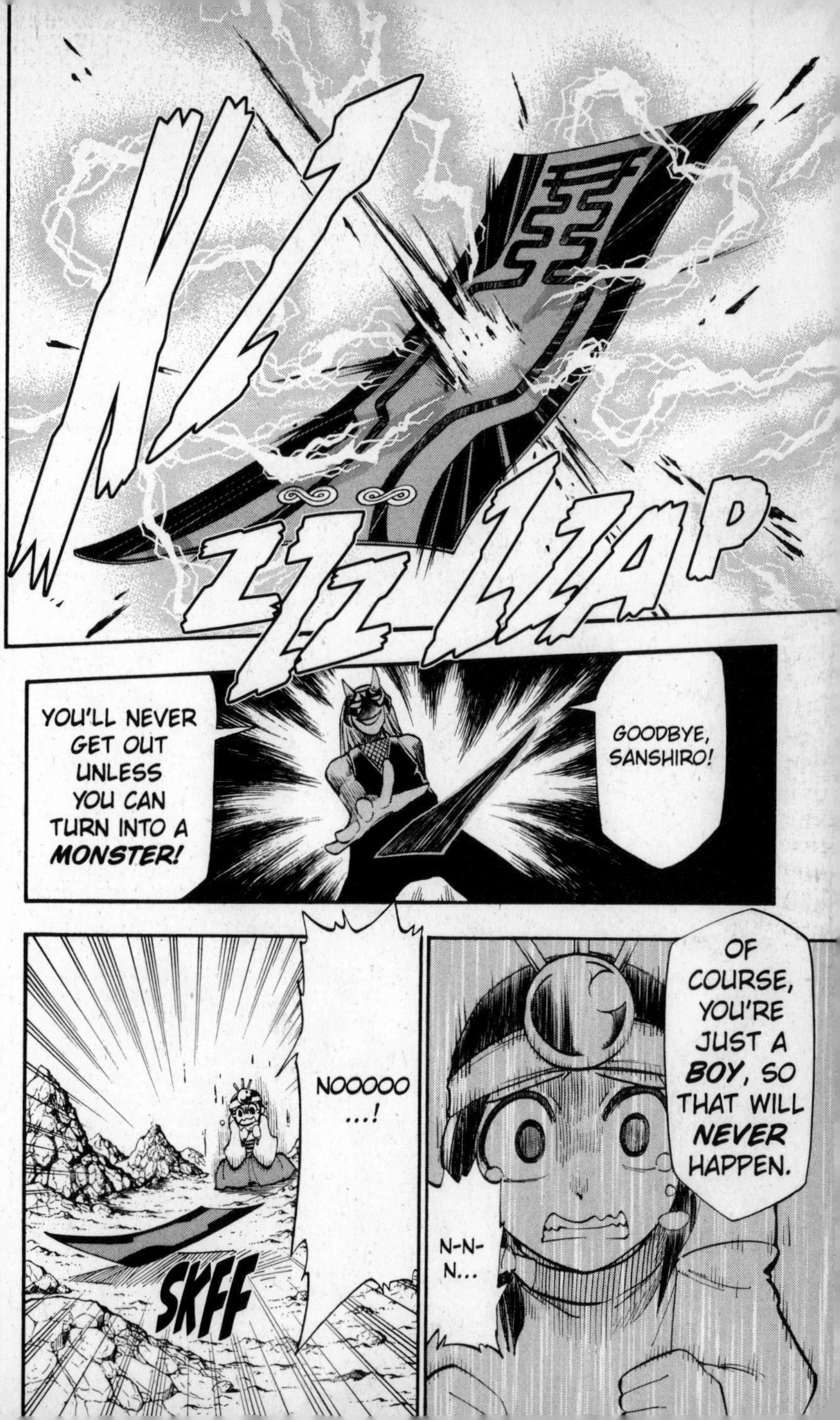
WZZZAP
GOODBYE, SANSHIRO!
YOU'LL NEVER GET OUT UNLESS YOU CAN TURN INTO A **MONSTER!**
OF COURSE, YOU'RE JUST A **BOY**, SO THAT WILL **NEVER** HAPPEN.
N-N-N...
NOOOOO ...!
SKFF

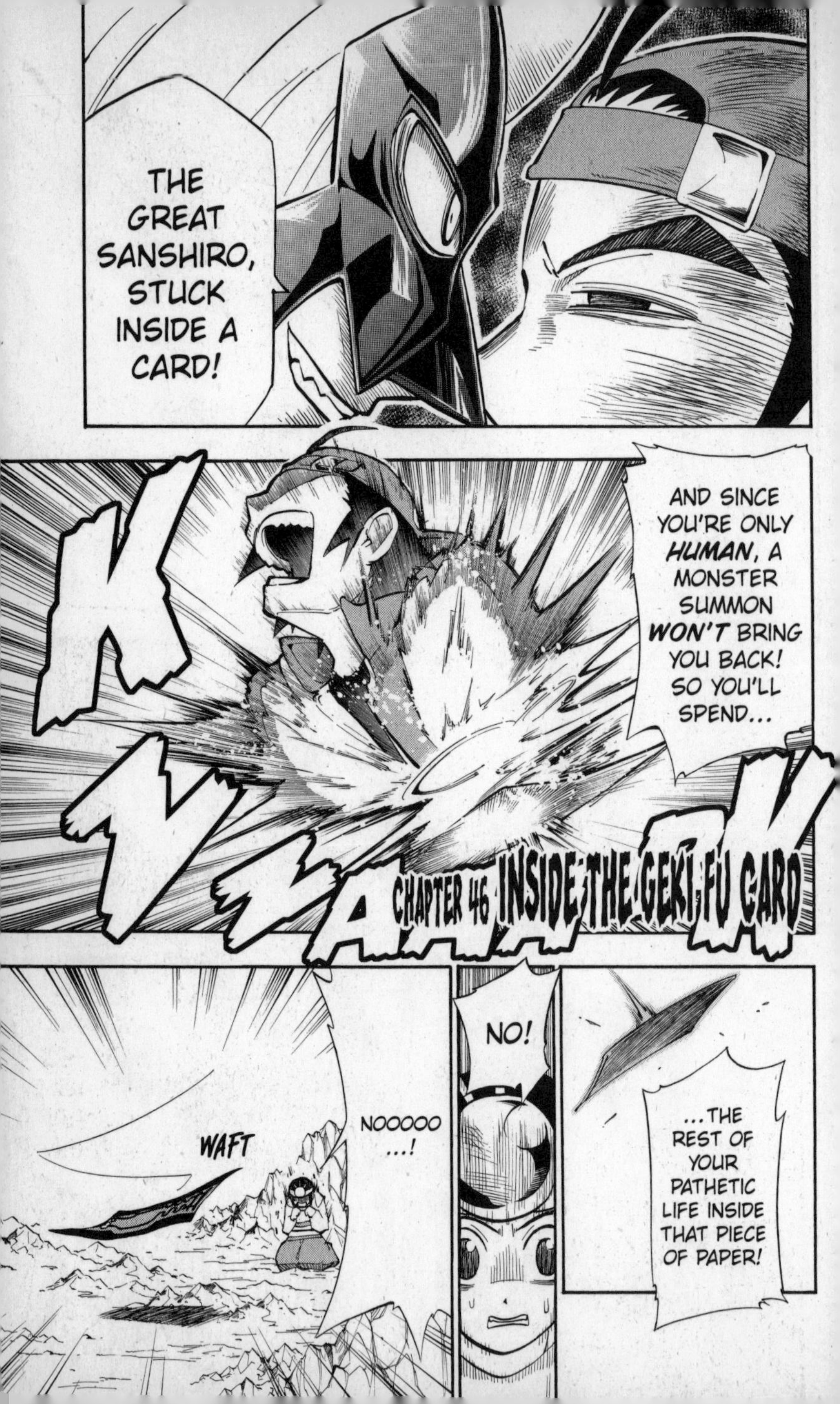
THE GREAT SANSHIRO, STUCK INSIDE A CARD!
AND SINCE YOU'RE ONLY HUMAN, A MONSTER SUMMON WON'T BRING YOU BACK! SO YOU'LL SPEND...
CHAPTER 46 INSIDE THE GEKI FU CARD
...THE REST OF YOUR PATHETIC LIFE INSIDE THAT PIECE OF PAPER!
NO!
NOOOOO ...!
WAFT

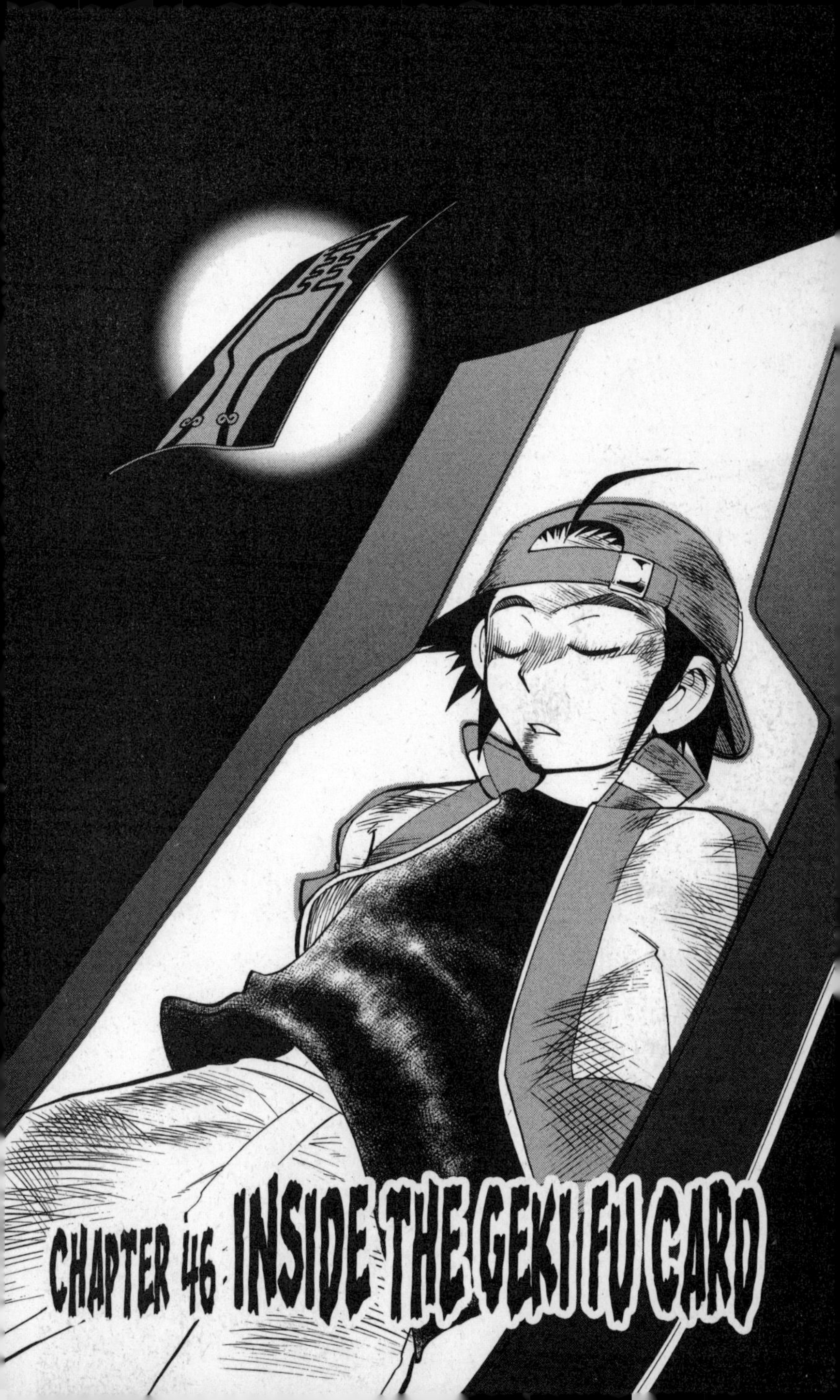
CHAPTER 46: INSIDE THE GEKI FU CARD

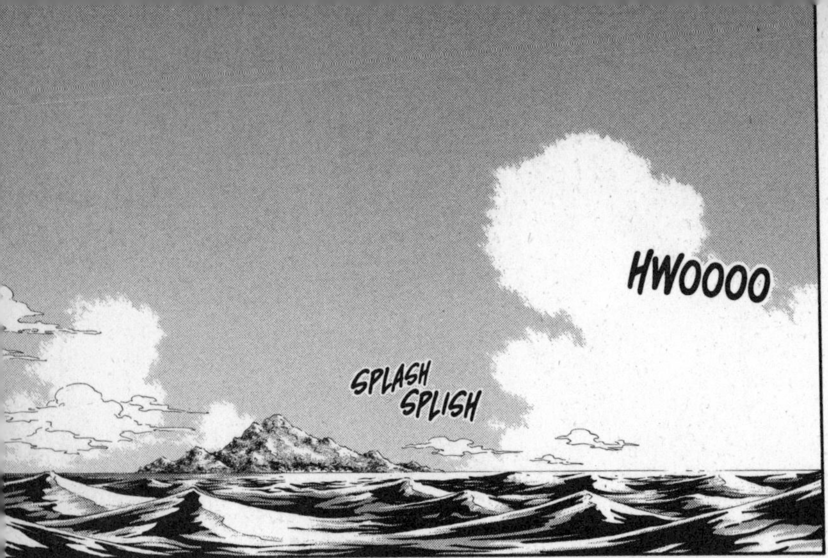
HWOOOO
SPLASH
SPLISH
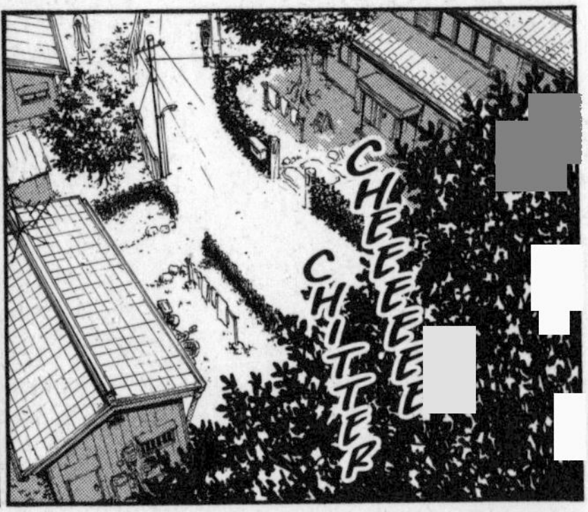
CHEEEEEE
CHITTER
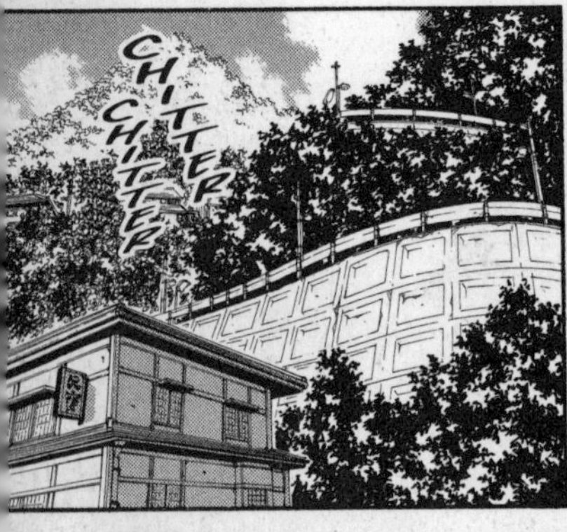
CHITTER
CHITTER
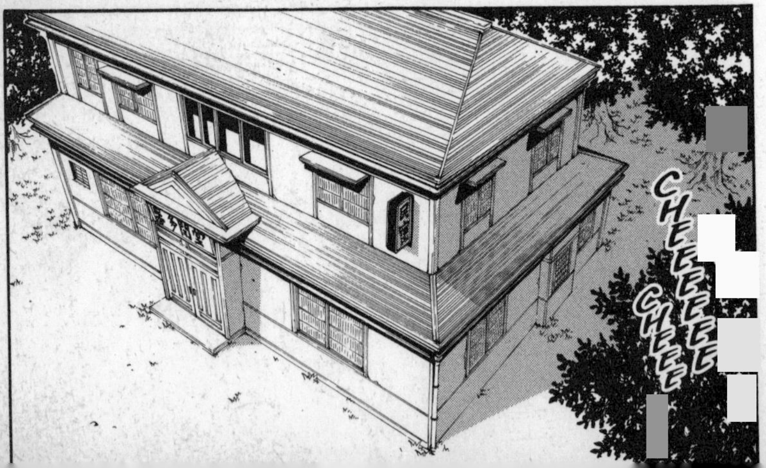
CHEEEEEEE
CHEEEE

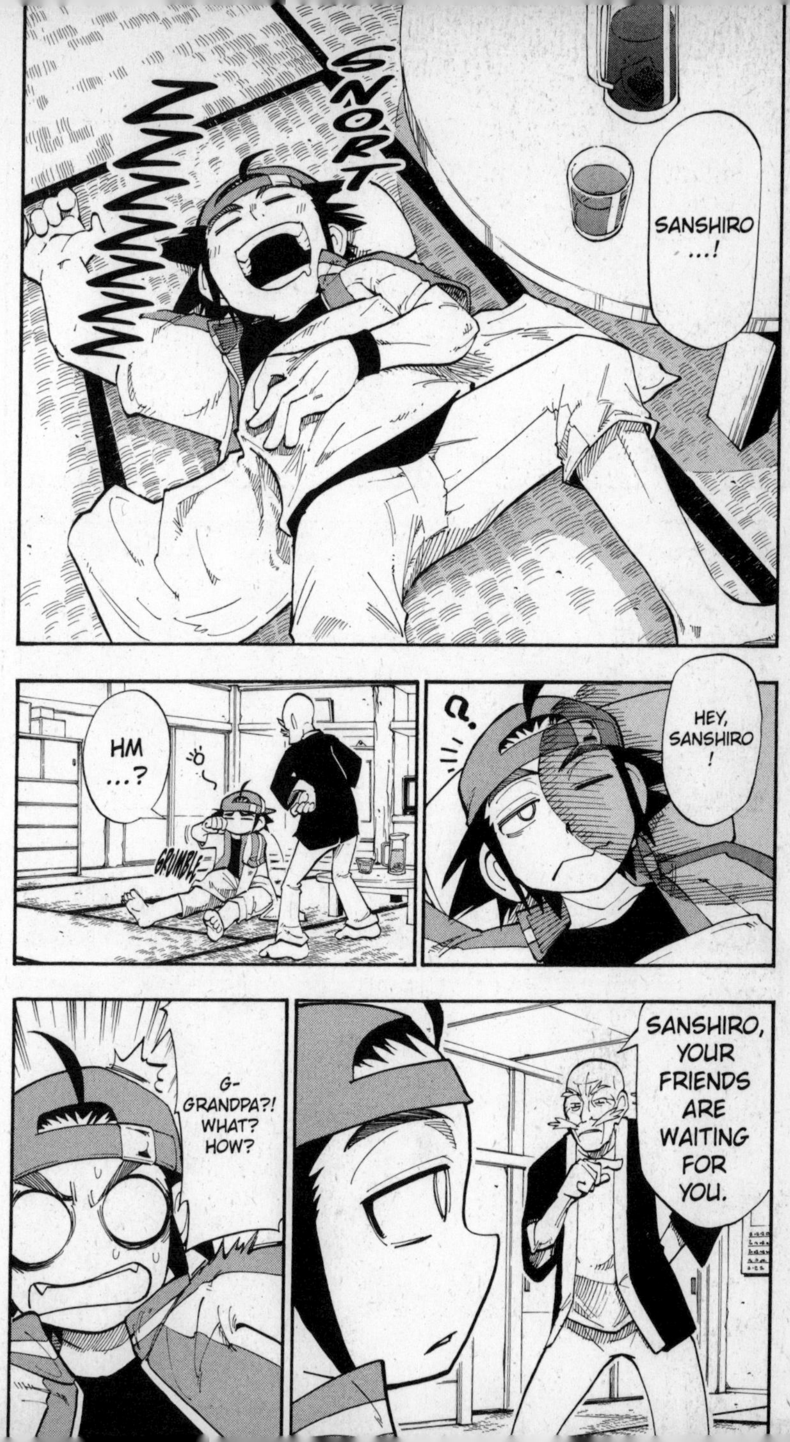
SNORT
SANSHIRO ...!
HEY, SANSHIRO!
HM ...?
GRUMBLE
SANSHIRO, YOUR FRIENDS ARE WAITING FOR YOU.
G-GRANDPA?! WHAT? HOW?

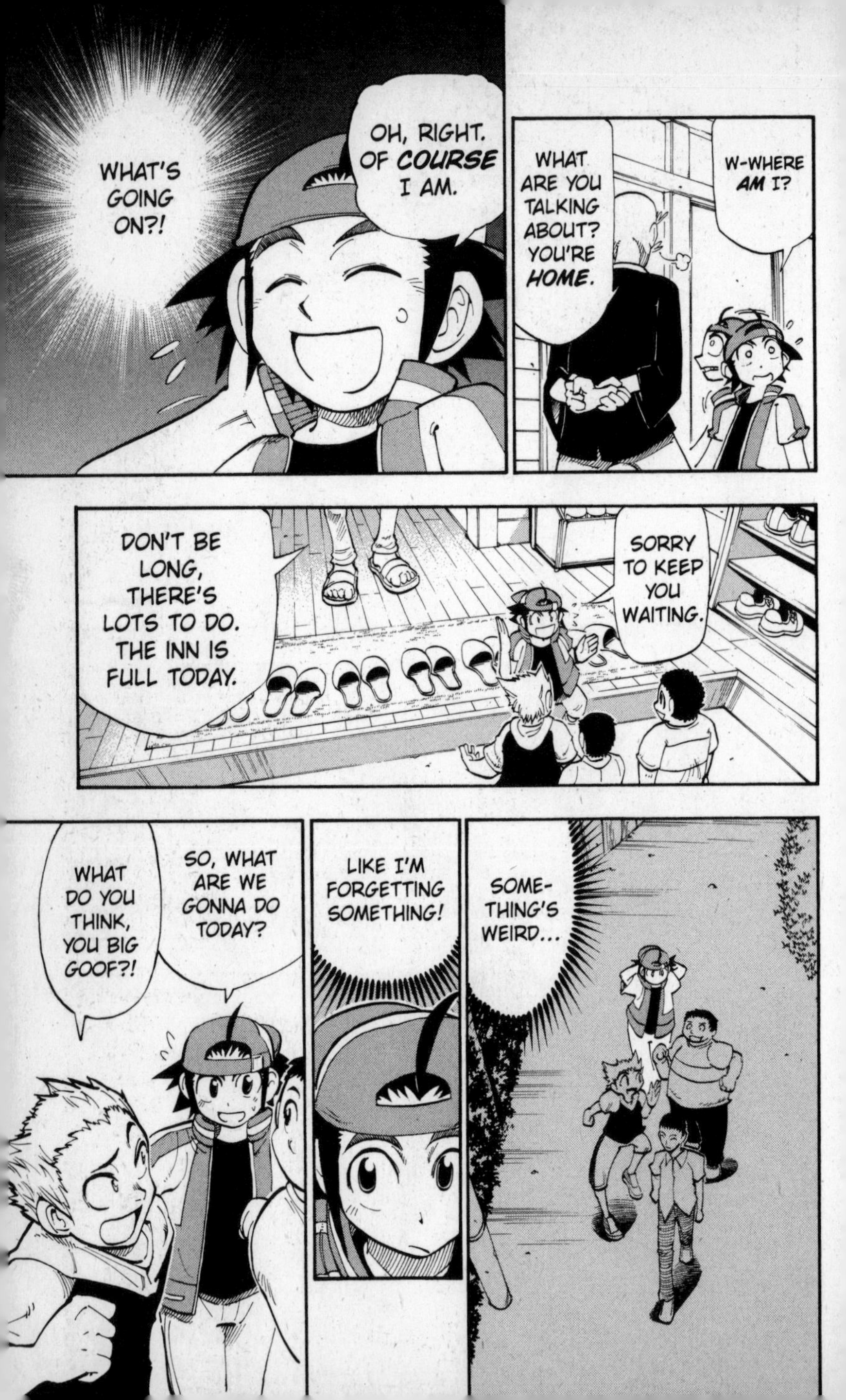
W-WHERE AM I?
WHAT ARE YOU TALKING ABOUT? YOU'RE HOME.
OH, RIGHT. OF COURSE I AM.
WHAT'S GOING ON?!
SORRY TO KEEP YOU WAITING.
DON'T BE LONG, THERE'S LOTS TO DO. THE INN IS FULL TODAY.
SOME-THING'S WEIRD...
LIKE I'M FORGETTING SOMETHING!
SO, WHAT ARE WE GONNA DO TODAY?
WHAT DO YOU THINK, YOU BIG GOOF?!

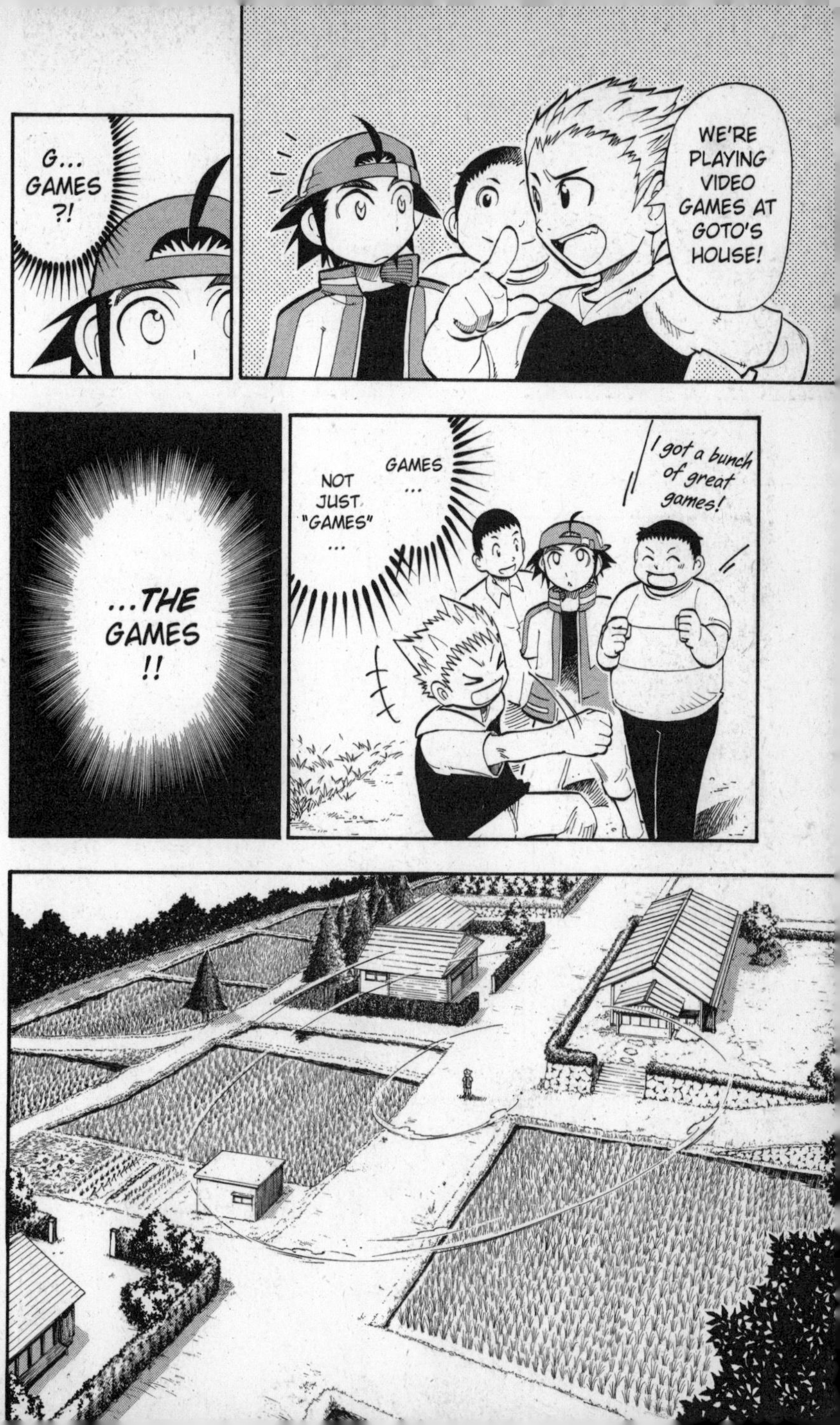
WE'RE PLAYING VIDEO GAMES AT GOTO'S HOUSE!
G... GAMES ?!
I got a bunch of great games!
GAMES ...
NOT JUST "GAMES" ...
...THE GAMES !!

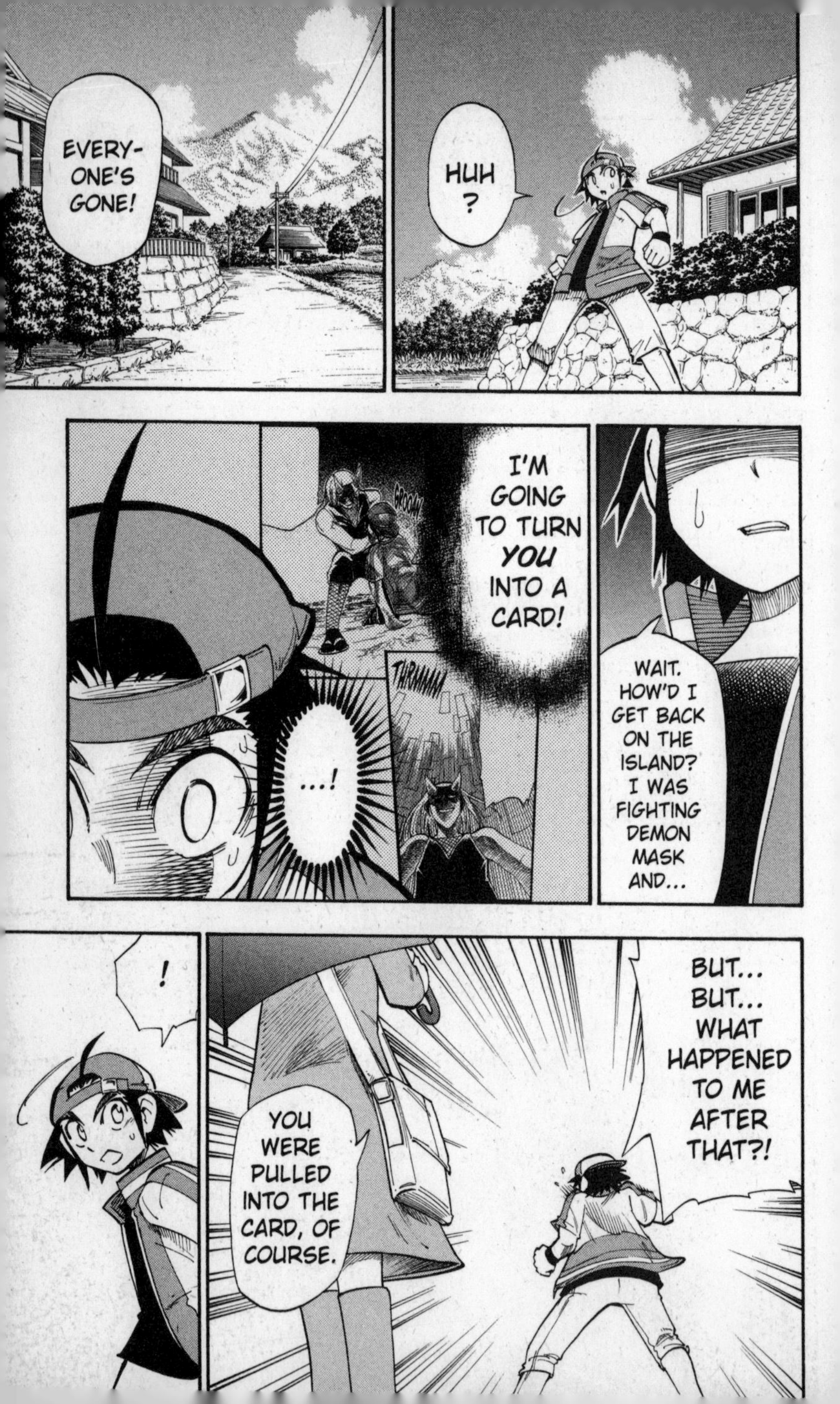
HUH?
EVERY-ONE'S GONE!
WAIT. HOW'D I GET BACK ON THE ISLAND? I WAS FIGHTING DEMON MASK AND...
I'M GOING TO TURN *YOU* INTO A CARD!
...!
BUT... BUT... WHAT HAPPENED TO ME AFTER THAT?!
YOU WERE PULLED INTO THE CARD, OF COURSE.
!

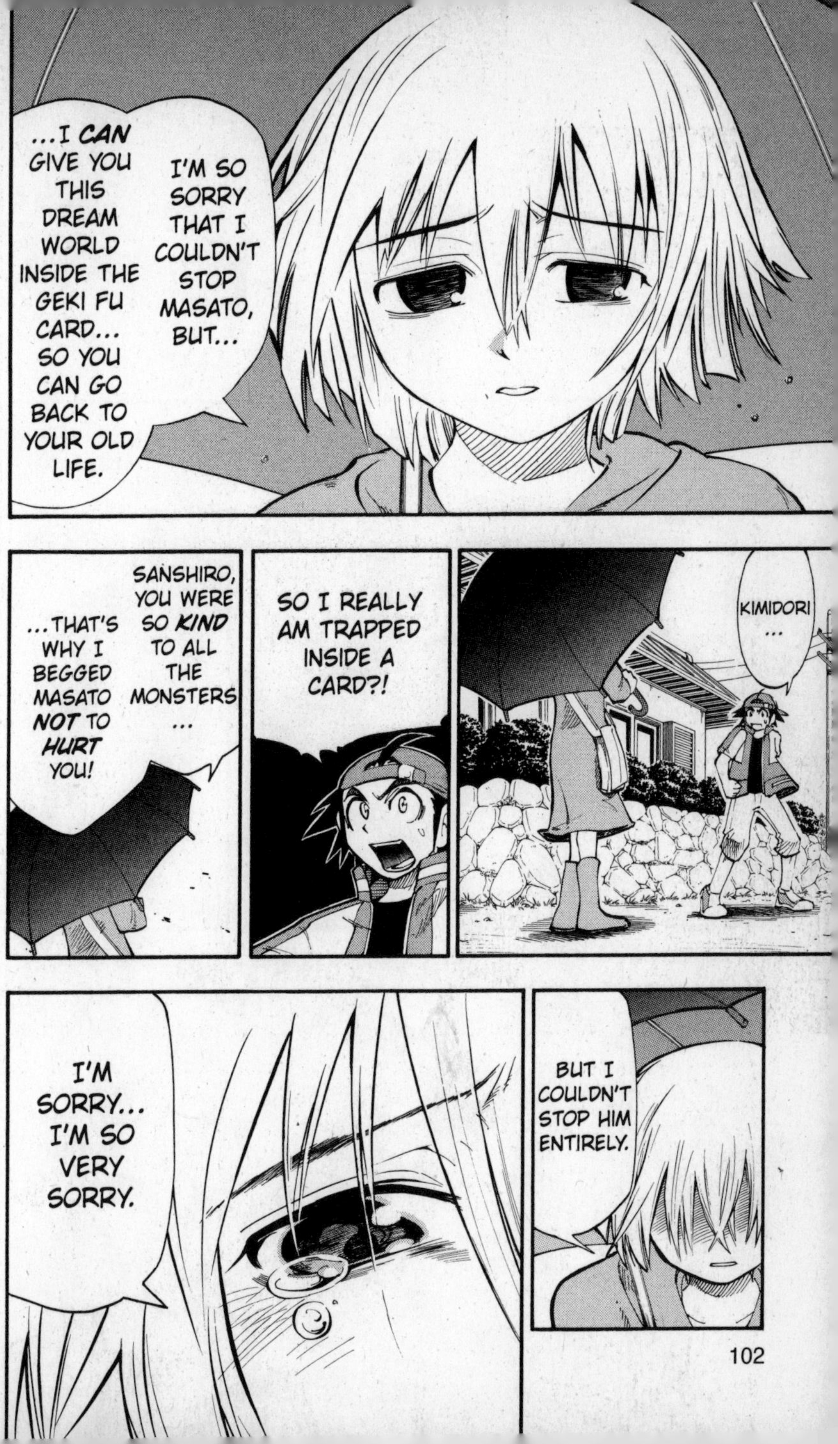
I'M SO SORRY THAT I COULDN'T STOP MASATO, BUT...
...I CAN GIVE YOU THIS DREAM WORLD INSIDE THE GEKI FU CARD... SO YOU CAN GO BACK TO YOUR OLD LIFE.
KIMIDORI...
SO I REALLY AM TRAPPED INSIDE A CARD?!
SANSHIRO, YOU WERE SO KIND TO ALL THE MONSTERS...
...THAT'S WHY I BEGGED MASATO NOT TO HURT YOU!
BUT I COULDN'T STOP HIM ENTIRELY.
I'M SORRY... I'M SO VERY SORRY.

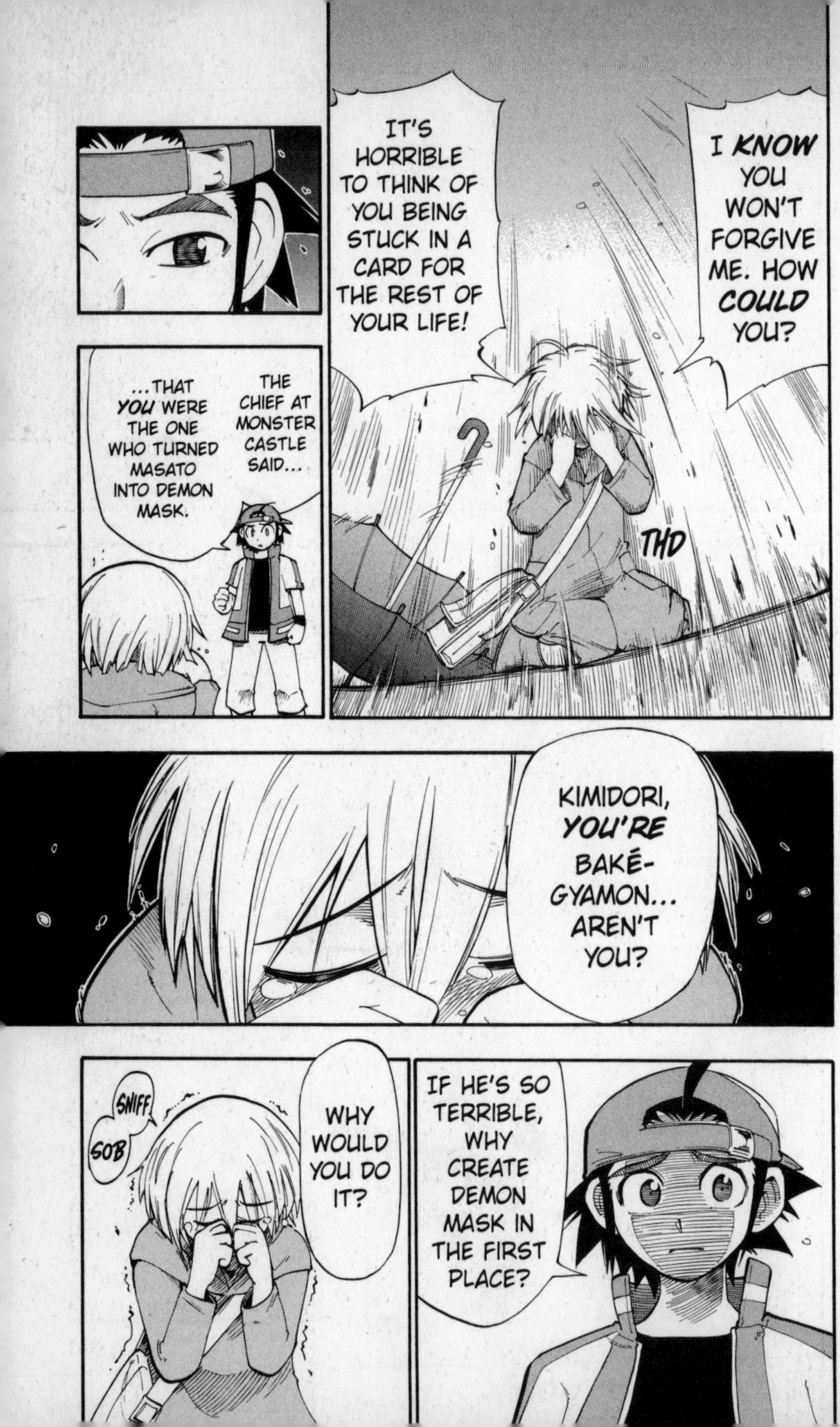
I KNOW YOU WON'T FORGIVE ME. HOW COULD YOU?
IT'S HORRIBLE TO THINK OF YOU BEING STUCK IN A CARD FOR THE REST OF YOUR LIFE!
THD
THE CHIEF AT MONSTER CASTLE SAID...
...THAT YOU WERE THE ONE WHO TURNED MASATO INTO DEMON MASK.
KIMIDORI, YOU'RE BAKÉ-GYAMON... AREN'T YOU?
IF HE'S SO TERRIBLE, WHY CREATE DEMON MASK IN THE FIRST PLACE?
WHY WOULD YOU DO IT?
SNIFF
SOB

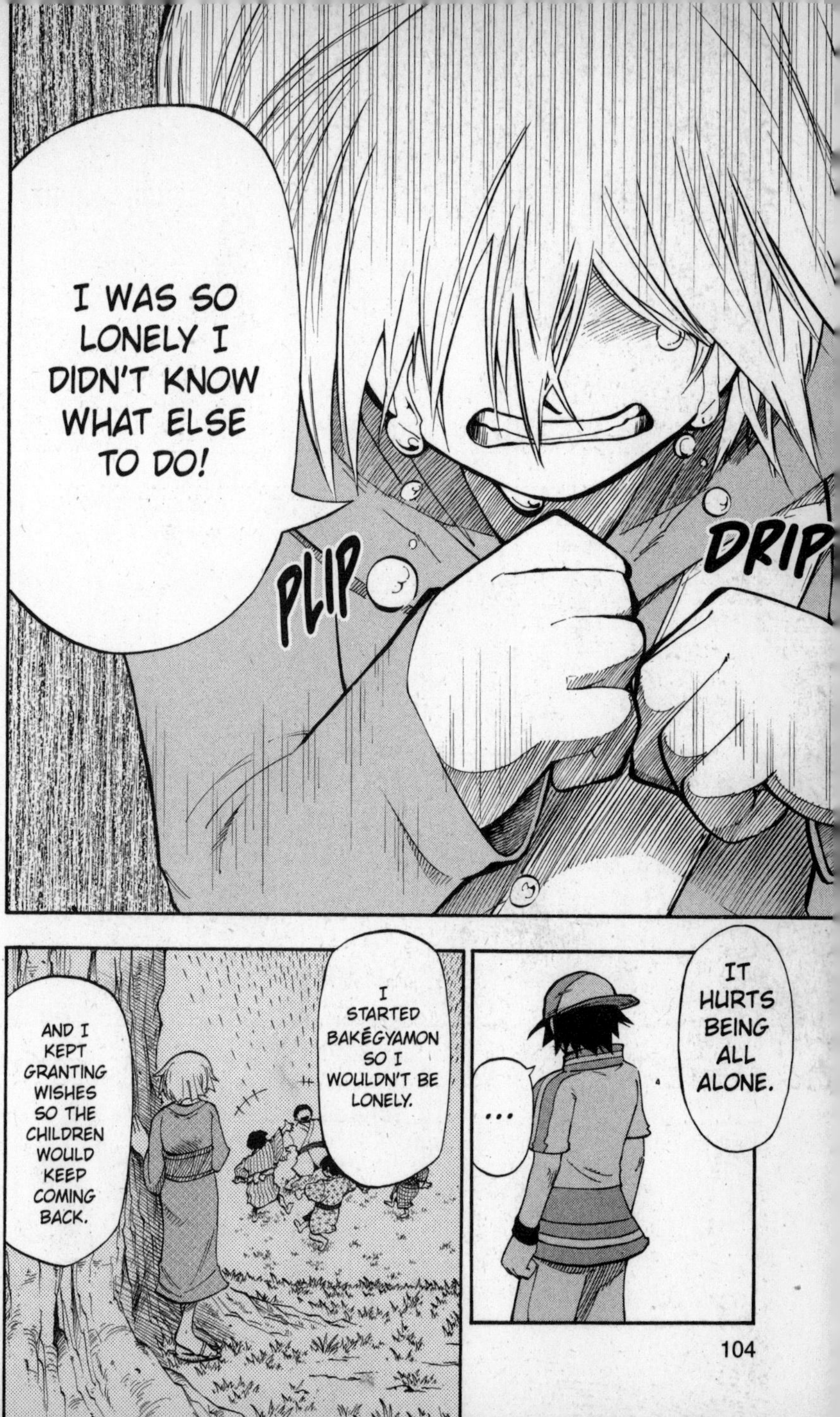
I WAS SO LONELY I DIDN'T KNOW WHAT ELSE TO DO!
DRIP
PLIP
IT HURTS BEING ALL ALONE.
...
I STARTED BAKÉGYAMON SO I WOULDN'T BE LONELY.
AND I KEPT GRANTING WISHES SO THE CHILDREN WOULD KEEP COMING BACK.

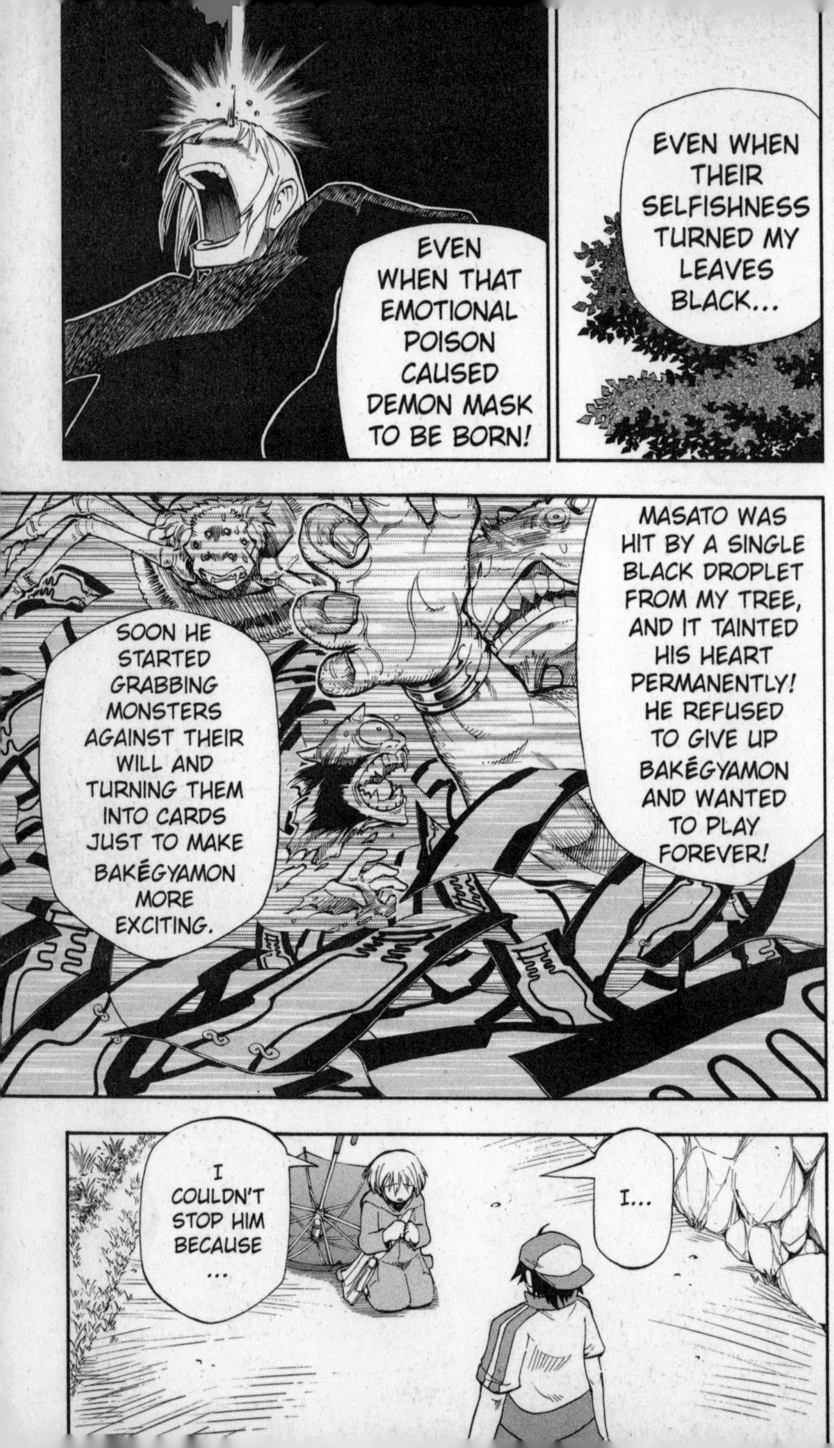
EVEN WHEN THEIR SELFISHNESS TURNED MY LEAVES BLACK...
EVEN WHEN THAT EMOTIONAL POISON CAUSED DEMON MASK TO BE BORN!
MASATO WAS HIT BY A SINGLE BLACK DROPLET FROM MY TREE, AND IT TAINTED HIS HEART PERMANENTLY! HE REFUSED TO GIVE UP BAKÉGYAMON AND WANTED TO PLAY FOREVER!
SOON HE STARTED GRABBING MONSTERS AGAINST THEIR WILL AND TURNING THEM INTO CARDS JUST TO MAKE BAKÉGYAMON MORE EXCITING.
I...
I COULDN'T STOP HIM BECAUSE ...

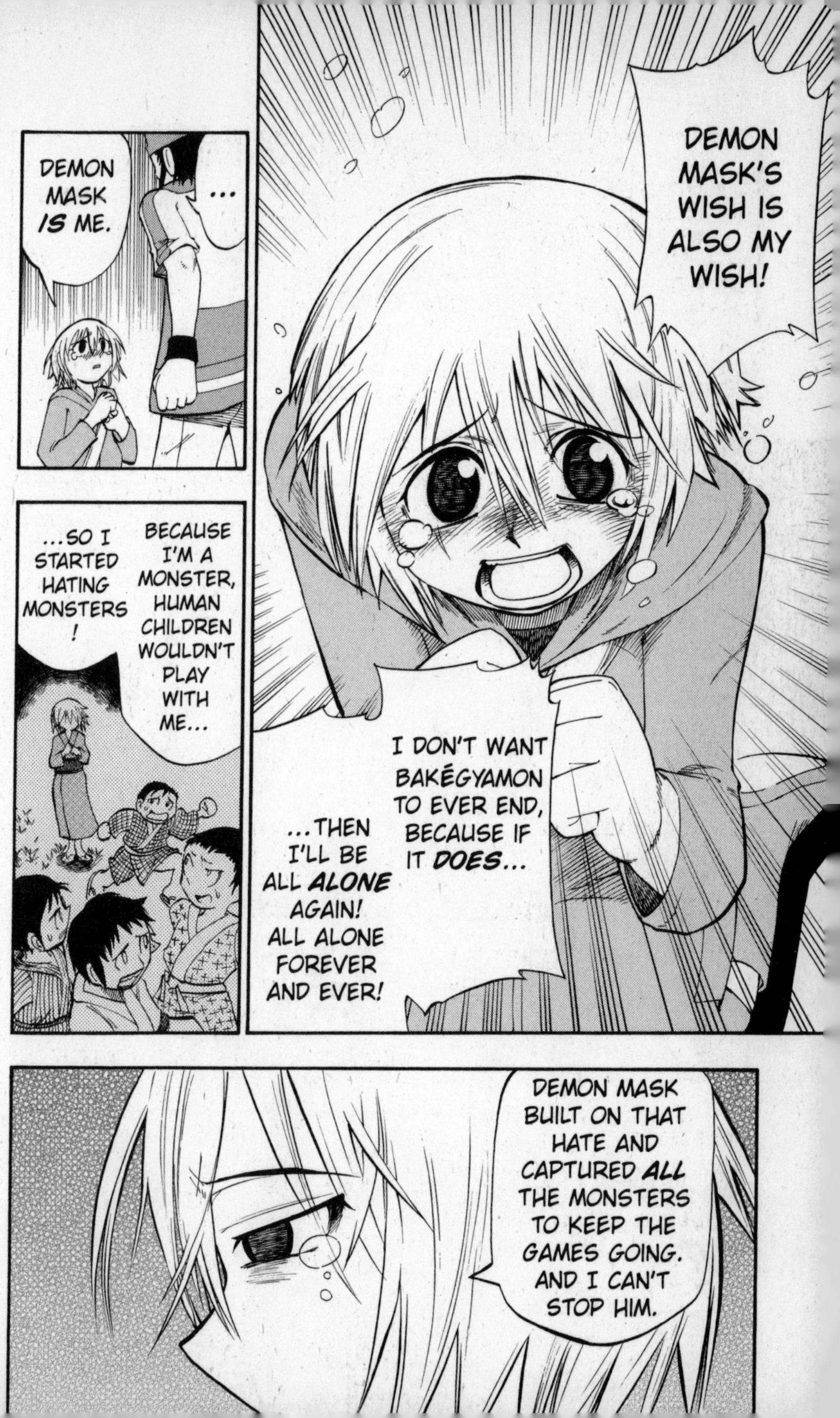
DEMON MASK *IS* ME.
...
BECAUSE I'M A MONSTER, HUMAN CHILDREN WOULDN'T PLAY WITH ME...
...SO I STARTED HATING MONSTERS!
DEMON MASK'S WISH IS ALSO MY WISH!
I DON'T WANT BAKÉGYAMON TO EVER END, BECAUSE IF IT *DOES*...
...THEN I'LL BE ALL *ALONE* AGAIN! ALL ALONE FOREVER AND EVER!
DEMON MASK BUILT ON THAT HATE AND CAPTURED *ALL* THE MONSTERS TO KEEP THE GAMES GOING. AND I CAN'T STOP HIM.

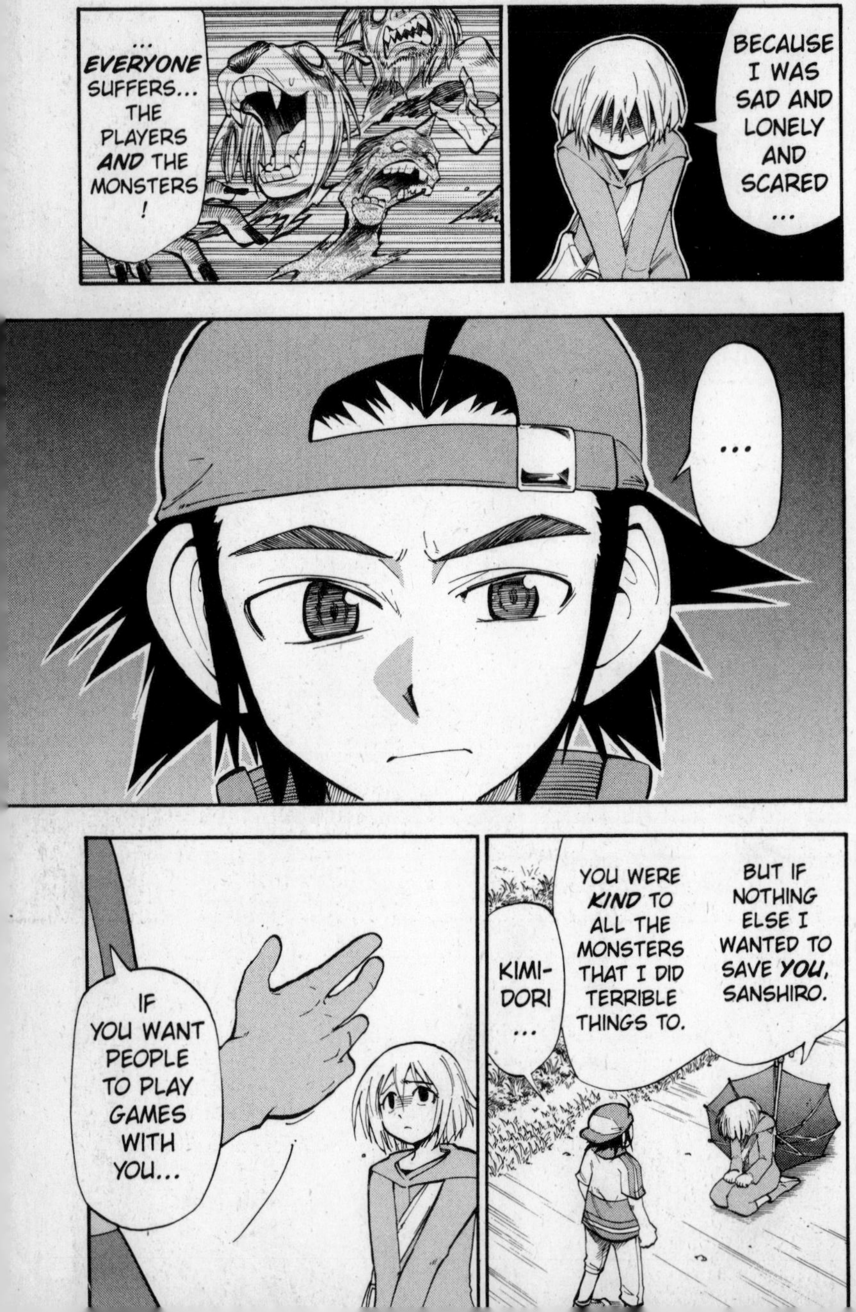
BECAUSE I WAS SAD AND LONELY AND SCARED ...
... *EVERYONE* SUFFERS... THE PLAYERS *AND* THE MONSTERS !
...
BUT IF NOTHING ELSE I WANTED TO SAVE *YOU*, SANSHIRO.
YOU WERE *KIND* TO ALL THE MONSTERS THAT I DID TERRIBLE THINGS TO.
KIMI-DORI ...
IF YOU WANT PEOPLE TO PLAY GAMES WITH YOU...

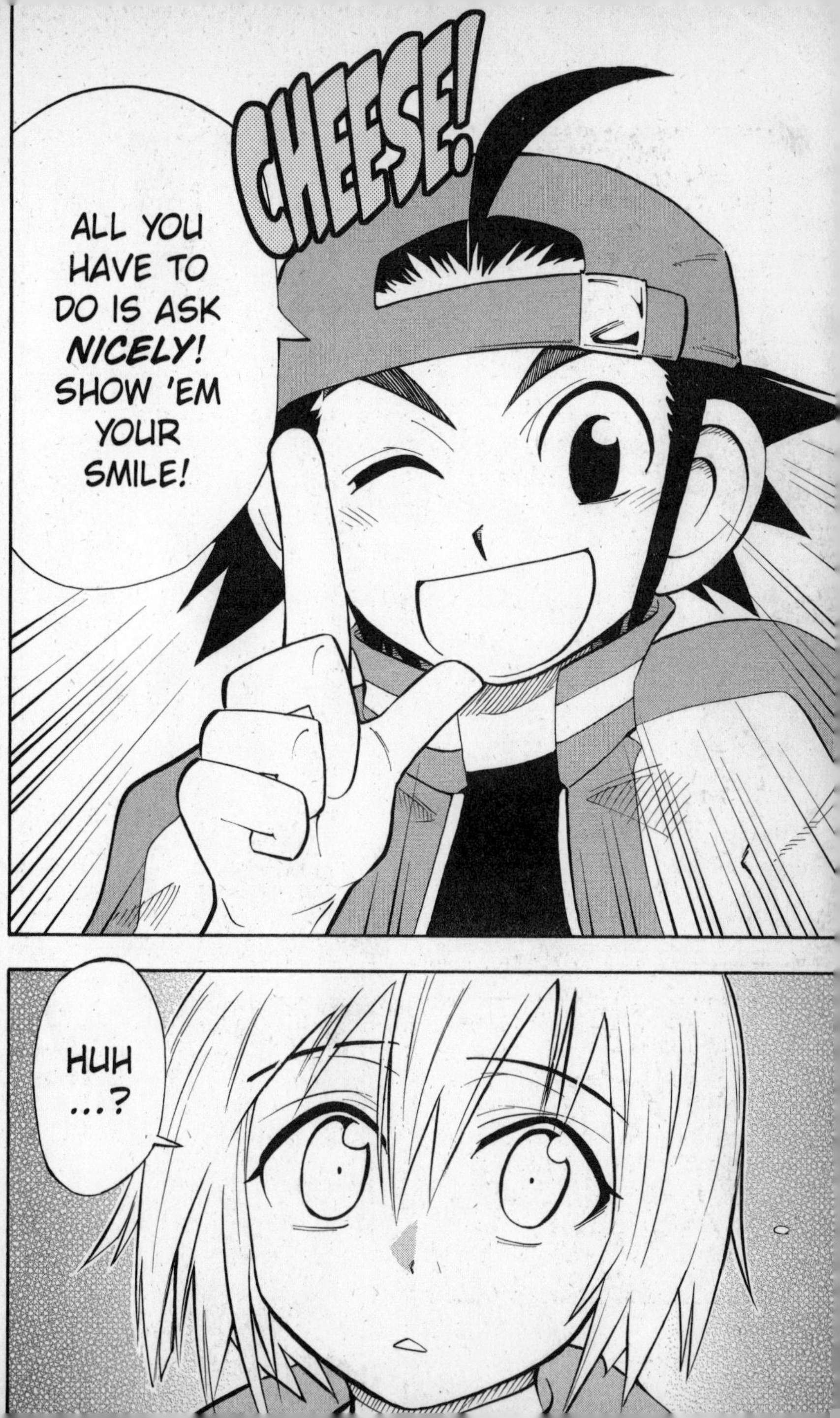
CHEESE!
ALL YOU HAVE TO DO IS ASK *NICELY*! SHOW 'EM YOUR SMILE!
HUH ...?

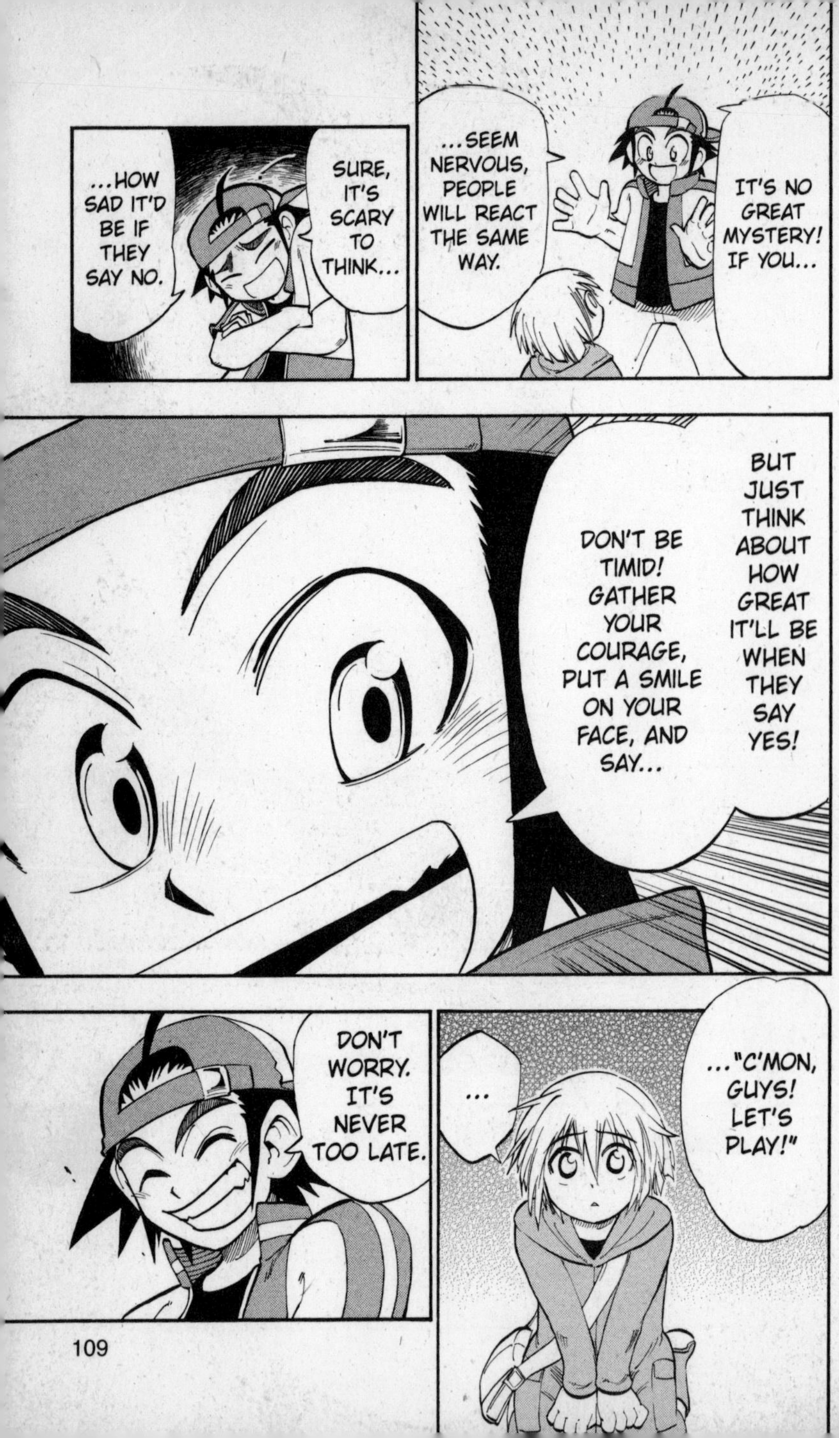
IT'S NO GREAT MYSTERY! IF YOU...
...SEEM NERVOUS, PEOPLE WILL REACT THE SAME WAY.
SURE, IT'S SCARY TO THINK...
...HOW SAD IT'D BE IF THEY SAY NO.
BUT JUST THINK ABOUT HOW GREAT IT'LL BE WHEN THEY SAY YES!
DON'T BE TIMID! GATHER YOUR COURAGE, PUT A SMILE ON YOUR FACE, AND SAY...
..."C'MON, GUYS! LET'S PLAY!"
...
DON'T WORRY. IT'S NEVER TOO LATE.

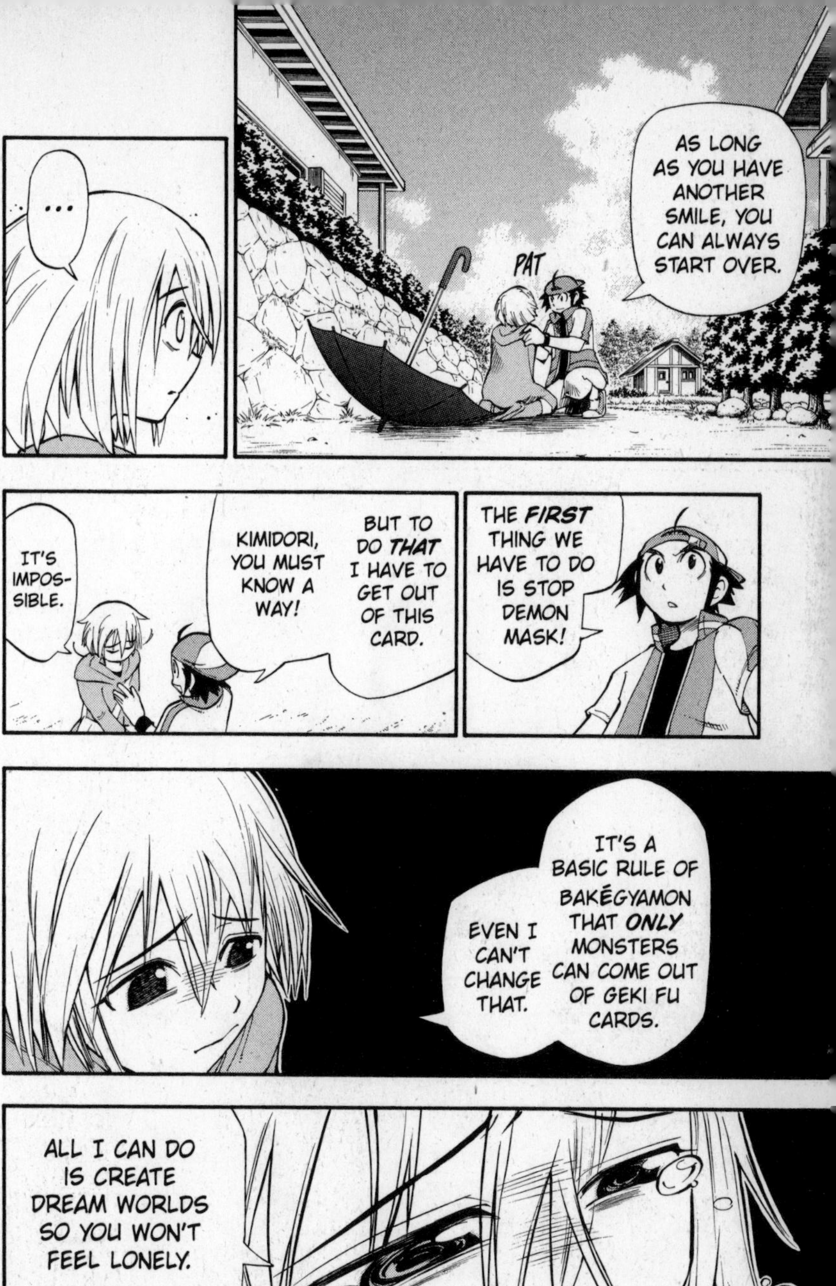
AS LONG AS YOU HAVE ANOTHER SMILE, YOU CAN ALWAYS START OVER.
PAT
...
THE *FIRST* THING WE HAVE TO DO IS STOP DEMON MASK!
BUT TO DO *THAT* I HAVE TO GET OUT OF THIS CARD.
KIMIDORI, YOU MUST KNOW A WAY!
IT'S IMPOS-SIBLE.
IT'S A BASIC RULE OF BAKÉGYAMON THAT *ONLY* MONSTERS CAN COME OUT OF GEKI FU CARDS.
EVEN I CAN'T CHANGE THAT.
ALL I CAN DO IS CREATE DREAM WORLDS SO YOU WON'T FEEL LONELY.

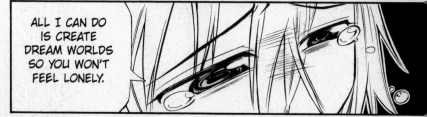

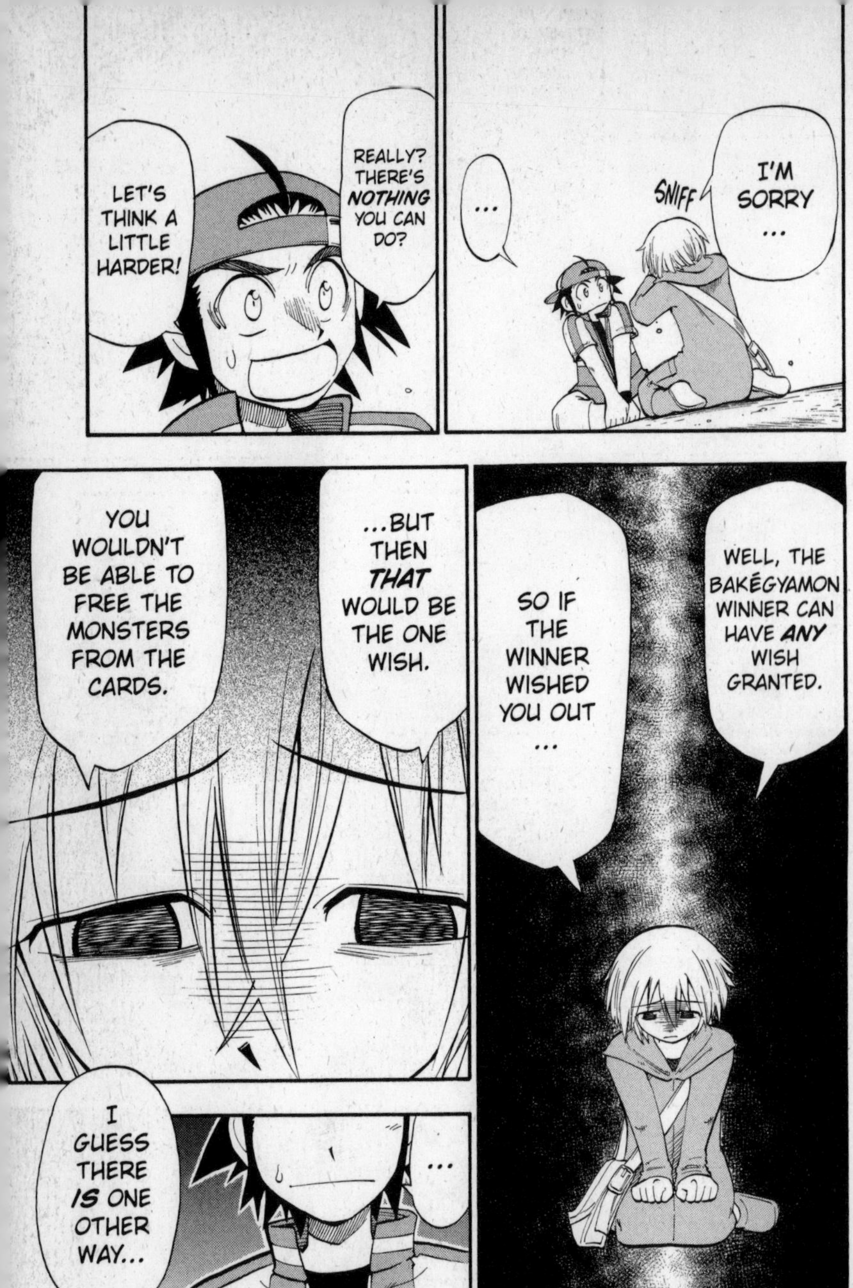
I'M SORRY ...
SNIFF
...
REALLY? THERE'S *NOTHING* YOU CAN DO?
LET'S THINK A LITTLE HARDER!
WELL, THE BAKÉGYAMON WINNER CAN HAVE *ANY* WISH GRANTED.
SO IF THE WINNER WISHED YOU OUT ...
...BUT THEN *THAT* WOULD BE THE ONE WISH.
YOU WOULDN'T BE ABLE TO FREE THE MONSTERS FROM THE CARDS.
...
I GUESS THERE *IS* ONE OTHER WAY...

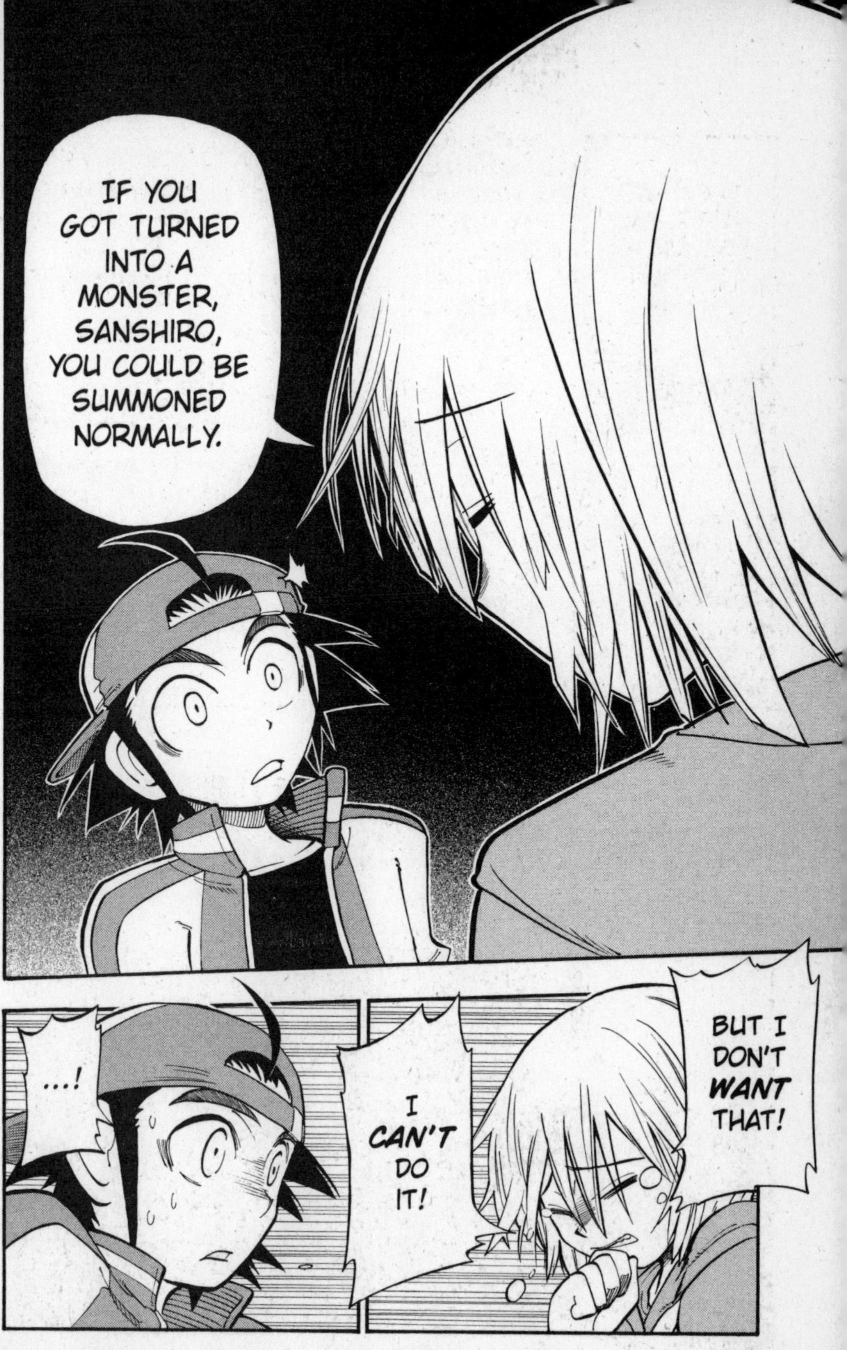
IF YOU GOT TURNED INTO A MONSTER, SANSHIRO, YOU COULD BE SUMMONED NORMALLY.
BUT I DON'T *WANT* THAT!
I *CAN'T* DO IT!
...!

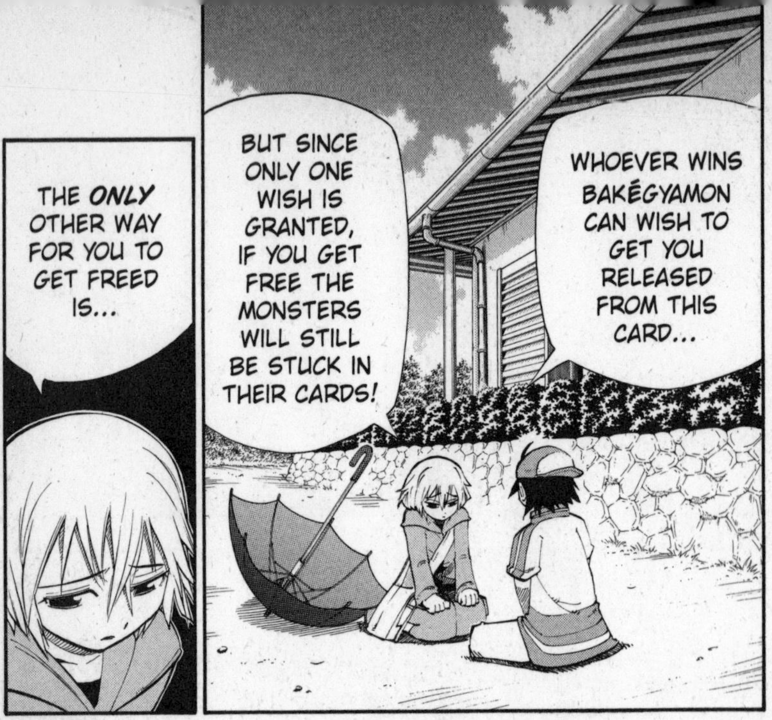
WHOEVER WINS BAKÉGYAMON CAN WISH TO GET YOU RELEASED FROM THIS CARD...
BUT SINCE ONLY ONE WISH IS GRANTED, IF YOU GET FREE THE MONSTERS WILL STILL BE STUCK IN THEIR CARDS!
THE *ONLY* OTHER WAY FOR YOU TO GET FREED IS...

CHAPTER 47 DECISION

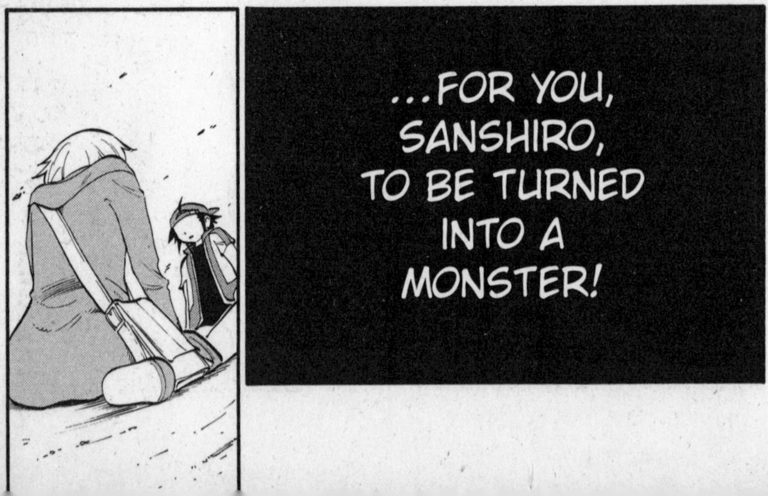
...FOR YOU, SANSHIRO, TO BE TURNED INTO A MONSTER!

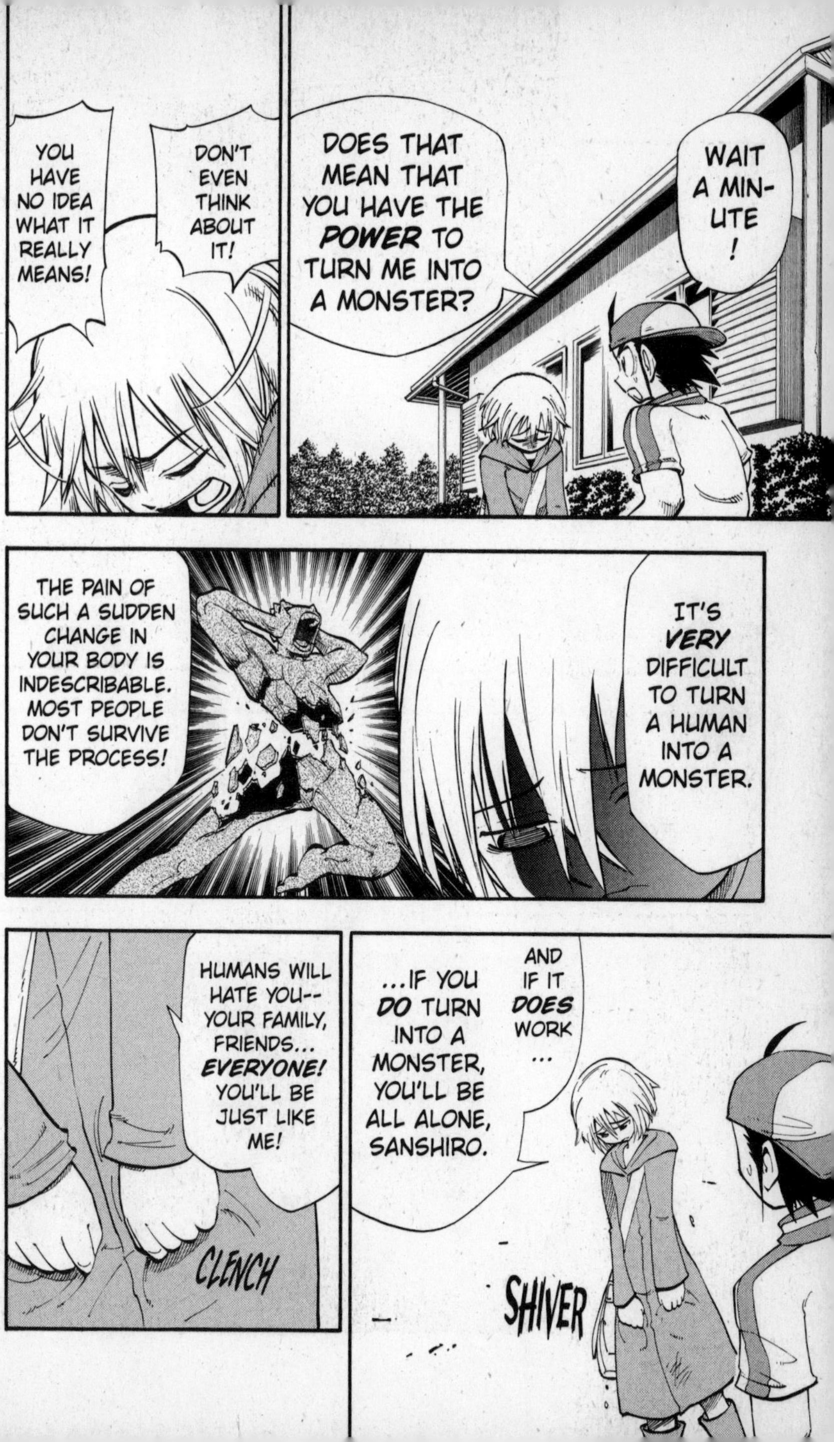
WAIT A MIN-UTE!
DOES THAT MEAN THAT YOU HAVE THE **POWER** TO TURN ME INTO A MONSTER?
DON'T EVEN THINK ABOUT IT!
YOU HAVE NO IDEA WHAT IT REALLY MEANS!
IT'S **VERY** DIFFICULT TO TURN A HUMAN INTO A MONSTER.
THE PAIN OF SUCH A SUDDEN CHANGE IN YOUR BODY IS INDESCRIBABLE. MOST PEOPLE DON'T SURVIVE THE PROCESS!
AND IF IT **DOES** WORK...
...IF YOU **DO** TURN INTO A MONSTER, YOU'LL BE ALL ALONE, SANSHIRO.
SHIVER
HUMANS WILL HATE YOU-- YOUR FAMILY, FRIENDS... **EVERYONE!** YOU'LL BE JUST LIKE ME!
CLENCH

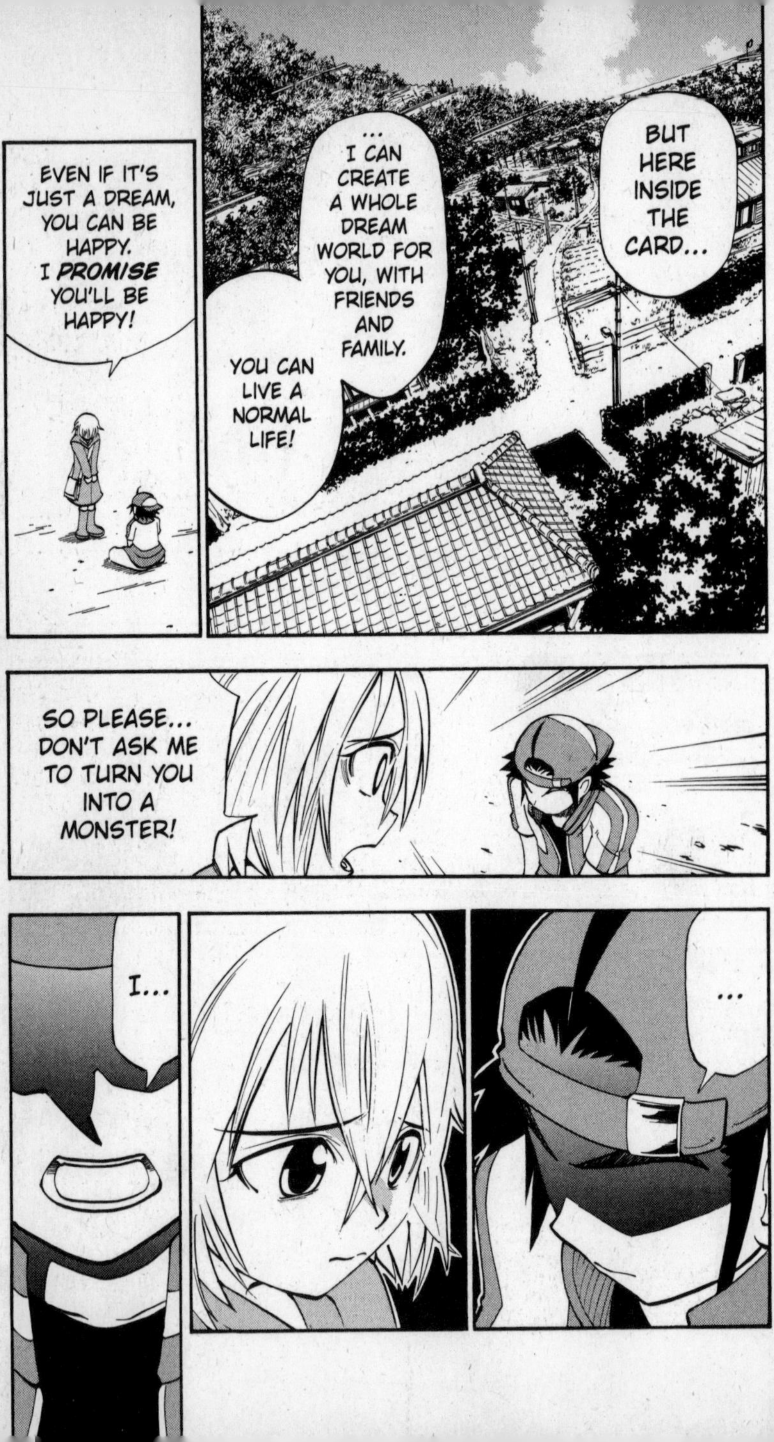
BUT HERE INSIDE THE CARD...
... I CAN CREATE A WHOLE DREAM WORLD FOR YOU, WITH FRIENDS AND FAMILY.
YOU CAN LIVE A NORMAL LIFE!
EVEN IF IT'S JUST A DREAM, YOU CAN BE HAPPY. I *PROMISE* YOU'LL BE HAPPY!
SO PLEASE... DON'T ASK ME TO TURN YOU INTO A MONSTER!
...
I...

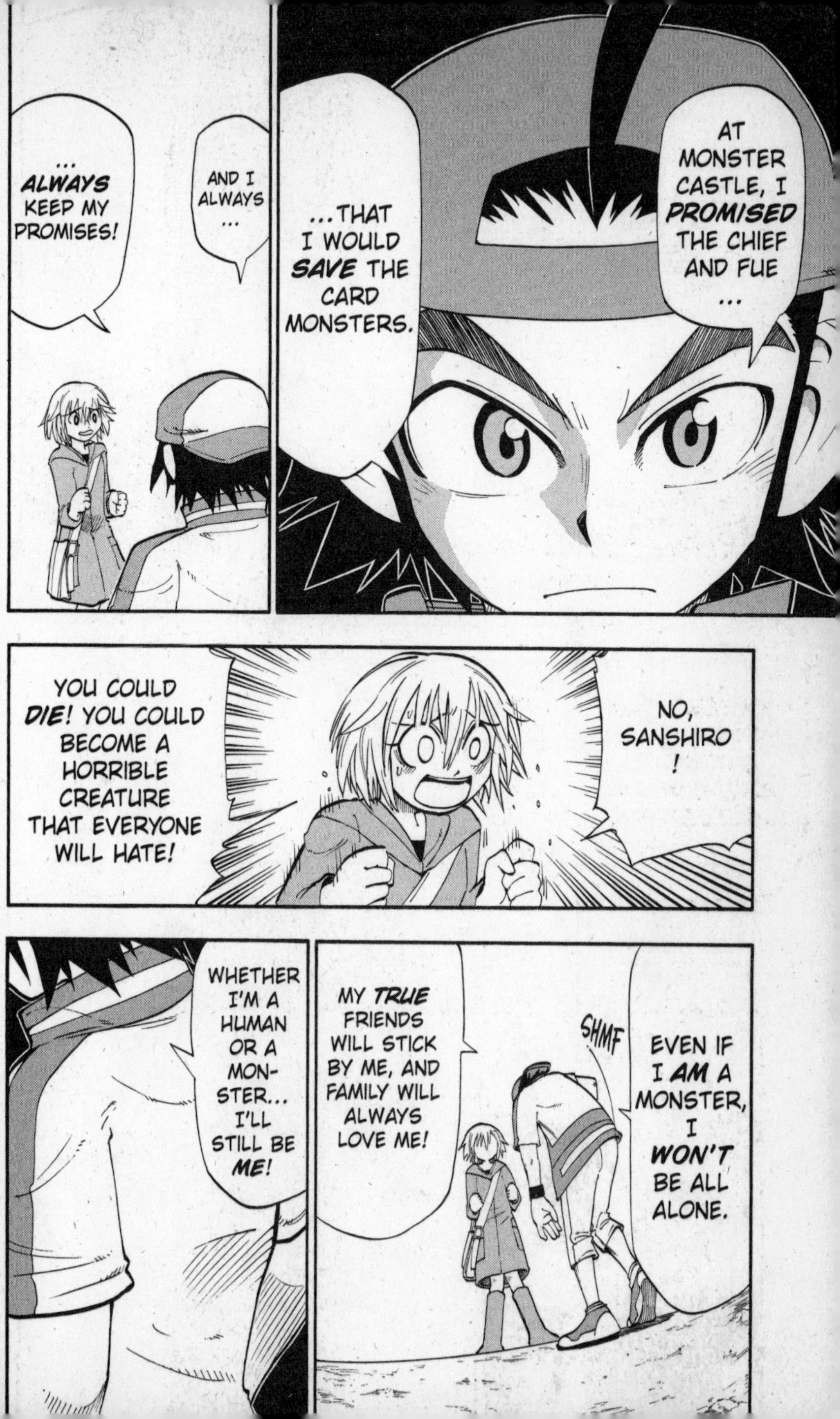
AT MONSTER CASTLE, I PROMISED THE CHIEF AND FUE...
...THAT I WOULD SAVE THE CARD MONSTERS.
AND I ALWAYS...
...ALWAYS KEEP MY PROMISES!
NO, SANSHIRO!
YOU COULD DIE! YOU COULD BECOME A HORRIBLE CREATURE THAT EVERYONE WILL HATE!
EVEN IF I AM A MONSTER, I WON'T BE ALL ALONE.
SHMF
MY TRUE FRIENDS WILL STICK BY ME, AND FAMILY WILL ALWAYS LOVE ME!
WHETHER I'M A HUMAN OR A MON-STER... I'LL STILL BE ME!

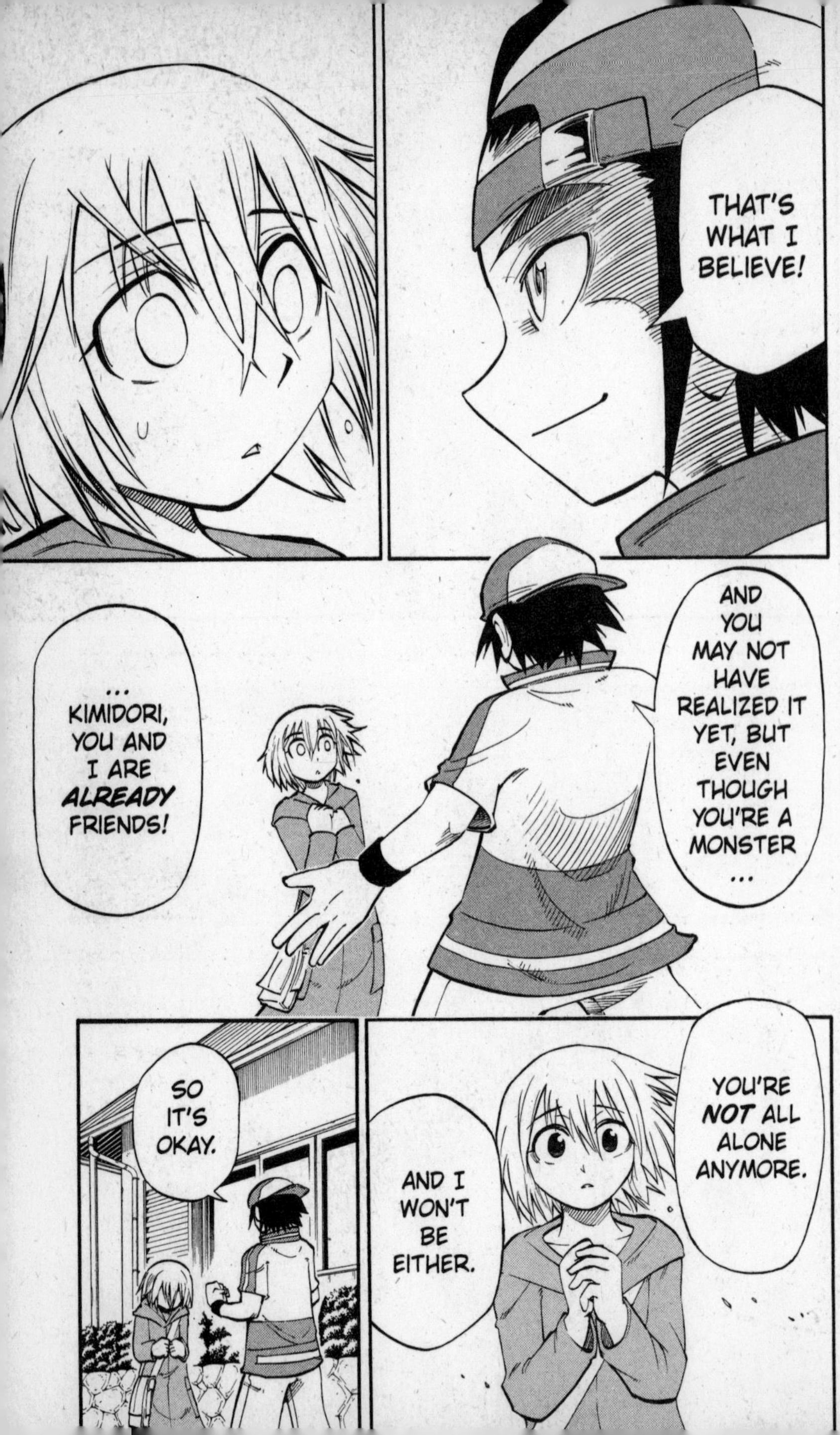
THAT'S WHAT I BELIEVE!
AND YOU MAY NOT HAVE REALIZED IT YET, BUT EVEN THOUGH YOU'RE A MONSTER ...
... KIMIDORI, YOU AND I ARE ALREADY FRIENDS!
YOU'RE NOT ALL ALONE ANYMORE.
AND I WON'T BE EITHER.
SO IT'S OKAY.

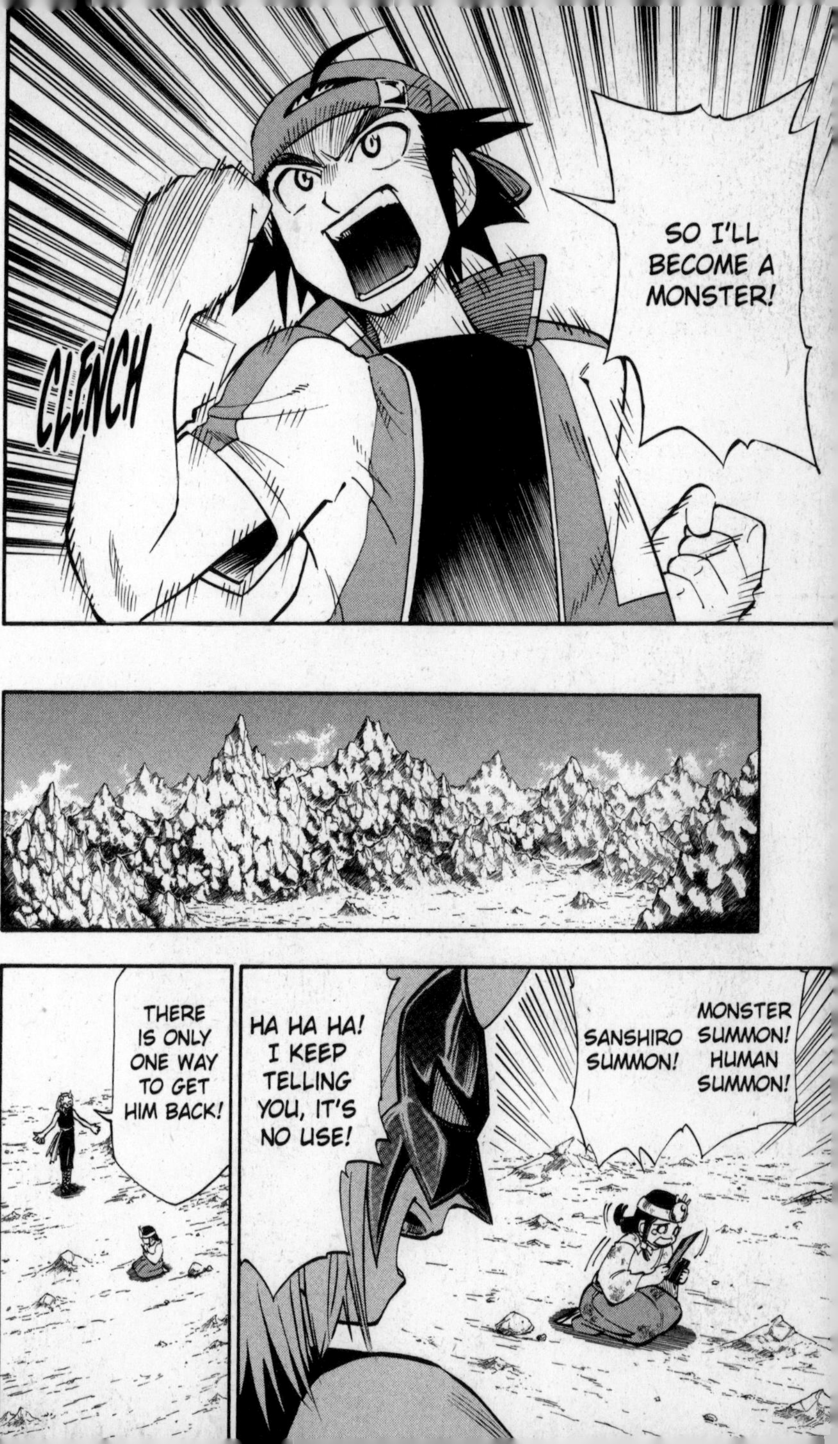
SO I'LL BECOME A MONSTER!
CLENCH
MONSTER SUMMON! HUMAN SUMMON!
SANSHIRO SUMMON!
HA HA HA! I KEEP TELLING YOU, IT'S NO USE!
THERE IS ONLY ONE WAY TO GET HIM BACK!

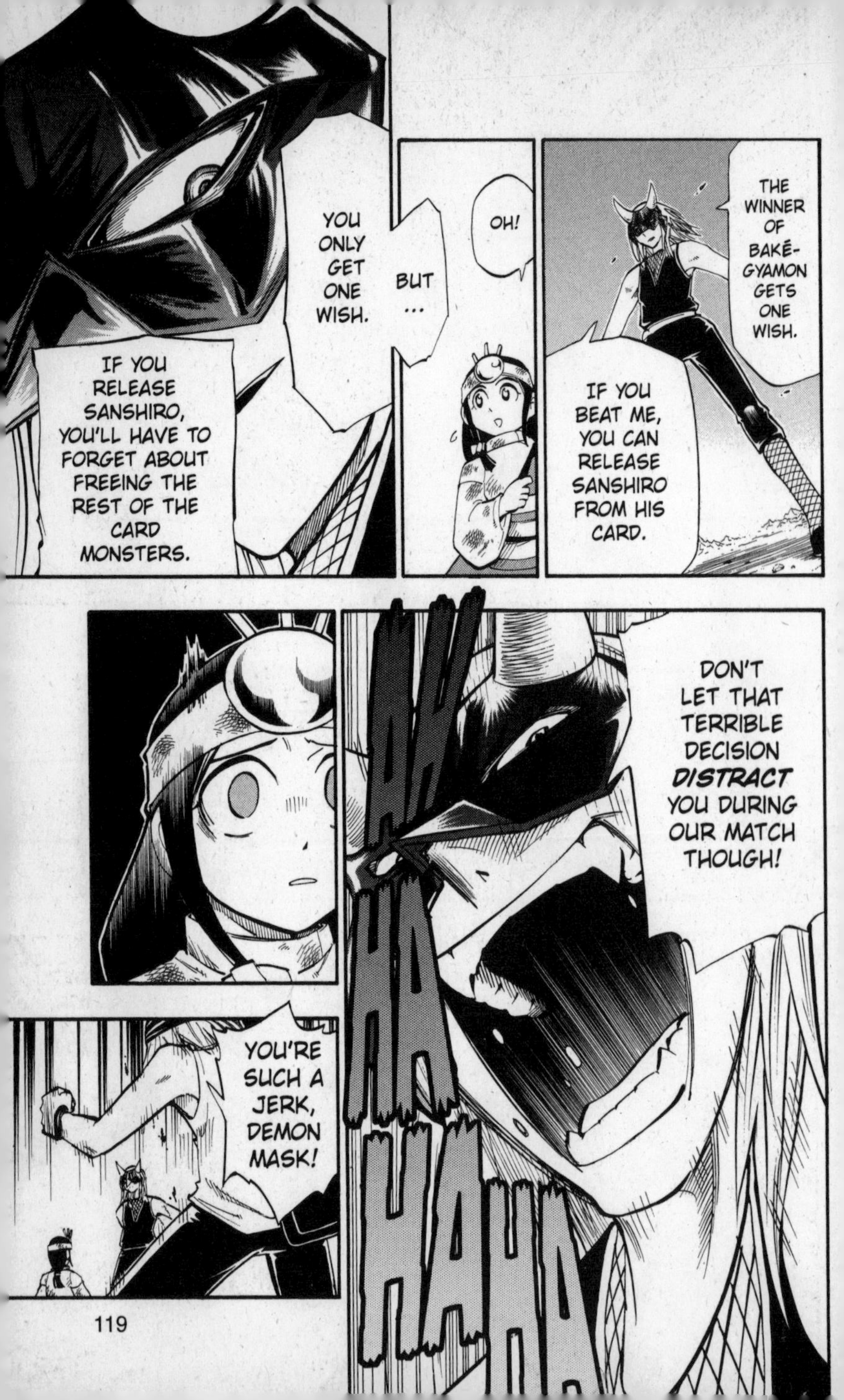
THE WINNER OF BAKÉ-GYAMON GETS ONE WISH.
IF YOU BEAT ME, YOU CAN RELEASE SANSHIRO FROM HIS CARD.
OH!
BUT ...
YOU ONLY GET ONE WISH.
IF YOU RELEASE SANSHIRO, YOU'LL HAVE TO FORGET ABOUT FREEING THE REST OF THE CARD MONSTERS.
DON'T LET THAT TERRIBLE DECISION *DISTRACT* YOU DURING OUR MATCH THOUGH!
YOU'RE SUCH A JERK, DEMON MASK!

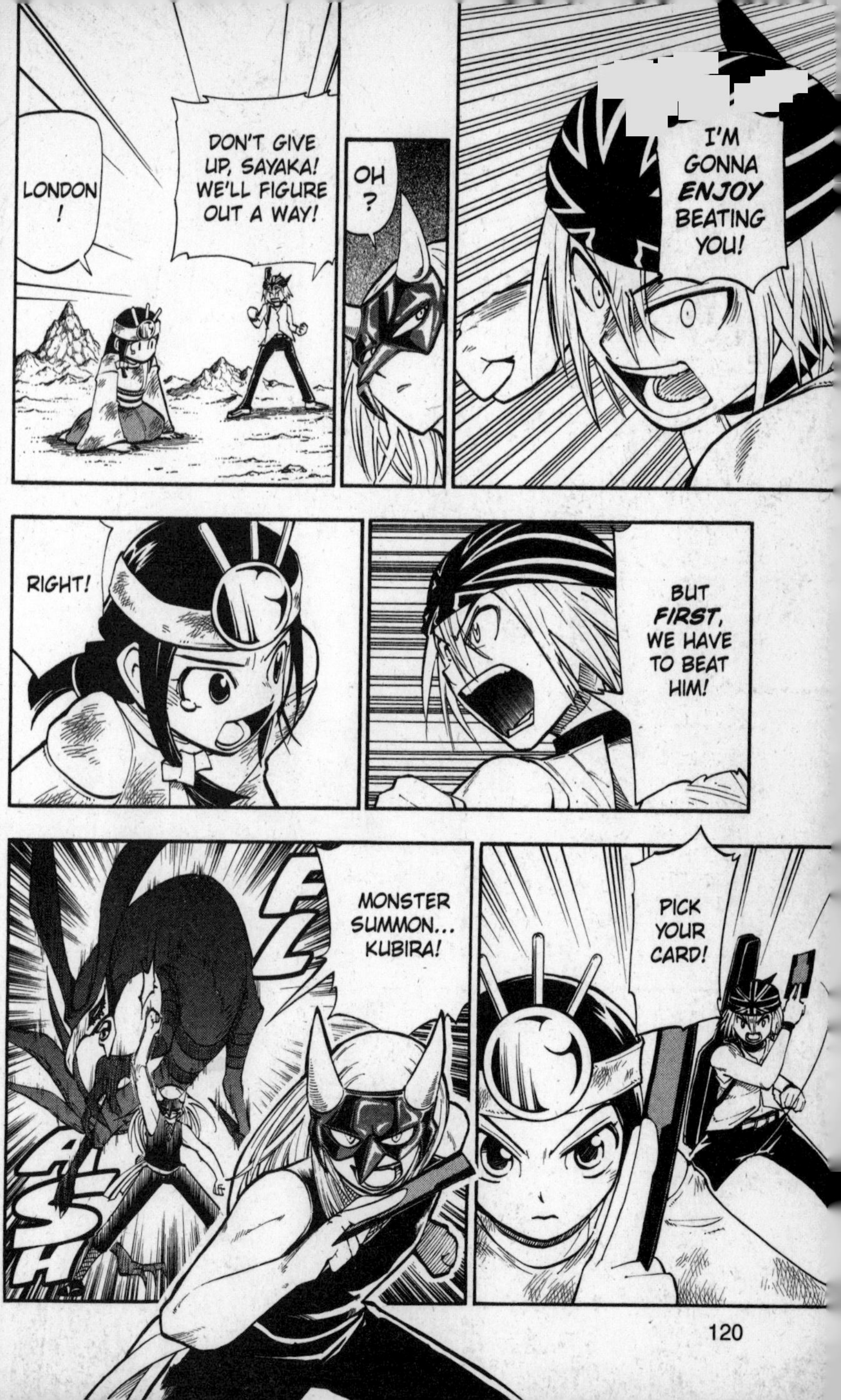
LONDON!
DON'T GIVE UP, SAYAKA! WE'LL FIGURE OUT A WAY!
OH?
I'M GONNA ENJOY BEATING YOU!
RIGHT!
BUT FIRST, WE HAVE TO BEAT HIM!
MONSTER SUMMON... KUBIRA!
PICK YOUR CARD!

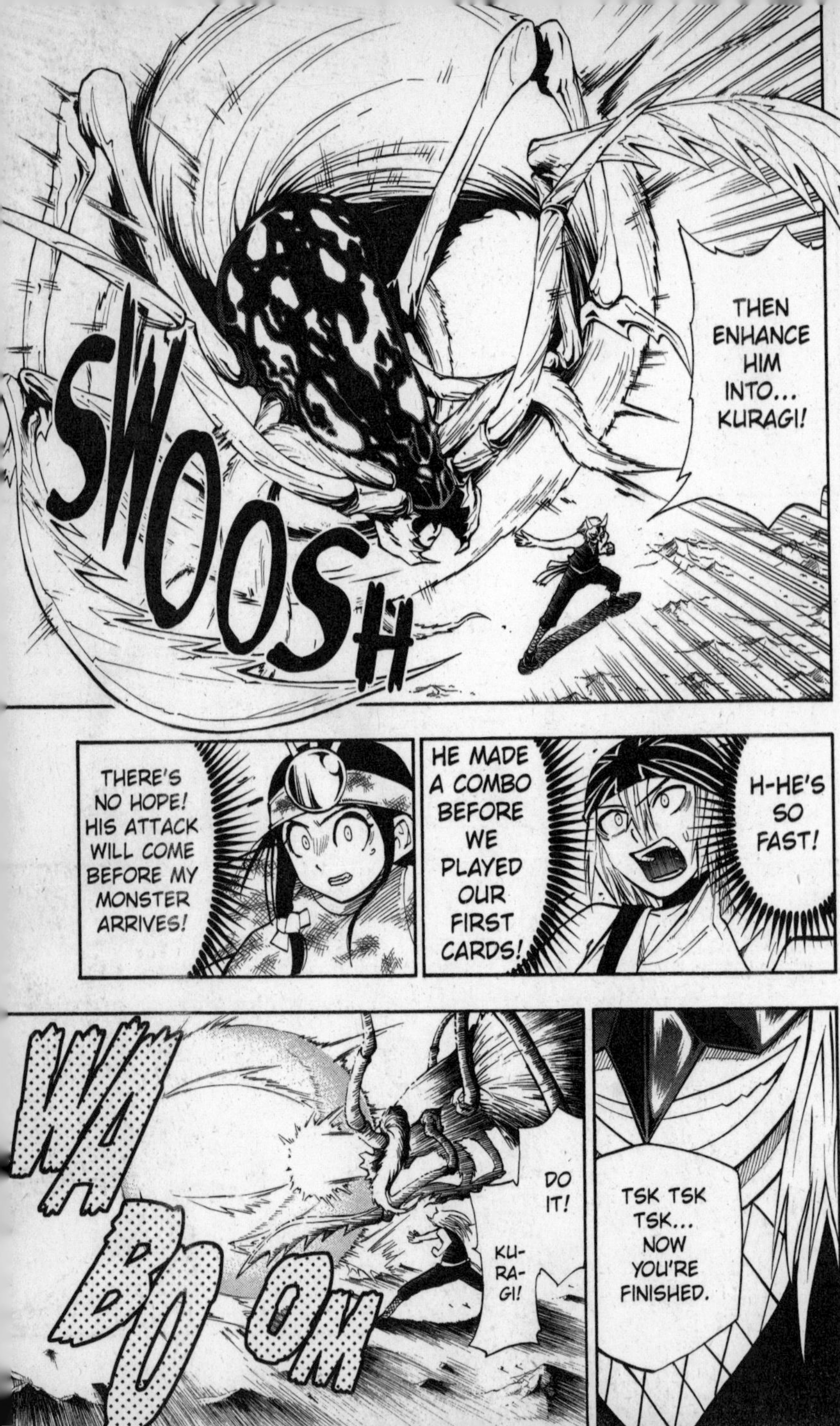
THEN ENHANCE HIM INTO... KURAGI!
SWOOSH
H-HE'S SO FAST!
HE MADE A COMBO BEFORE WE PLAYED OUR FIRST CARDS!
THERE'S NO HOPE! HIS ATTACK WILL COME BEFORE MY MONSTER ARRIVES!
TSK TSK TSK... NOW YOU'RE FINISHED.
DO IT!
KU-RA-GI!
WABOOM

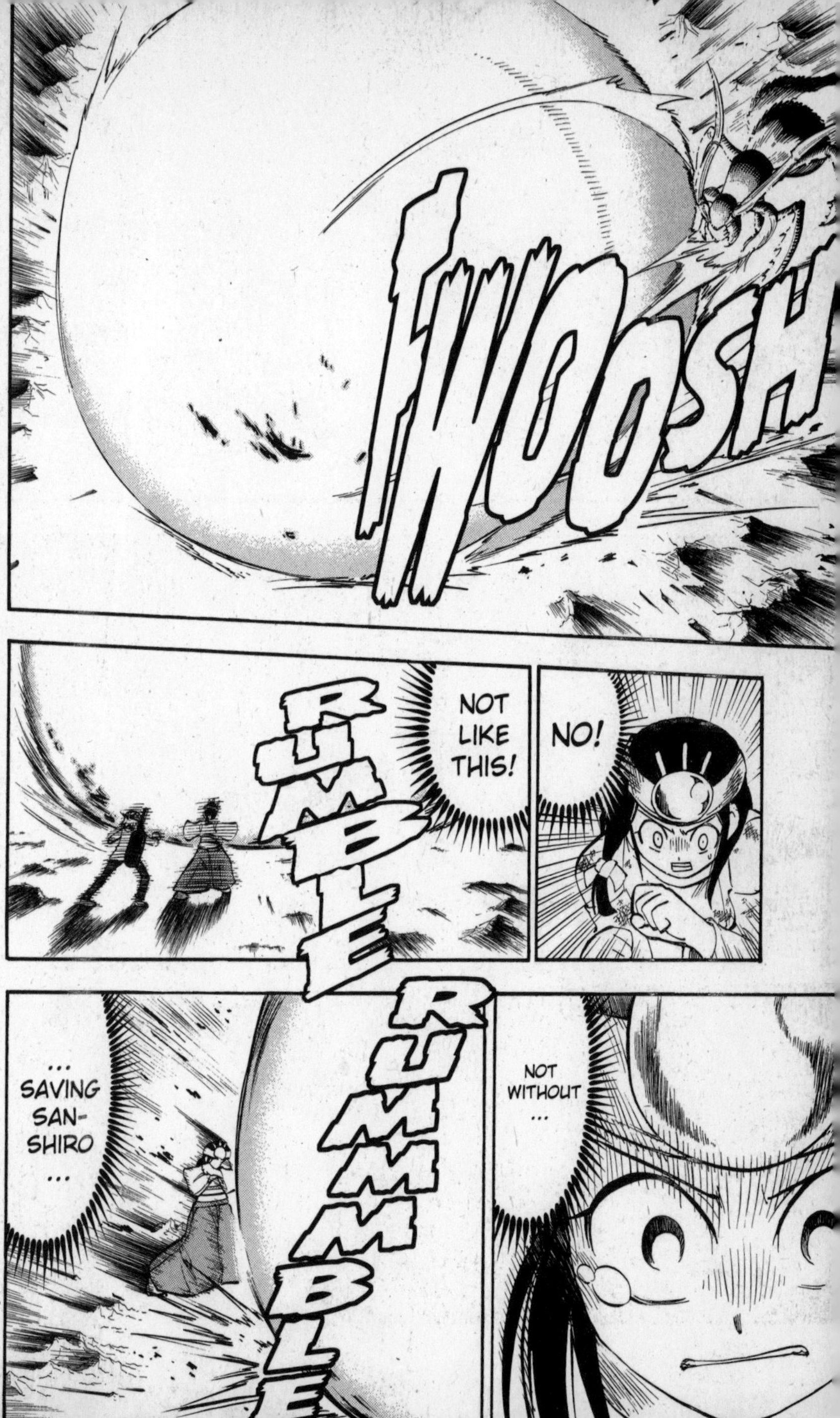
WHOOSH
NO!
NOT LIKE THIS!
RUMBLE
NOT WITHOUT ...
... SAVING SAN-SHIRO ...
RUMMMBLE

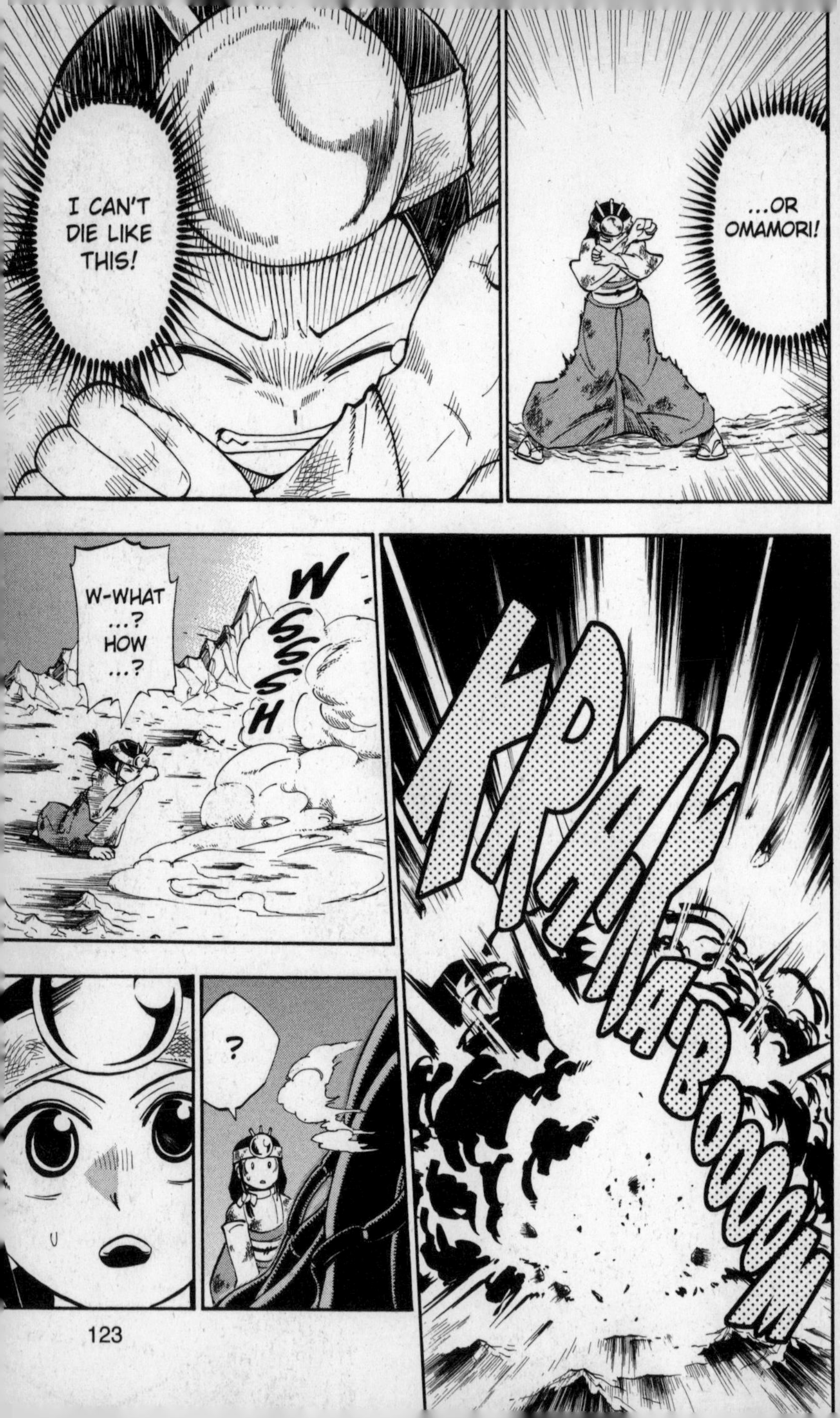
...OR OMAMORI!
I CAN'T DIE LIKE THIS!
KRAKABOOOOM
WSSSSH
W-WHAT ...? HOW ...?
?

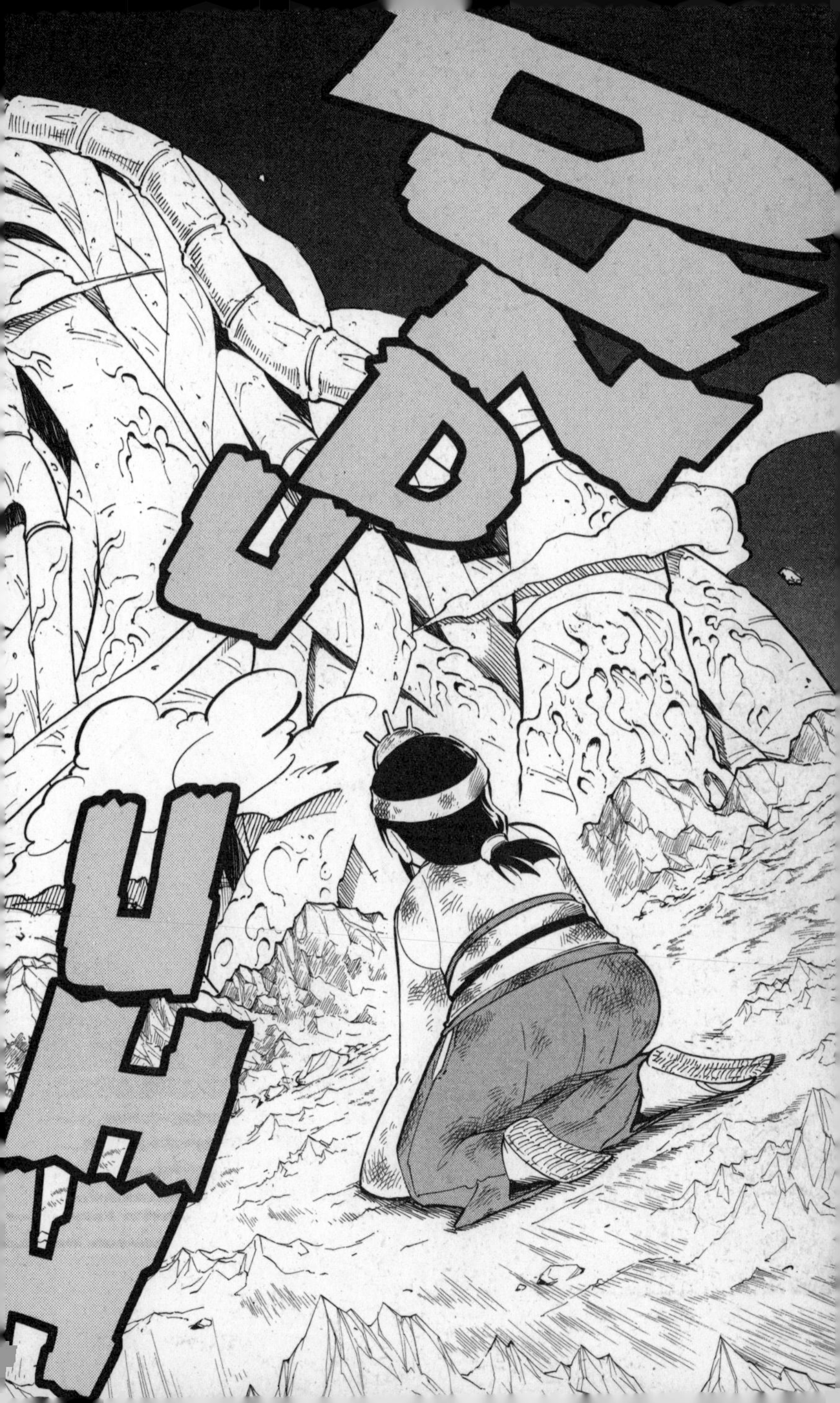

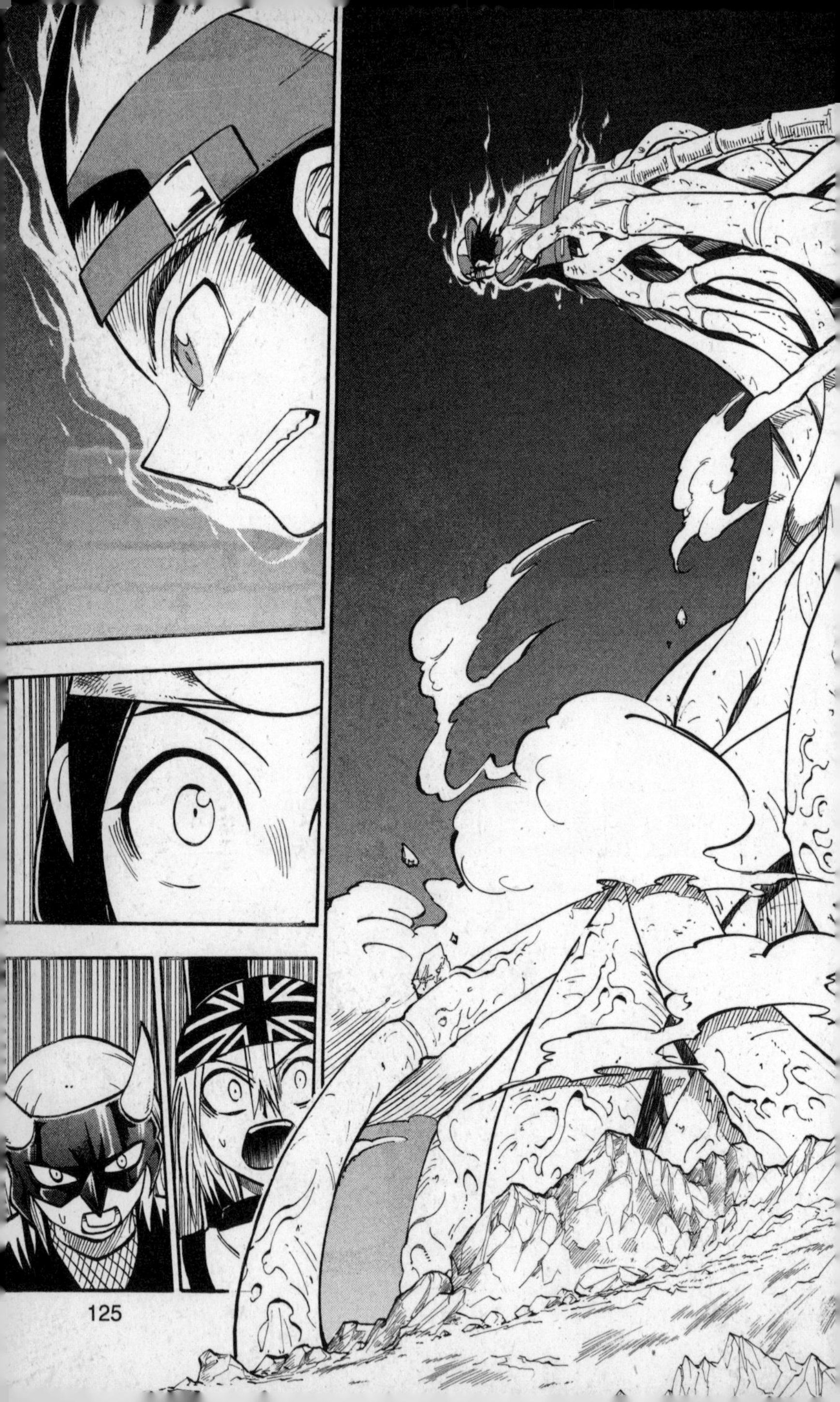

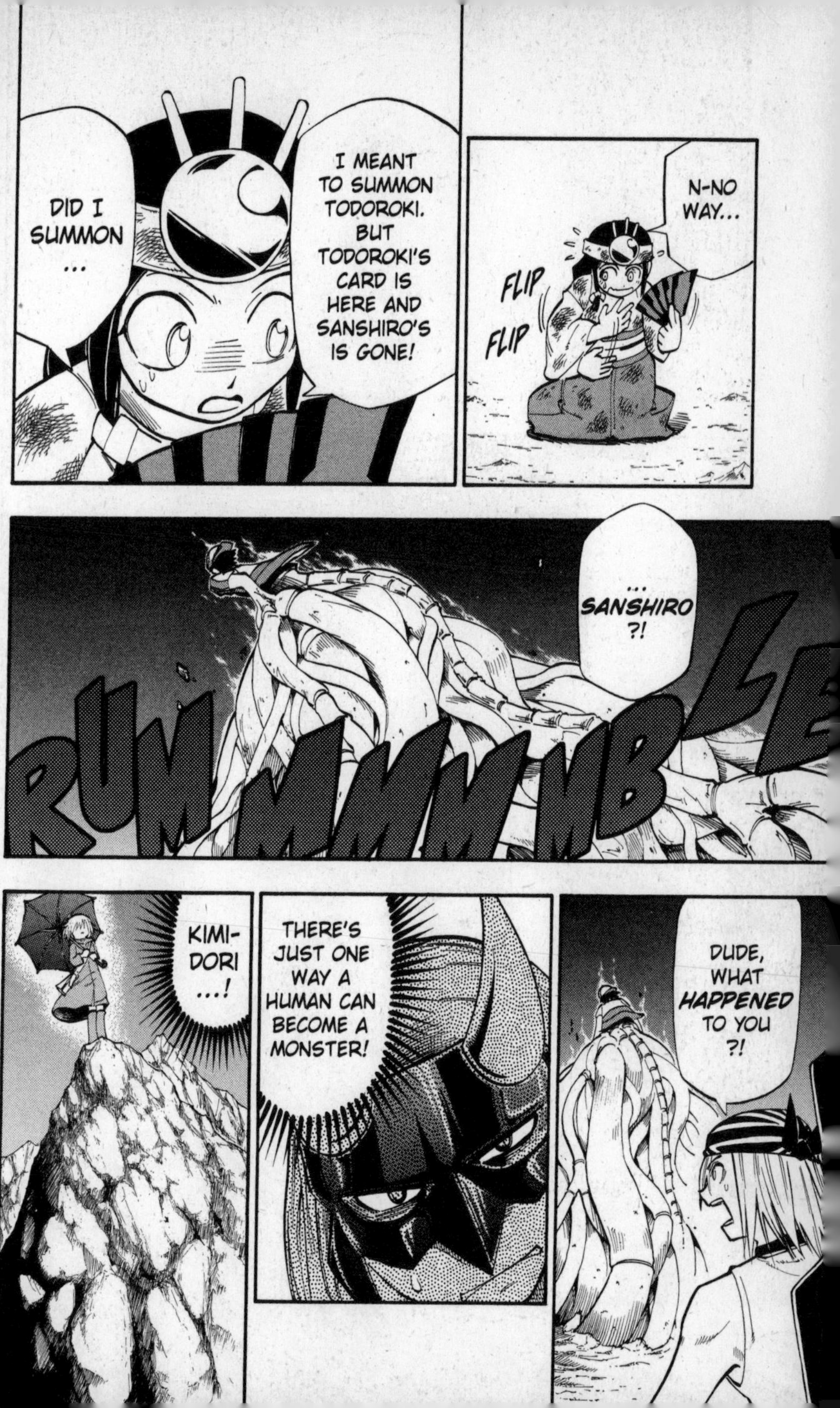
N-NO WAY...
FLIP
FLIP
I MEANT TO SUMMON TODOROKI. BUT TODOROKI'S CARD IS HERE AND SANSHIRO'S IS GONE!
DID I SUMMON ...
...SANSHIRO ?!
RUMMMMBLE
DUDE, WHAT HAPPENED TO YOU ?!
THERE'S JUST ONE WAY A HUMAN CAN BECOME A MONSTER!
KIMI-DORI ...!

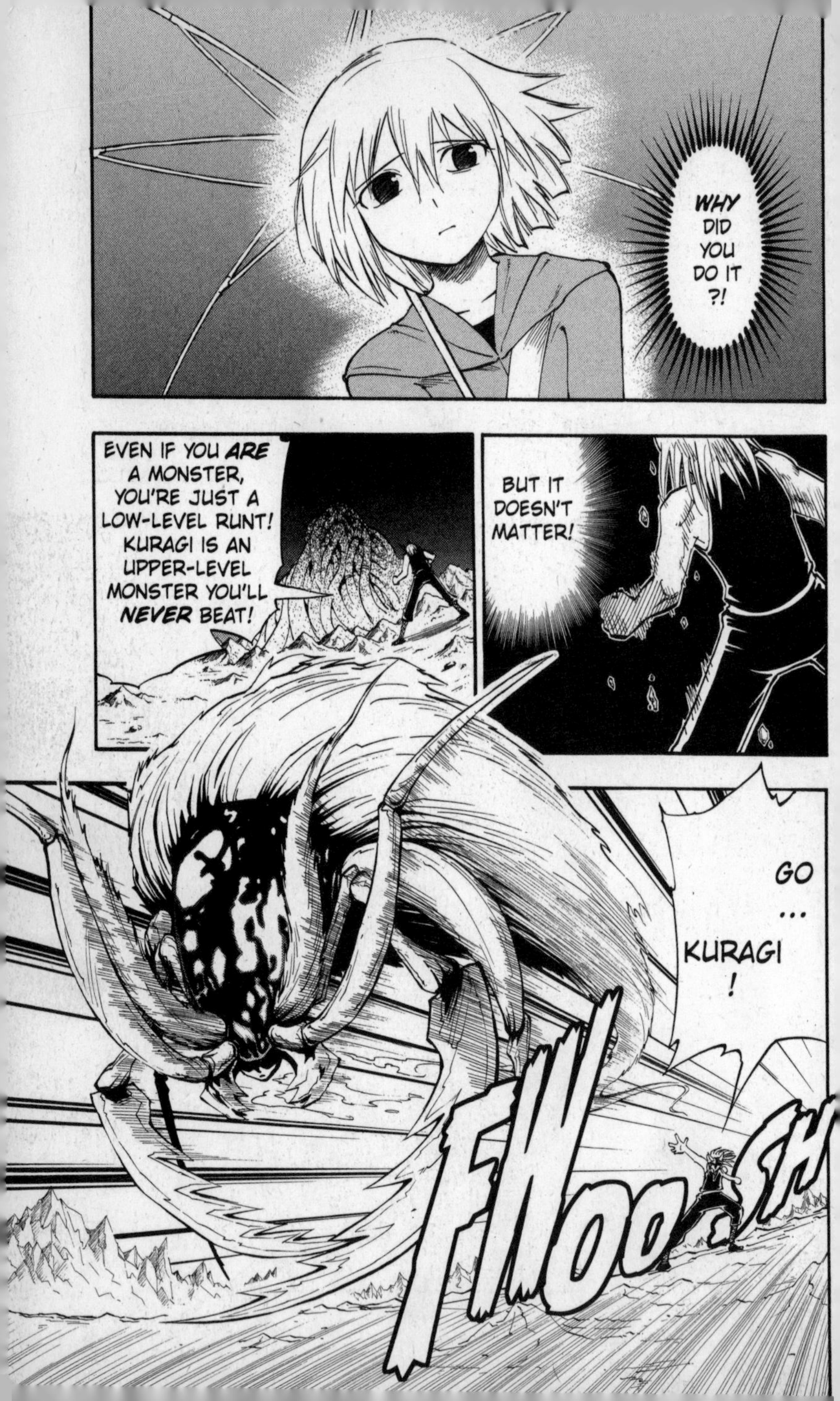
WHY DID YOU DO IT ?!
BUT IT DOESN'T MATTER!
EVEN IF YOU ARE A MONSTER, YOU'RE JUST A LOW-LEVEL RUNT! KURAGI IS AN UPPER-LEVEL MONSTER YOU'LL NEVER BEAT!
GO ... KURAGI !
FWOOSH

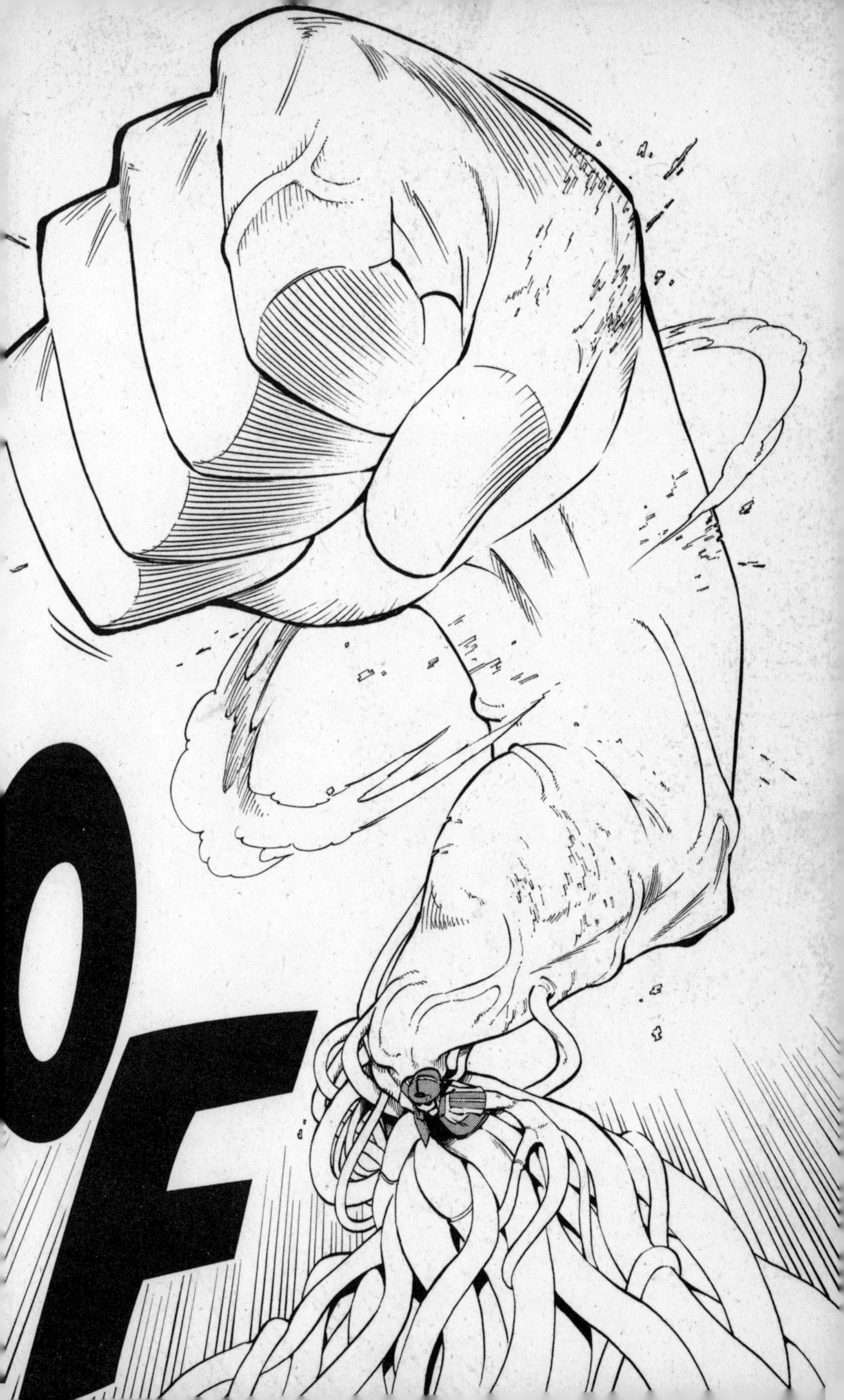
OF

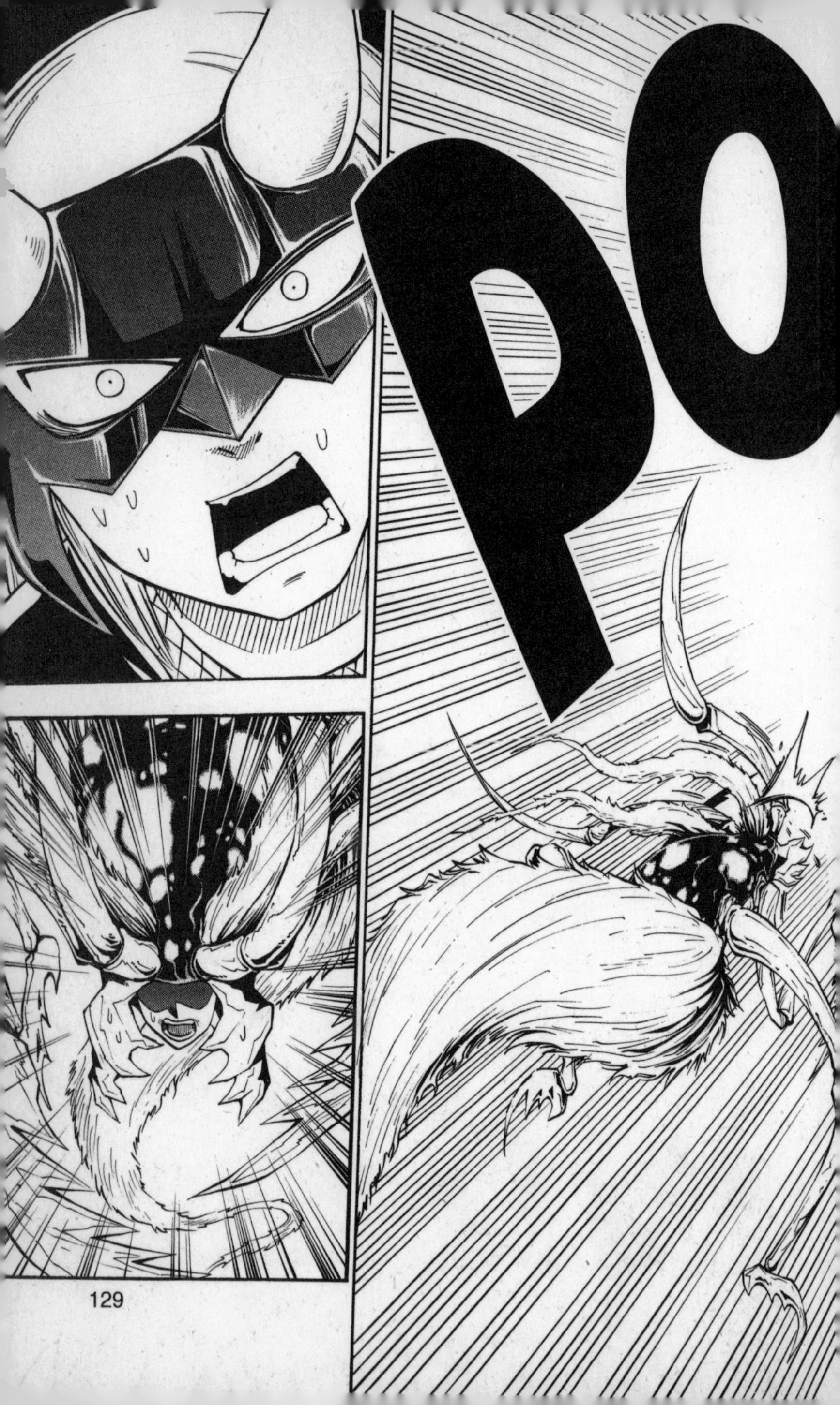
PO

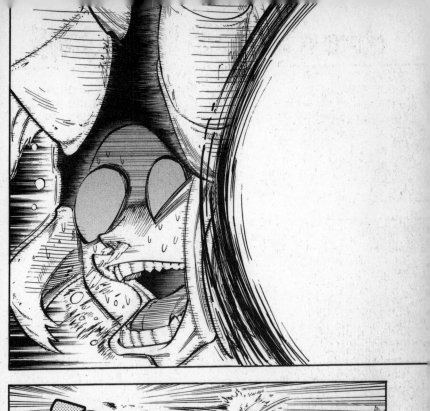

ZOOOOM

PING

CHAPTER 48 SANSHIRO BREAKS DOWN

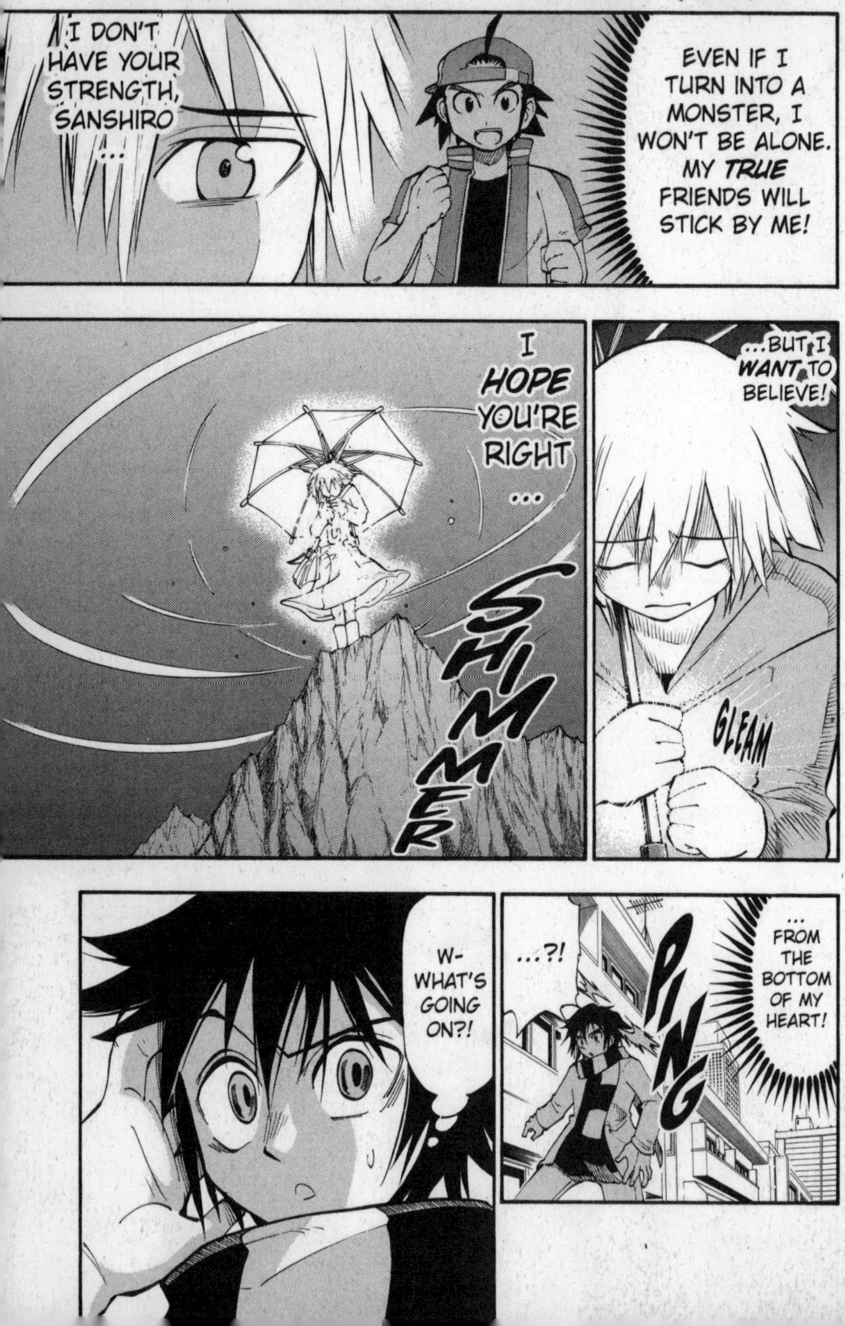
EVEN IF I TURN INTO A MONSTER, I WON'T BE ALONE. MY TRUE FRIENDS WILL STICK BY ME!
I DON'T HAVE YOUR STRENGTH, SANSHIRO ...
...BUT I WANT TO BELIEVE!
GLEAM
I HOPE YOU'RE RIGHT ...
SHIMMER
... FROM THE BOTTOM OF MY HEART!
PING
...?!
W-WHAT'S GOING ON?!

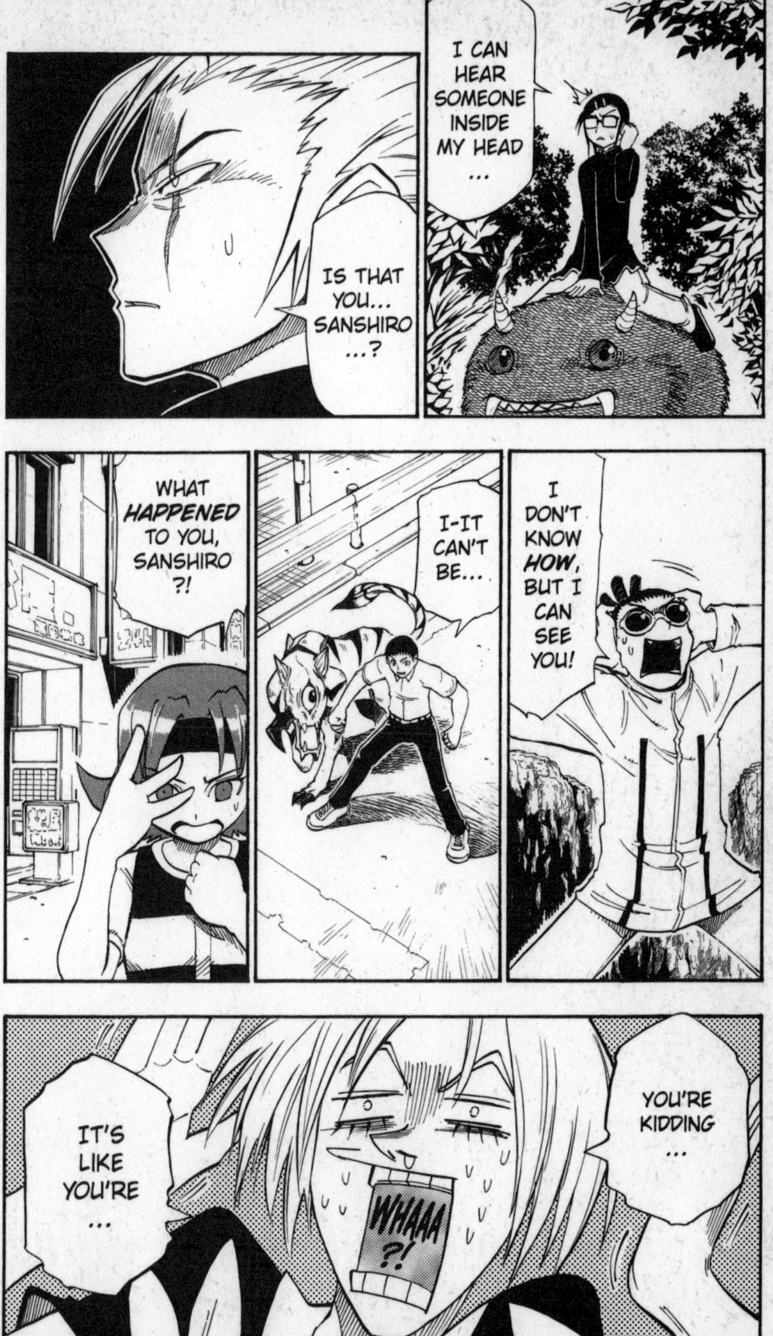
I CAN HEAR SOMEONE INSIDE MY HEAD ...
IS THAT YOU... SANSHIRO ...?
I DON'T KNOW **HOW**, BUT I CAN SEE YOU!
I-IT CAN'T BE...
WHAT **HAPPENED** TO YOU, SANSHIRO ?!
YOU'RE KIDDING ...
WHAAA ?!
IT'S LIKE YOU'RE ...

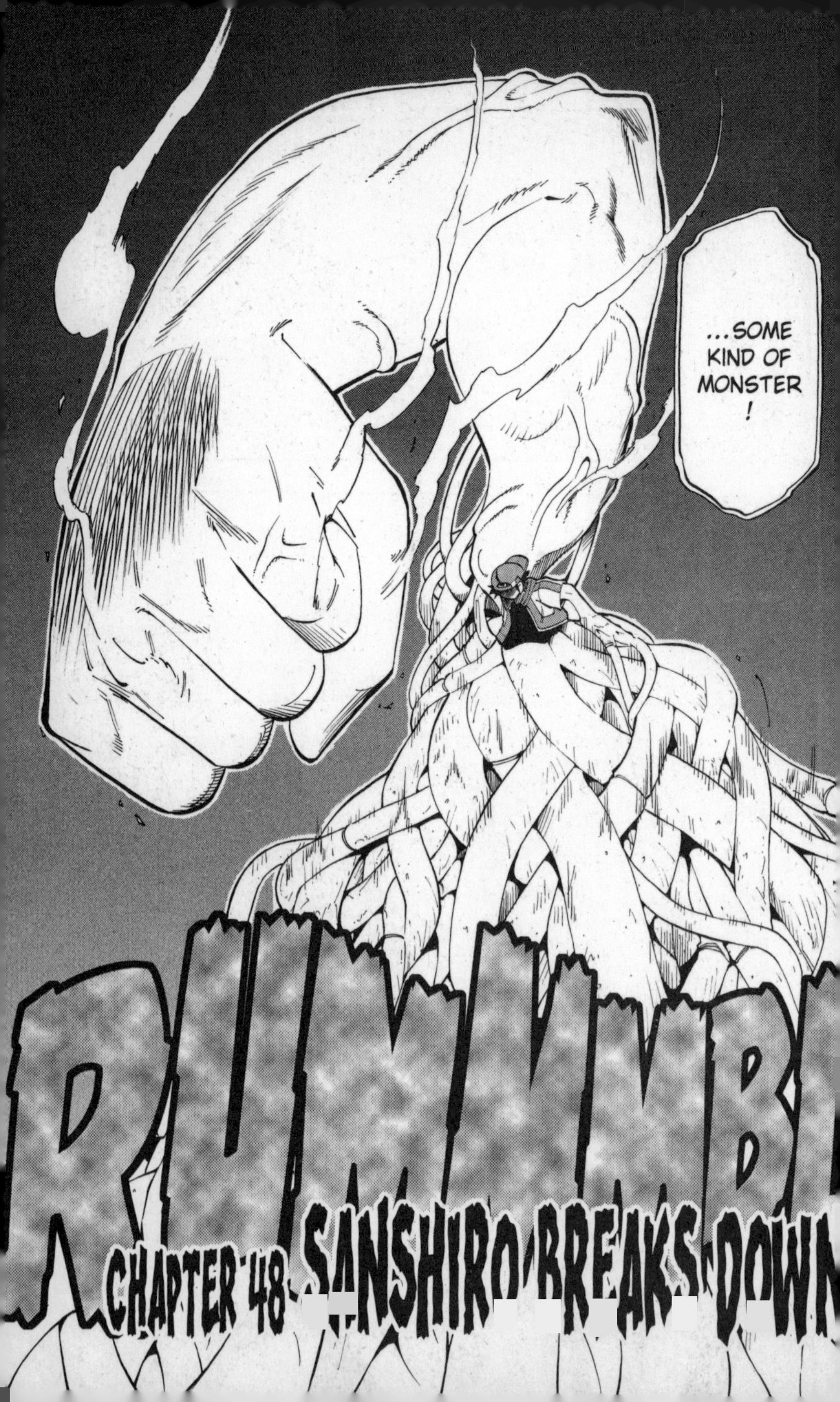
...SOME KIND OF MONSTER !
RUMMBL
CHAPTER 48: SANSHIRO BREAKS DOWN

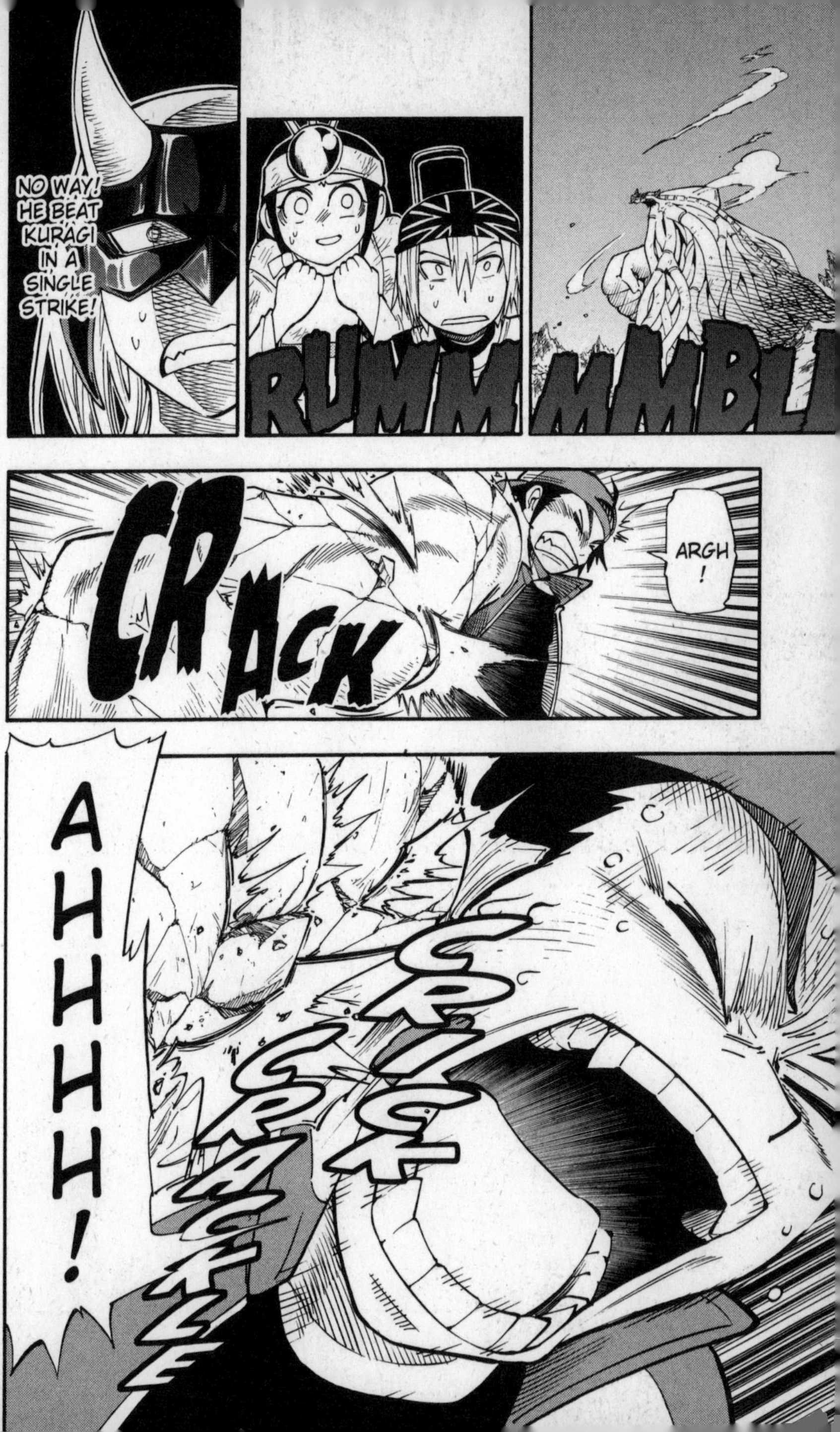
RUMMMBL
NO WAY! HE BEAT KURAGI IN A SINGLE STRIKE!
CRACK
ARGH!
AHHHH!
CRICK
CRACKLE

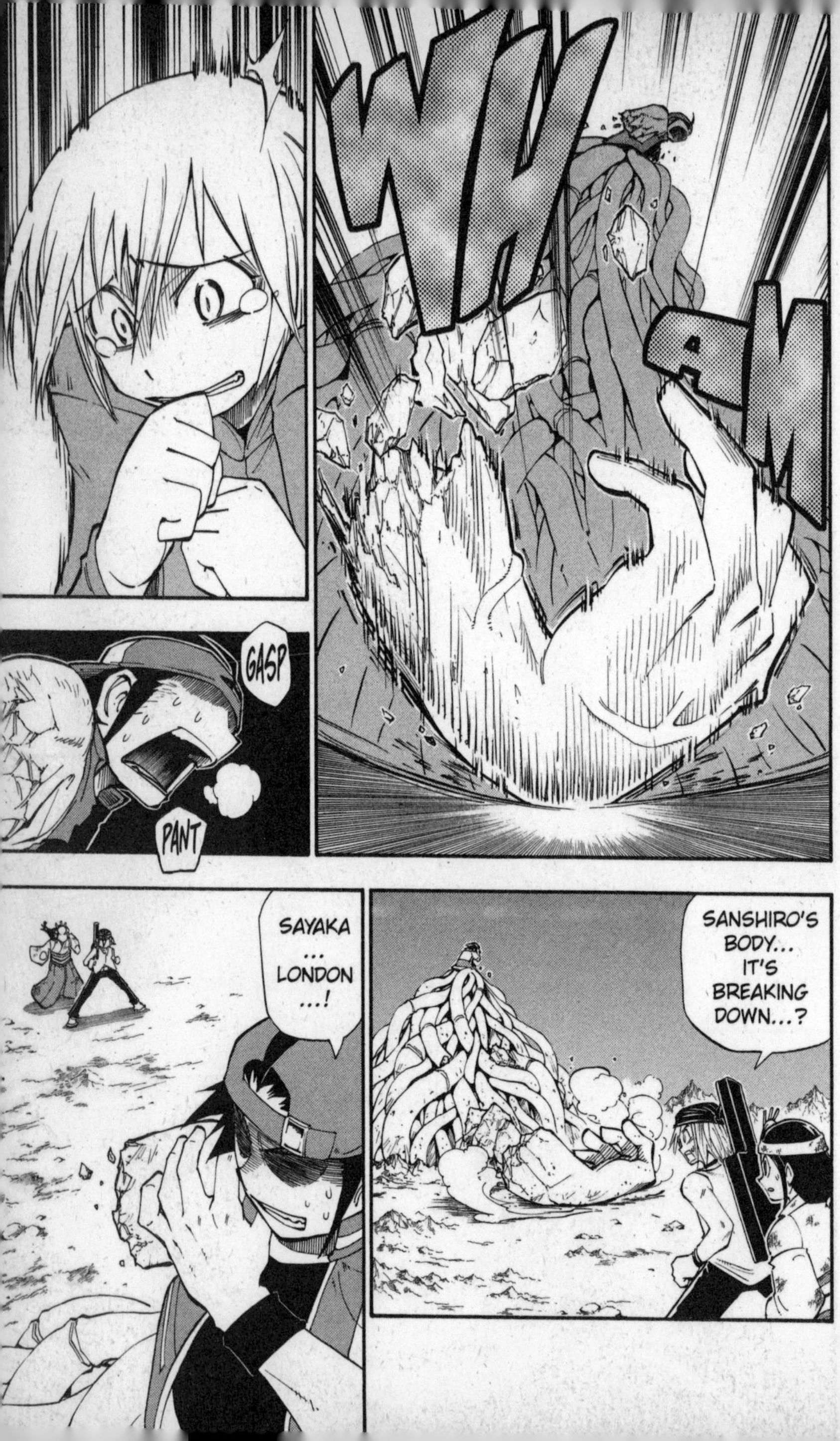
WHAM
GASP
PANT
SANSHIRO'S BODY... IT'S BREAKING DOWN...?
SAYAKA ... LONDON ...!

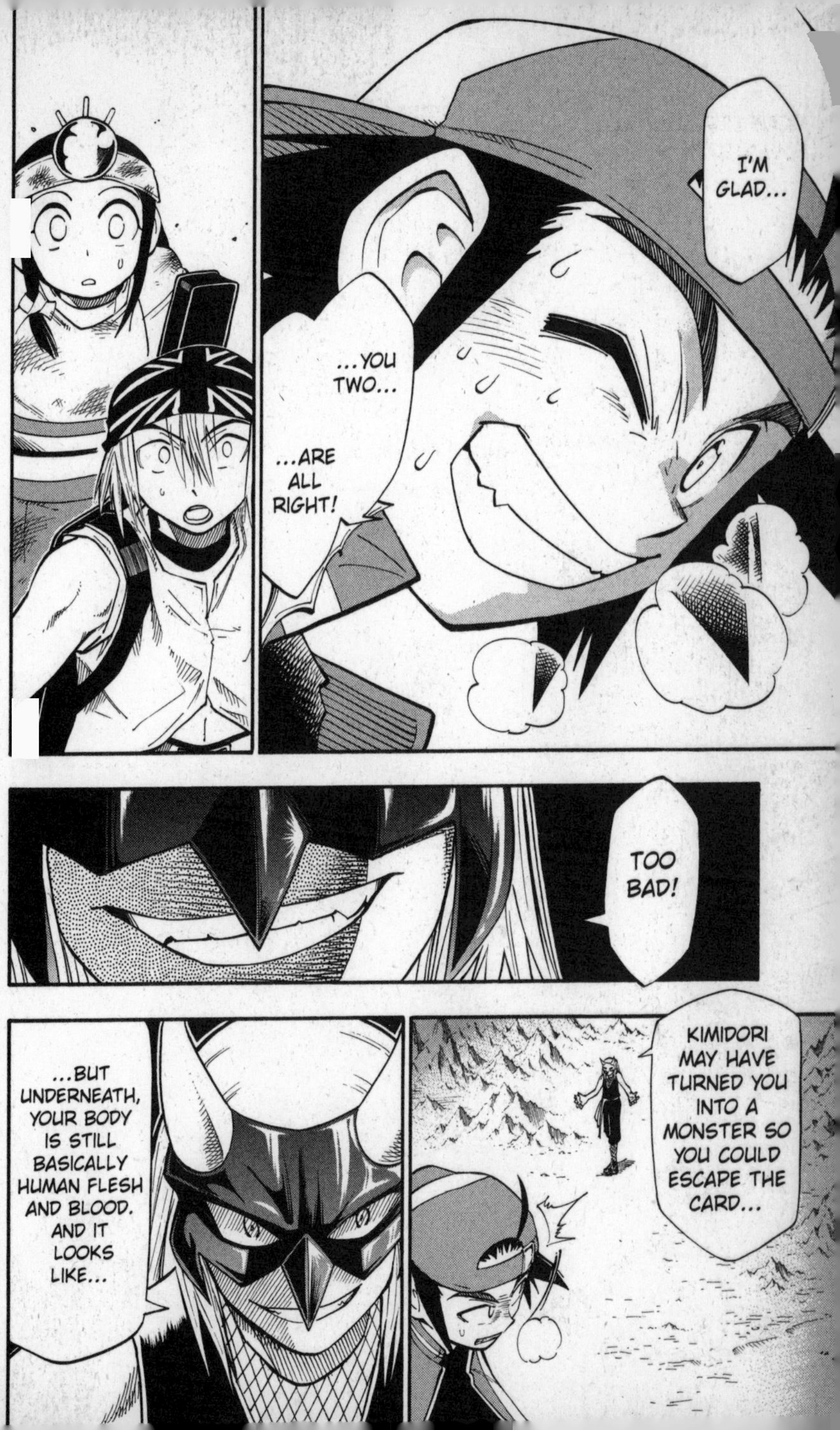
I'M GLAD...
...YOU TWO...
...ARE ALL RIGHT!
TOO BAD!
KIMIDORI MAY HAVE TURNED YOU INTO A MONSTER SO YOU COULD ESCAPE THE CARD...
...BUT UNDERNEATH, YOUR BODY IS STILL BASICALLY HUMAN FLESH AND BLOOD. AND IT LOOKS LIKE...

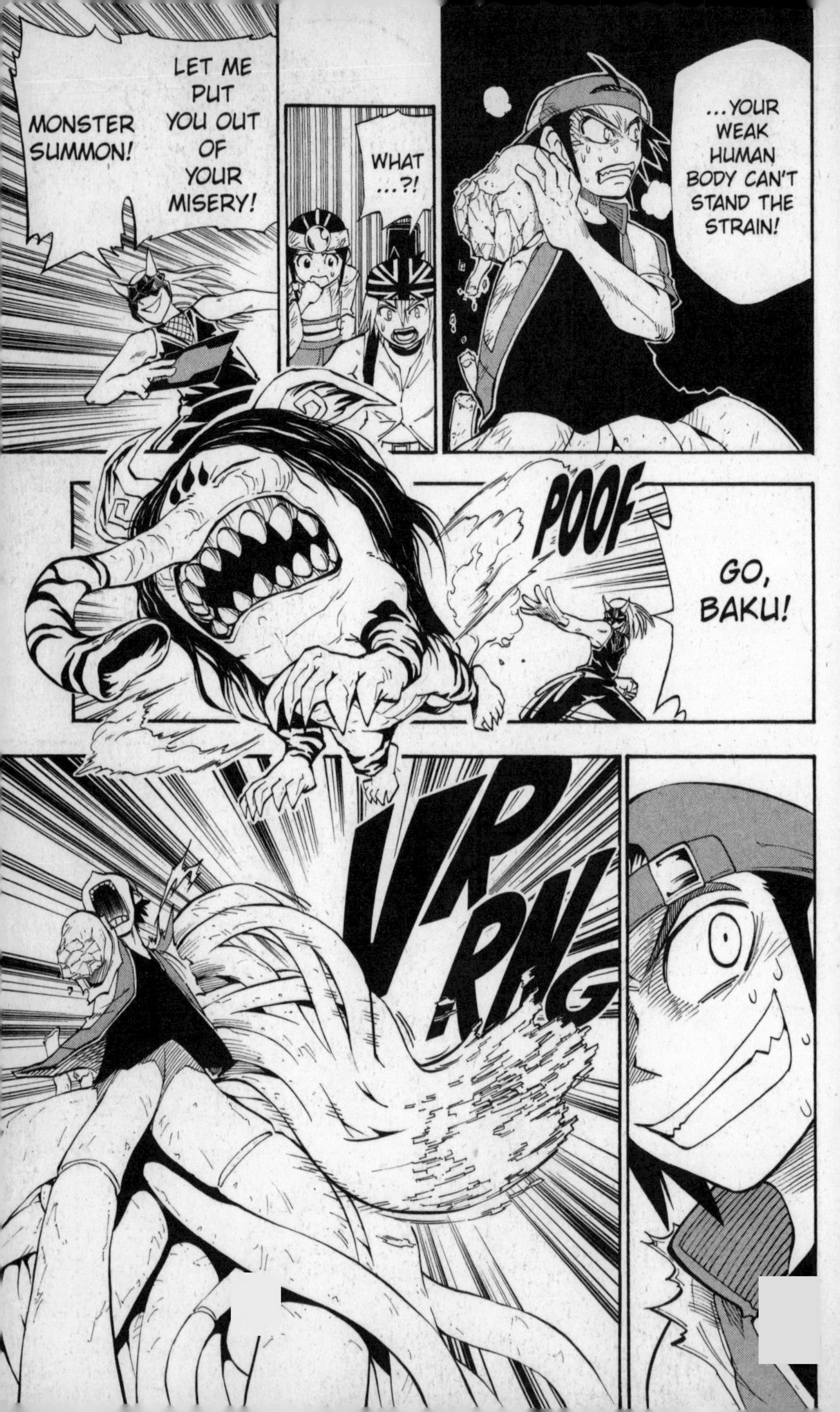
...YOUR WEAK HUMAN BODY CAN'T STAND THE STRAIN!
WHAT ...?!
LET ME PUT YOU OUT OF YOUR MISERY!
MONSTER SUMMON!
GO, BAKU!
POOF

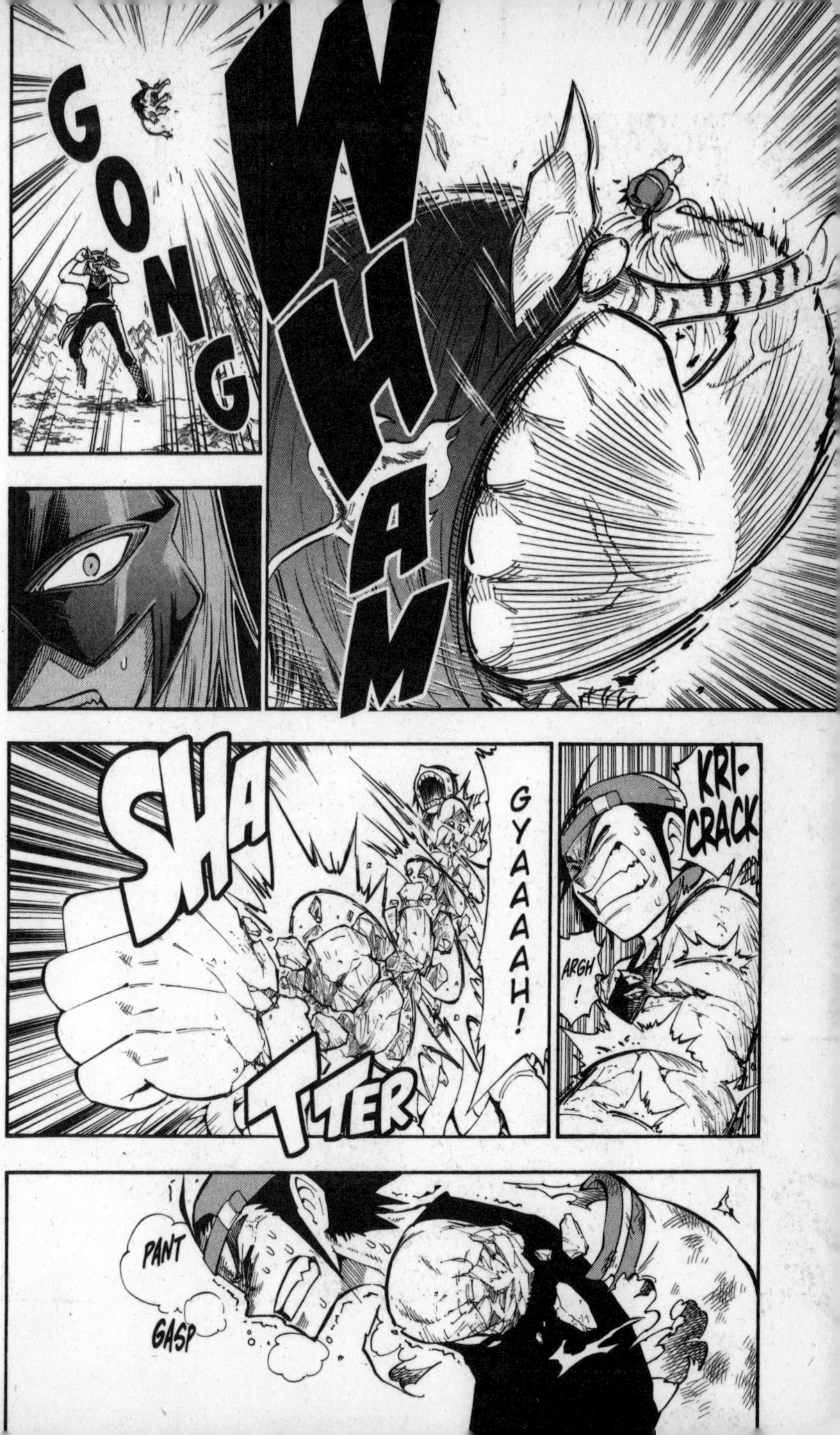
WHAM
GONG
KRI-CRACK
ARGH!
GYAAAAAH!
SHATTER
PANT
GASP

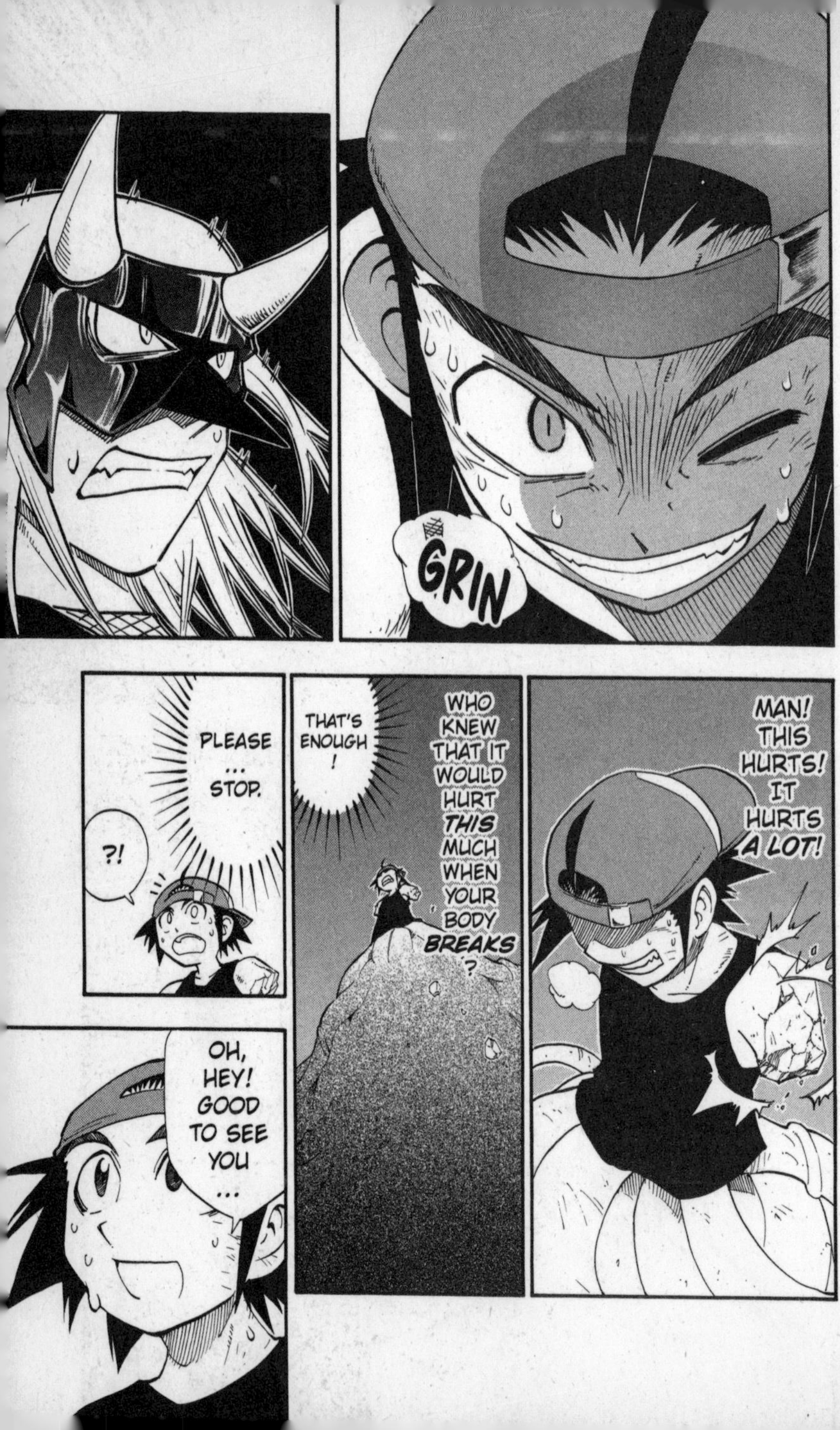
GRIN
MAN! THIS HURTS! IT HURTS A LOT!
WHO KNEW THAT IT WOULD HURT THIS MUCH WHEN YOUR BODY BREAKS?
THAT'S ENOUGH!
PLEASE... STOP.
?!
OH, HEY! GOOD TO SEE YOU...

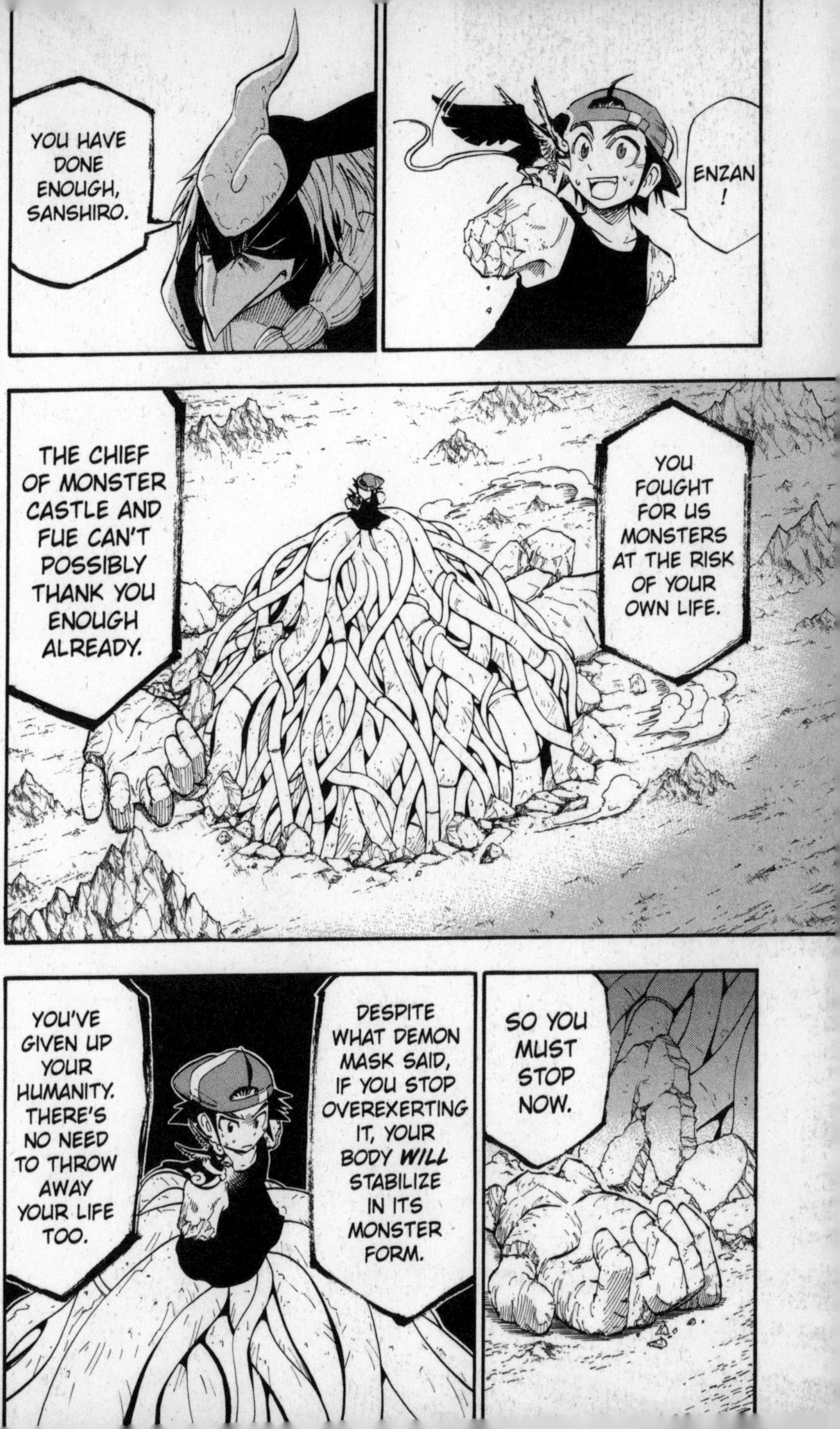
YOU HAVE DONE ENOUGH, SANSHIRO.
ENZAN!
THE CHIEF OF MONSTER CASTLE AND FUE CAN'T POSSIBLY THANK YOU ENOUGH ALREADY.
YOU FOUGHT FOR US MONSTERS AT THE RISK OF YOUR OWN LIFE.
YOU'VE GIVEN UP YOUR HUMANITY. THERE'S NO NEED TO THROW AWAY YOUR LIFE TOO.
DESPITE WHAT DEMON MASK SAID, IF YOU STOP OVEREXERTING IT, YOUR BODY WILL STABILIZE IN ITS MONSTER FORM.
SO YOU MUST STOP NOW.

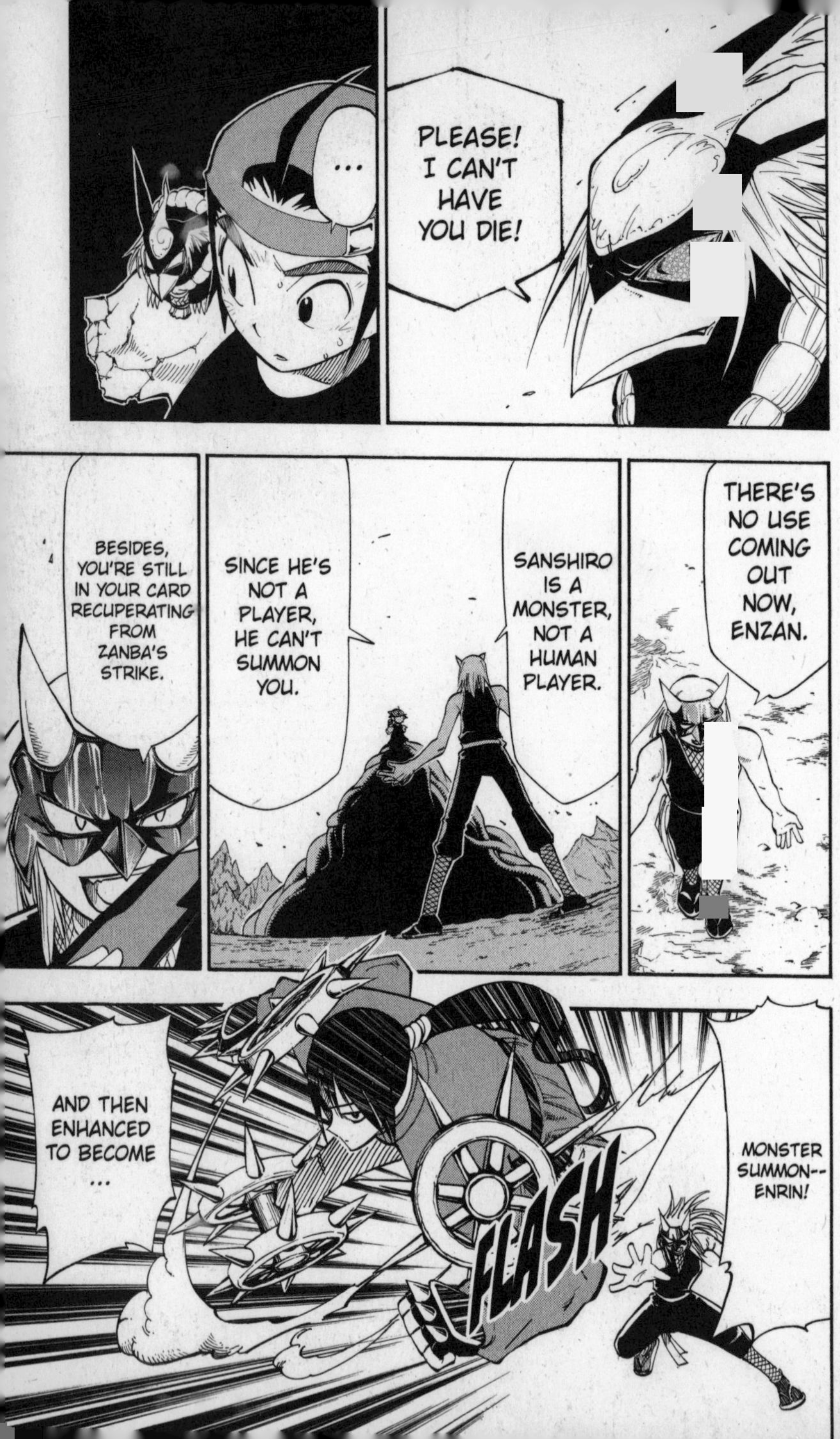
PLEASE! I CAN'T HAVE YOU DIE!
...
THERE'S NO USE COMING OUT NOW, ENZAN.
SANSHIRO IS A MONSTER, NOT A HUMAN PLAYER.
SINCE HE'S NOT A PLAYER, HE CAN'T SUMMON YOU.
BESIDES, YOU'RE STILL IN YOUR CARD RECUPERATING FROM ZANBA'S STRIKE.
MONSTER SUMMON--ENRIN!
FLASH
AND THEN ENHANCED TO BECOME ...

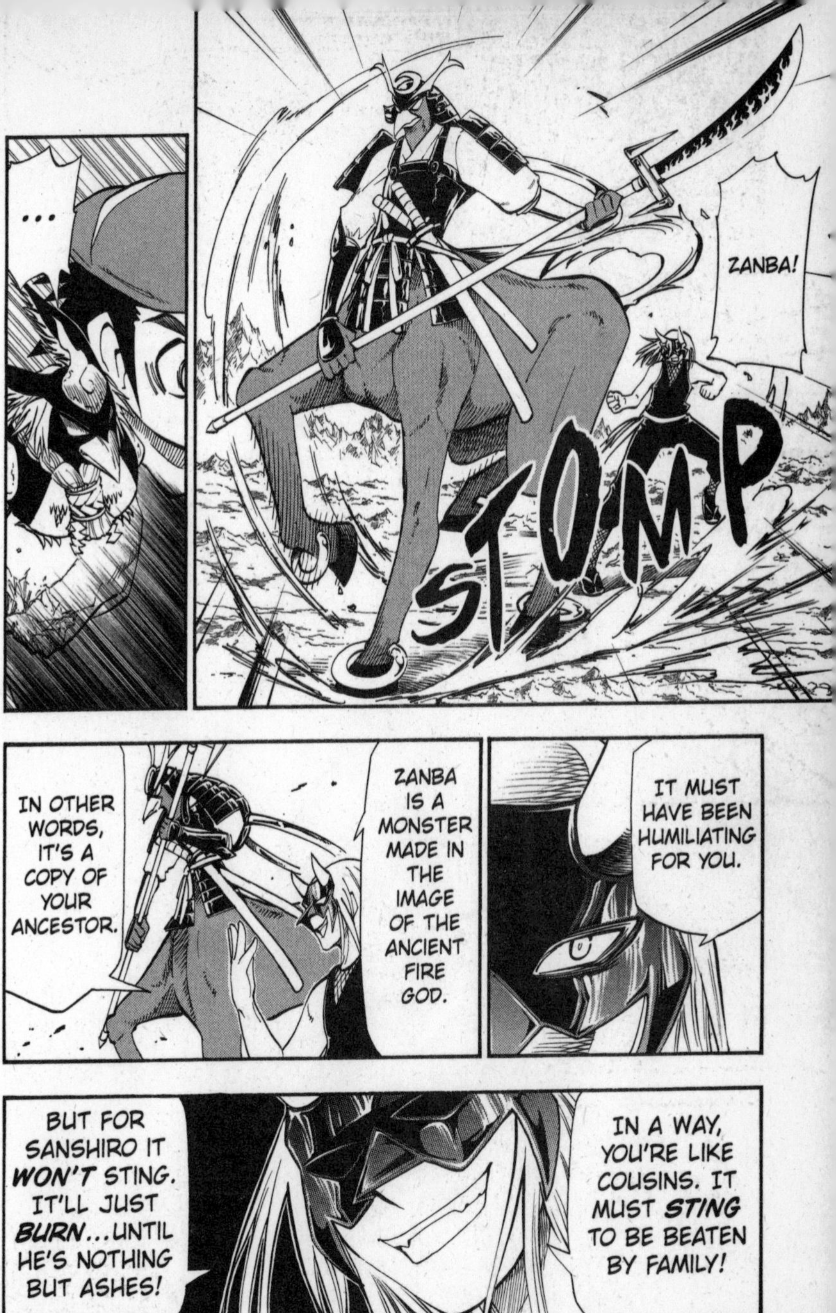
ZANBA!
STOMP
...
IT MUST HAVE BEEN HUMILIATING FOR YOU.
ZANBA IS A MONSTER MADE IN THE IMAGE OF THE ANCIENT FIRE GOD.
IN OTHER WORDS, IT'S A COPY OF YOUR ANCESTOR.
IN A WAY, YOU'RE LIKE COUSINS. IT MUST *STING* TO BE BEATEN BY FAMILY!
BUT FOR SANSHIRO IT *WON'T* STING. IT'LL JUST *BURN*...UNTIL HE'S NOTHING BUT ASHES!

GO, ZANBA!

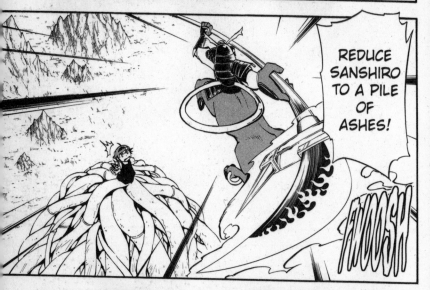

REDUCE SANSHIRO TO A PILE OF ASHES!

FWOOSH

I CAN'T *DO* ANYTHING!

TOO FAST!

SQURCH

THANK YOU FOR PROTECTING ME ALL THIS TIME ...

ENZAN...

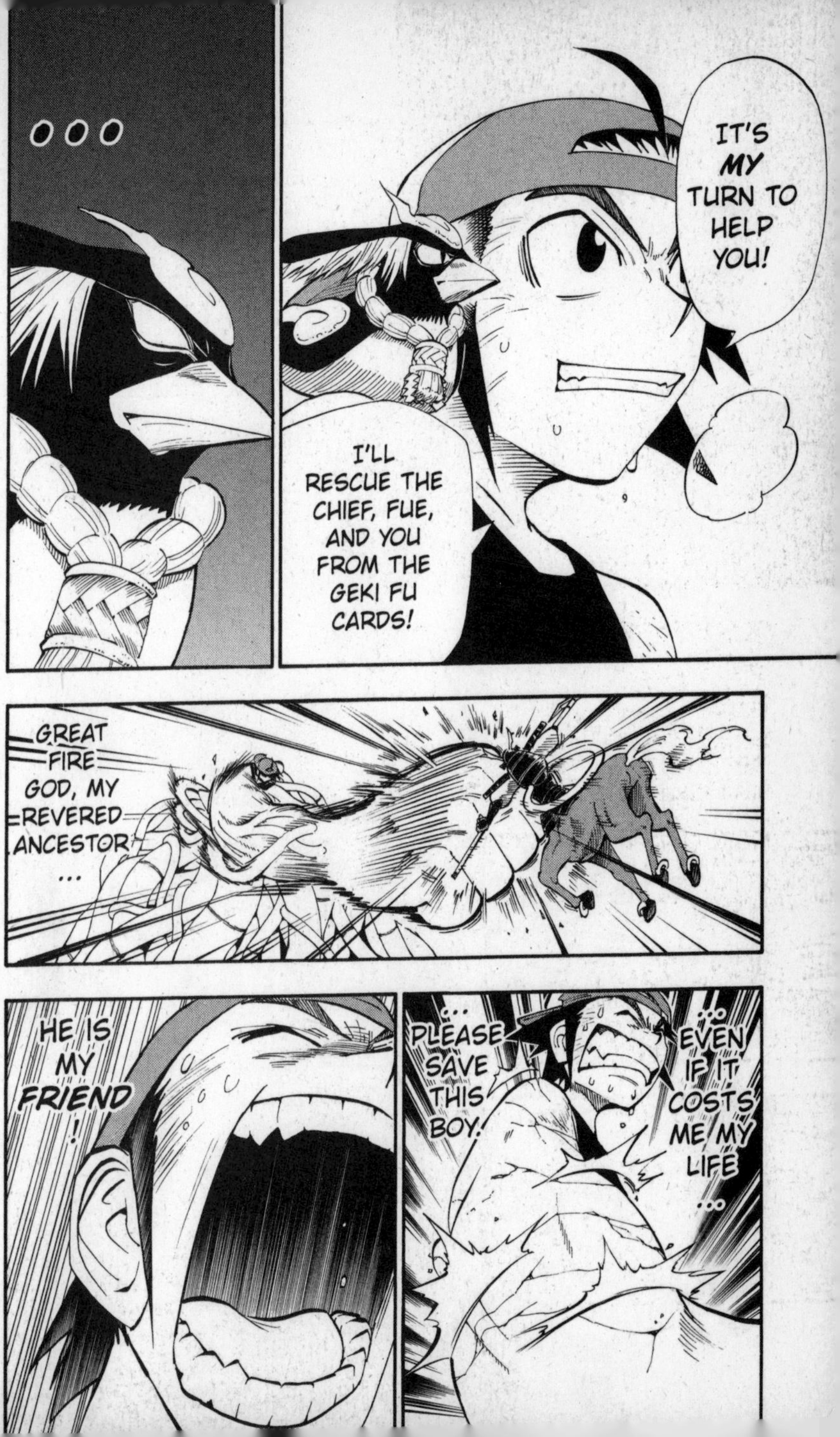
IT'S MY TURN TO HELP YOU!
I'LL RESCUE THE CHIEF, FUE, AND YOU FROM THE GEKI FU CARDS!
ooo
GREAT FIRE GOD, MY REVERED ANCESTOR...
...EVEN IF IT COSTS ME MY LIFE...
...PLEASE SAVE THIS BOY.
HE IS MY FRIEND!

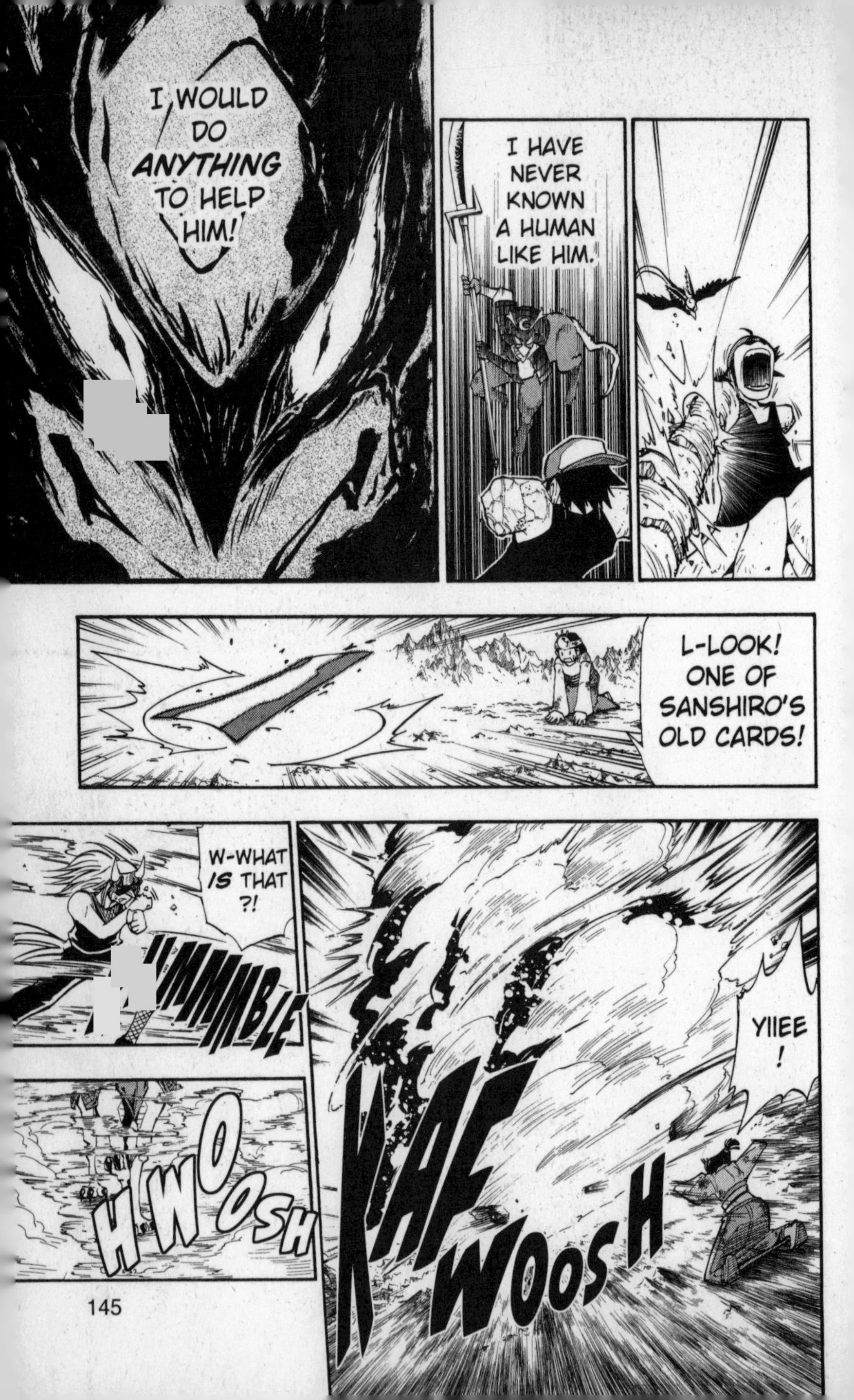
I HAVE NEVER KNOWN A HUMAN LIKE HIM.
I WOULD DO ANYTHING TO HELP HIM!
L-LOOK! ONE OF SANSHIRO'S OLD CARDS!
YIIEE!
WOOSH
W-WHAT IS THAT?!
HWOOSH

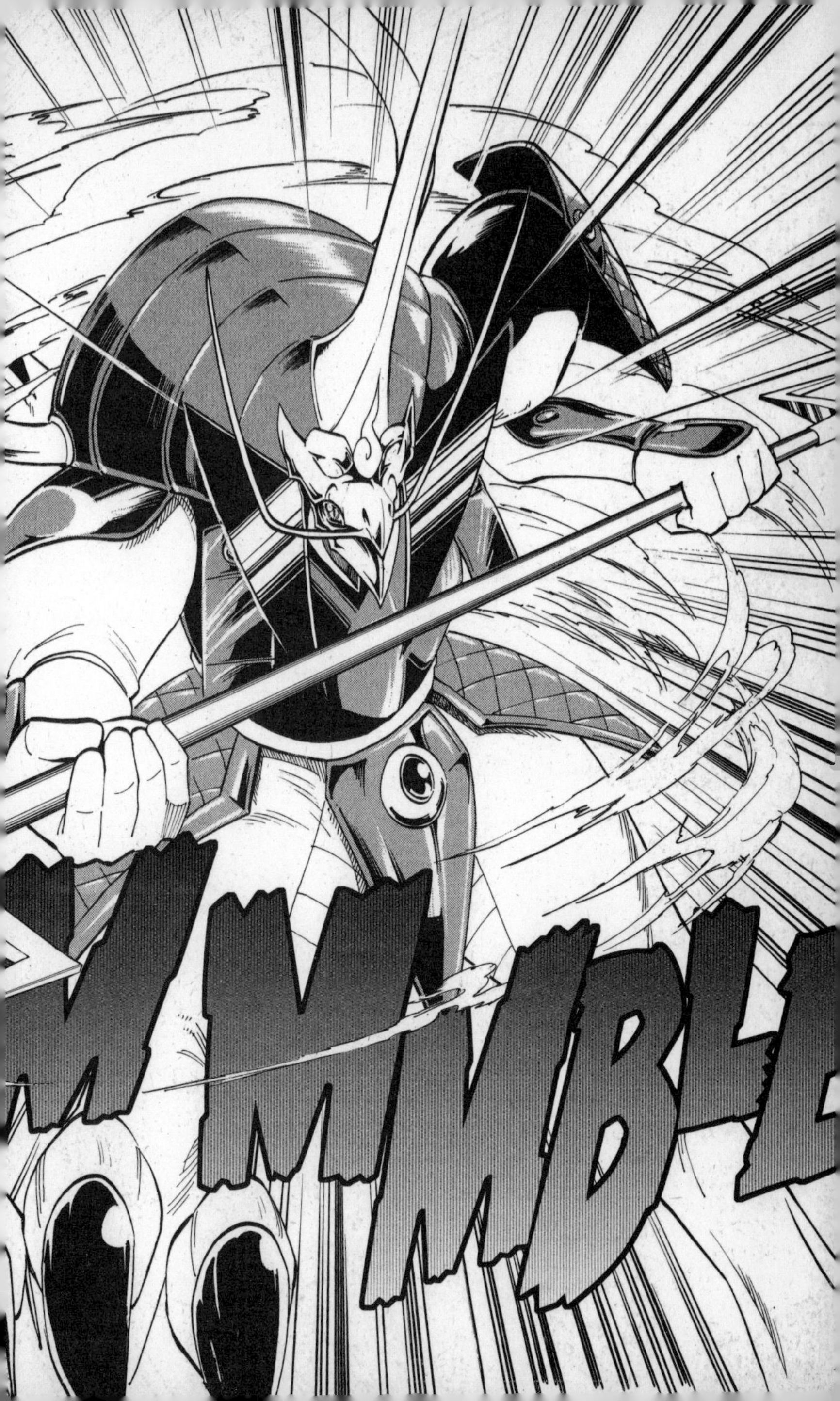
MMMBL

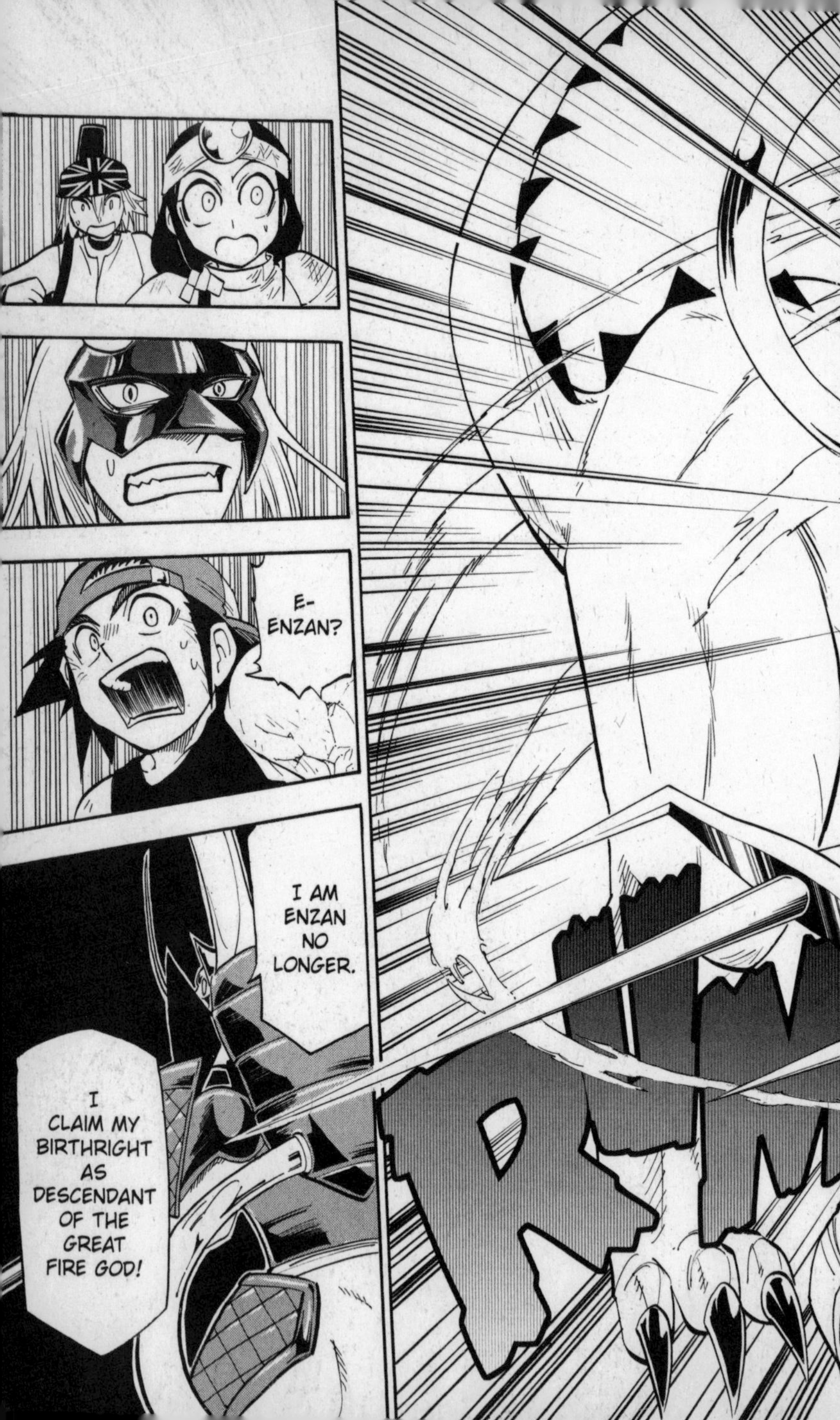
E-
ENZAN?
I AM
ENZAN
NO
LONGER.
I
CLAIM MY
BIRTHRIGHT
AS
DESCENDANT
OF THE
GREAT
FIRE GOD!

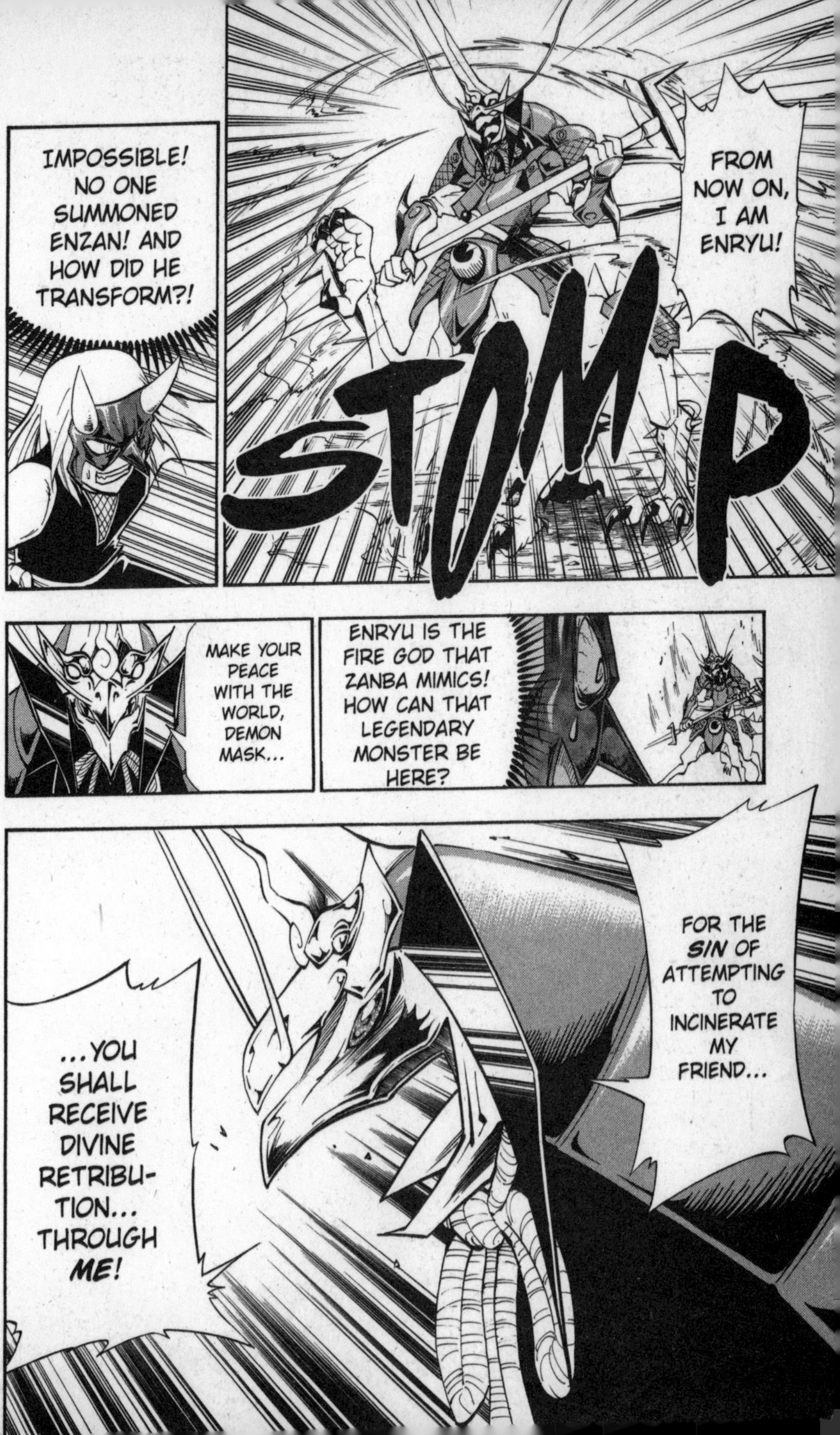
FROM NOW ON, I AM ENRYU!
STOMP
IMPOSSIBLE! NO ONE SUMMONED ENZAN! AND HOW DID HE TRANSFORM?!
ENRYU IS THE FIRE GOD THAT ZANBA MIMICS! HOW CAN THAT LEGENDARY MONSTER BE HERE?
MAKE YOUR PEACE WITH THE WORLD, DEMON MASK...
FOR THE *SIN* OF ATTEMPTING TO INCINERATE MY FRIEND...
...YOU SHALL RECEIVE DIVINE RETRIBUTION... THROUGH *ME*!

CHAPTER 49 A MASK OF EVIL DESIRES

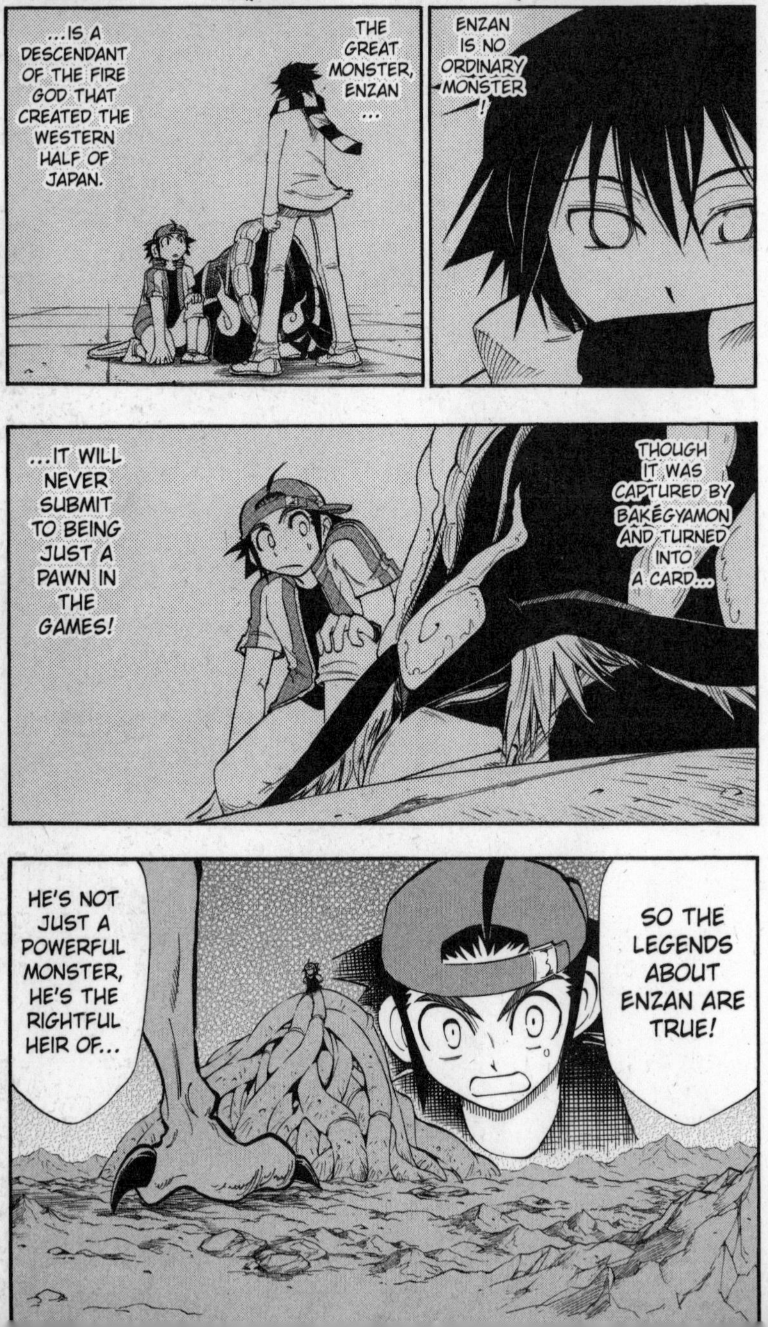
ENZAN IS NO ORDINARY MONSTER!
THE GREAT MONSTER, ENZAN...
...IS A DESCENDANT OF THE FIRE GOD THAT CREATED THE WESTERN HALF OF JAPAN.
THOUGH IT WAS CAPTURED BY BAKÉGYAMON AND TURNED INTO A CARD...
...IT WILL NEVER SUBMIT TO BEING JUST A PAWN IN THE GAMES!
SO THE LEGENDS ABOUT ENZAN ARE TRUE!
HE'S NOT JUST A POWERFUL MONSTER, HE'S THE RIGHTFUL HEIR OF...

CHAPTER 49 A MASK OF EVIL DESIRES

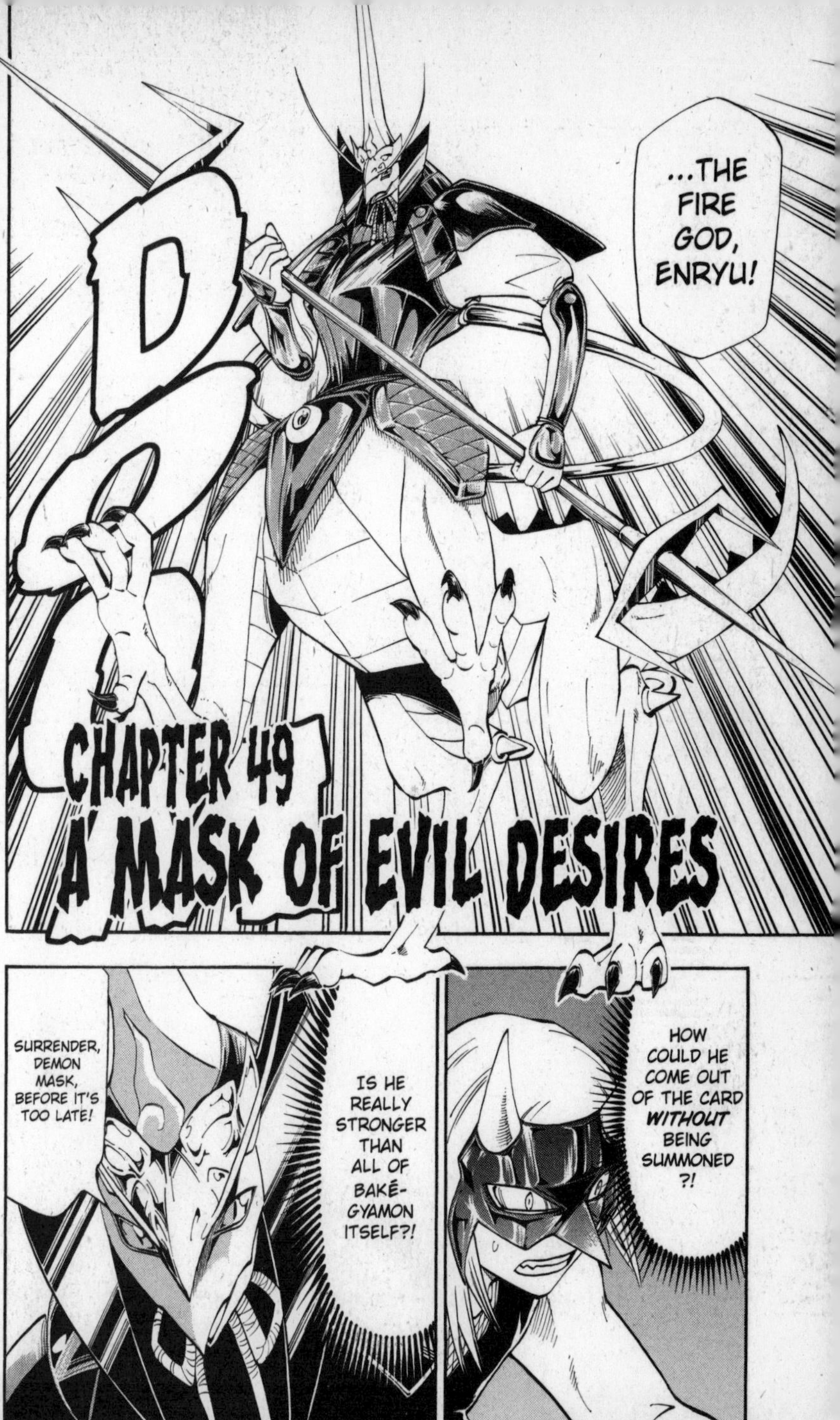
...THE FIRE GOD, ENRYU!
CHAPTER 49
A MASK OF EVIL DESIRES
HOW COULD HE COME OUT OF THE CARD *WITHOUT* BEING SUMMONED ?!
IS HE REALLY STRONGER THAN ALL OF BAKÉ-GYAMON ITSELF?!
SURRENDER, DEMON MASK, BEFORE IT'S TOO LATE!

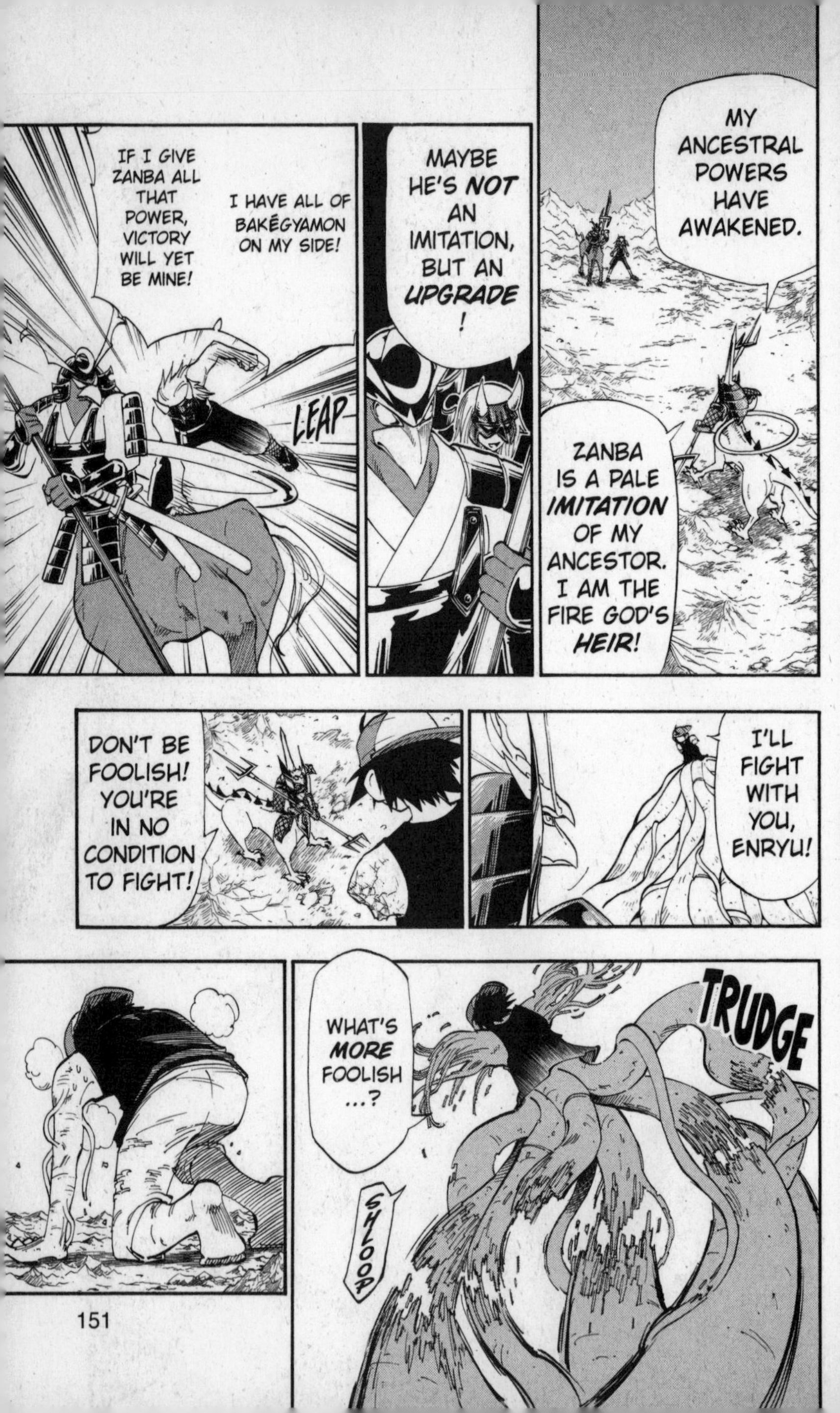
MY ANCESTRAL POWERS HAVE AWAKENED.
ZANBA IS A PALE *IMITATION* OF MY ANCESTOR. I AM THE FIRE GOD'S *HEIR*!
MAYBE HE'S *NOT* AN IMITATION, BUT AN *UPGRADE*!
I HAVE ALL OF BAKÉGYAMON ON MY SIDE!
IF I GIVE ZANBA ALL THAT POWER, VICTORY WILL YET BE MINE!
LEAP
I'LL FIGHT WITH YOU, ENRYU!
DON'T BE FOOLISH! YOU'RE IN NO CONDITION TO FIGHT!
TRUDGE
WHAT'S *MORE* FOOLISH ...?
SHLOOP

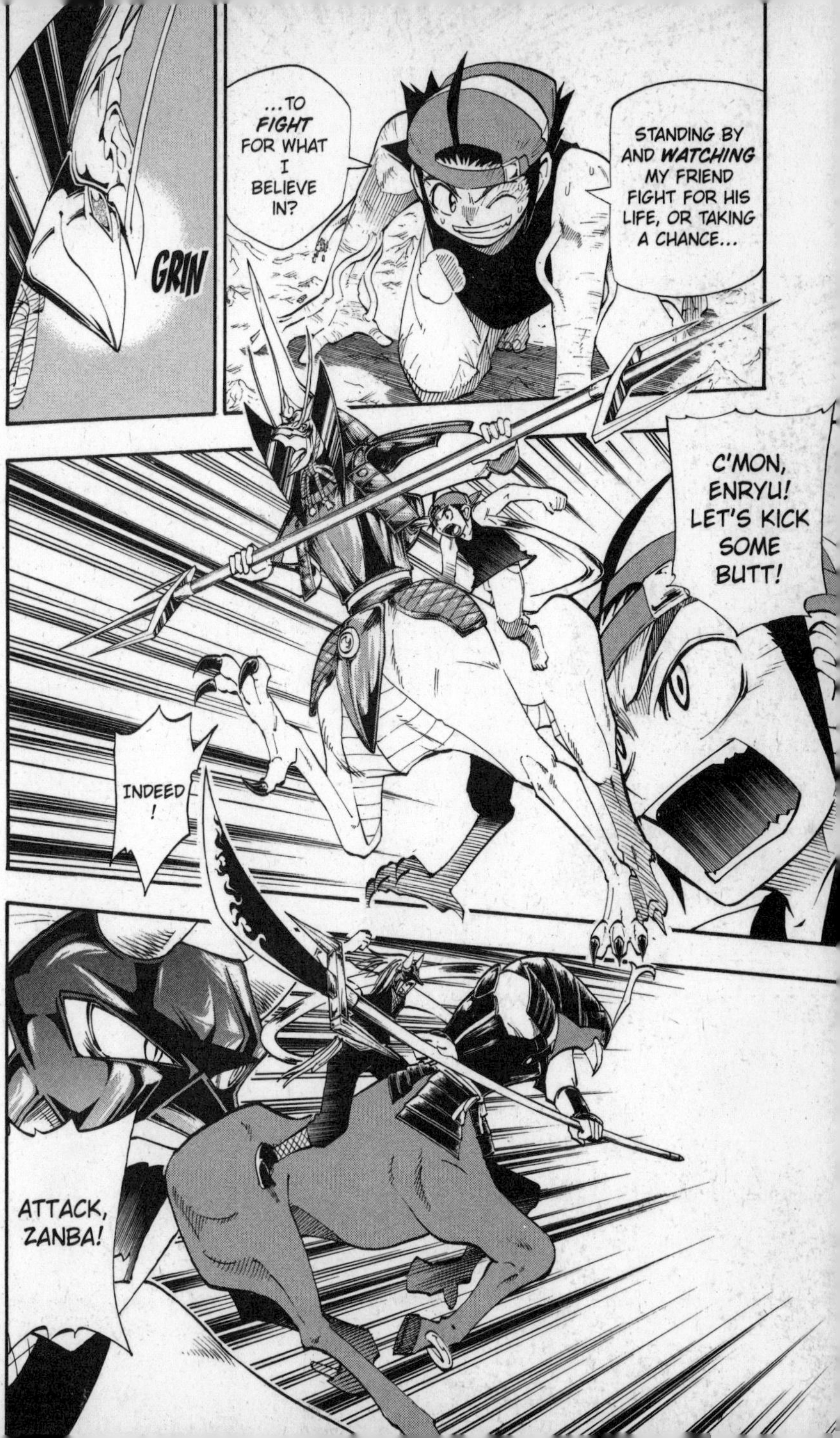
STANDING BY AND WATCHING MY FRIEND FIGHT FOR HIS LIFE, OR TAKING A CHANCE...
...TO FIGHT FOR WHAT I BELIEVE IN?
GRIN
C'MON, ENRYU! LET'S KICK SOME BUTT!
INDEED!
ATTACK, ZANBA!

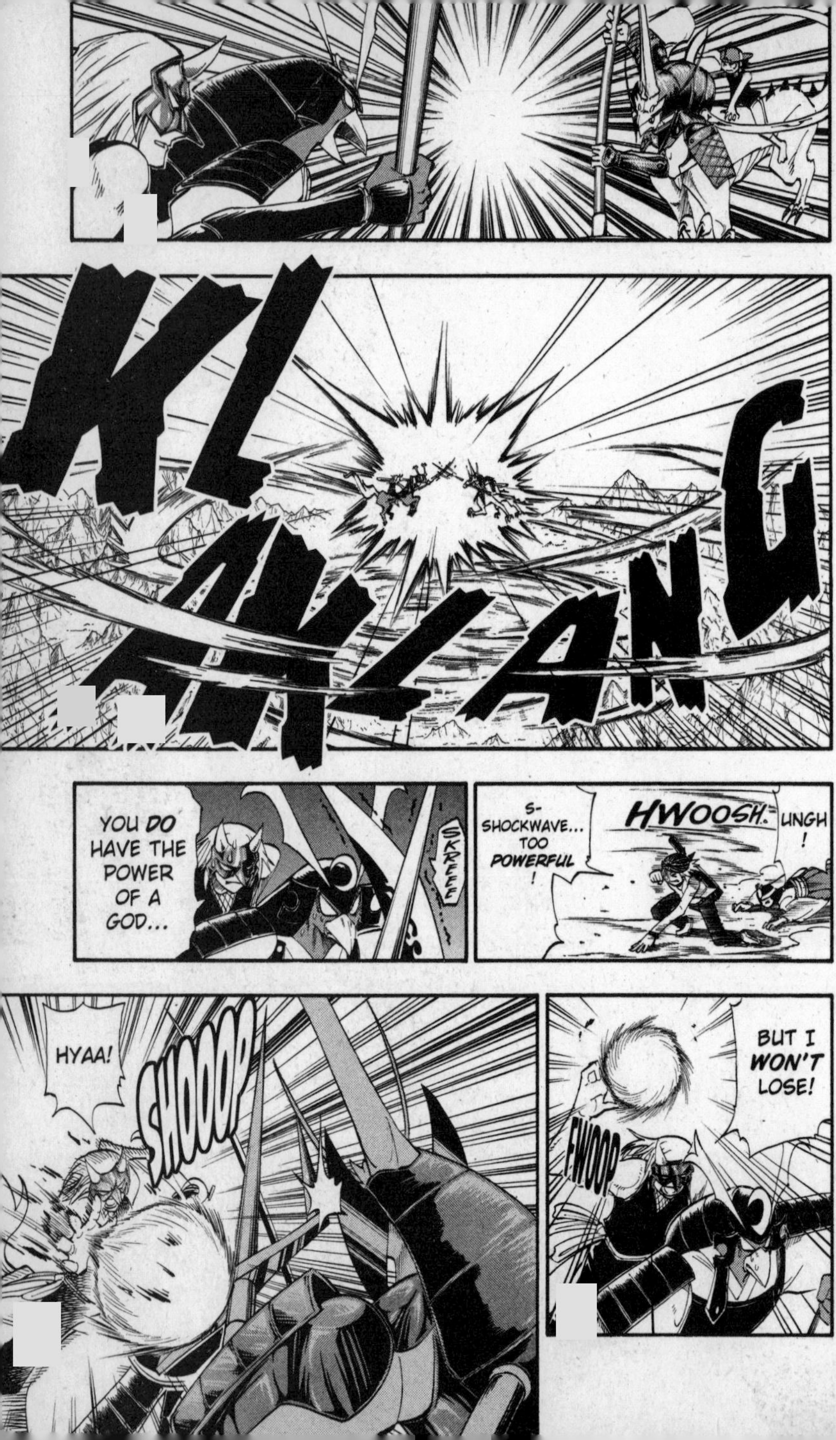
KLANNNGG
UNGH!
HWOOSH
S-SHOCKWAVE... TOO POWERFUL!
SKREEEE
YOU DO HAVE THE POWER OF A GOD...
BUT I WON'T LOSE!
FWOOP
HYAA!
SHOOOP

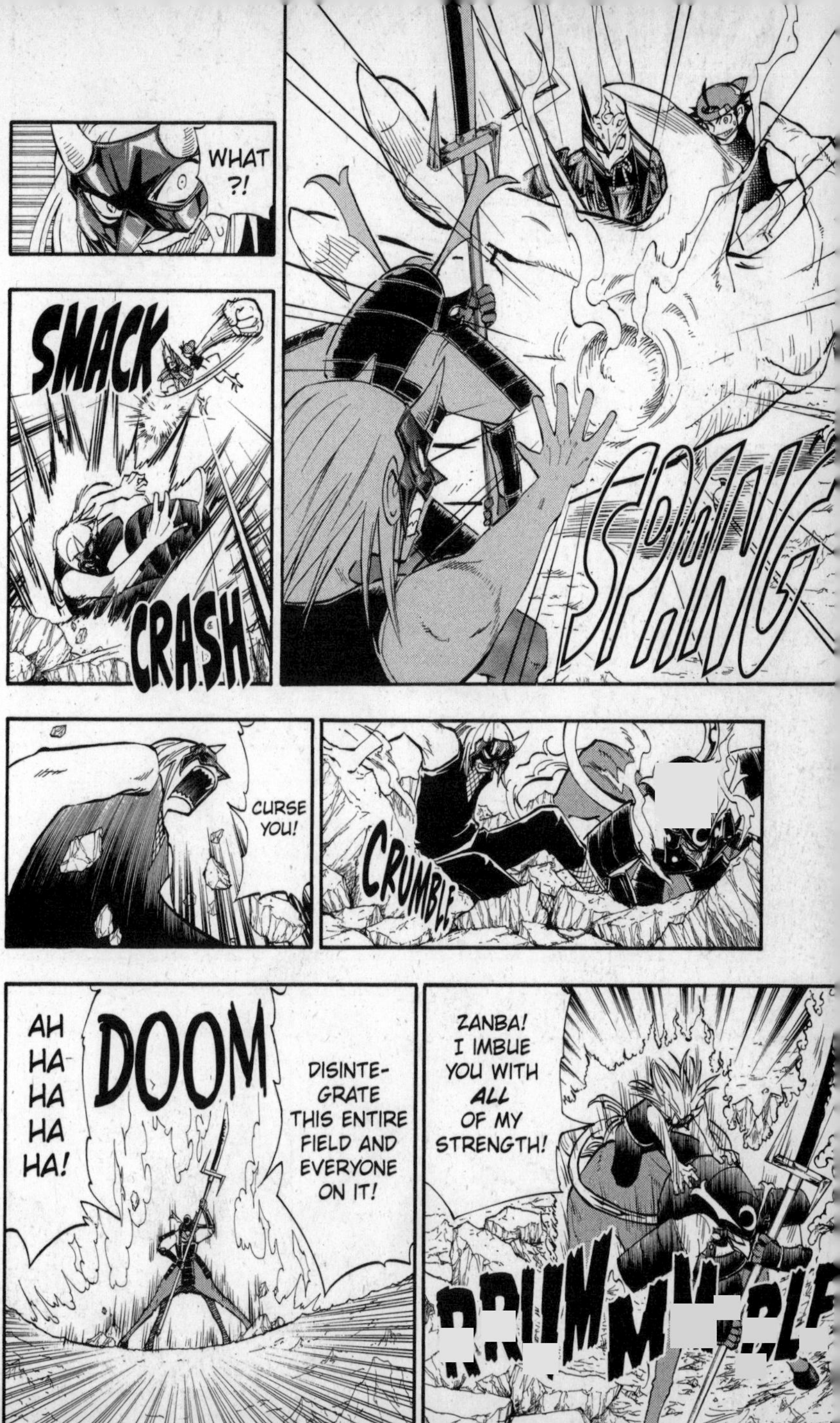
SPANG
WHAT?!
SMACK
CRASH
CRUMBLE
CURSE YOU!
ZANBA! I IMBUE YOU WITH ALL OF MY STRENGTH!
DISINTE-GRATE THIS ENTIRE FIELD AND EVERYONE ON IT!
DOOM
AH HA HA HA HA!

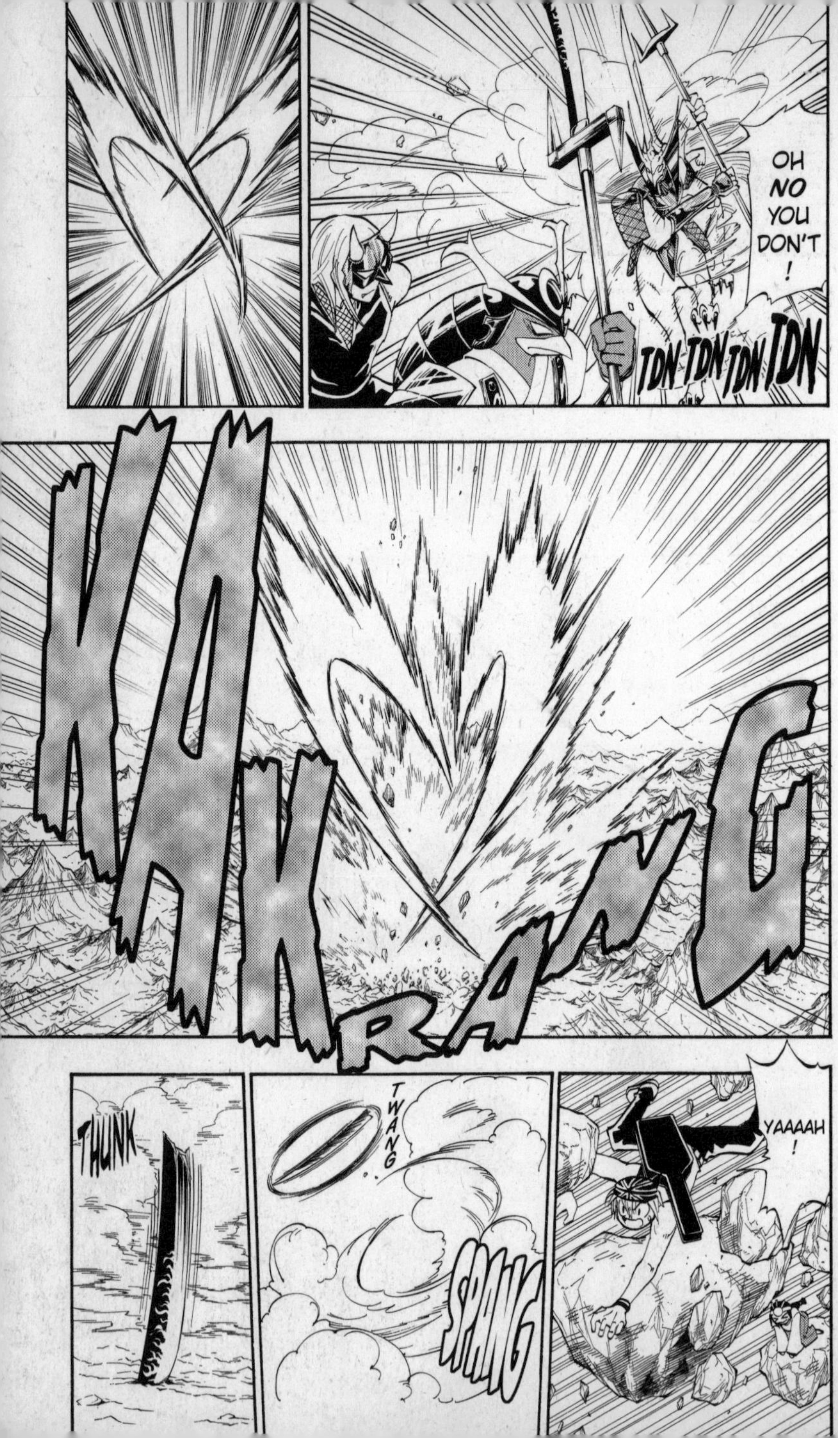
OH NO YOU DON'T!
TDN TDN TDN TDN
KAKRANG
YAAAAH!
TWANG
SPANG
THUNK

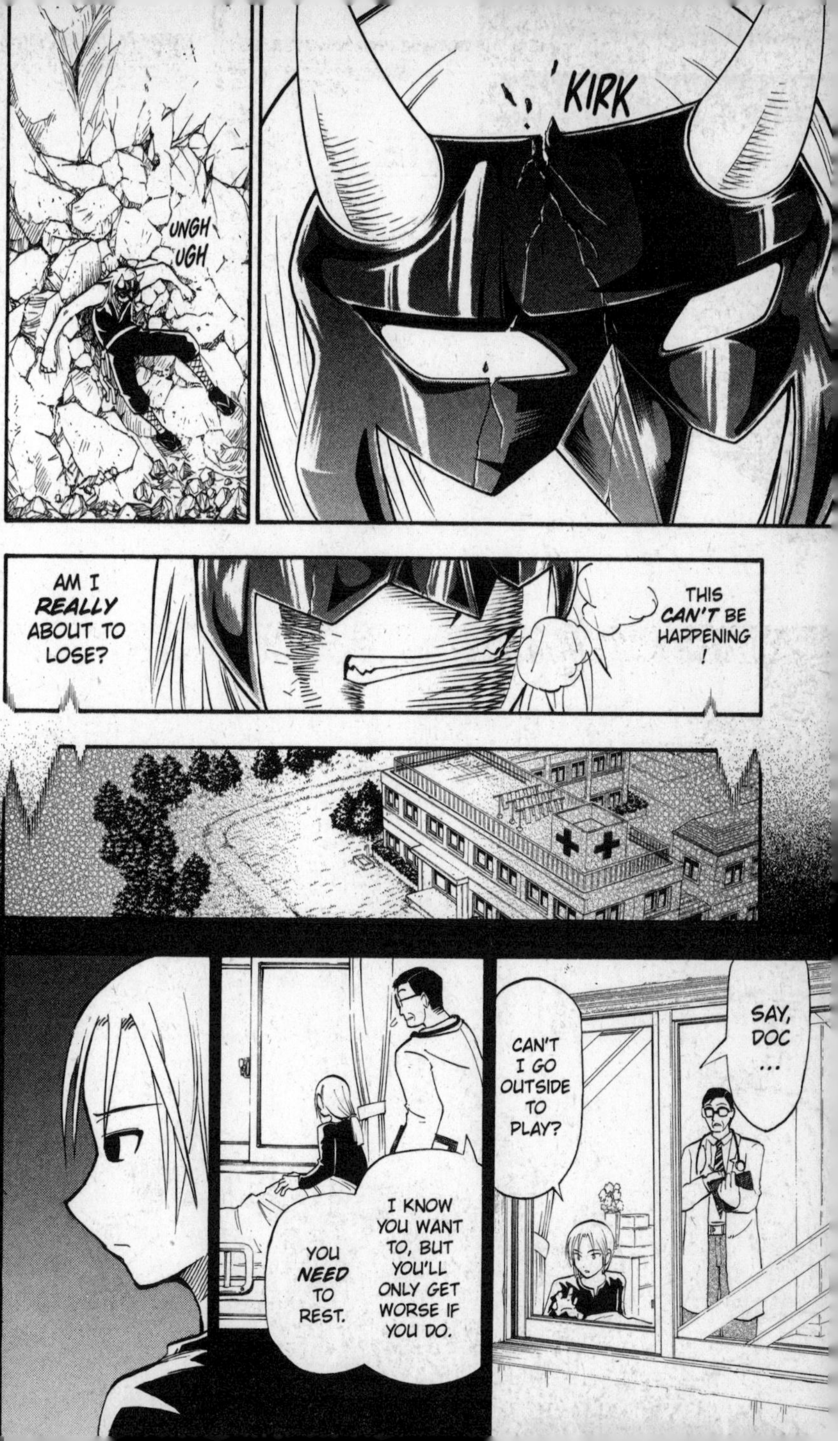
KIRK
UNGH UGH
THIS CAN'T BE HAPPENING!
AM I REALLY ABOUT TO LOSE?
SAY, DOC...
CAN'T I GO OUTSIDE TO PLAY?
I KNOW YOU WANT TO, BUT YOU'LL ONLY GET WORSE IF YOU DO.
YOU NEED TO REST.

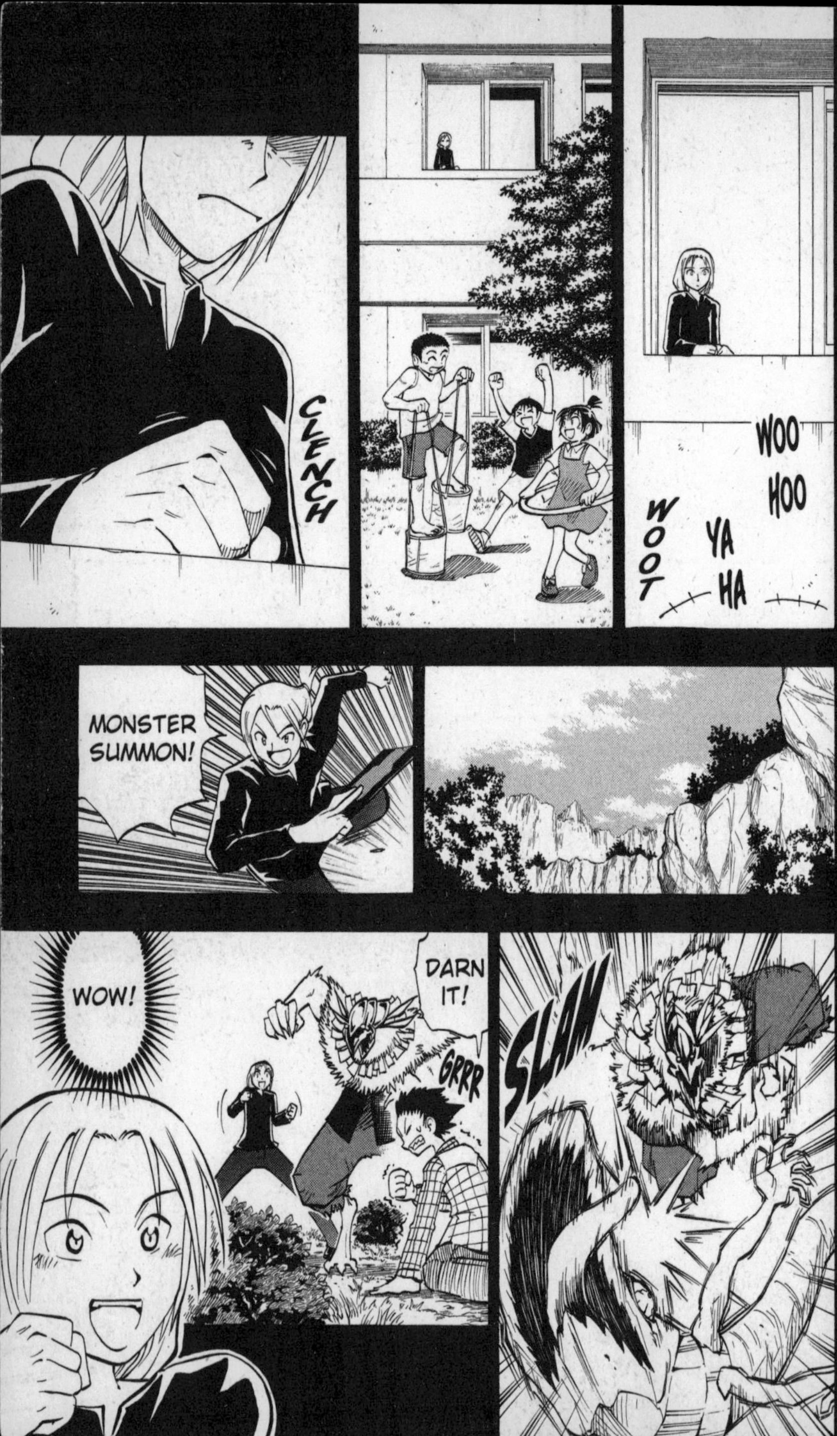
WOO HOO
YA HA
WOOT
CLENCH
MONSTER SUMMON!
SLAM
WOW!
DARN IT!
GRRR

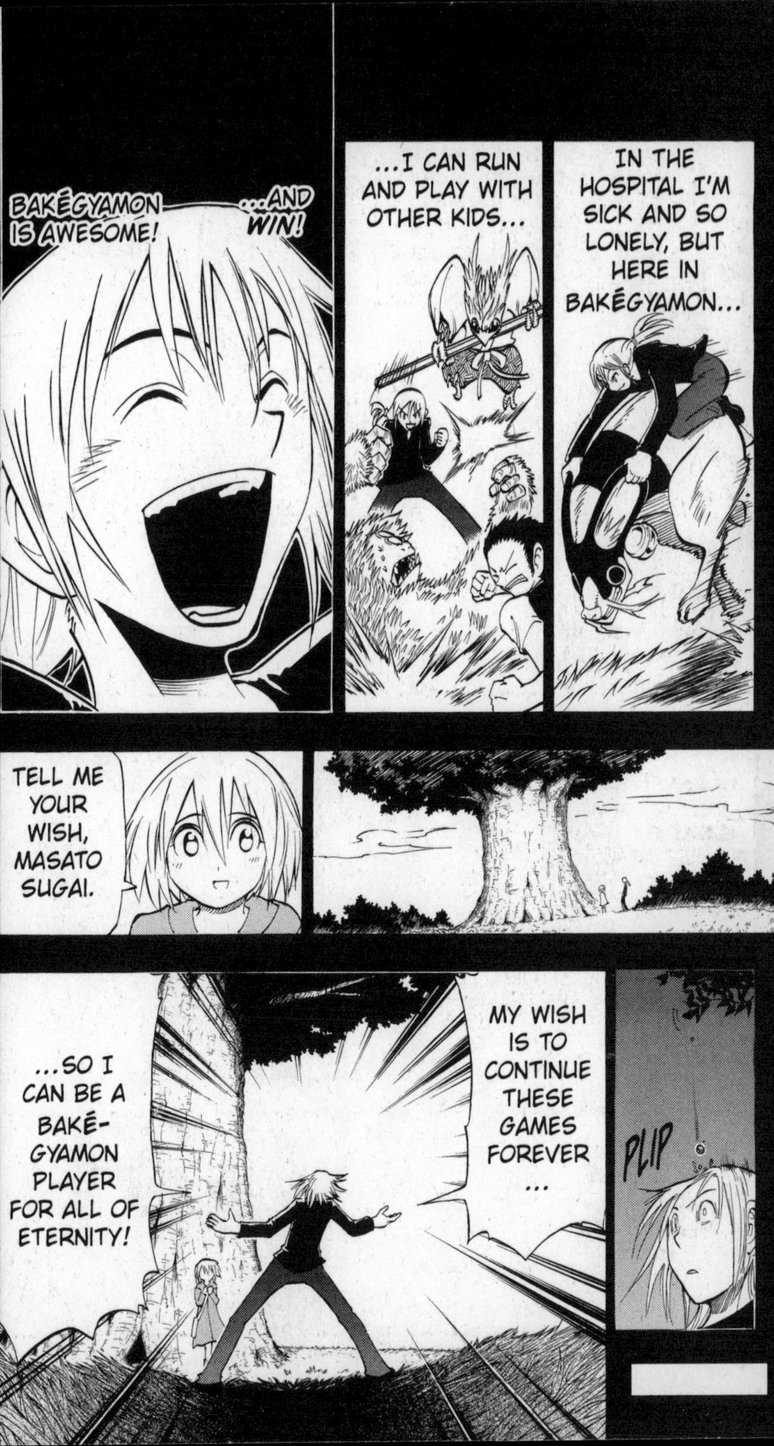
IN THE HOSPITAL I'M SICK AND SO LONELY, BUT HERE IN BAKÉGYAMON...
...I CAN RUN AND PLAY WITH OTHER KIDS...
...AND WIN!
BAKÉGYAMON IS AWESOME!
TELL ME YOUR WISH, MASATO SUGAI.
PLIP
MY WISH IS TO CONTINUE THESE GAMES FOREVER...
...SO I CAN BE A BAKÉ-GYAMON PLAYER FOR ALL OF ETERNITY!

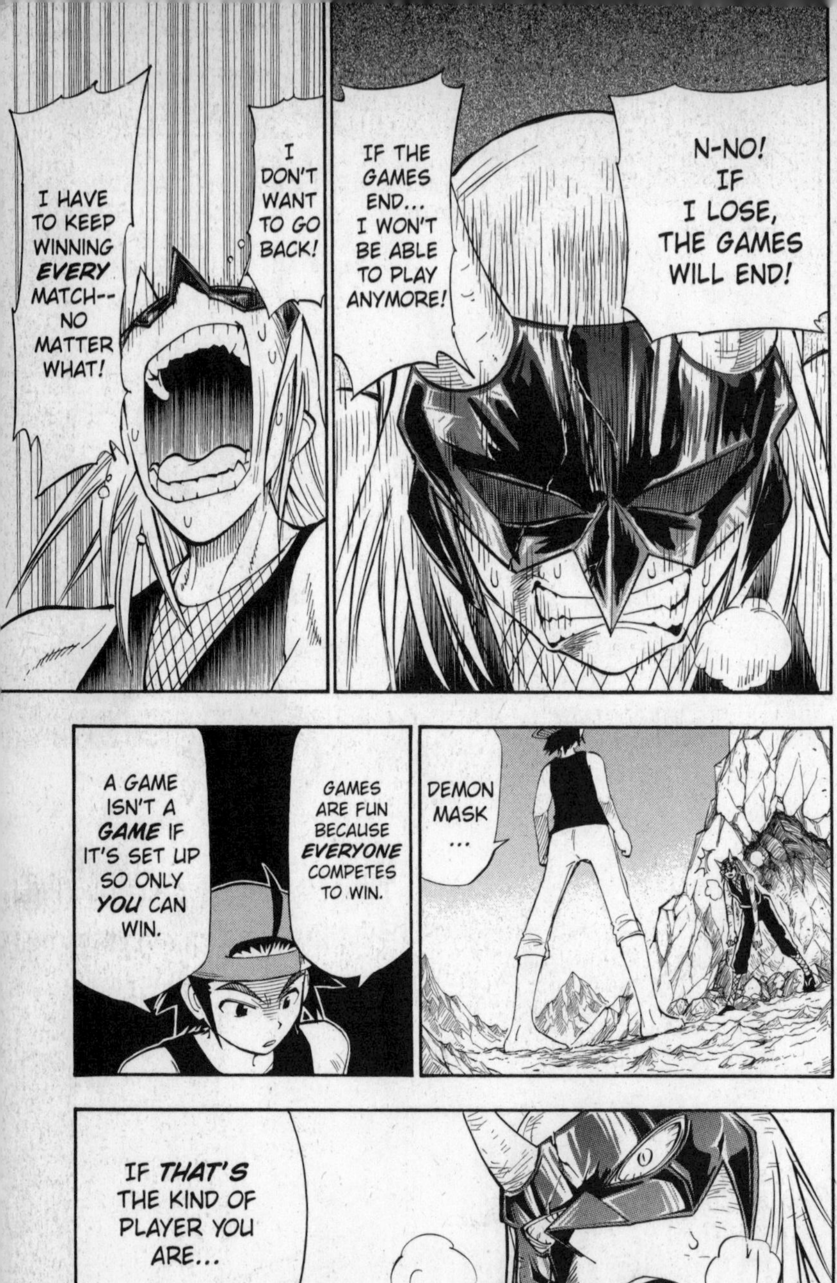
N-NO! IF I LOSE, THE GAMES WILL END!
IF THE GAMES END... I WON'T BE ABLE TO PLAY ANYMORE!
I DON'T WANT TO GO BACK!
I HAVE TO KEEP WINNING *EVERY* MATCH-- NO MATTER WHAT!
DEMON MASK ...
GAMES ARE FUN BECAUSE *EVERYONE* COMPETES TO WIN.
A GAME ISN'T A *GAME* IF IT'S SET UP SO ONLY *YOU* CAN WIN.
IF *THAT'S* THE KIND OF PLAYER YOU ARE...

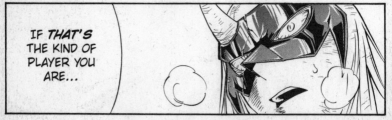

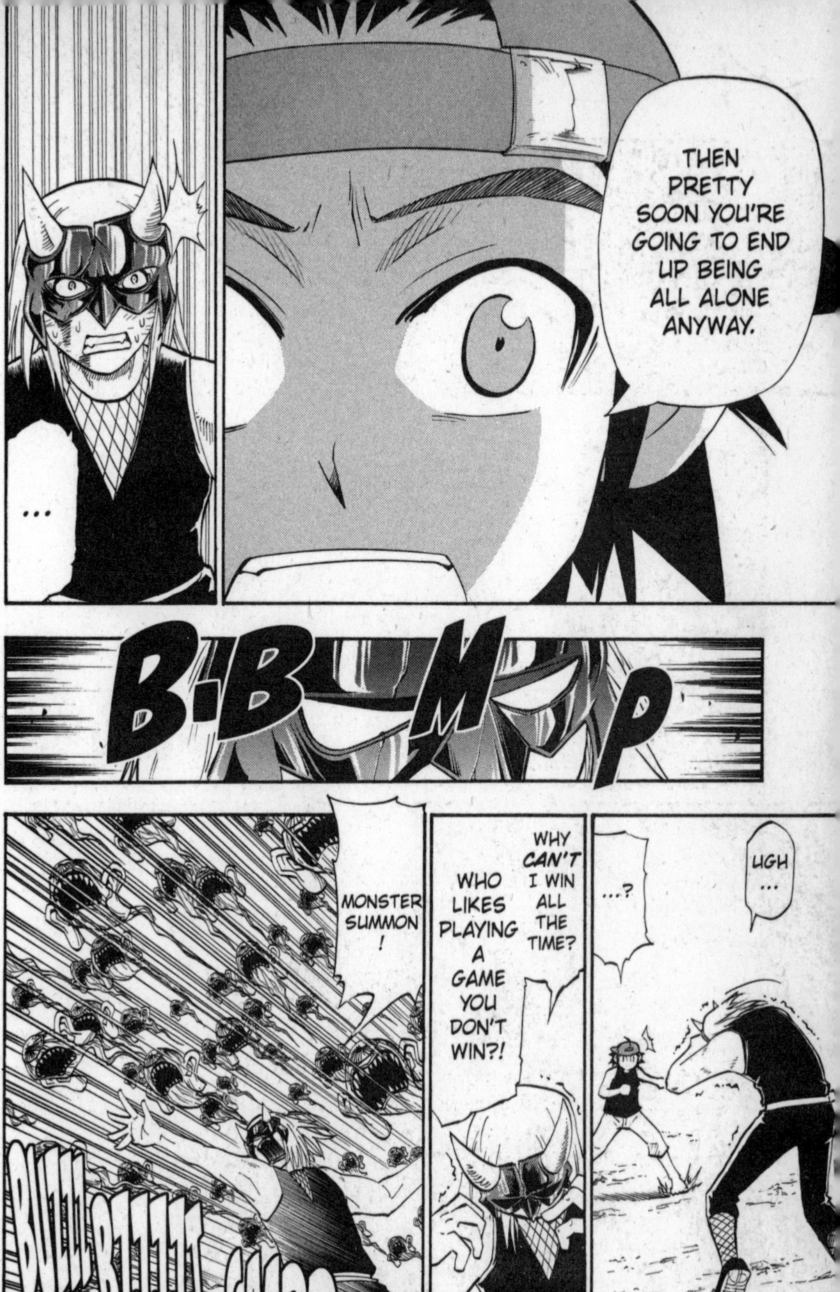
THEN PRETTY SOON YOU'RE GOING TO END UP BEING ALL ALONE ANYWAY.
...
UGH ...
...?
WHY CAN'T I WIN ALL THE TIME?
WHO LIKES PLAYING A GAME YOU DON'T WIN?!
MONSTER SUMMON!
GARR

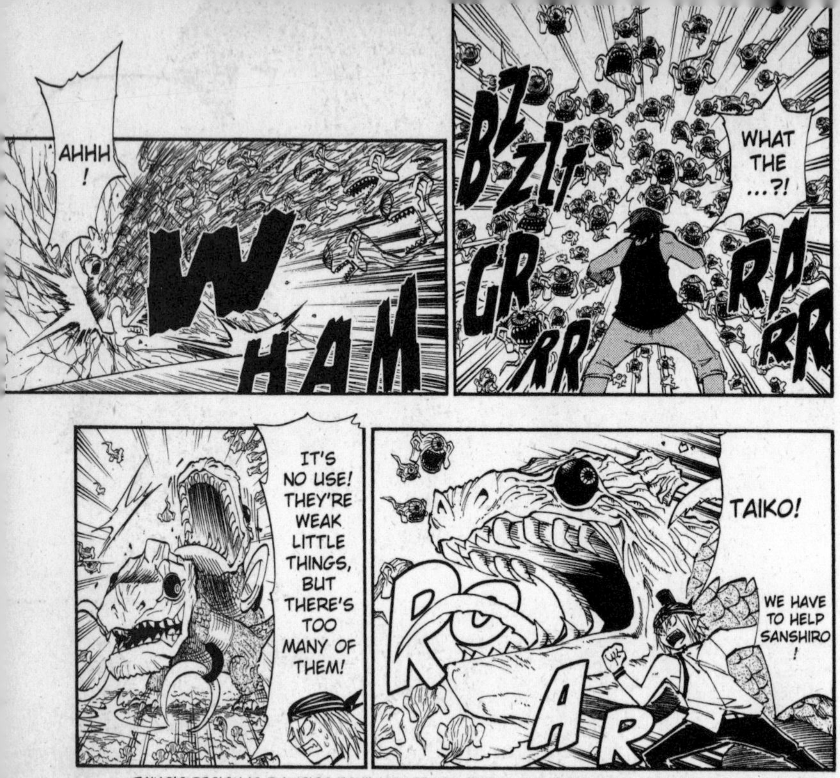
BZZLT
WHAT THE ...?!
GRRR
RARRR
AHHH!
WHAM
TAIKO!
WE HAVE TO HELP SANSHIRO!
ROAR
IT'S NO USE! THEY'RE WEAK LITTLE THINGS, BUT THERE'S TOO MANY OF THEM!

TAIKO'S DESIGN IS BY KEIGO ISHII. CONGRATULATIONS ON WINNING THE MONSTER DESIGN CONTEST!

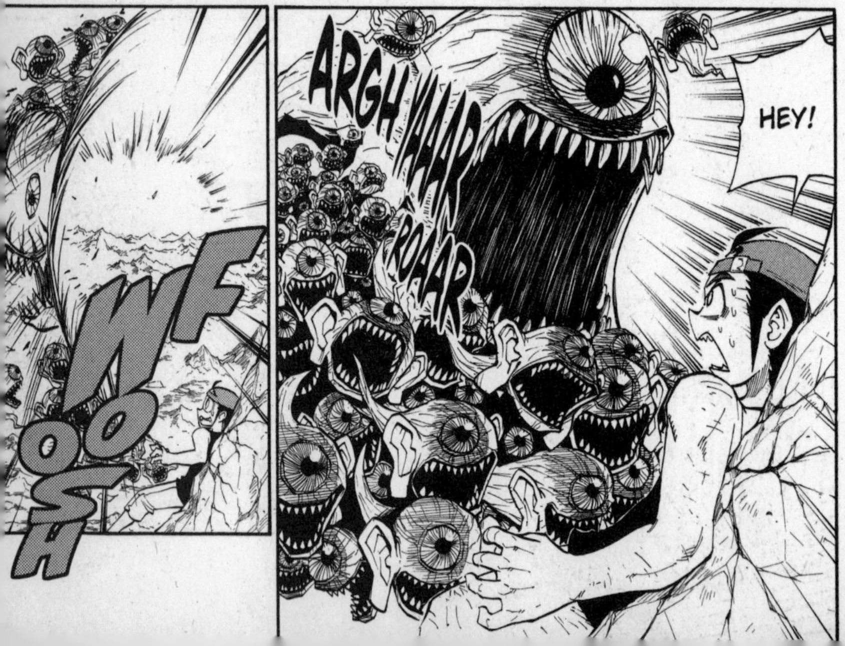
HEY!
ARGH
YAAAR
ROAAR
WHOOSH

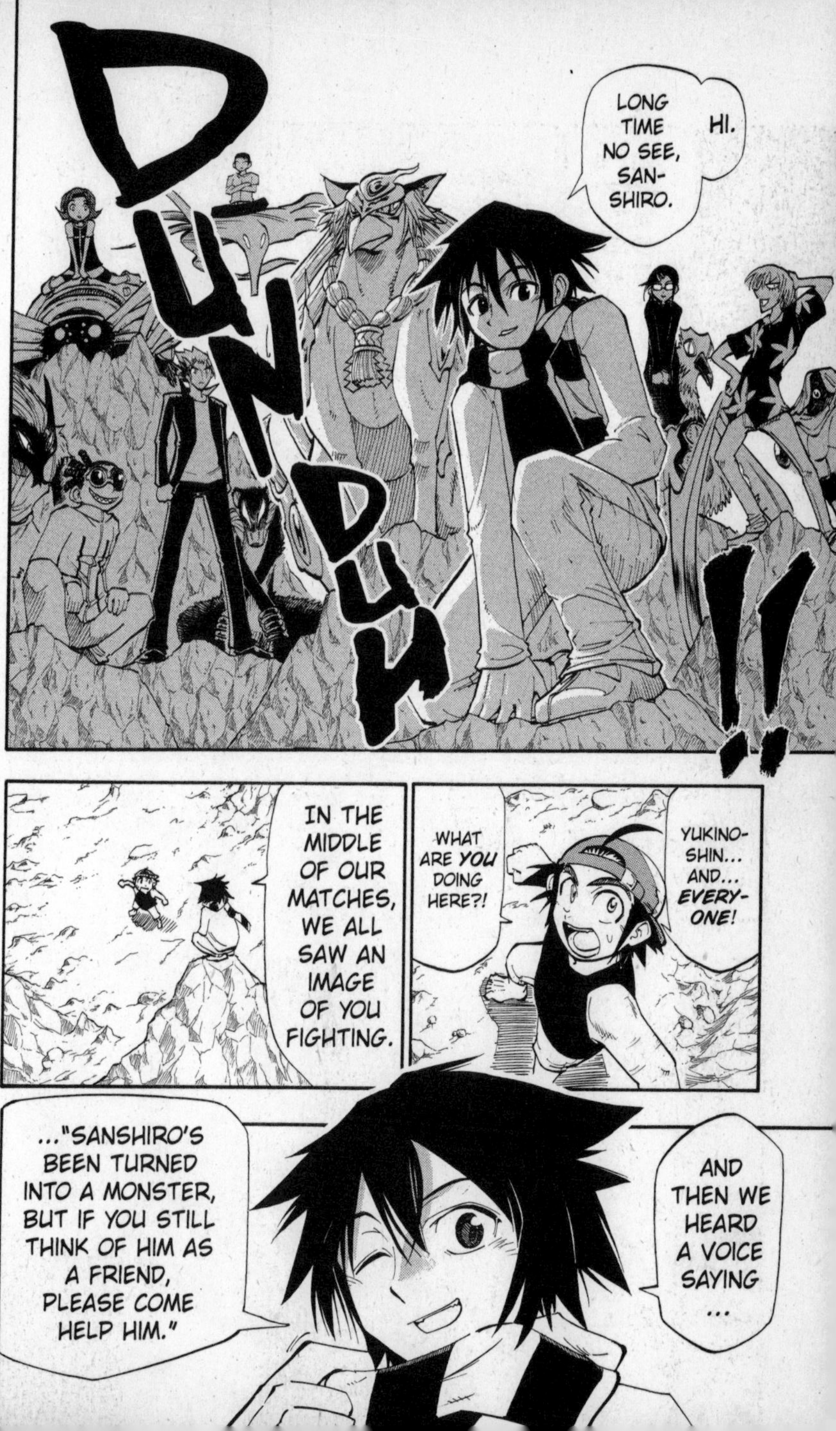
HI.
LONG TIME NO SEE, SAN-SHIRO.
DUNDUH!!
YUKINO-SHIN... AND... EVERY-ONE!
WHAT ARE YOU DOING HERE?!
IN THE MIDDLE OF OUR MATCHES, WE ALL SAW AN IMAGE OF YOU FIGHTING.
AND THEN WE HEARD A VOICE SAYING ...
..."SANSHIRO'S BEEN TURNED INTO A MONSTER, BUT IF YOU STILL THINK OF HIM AS A FRIEND, PLEASE COME HELP HIM."

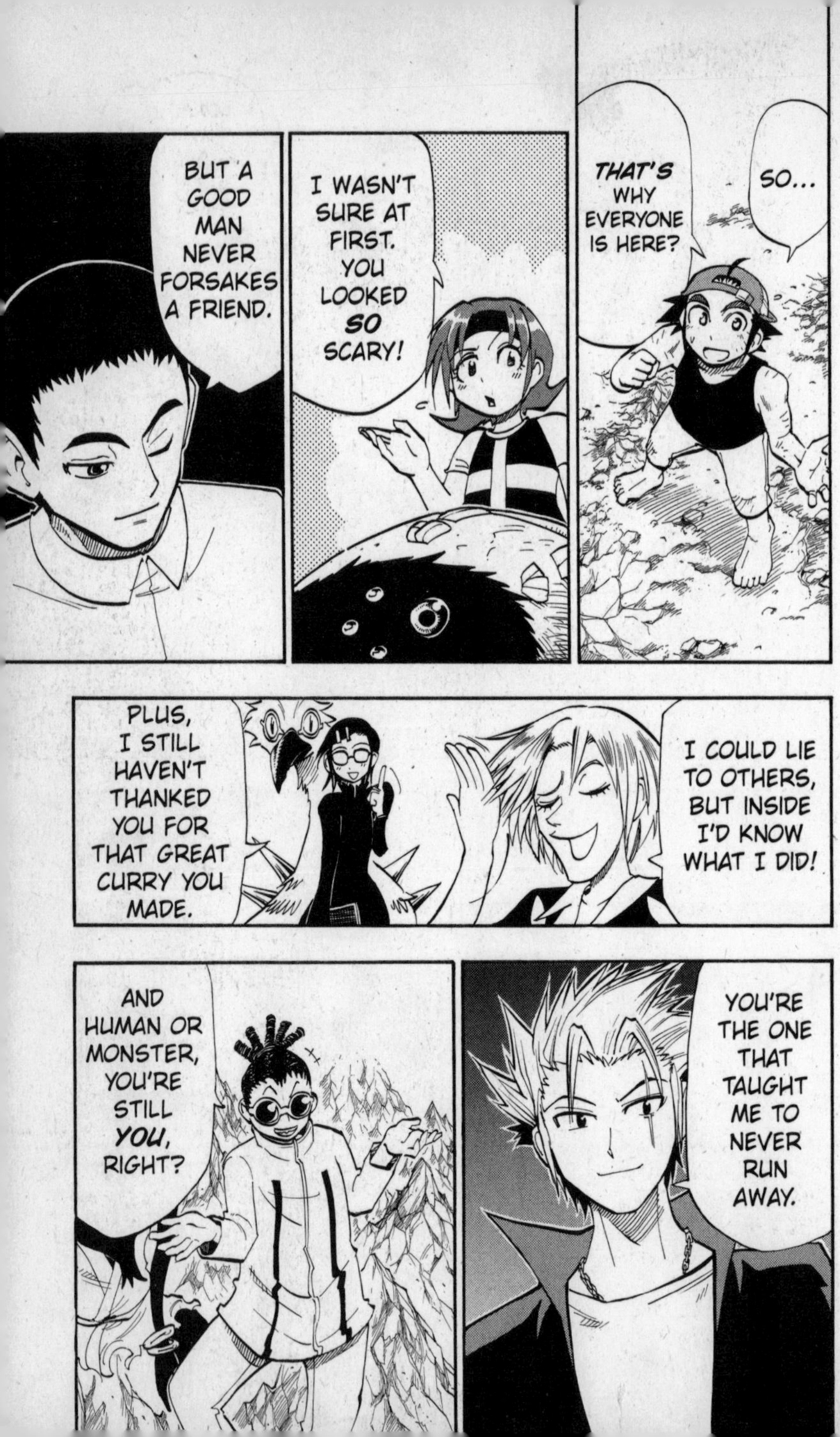
SO...
THAT'S WHY EVERYONE IS HERE?
I WASN'T SURE AT FIRST. YOU LOOKED SO SCARY!
BUT A GOOD MAN NEVER FORSAKES A FRIEND.
I COULD LIE TO OTHERS, BUT INSIDE I'D KNOW WHAT I DID!
PLUS, I STILL HAVEN'T THANKED YOU FOR THAT GREAT CURRY YOU MADE.
YOU'RE THE ONE THAT TAUGHT ME TO NEVER RUN AWAY.
AND HUMAN OR MONSTER, YOU'RE STILL YOU, RIGHT?

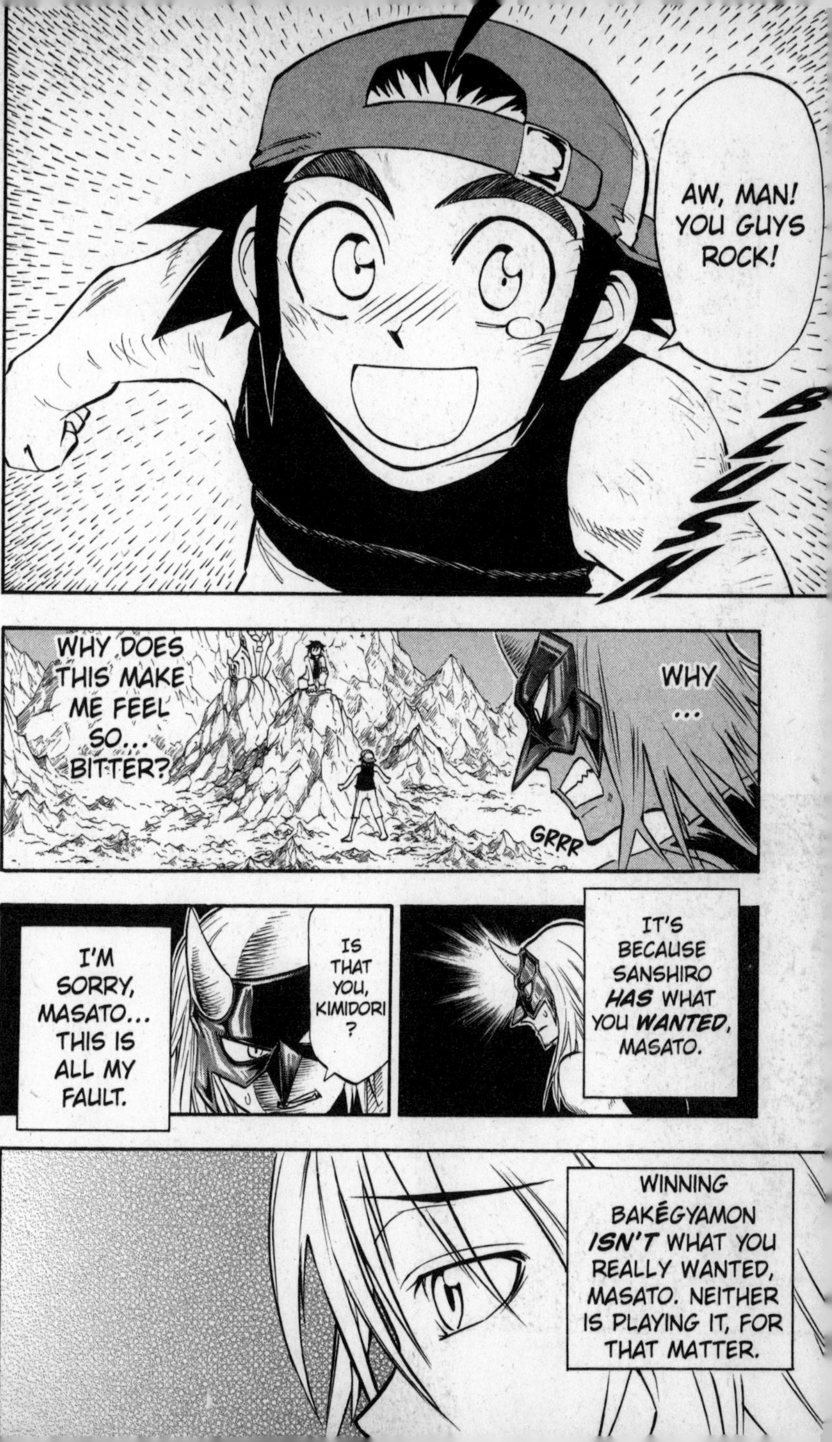
AW, MAN! YOU GUYS ROCK!
BLUSH
WHY ...
GRRR
WHY DOES THIS MAKE ME FEEL SO... BITTER?
IT'S BECAUSE SANSHIRO HAS WHAT YOU WANTED, MASATO.
IS THAT YOU, KIMIDORI ?
I'M SORRY, MASATO... THIS IS ALL MY FAULT.
WINNING BAKÉGYAMON ISN'T WHAT YOU REALLY WANTED, MASATO. NEITHER IS PLAYING IT, FOR THAT MATTER.

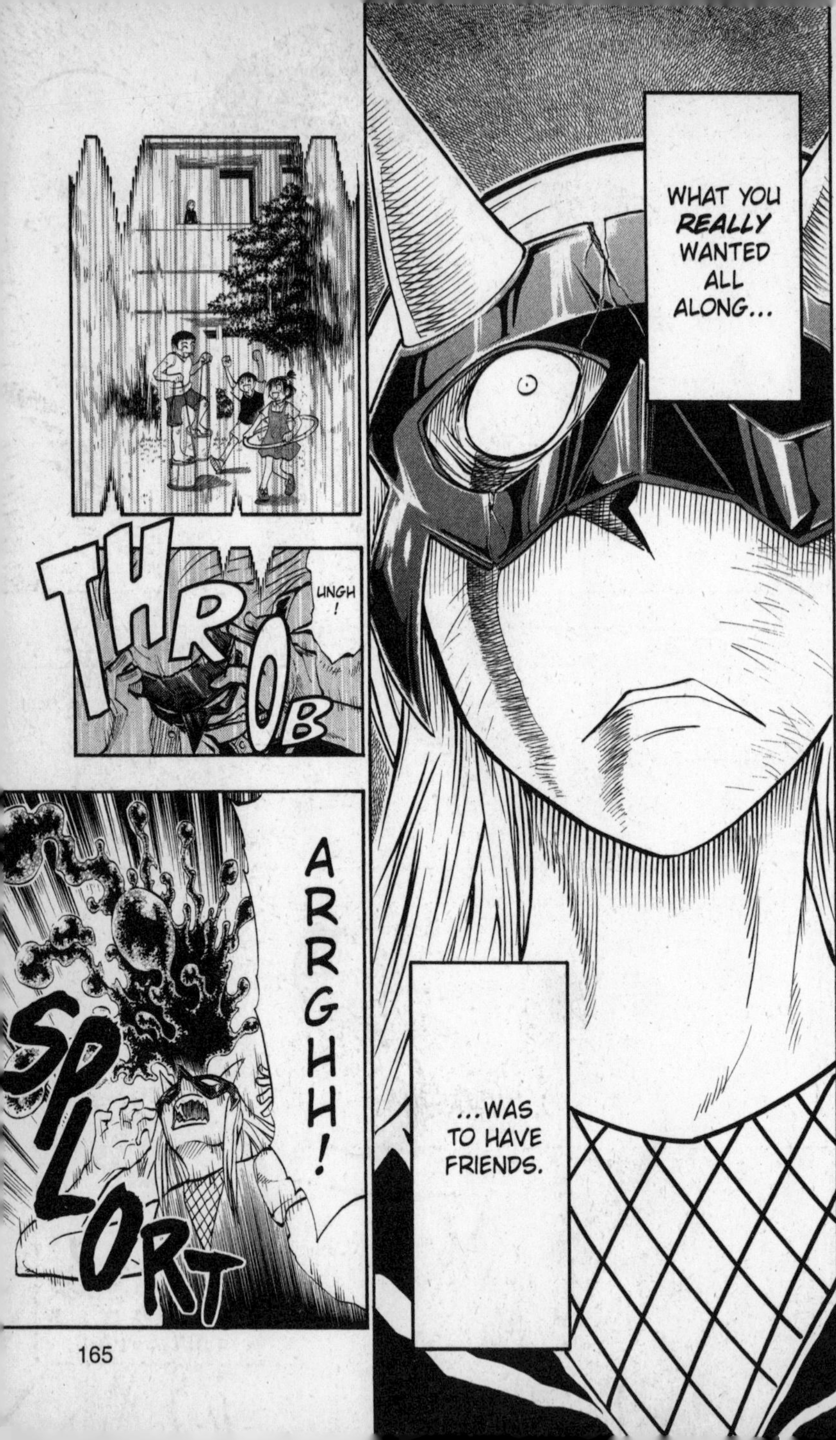
WHAT YOU *REALLY* WANTED ALL ALONG...
...WAS TO HAVE FRIENDS.
THROB
UNGH!
ARRGHH!
SPLORT

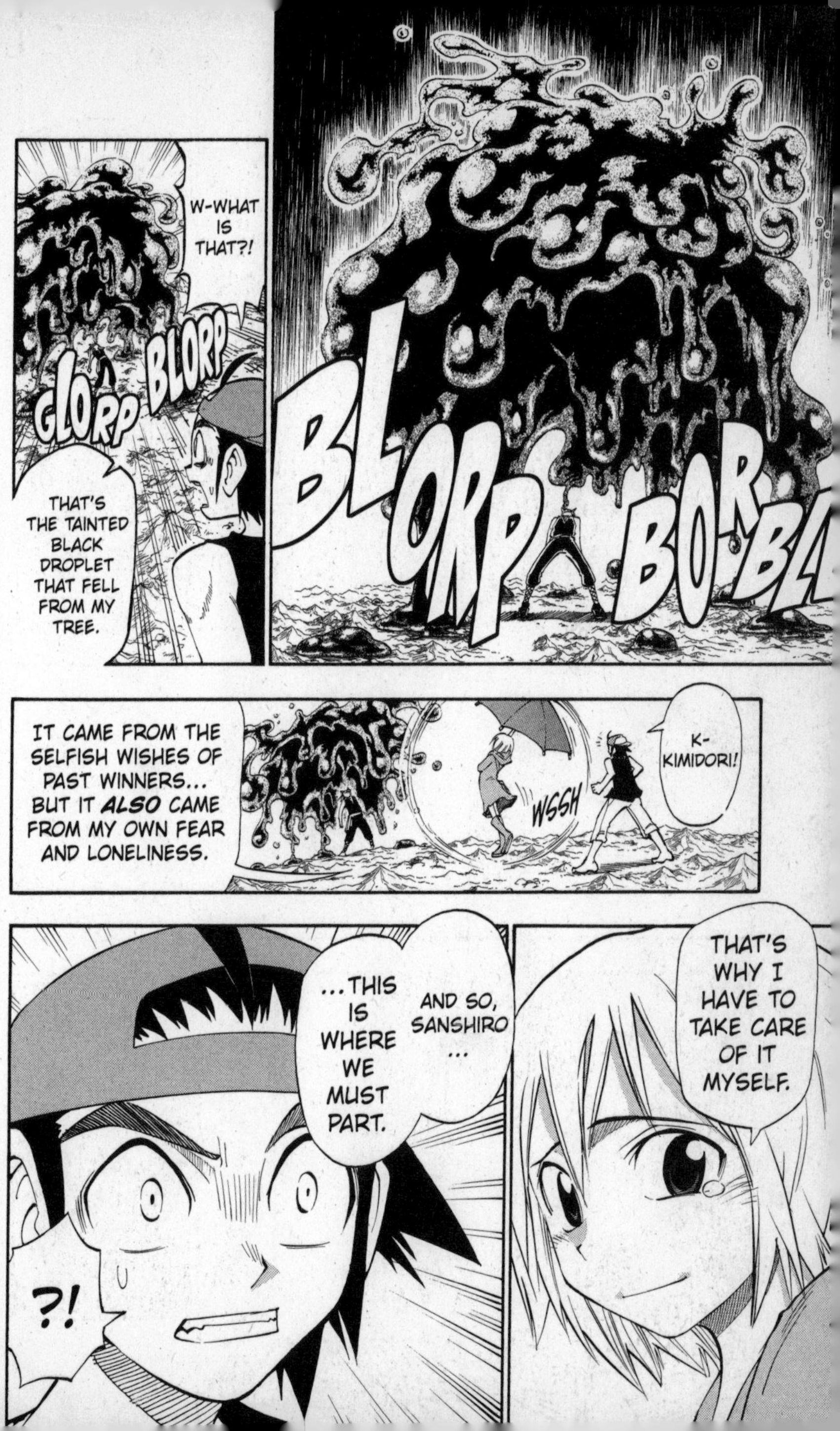
BLORP
BORBL
W-WHAT IS THAT?!
GLORP
BLORP
THAT'S THE TAINTED BLACK DROPLET THAT FELL FROM MY TREE.
K-KIMIDORI!
WSSH
IT CAME FROM THE SELFISH WISHES OF PAST WINNERS... BUT IT *ALSO* CAME FROM MY OWN FEAR AND LONELINESS.
THAT'S WHY I HAVE TO TAKE CARE OF IT MYSELF.
AND SO, SANSHIRO...
...THIS IS WHERE WE MUST PART.
?!

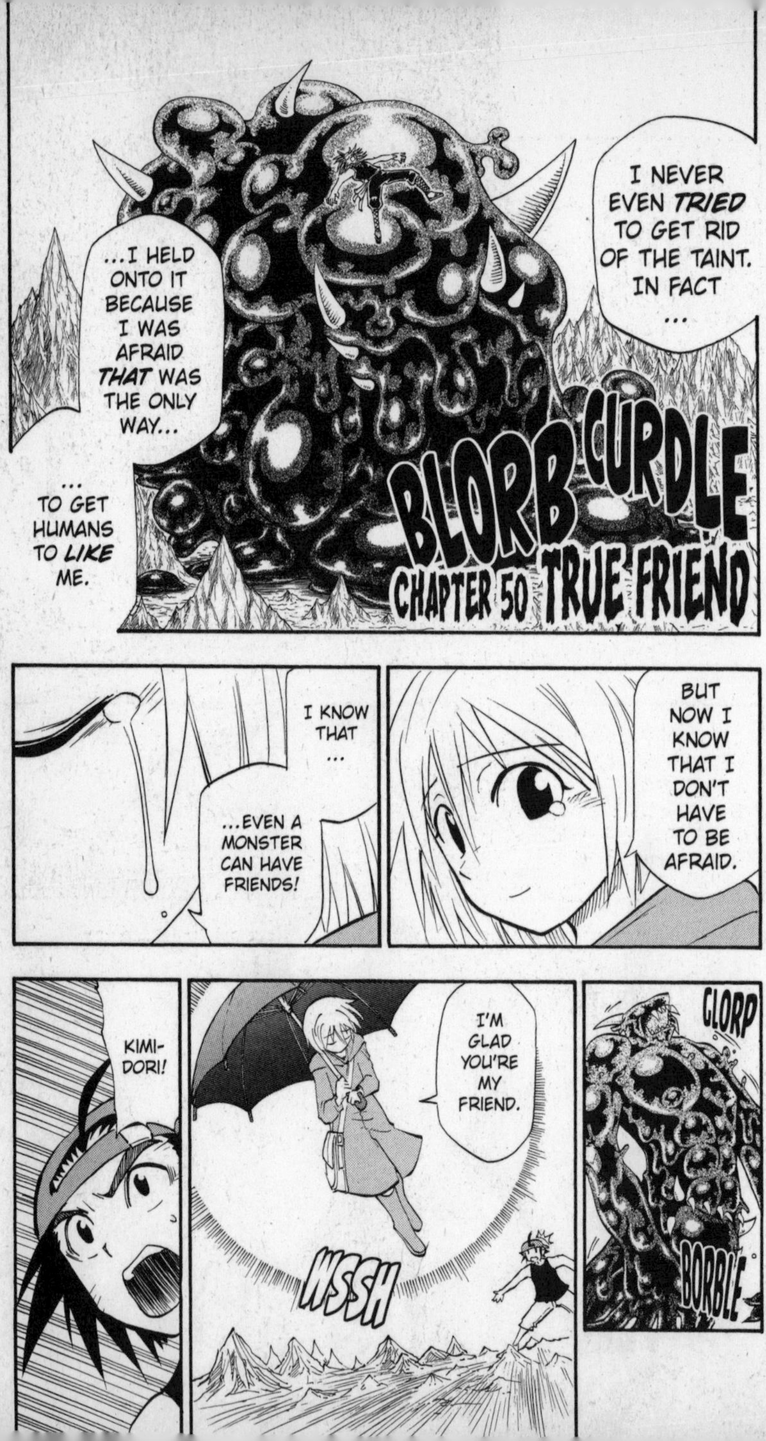
I NEVER EVEN *TRIED* TO GET RID OF THE TAINT. IN FACT ...
...I HELD ONTO IT BECAUSE I WAS AFRAID *THAT* WAS THE ONLY WAY...
... TO GET HUMANS TO *LIKE* ME.
BLORB CURDLE
CHAPTER 50 TRUE FRIEND
BUT NOW I KNOW THAT I DON'T HAVE TO BE AFRAID.
I KNOW THAT ...
...EVEN A MONSTER CAN HAVE FRIENDS!
GLORP
BORBLE
I'M GLAD YOU'RE MY FRIEND.
WSSH
KIMI-DORI!

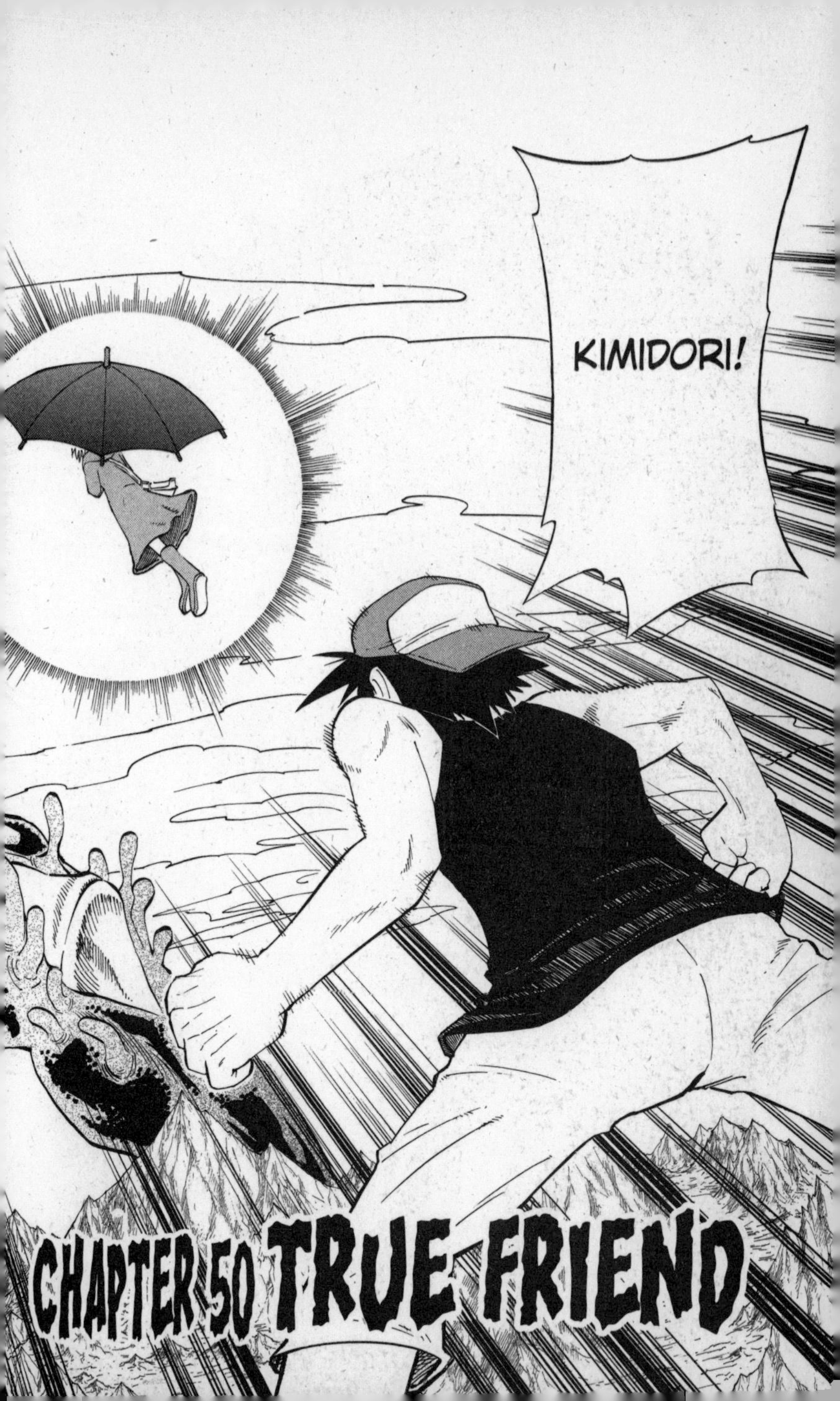
KIMIDORI!
CHAPTER 50 TRUE FRIEND

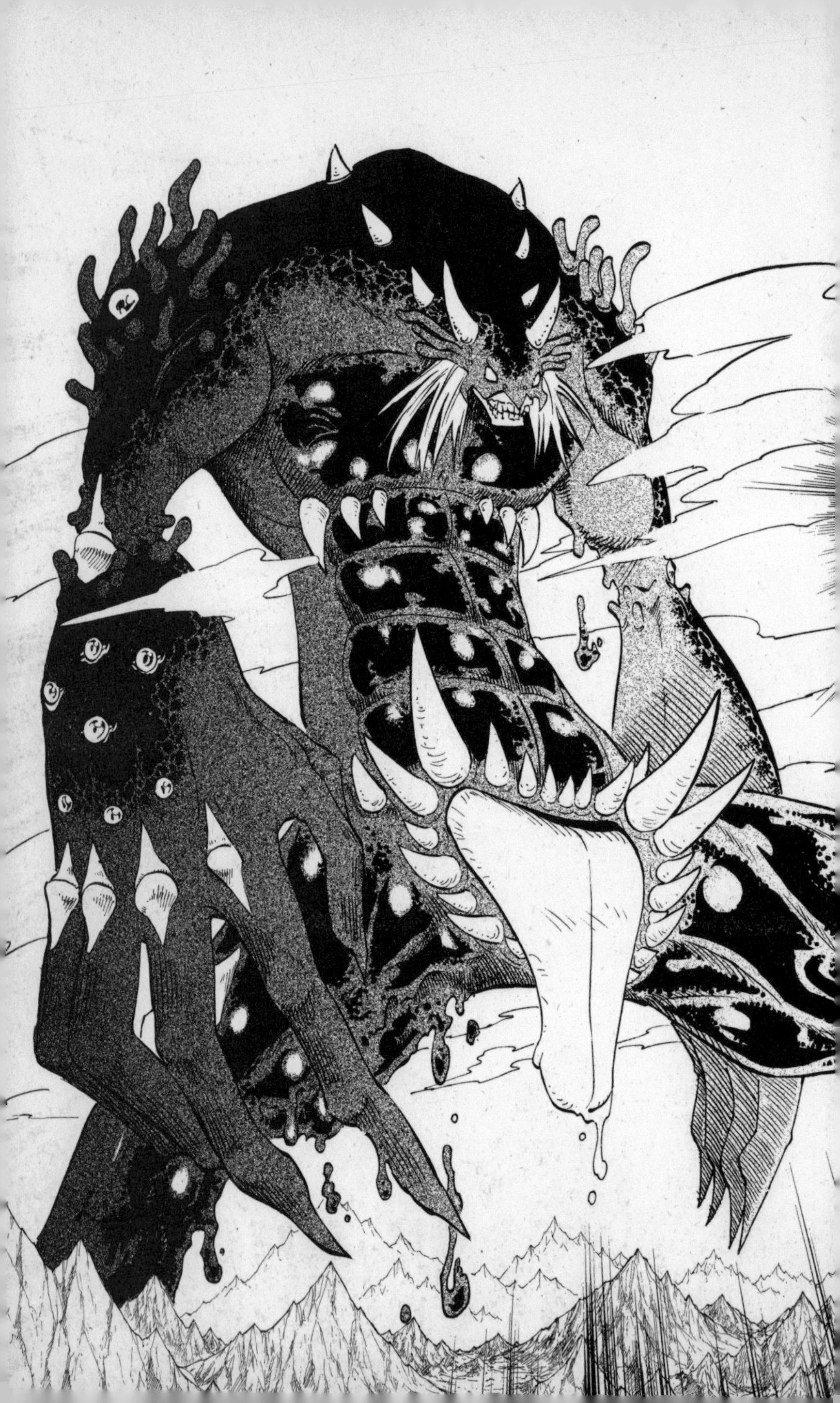

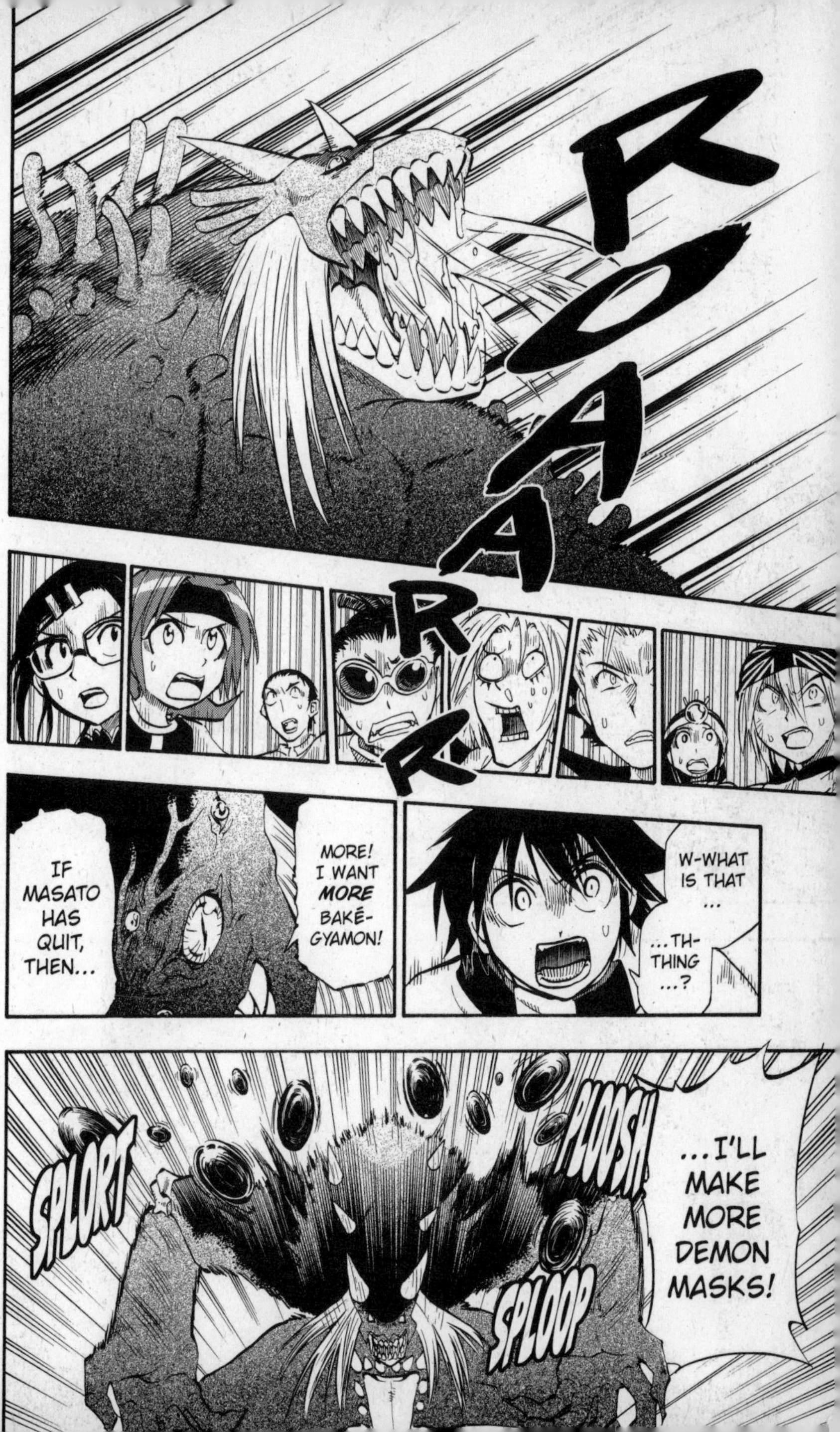
RROAAARR
W-WHAT IS THAT ...
...TH-THING ...?
MORE! I WANT MORE BAKÉ-GYAMON!
IF MASATO HAS QUIT, THEN...
...I'LL MAKE MORE DEMON MASKS!
PLOOSH
SPLORT
SPLOOP

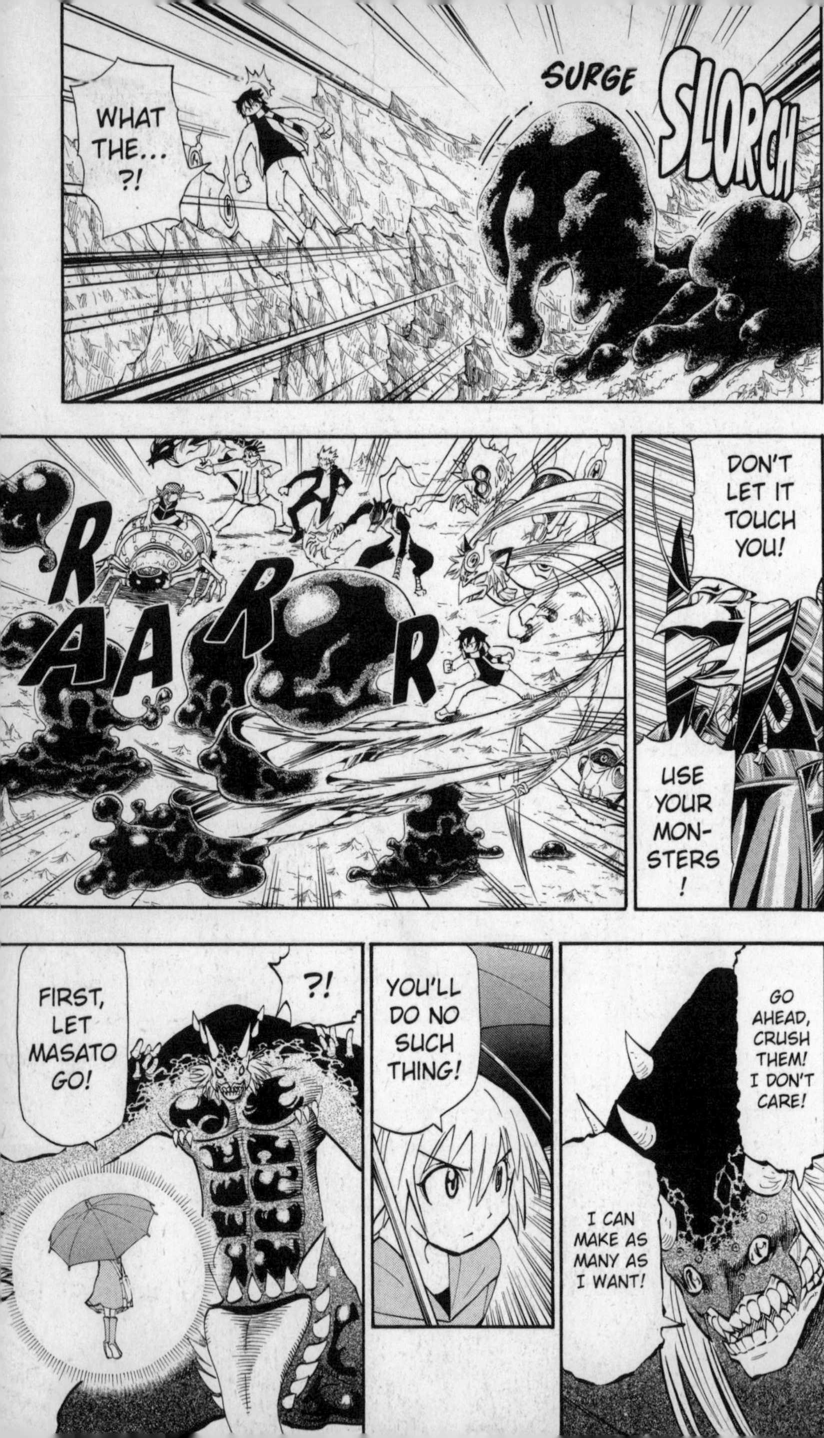
SLORCH
SURGE
WHAT THE... ?!
DON'T LET IT TOUCH YOU!
USE YOUR MON-STERS!
RAAARR
GO AHEAD, CRUSH THEM! I DON'T CARE!
I CAN MAKE AS MANY AS I WANT!
YOU'LL DO NO SUCH THING!
?!
FIRST, LET MASATO GO!

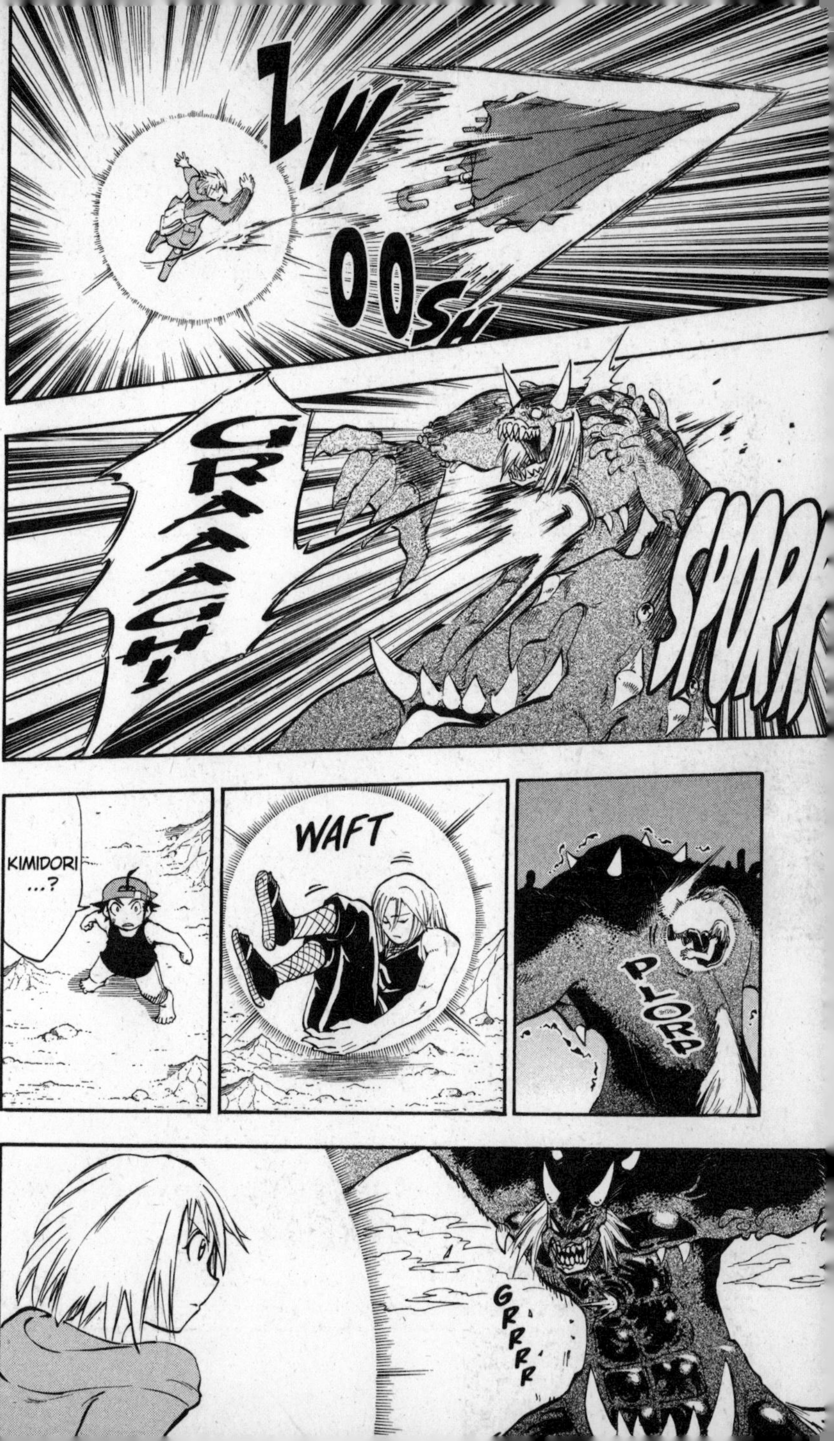
ZWOOSH
GRAAACH!!
SPORK
PLORP
WAFT
KIMIDORI ...?
GRRR

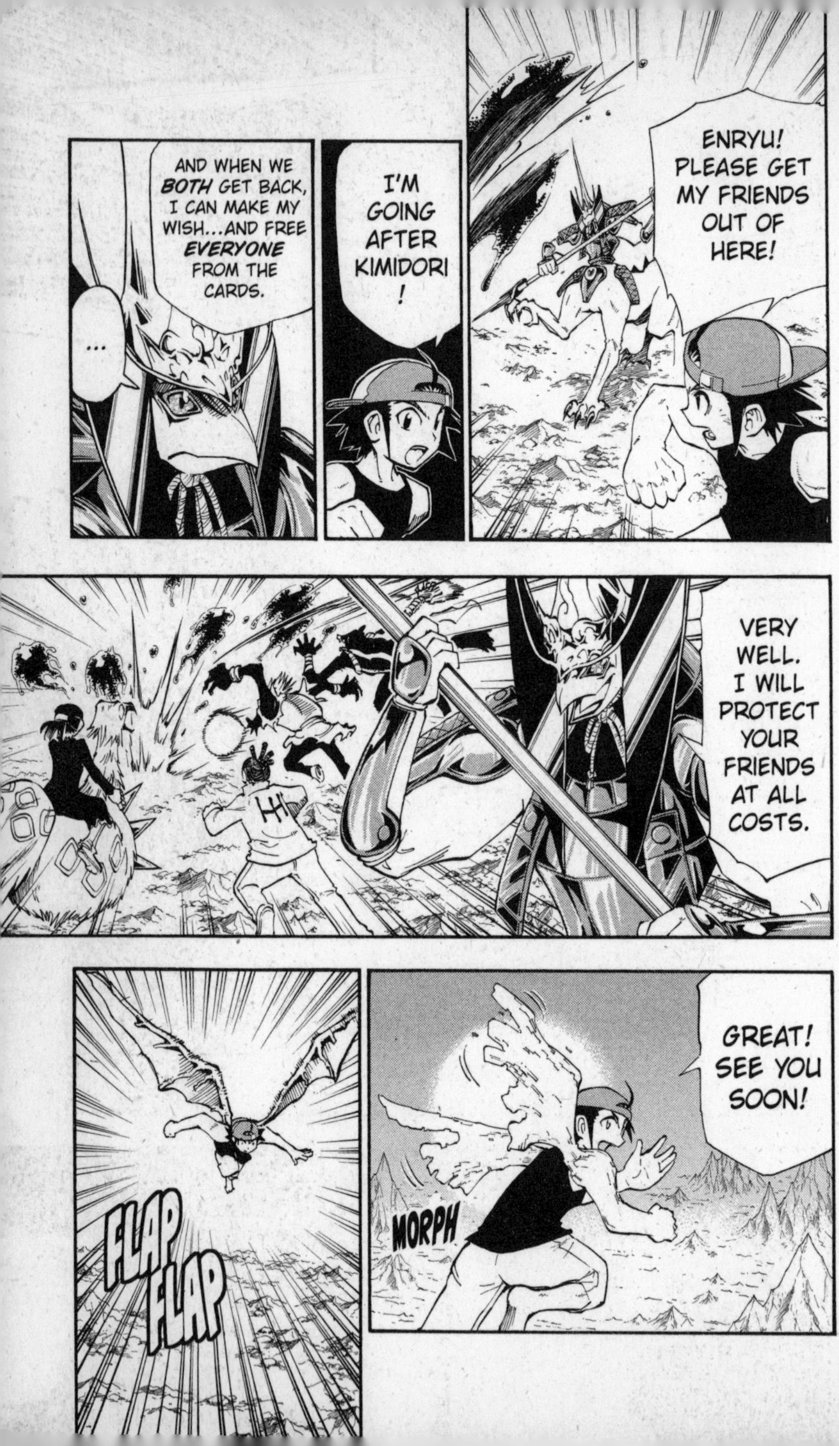
ENRYU! PLEASE GET MY FRIENDS OUT OF HERE!
I'M GOING AFTER KIMIDORI!
AND WHEN WE BOTH GET BACK, I CAN MAKE MY WISH...AND FREE EVERYONE FROM THE CARDS.
...
VERY WELL. I WILL PROTECT YOUR FRIENDS AT ALL COSTS.
GREAT! SEE YOU SOON!
MORPH
FLAP FLAP

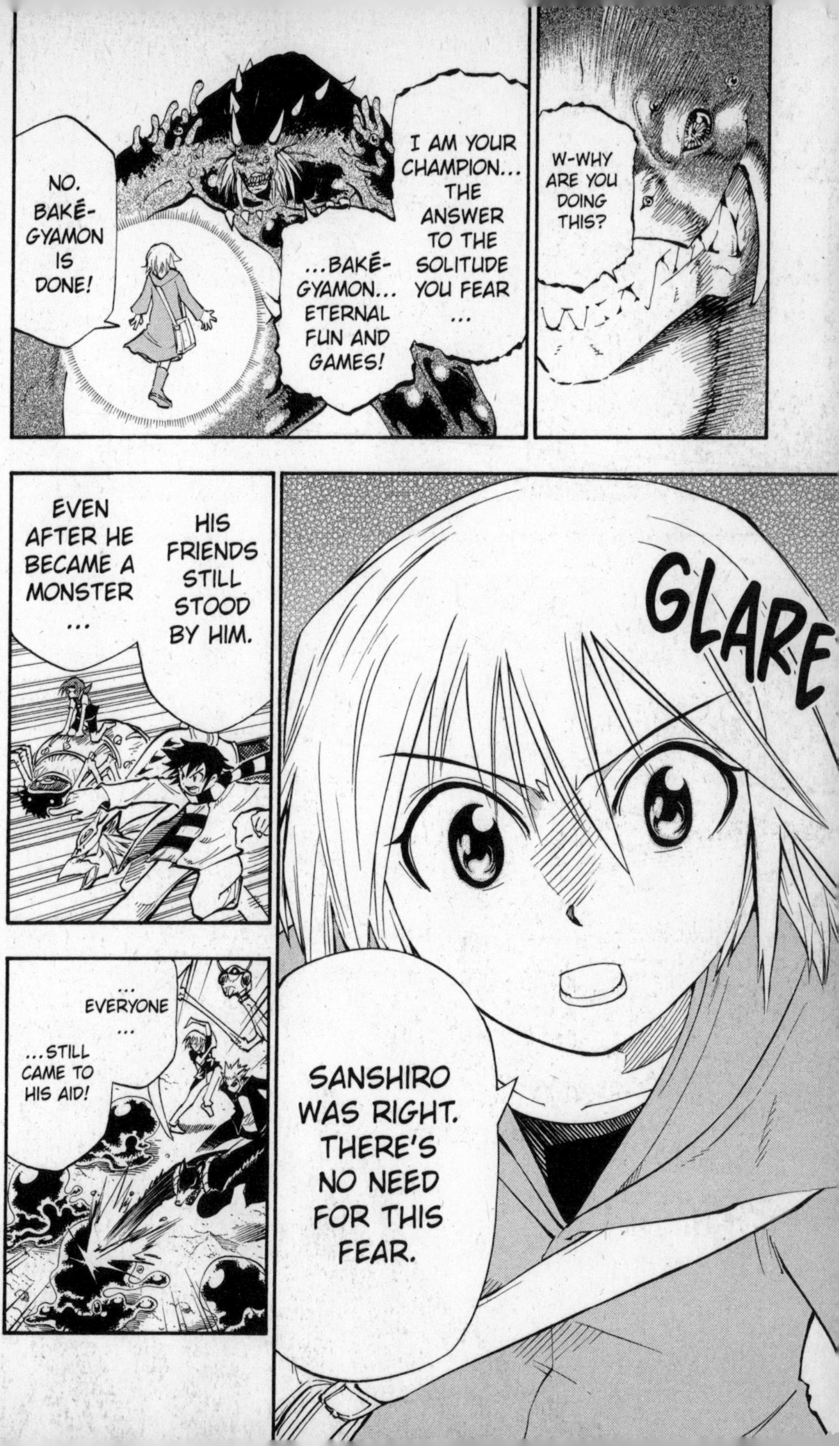
W-WHY ARE YOU DOING THIS?
I AM YOUR CHAMPION... THE ANSWER TO THE SOLITUDE YOU FEAR ...
...BAKÉ-GYAMON... ETERNAL FUN AND GAMES!
NO. BAKÉ-GYAMON IS DONE!
GLARE
HIS FRIENDS STILL STOOD BY HIM.
EVEN AFTER HE BECAME A MONSTER ...
... EVERYONE ...
...STILL CAME TO HIS AID!
SANSHIRO WAS RIGHT. THERE'S NO NEED FOR THIS FEAR.

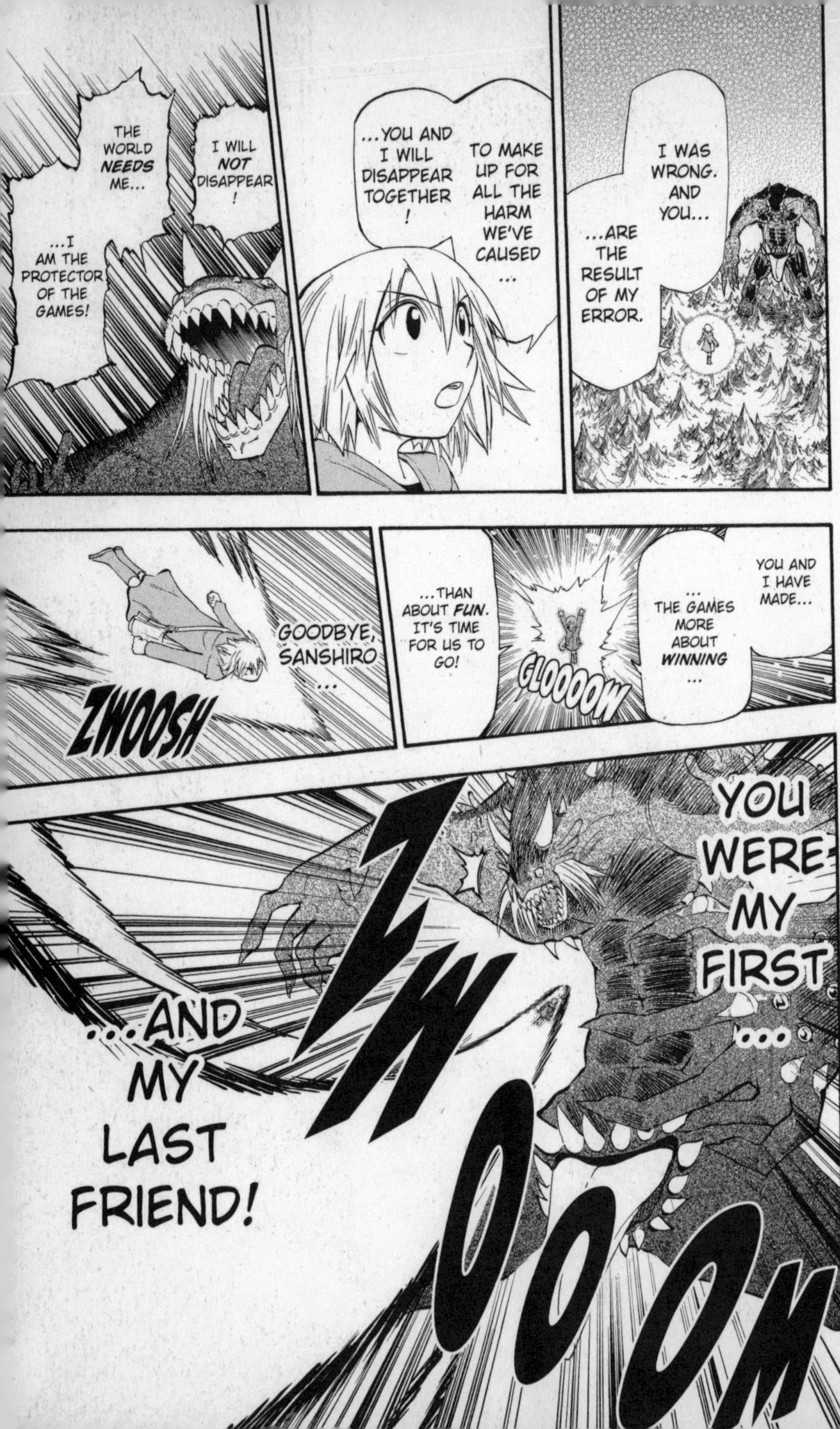
I WAS WRONG. AND YOU...
...ARE THE RESULT OF MY ERROR.
TO MAKE UP FOR ALL THE HARM WE'VE CAUSED...
...YOU AND I WILL DISAPPEAR TOGETHER!
I WILL NOT DISAPPEAR!
THE WORLD NEEDS ME...
...I AM THE PROTECTOR OF THE GAMES!
YOU AND I HAVE MADE...
...THE GAMES MORE ABOUT WINNING...
...THAN ABOUT FUN. IT'S TIME FOR US TO GO!
GLOOOOW
GOODBYE, SANSHIRO...
ZWOOSH
YOU WERE MY FIRST...
...AND MY LAST FRIEND!
ZWOOOOM

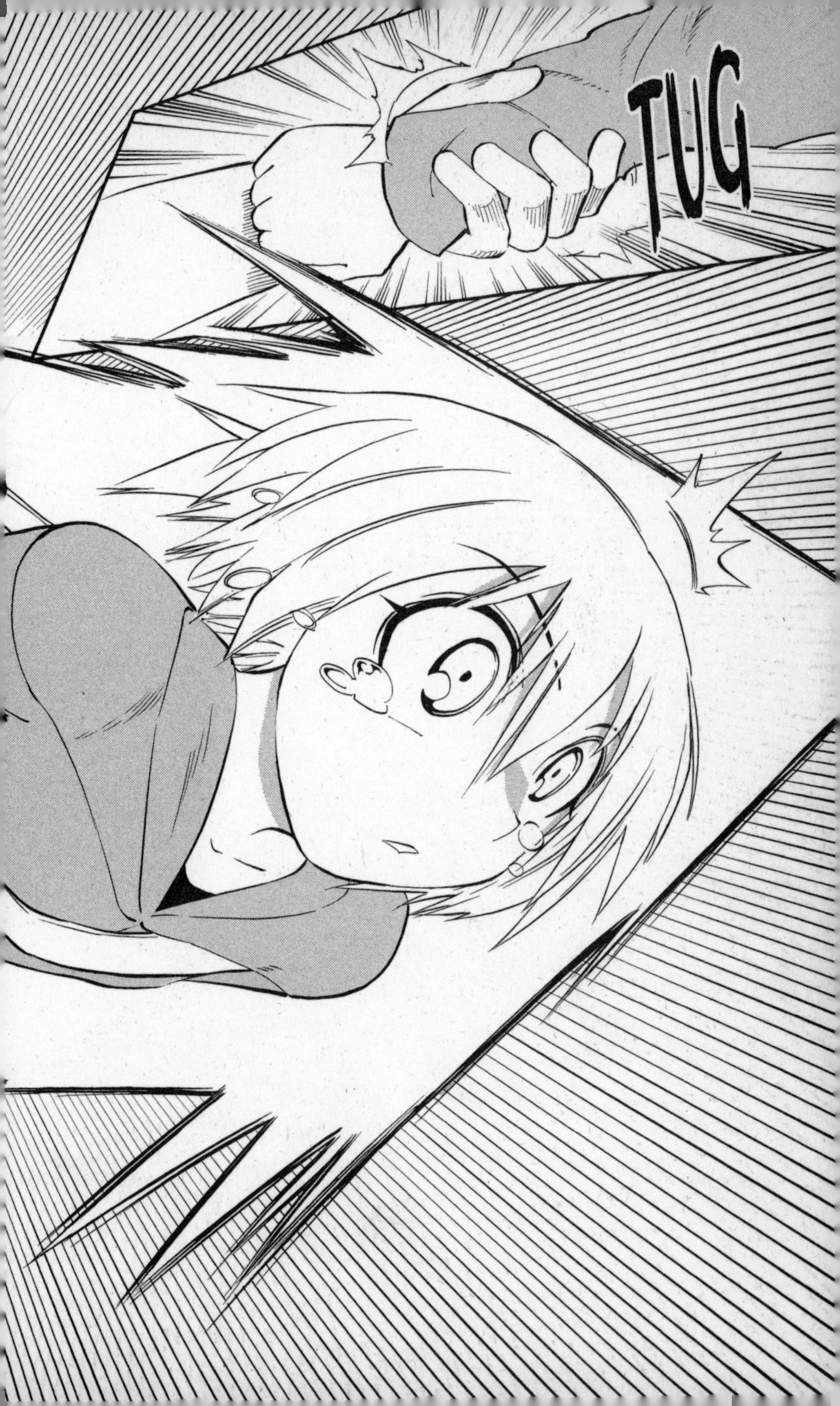
TUG

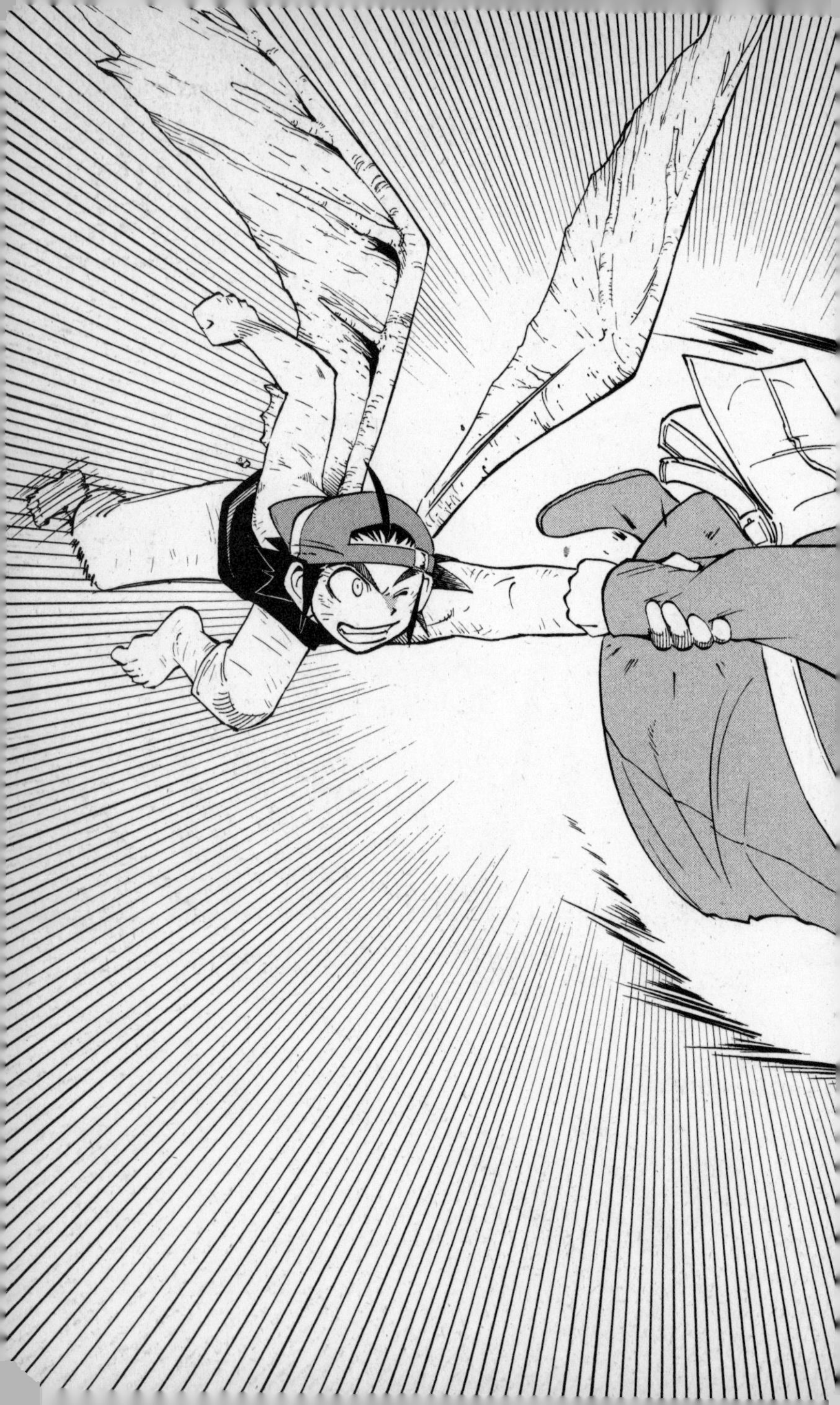

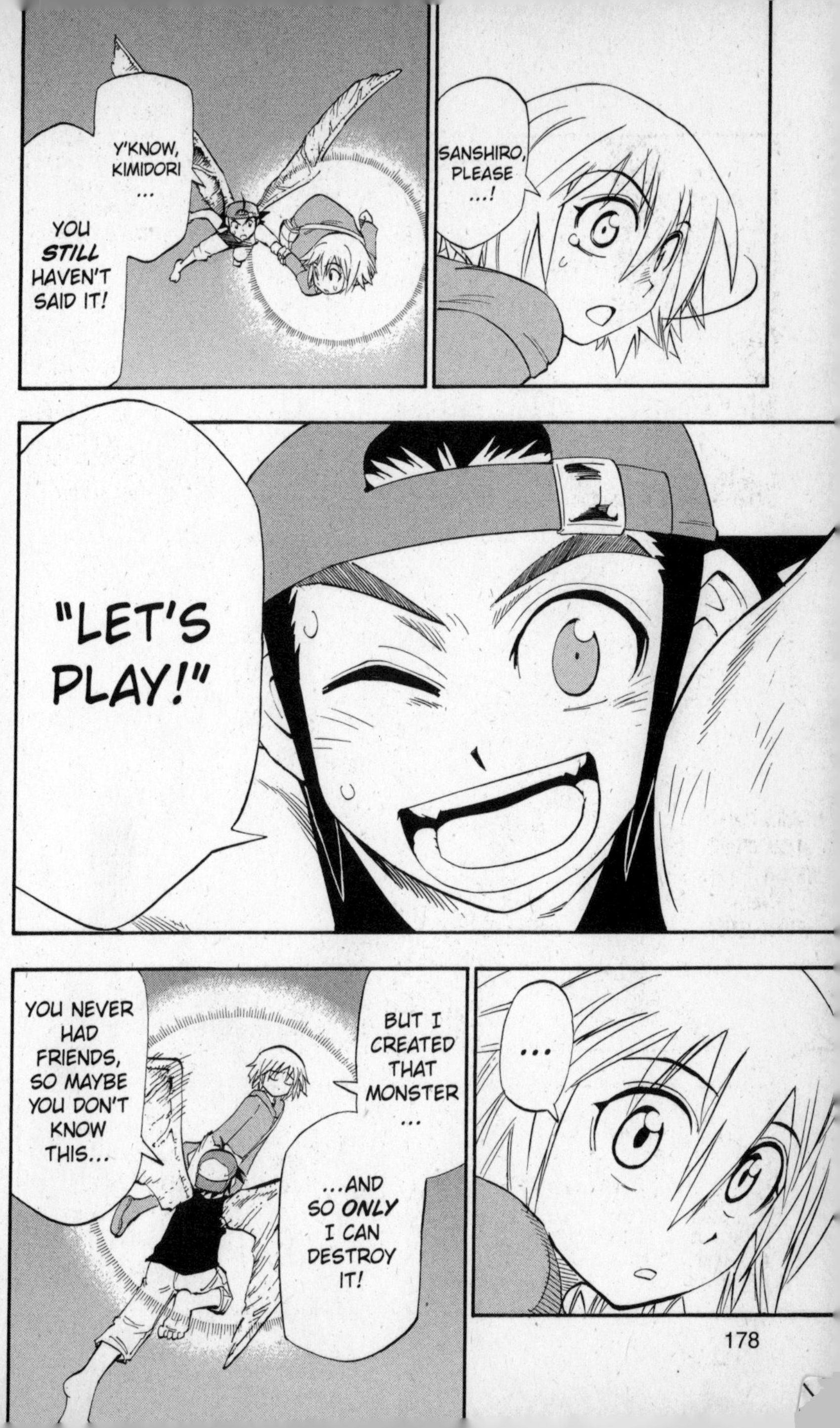
SANSHIRO, PLEASE ...!
Y'KNOW, KIMIDORI ...
YOU **STILL** HAVEN'T SAID IT!
"LET'S PLAY!"
...
YOU NEVER HAD FRIENDS, SO MAYBE YOU DON'T KNOW THIS...
BUT I CREATED THAT MONSTER ...
...AND SO **ONLY** I CAN DESTROY IT!

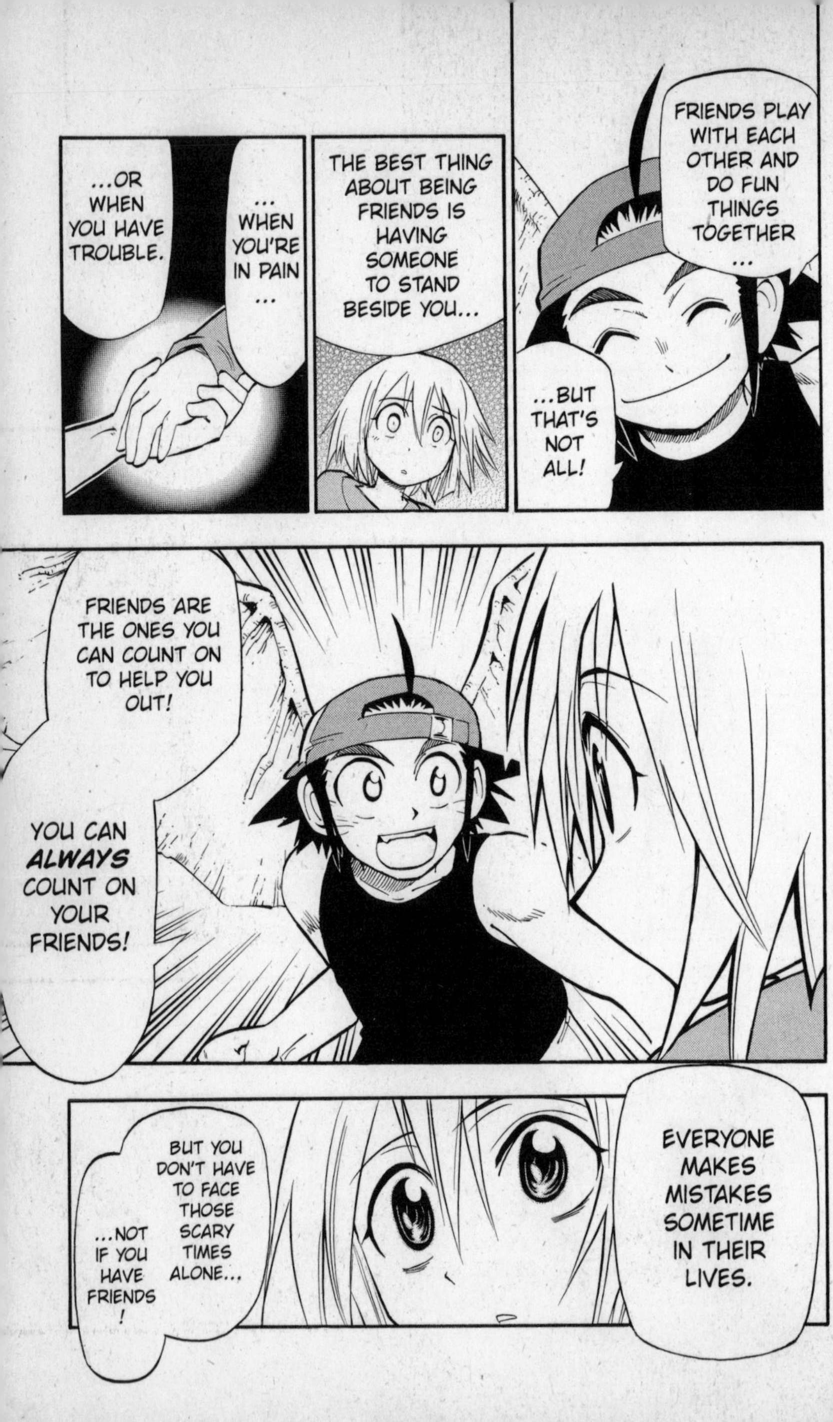
FRIENDS PLAY WITH EACH OTHER AND DO FUN THINGS TOGETHER ...
...BUT THAT'S NOT ALL!
THE BEST THING ABOUT BEING FRIENDS IS HAVING SOMEONE TO STAND BESIDE YOU...
... WHEN YOU'RE IN PAIN ...
...OR WHEN YOU HAVE TROUBLE.
FRIENDS ARE THE ONES YOU CAN COUNT ON TO HELP YOU OUT!
YOU CAN *ALWAYS* COUNT ON YOUR FRIENDS!
EVERYONE MAKES MISTAKES SOMETIME IN THEIR LIVES.
BUT YOU DON'T HAVE TO FACE THOSE SCARY TIMES ALONE...
...NOT IF YOU HAVE FRIENDS!

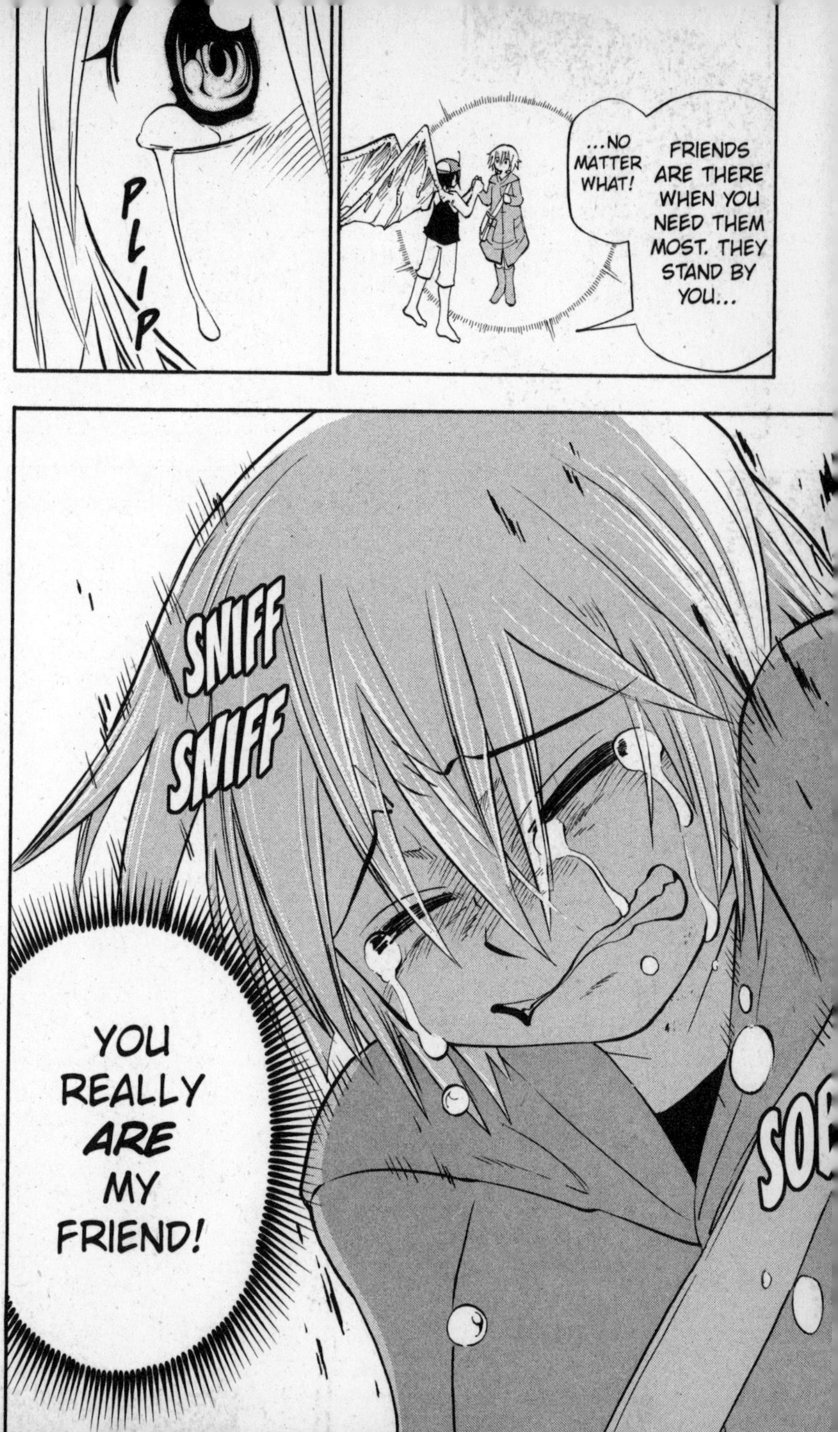
FRIENDS ARE THERE WHEN YOU NEED THEM MOST. THEY STAND BY YOU...
...NO MATTER WHAT!
PLIP
SNIFF SNIFF
YOU REALLY ARE MY FRIEND!

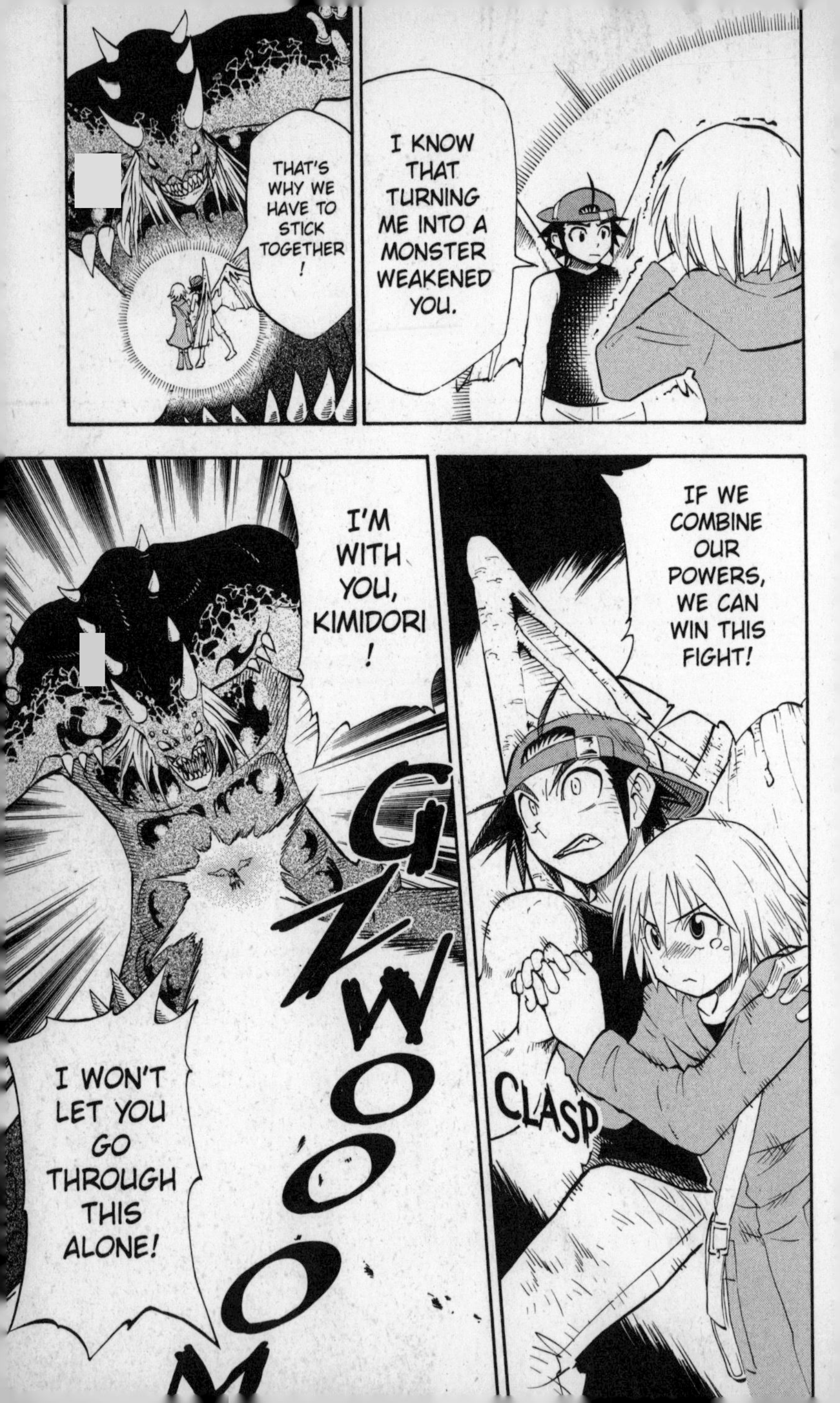
I KNOW THAT TURNING ME INTO A MONSTER WEAKENED YOU.
THAT'S WHY WE HAVE TO STICK TOGETHER!
IF WE COMBINE OUR POWERS, WE CAN WIN THIS FIGHT!
CLASP
I'M WITH YOU, KIMIDORI!
I WON'T LET YOU GO THROUGH THIS ALONE!

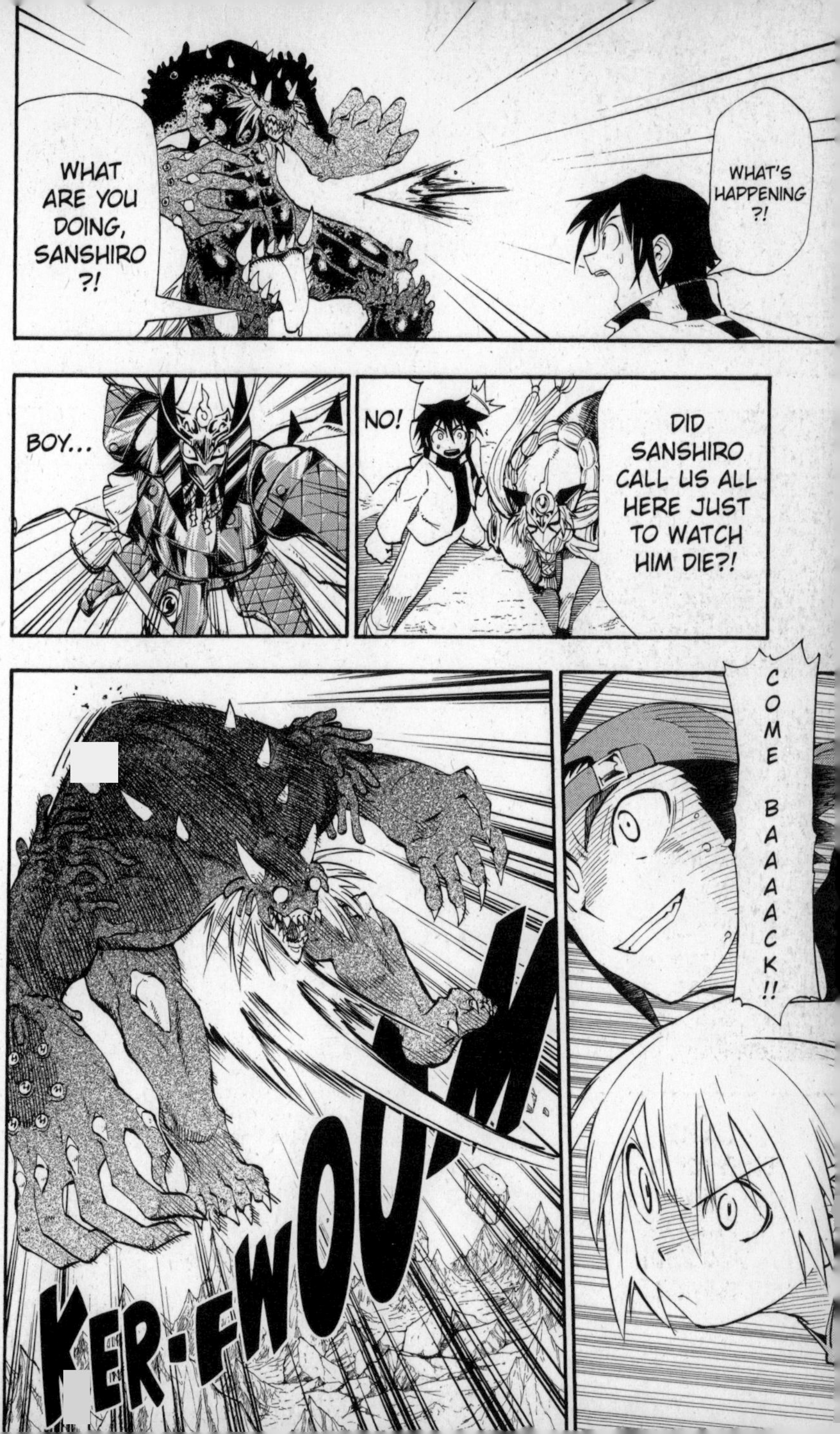
WHAT'S HAPPENING ?!
WHAT ARE YOU DOING, SANSHIRO ?!
DID SANSHIRO CALL US ALL HERE JUST TO WATCH HIM DIE?!
NO!
BOY...
COME BAAAACK!!
KER-FWOOM

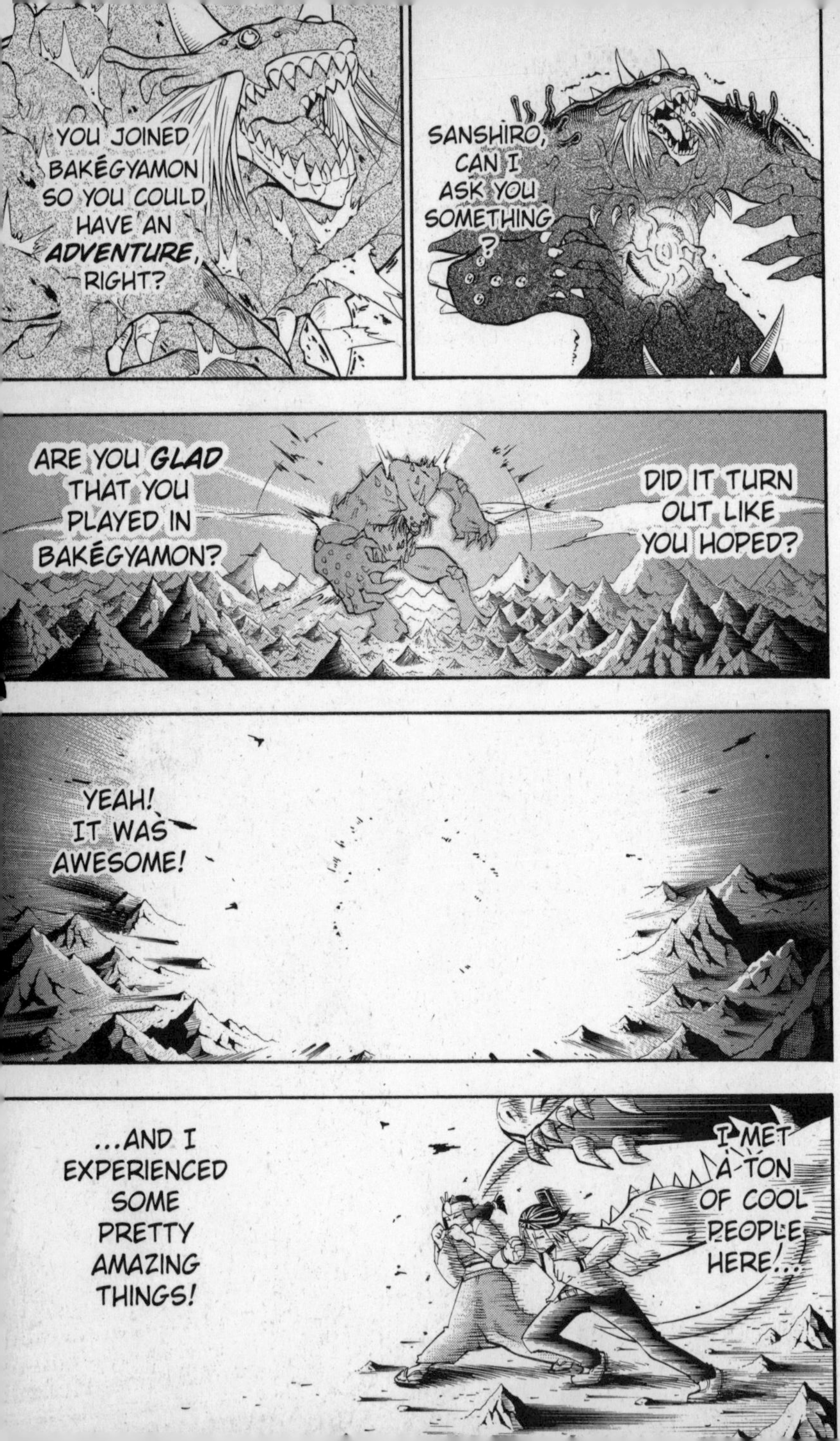
SANSHIRO, CAN I ASK YOU SOMETHING?
YOU JOINED BAKÉGYAMON SO YOU COULD HAVE AN ADVENTURE, RIGHT?
DID IT TURN OUT LIKE YOU HOPED?
ARE YOU GLAD THAT YOU PLAYED IN BAKÉGYAMON?
YEAH! IT WAS AWESOME!
I MET A TON OF COOL PEOPLE HERE!...
...AND I EXPERIENCED SOME PRETTY AMAZING THINGS!

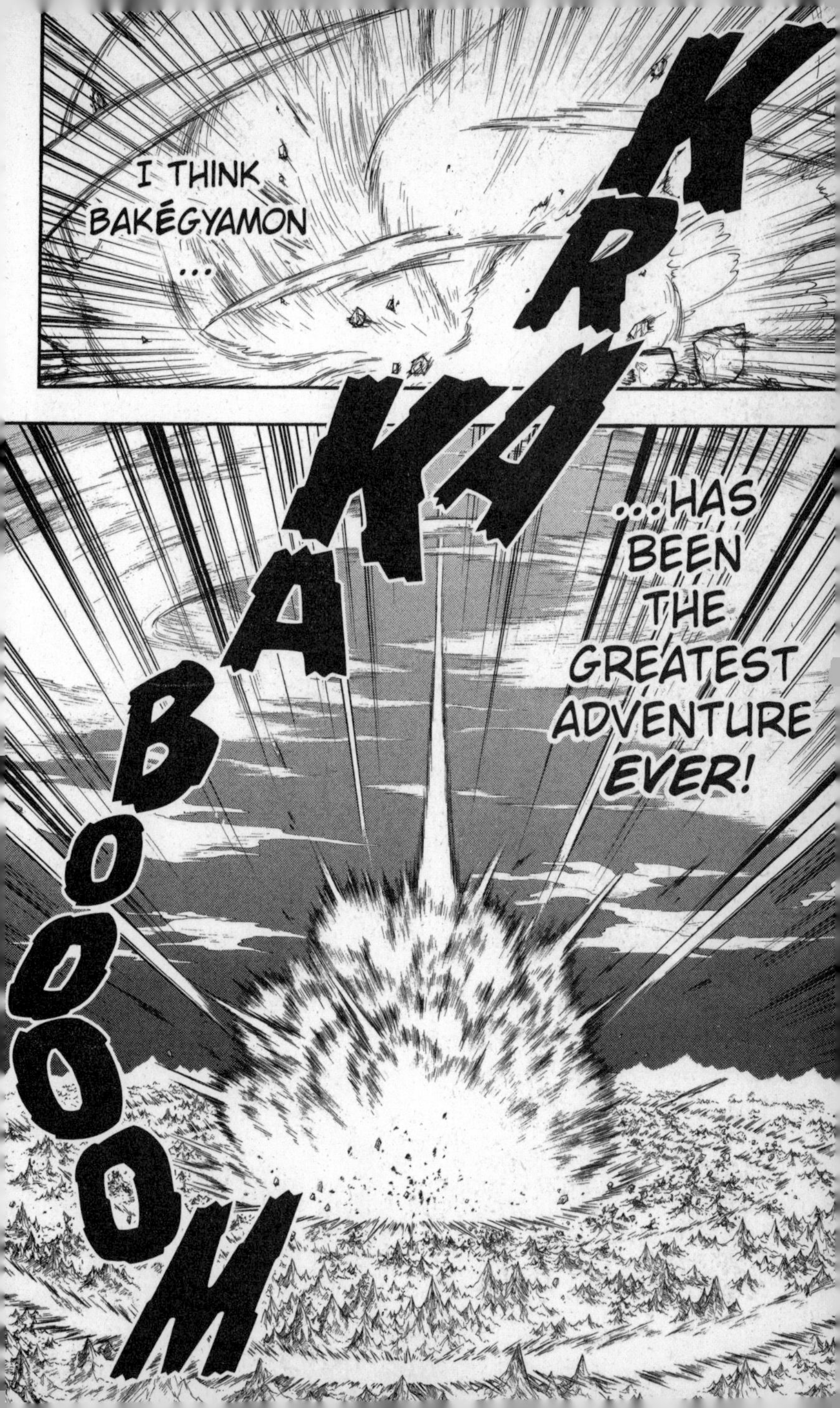
I THINK BAKÉGYAMON ...
KRAKABOOOOM
...HAS BEEN THE GREATEST ADVENTURE EVER!

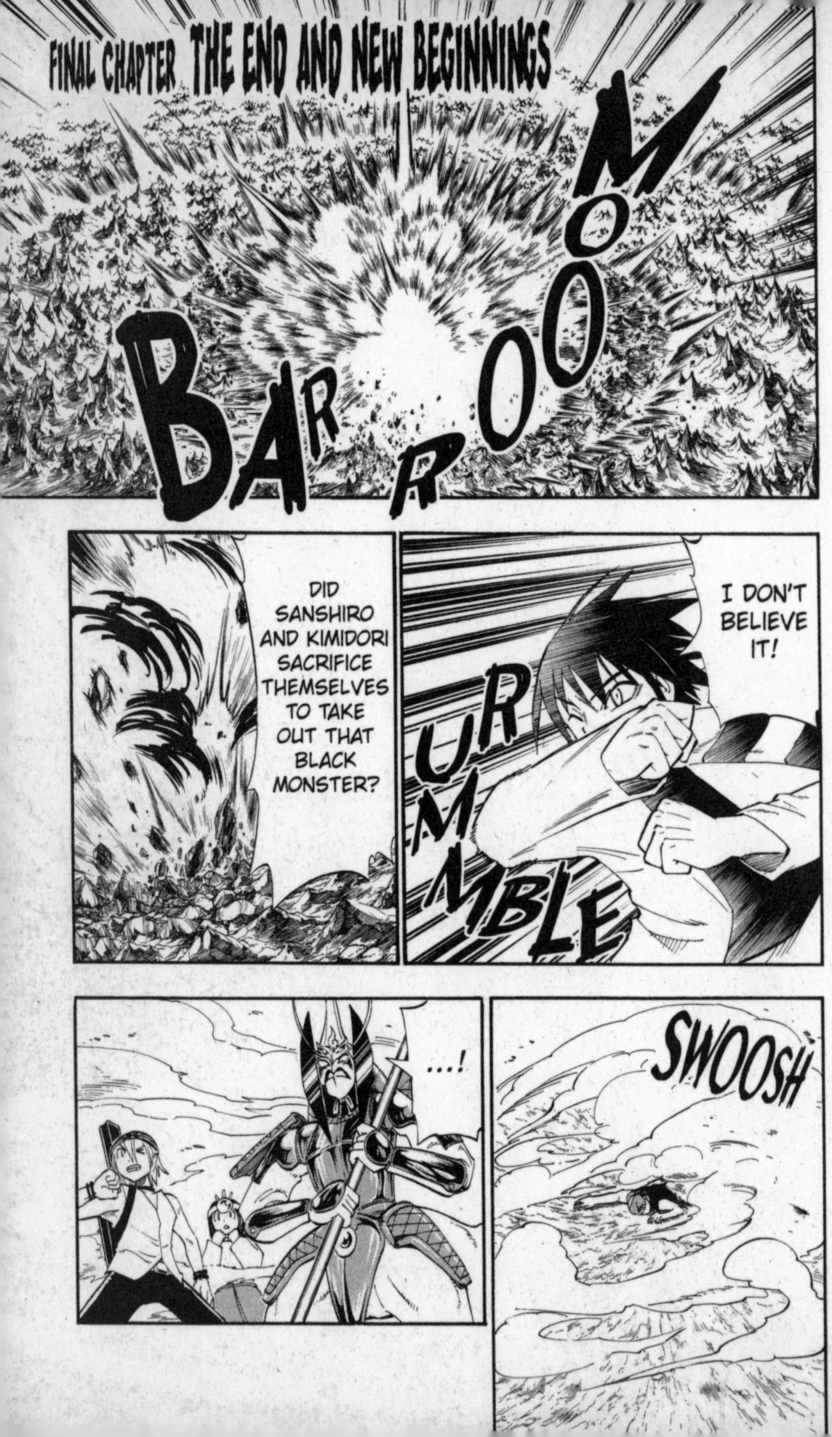
FINAL CHAPTER THE END AND NEW BEGINNINGS
BARROOOOM
I DON'T BELIEVE IT!
RUMMBLE
DID SANSHIRO AND KIMIDORI SACRIFICE THEMSELVES TO TAKE OUT THAT BLACK MONSTER?
SWOOSH
...!

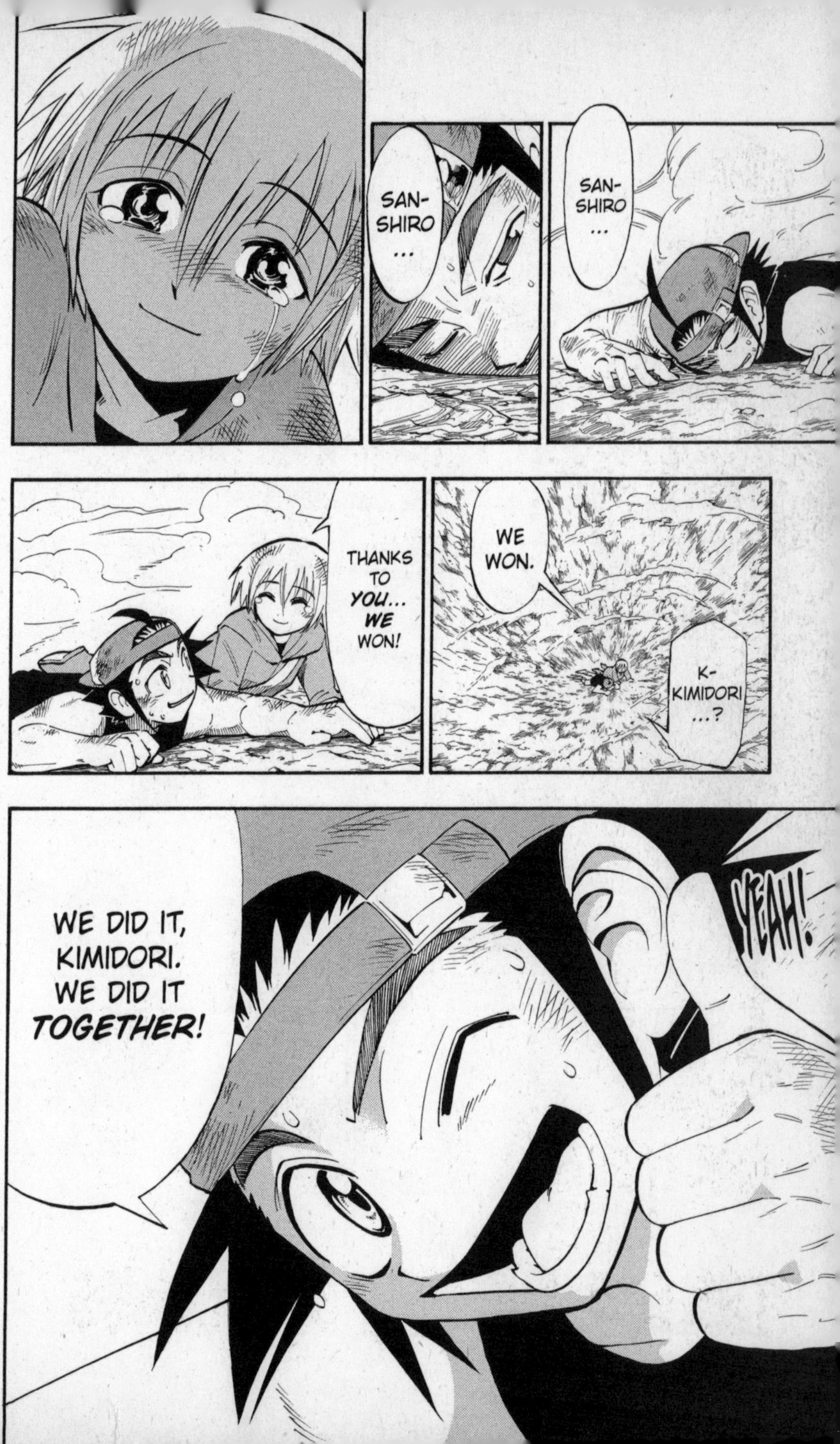
SAN-SHIRO ...
SAN-SHIRO ...
WE WON.
K-KIMIDORI ...?
THANKS TO *YOU*... *WE* WON!
YEAH!
WE DID IT, KIMIDORI. WE DID IT *TOGETHER*!

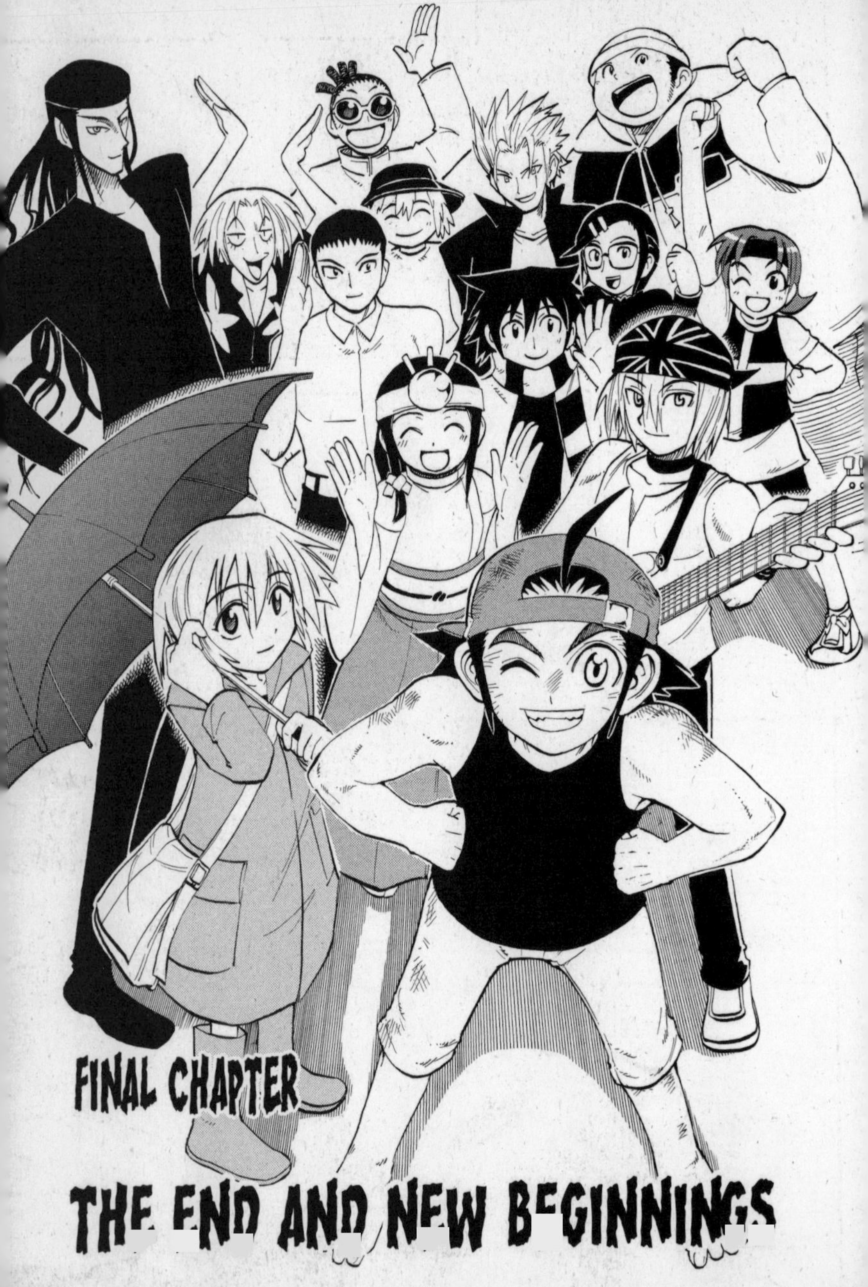
FINAL CHAPTER
THE END AND NEW BEGINNINGS

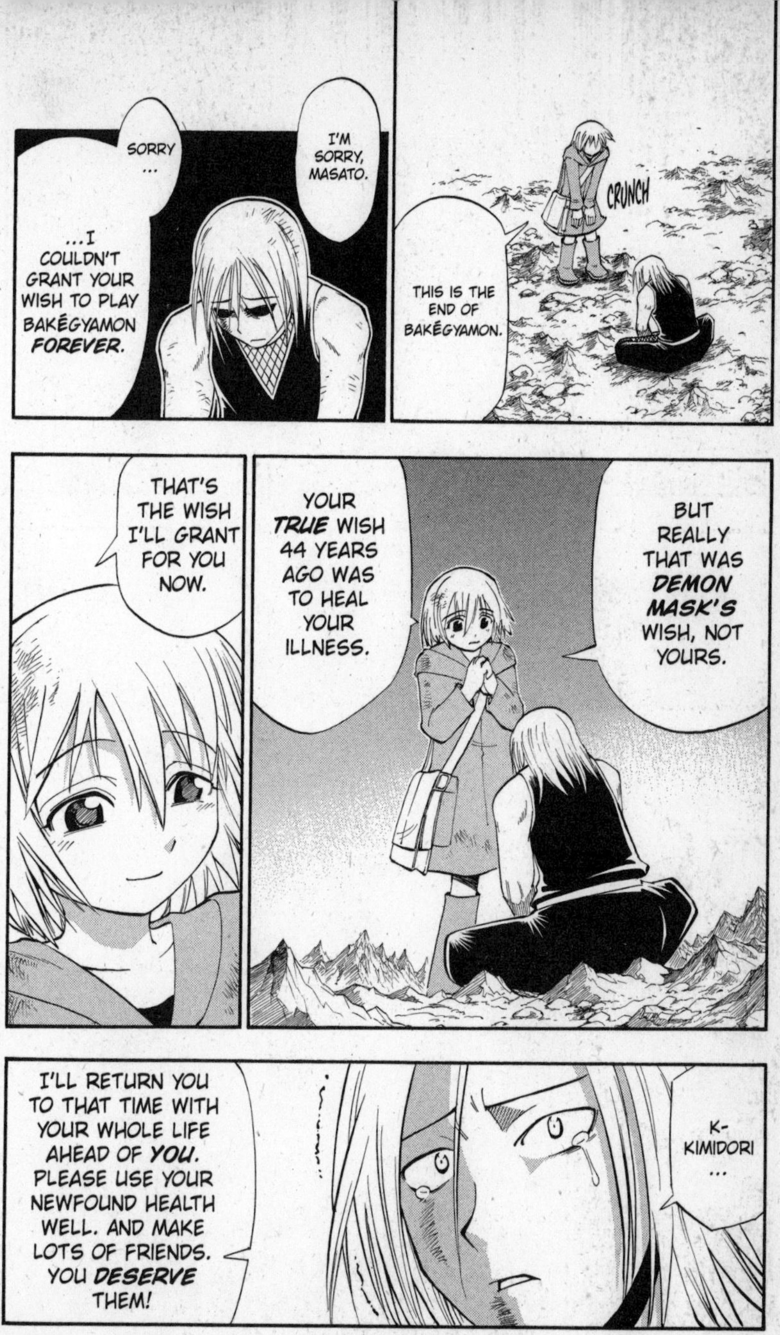
CRUNCH
THIS IS THE END OF BAKÉGYAMON.
I'M SORRY, MASATO.
SORRY ...
...I COULDN'T GRANT YOUR WISH TO PLAY BAKÉGYAMON *FOREVER*.
BUT REALLY THAT WAS *DEMON MASK'S* WISH, NOT YOURS.
YOUR *TRUE* WISH 44 YEARS AGO WAS TO HEAL YOUR ILLNESS.
THAT'S THE WISH I'LL GRANT FOR YOU NOW.
K-KIMIDORI ...
I'LL RETURN YOU TO THAT TIME WITH YOUR WHOLE LIFE AHEAD OF *YOU*. PLEASE USE YOUR NEWFOUND HEALTH WELL. AND MAKE LOTS OF FRIENDS. YOU *DESERVE* THEM!

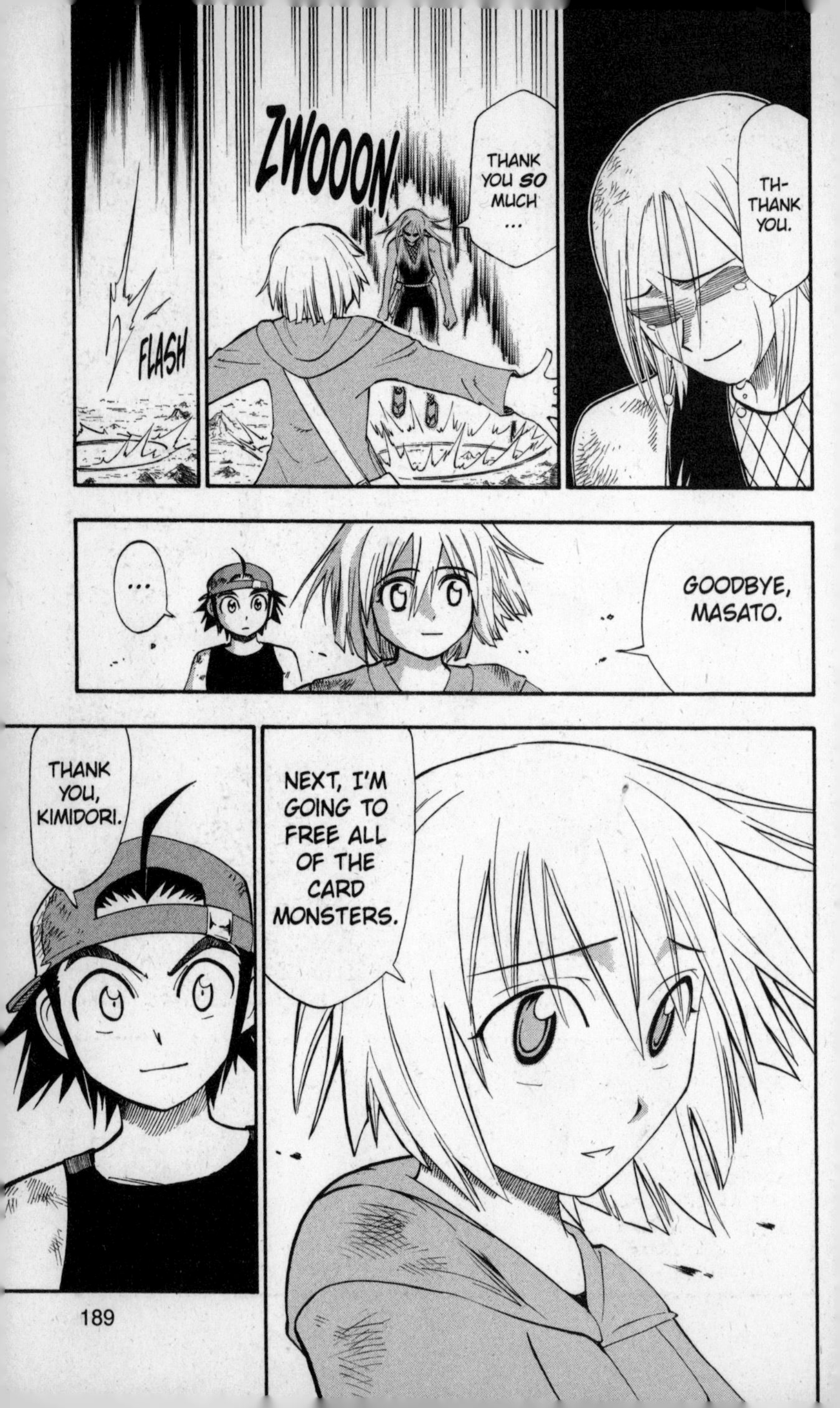
TH- THANK YOU.
THANK YOU SO MUCH ...
ZWOOON
FLASH
GOODBYE, MASATO.
...
NEXT, I'M GOING TO FREE ALL OF THE CARD MONSTERS.
THANK YOU, KIMIDORI.

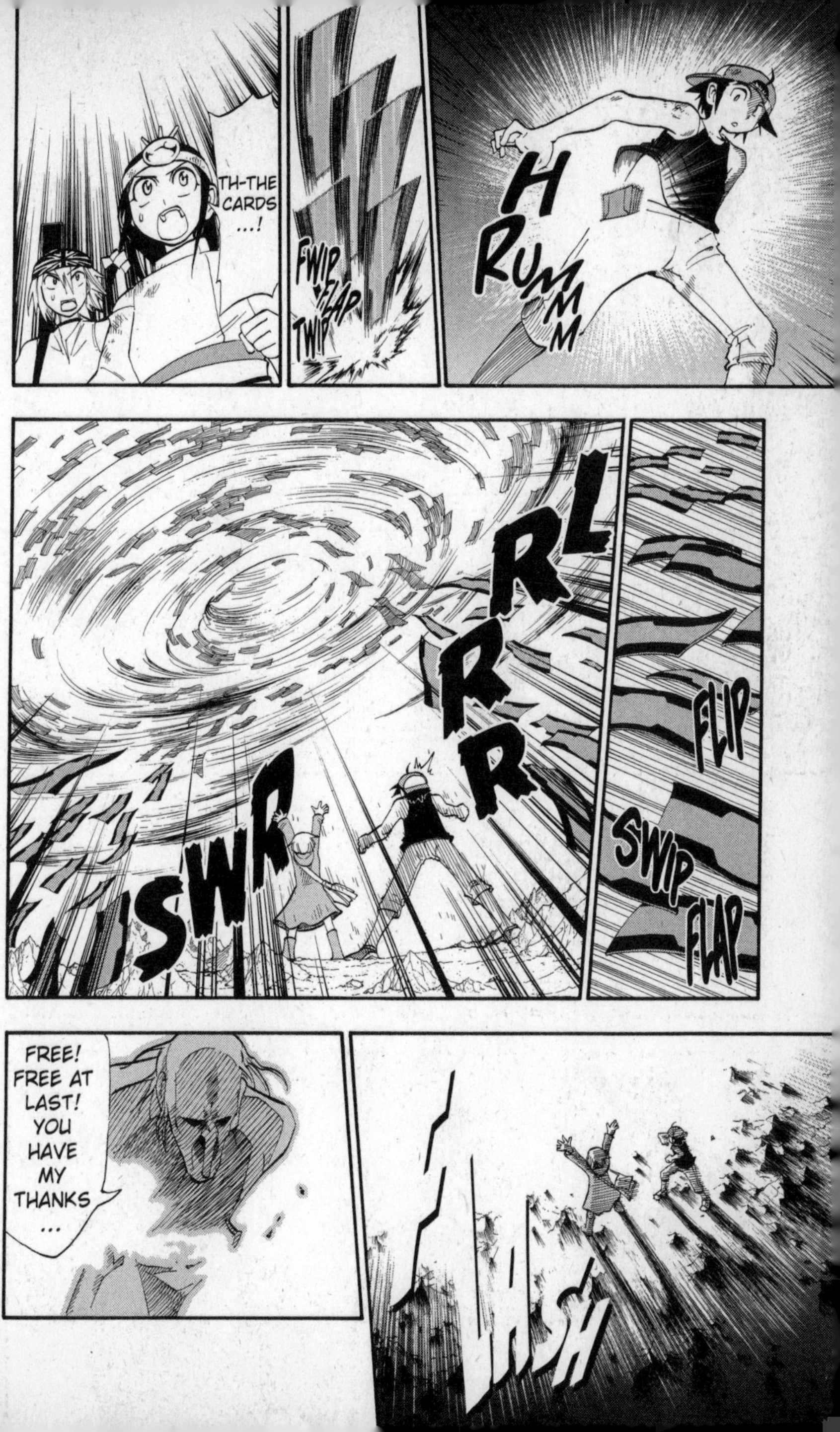
HRUMMM
FWIP FLAP TWIP
TH-THE CARDS ...!
FLIP
SWIP
FLAP
RRRL
SWR
FREE! FREE AT LAST! YOU HAVE MY THANKS ...

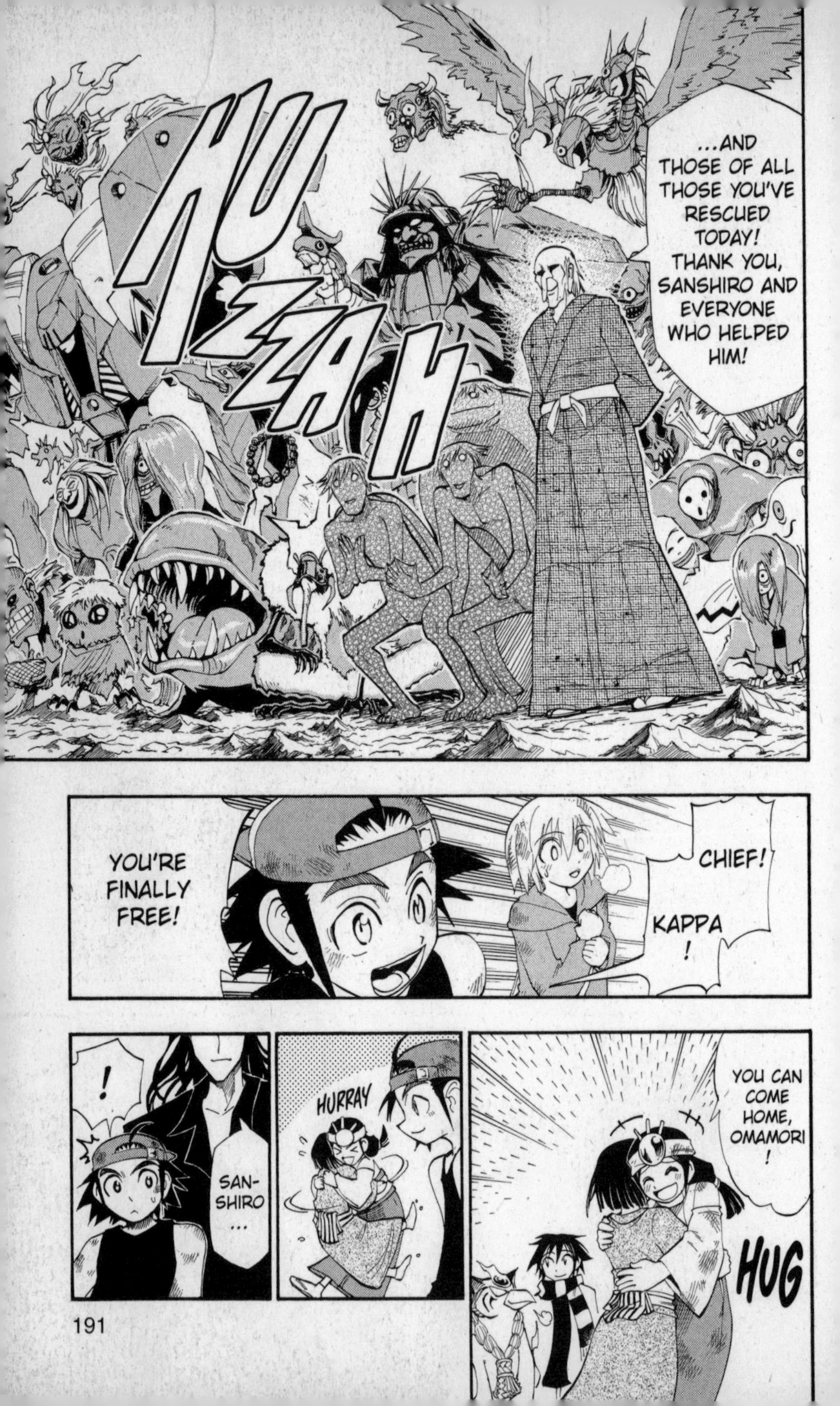
...AND THOSE OF ALL THOSE YOU'VE RESCUED TODAY! THANK YOU, SANSHIRO AND EVERYONE WHO HELPED HIM!
HUZZAH
CHIEF!
KAPPA!
YOU'RE FINALLY FREE!
YOU CAN COME HOME, OMAMORI!
HUG
HURRAY
!
SANSHIRO...

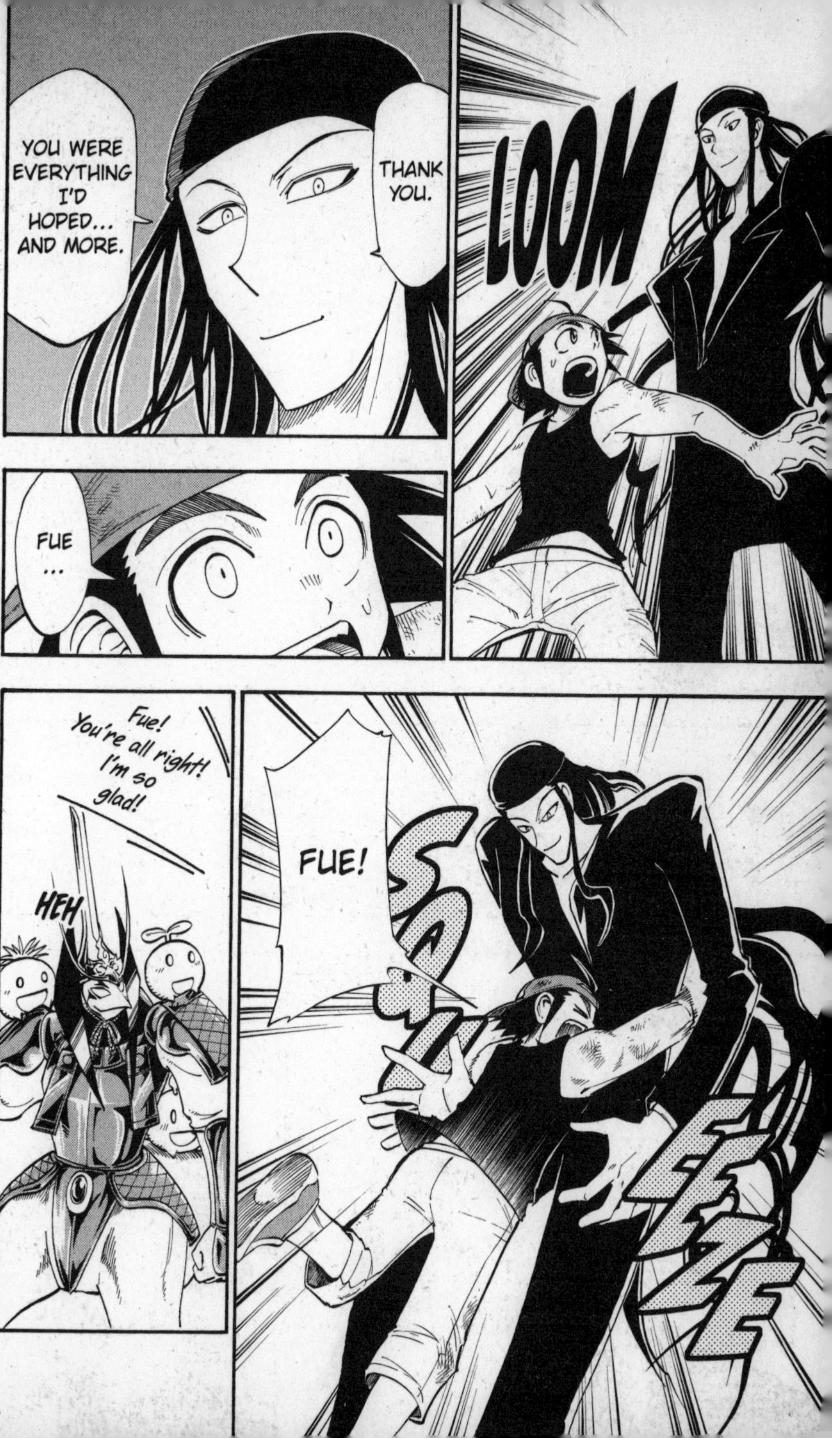
LOOM
THANK YOU.
YOU WERE EVERYTHING I'D HOPED... AND MORE.
FUE ...
FUE!
SQUEEZE
Fue! You're all right! I'm so glad!
HEH

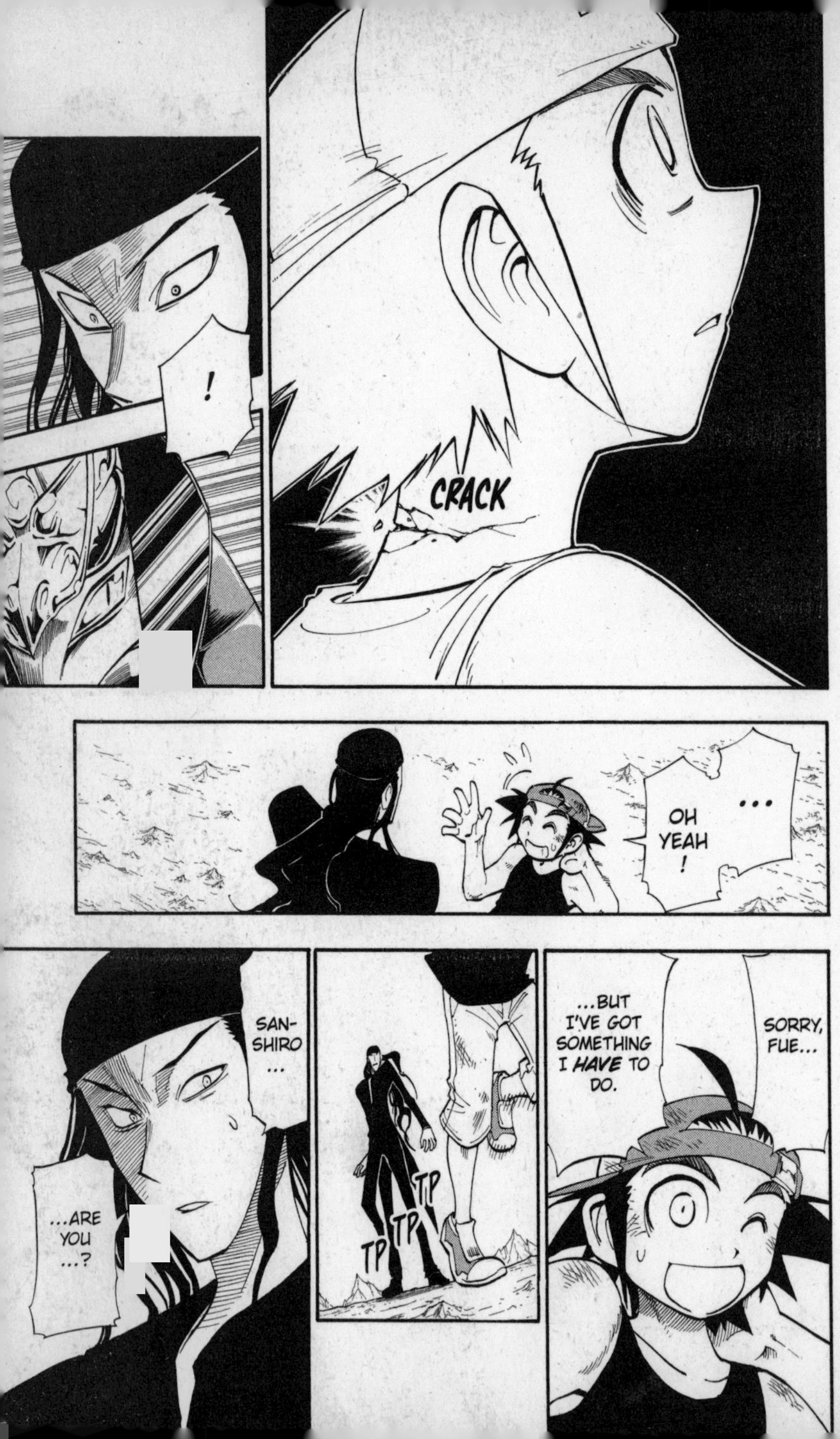
CRACK
!
... OH YEAH!
SORRY, FUE...
...BUT I'VE GOT SOMETHING I *HAVE* TO DO.
TP TP TP
SAN-SHIRO...
...ARE YOU ...?

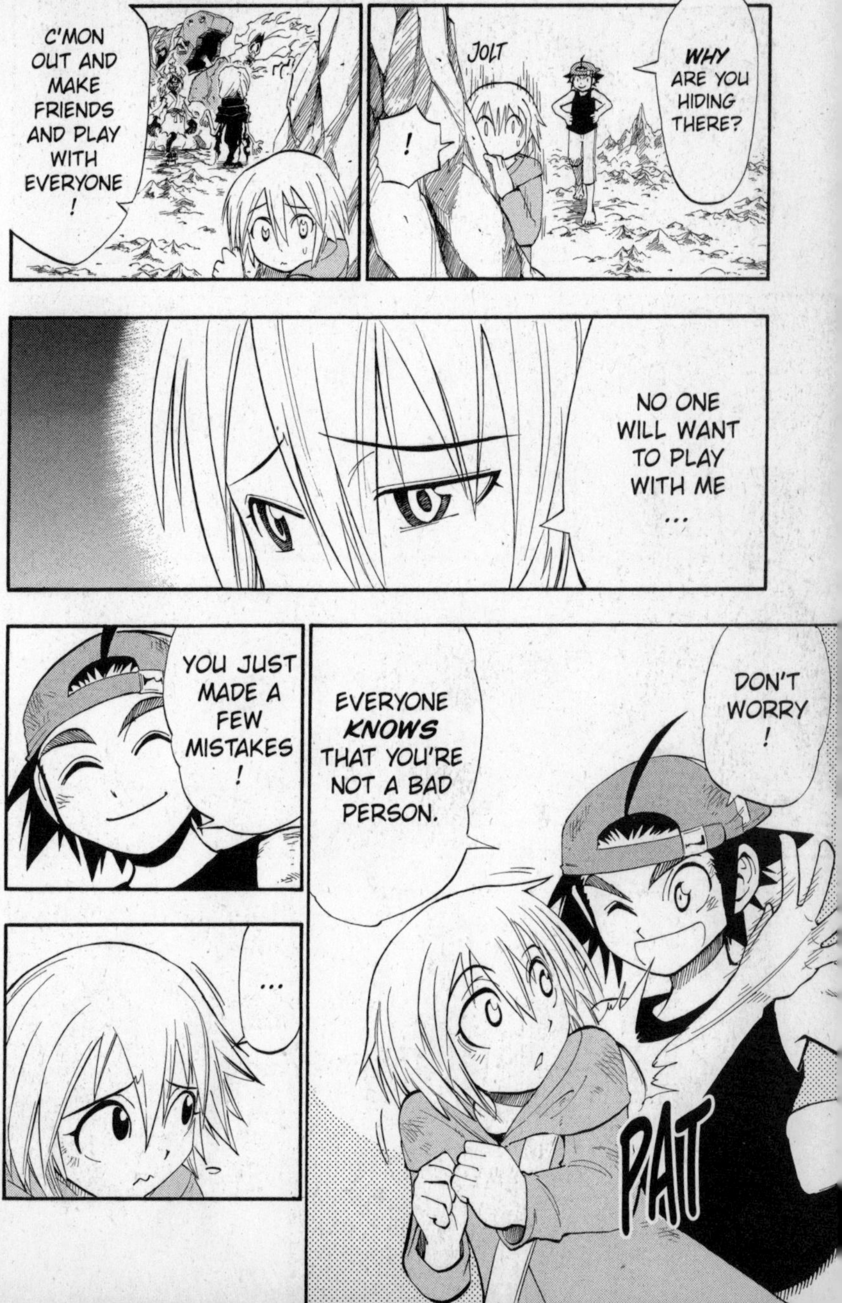
WHY ARE YOU HIDING THERE?
JOLT
!
C'MON OUT AND MAKE FRIENDS AND PLAY WITH EVERYONE!
NO ONE WILL WANT TO PLAY WITH ME...
DON'T WORRY!
EVERYONE KNOWS THAT YOU'RE NOT A BAD PERSON.
PAT
YOU JUST MADE A FEW MISTAKES!
...

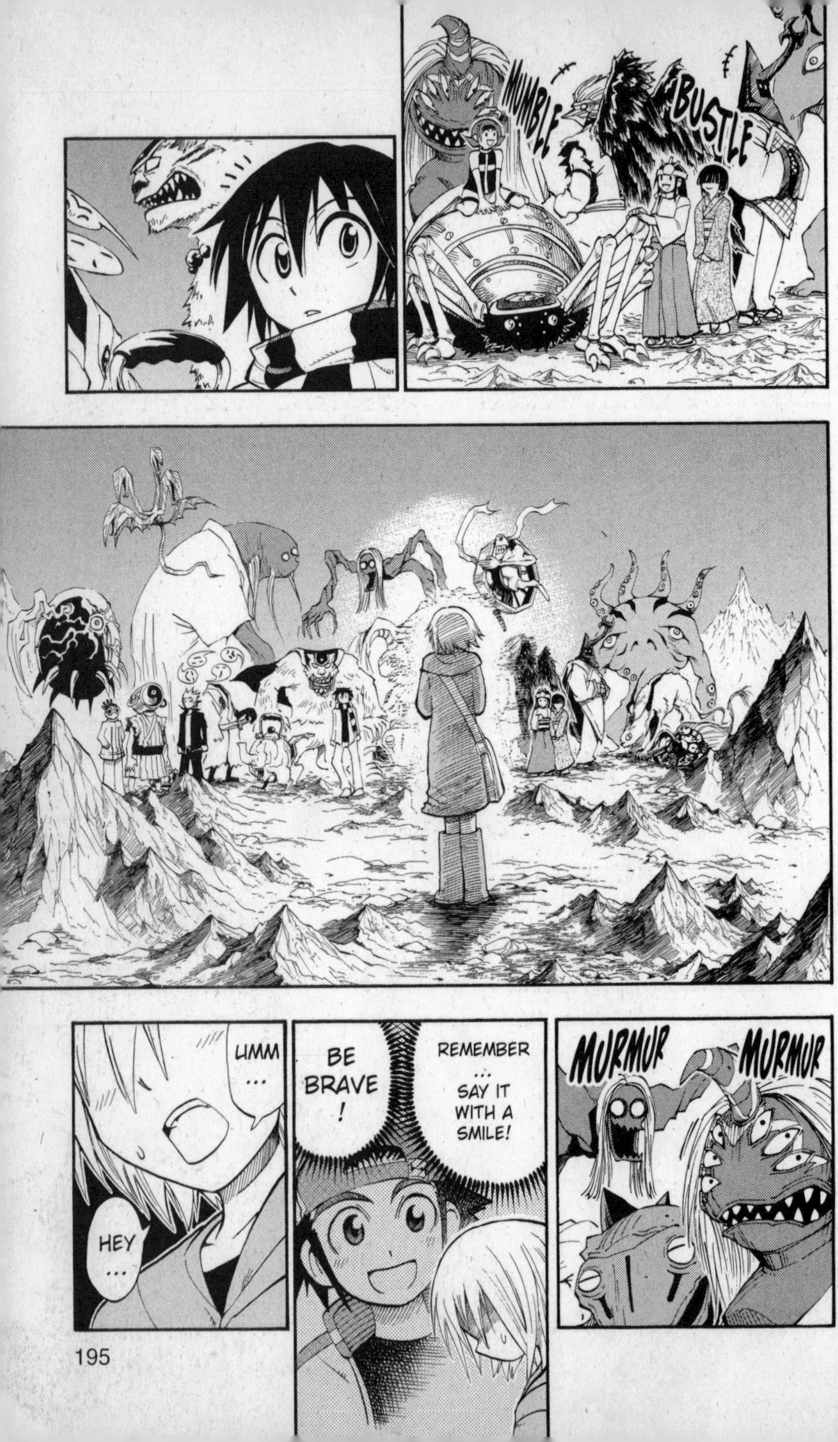
MUMBLE
BUSTLE
MURMUR
MURMUR
REMEMBER ... SAY IT WITH A SMILE!
BE BRAVE!
UMM ...
HEY ...

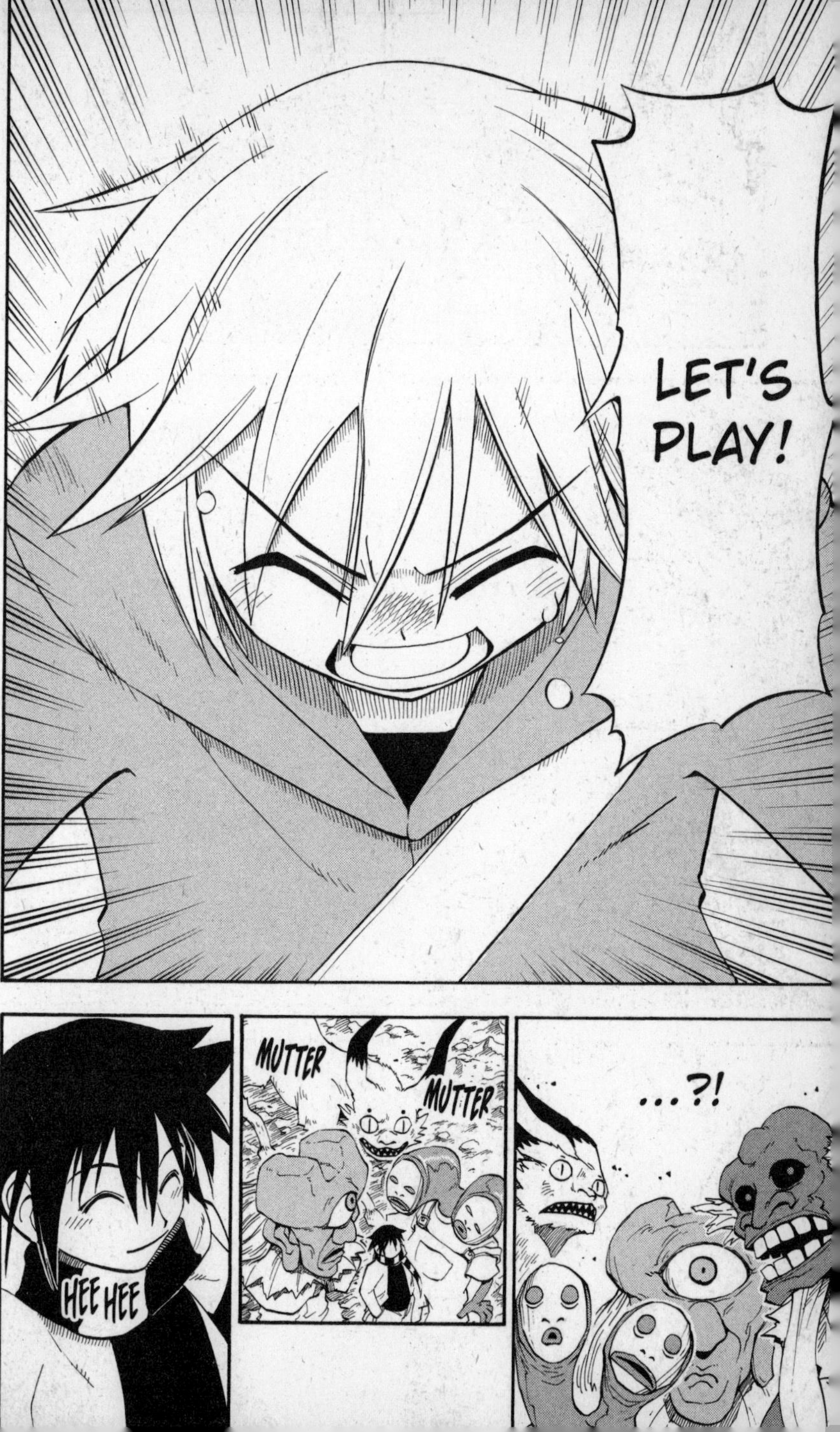
LET'S PLAY!
...?!
MUTTER
MUTTER
HEE HEE

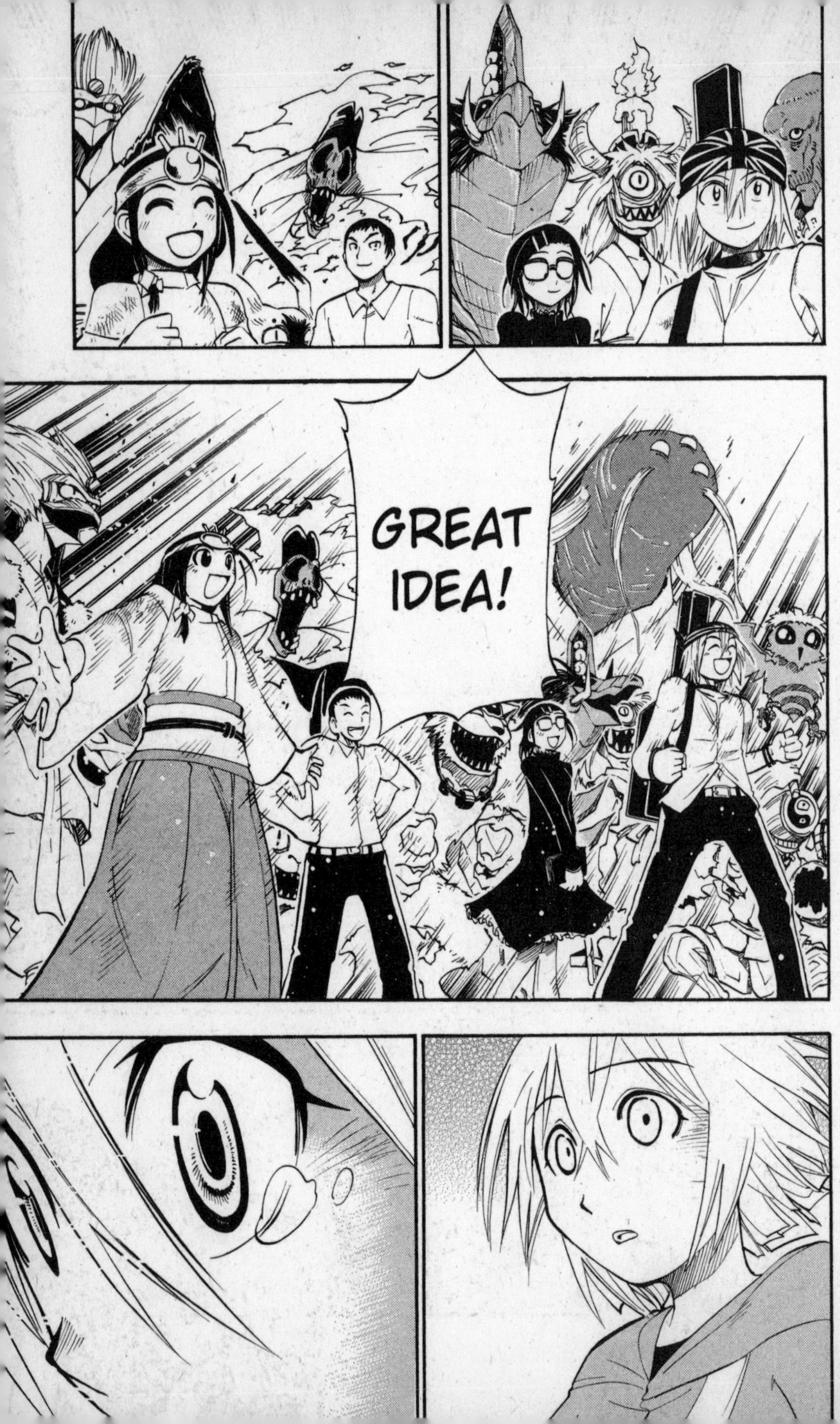
GREAT IDEA!

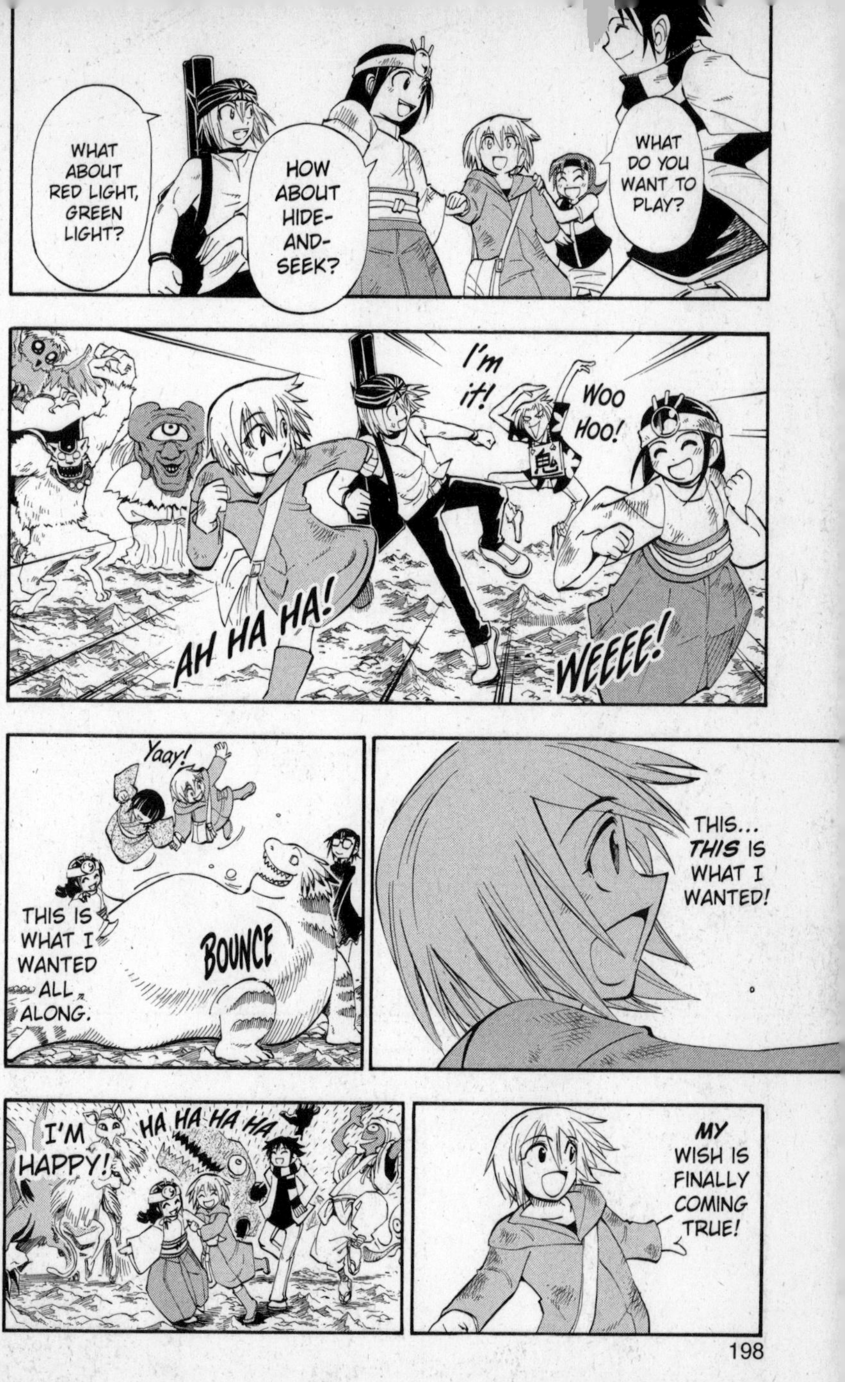
WHAT DO YOU WANT TO PLAY?
HOW ABOUT HIDE-AND-SEEK?
WHAT ABOUT RED LIGHT, GREEN LIGHT?
WOO HOO!
I'm it!
WEEEE!
AH HA HA!
THIS... THIS IS WHAT I WANTED!
Yaay!
THIS IS WHAT I WANTED ALL ALONG.
BOUNCE
MY WISH IS FINALLY COMING TRUE!
HA HA HA HA
I'M HAPPY!

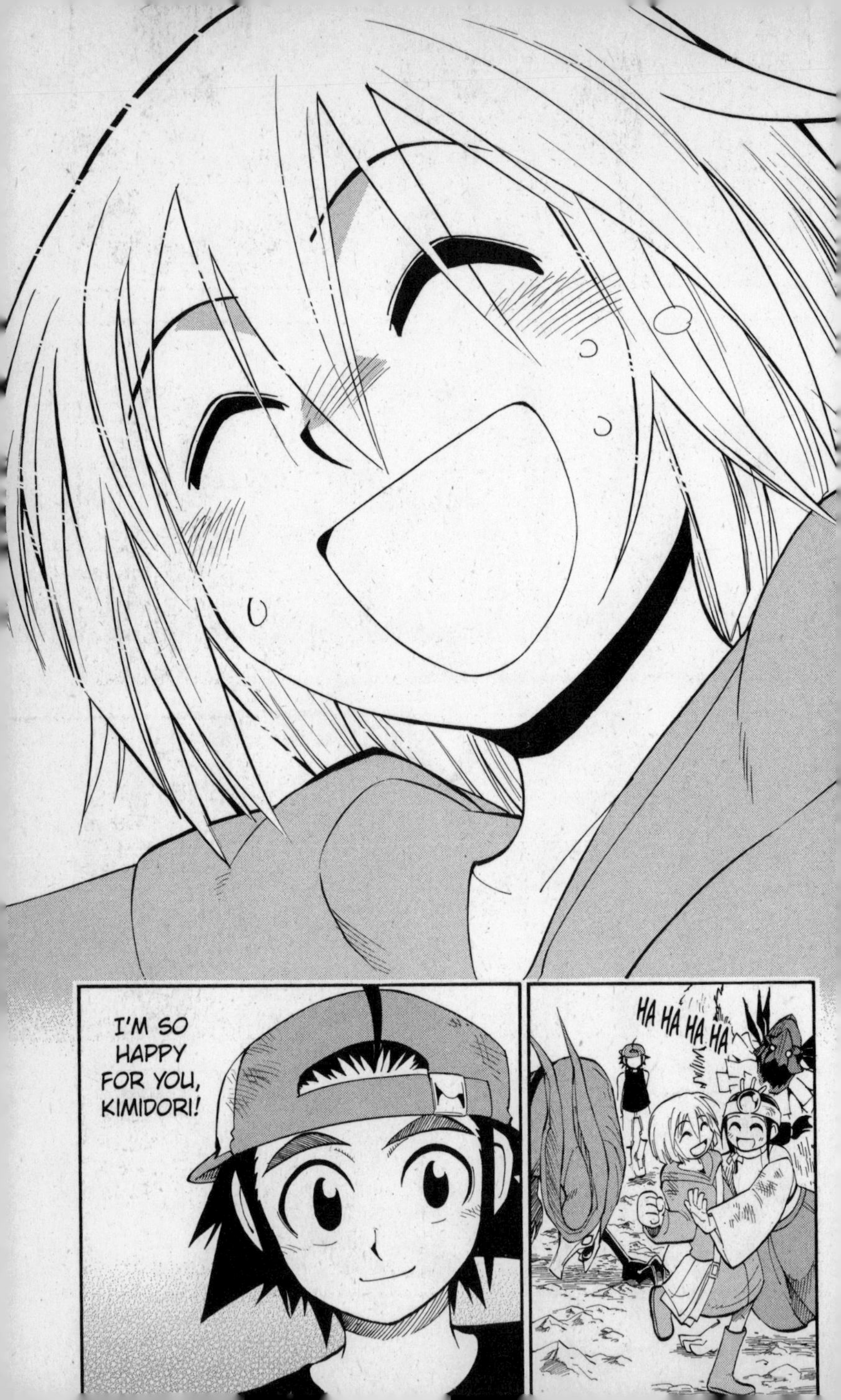
HA HA HA HA
I'M SO HAPPY FOR YOU, KIMIDORI!

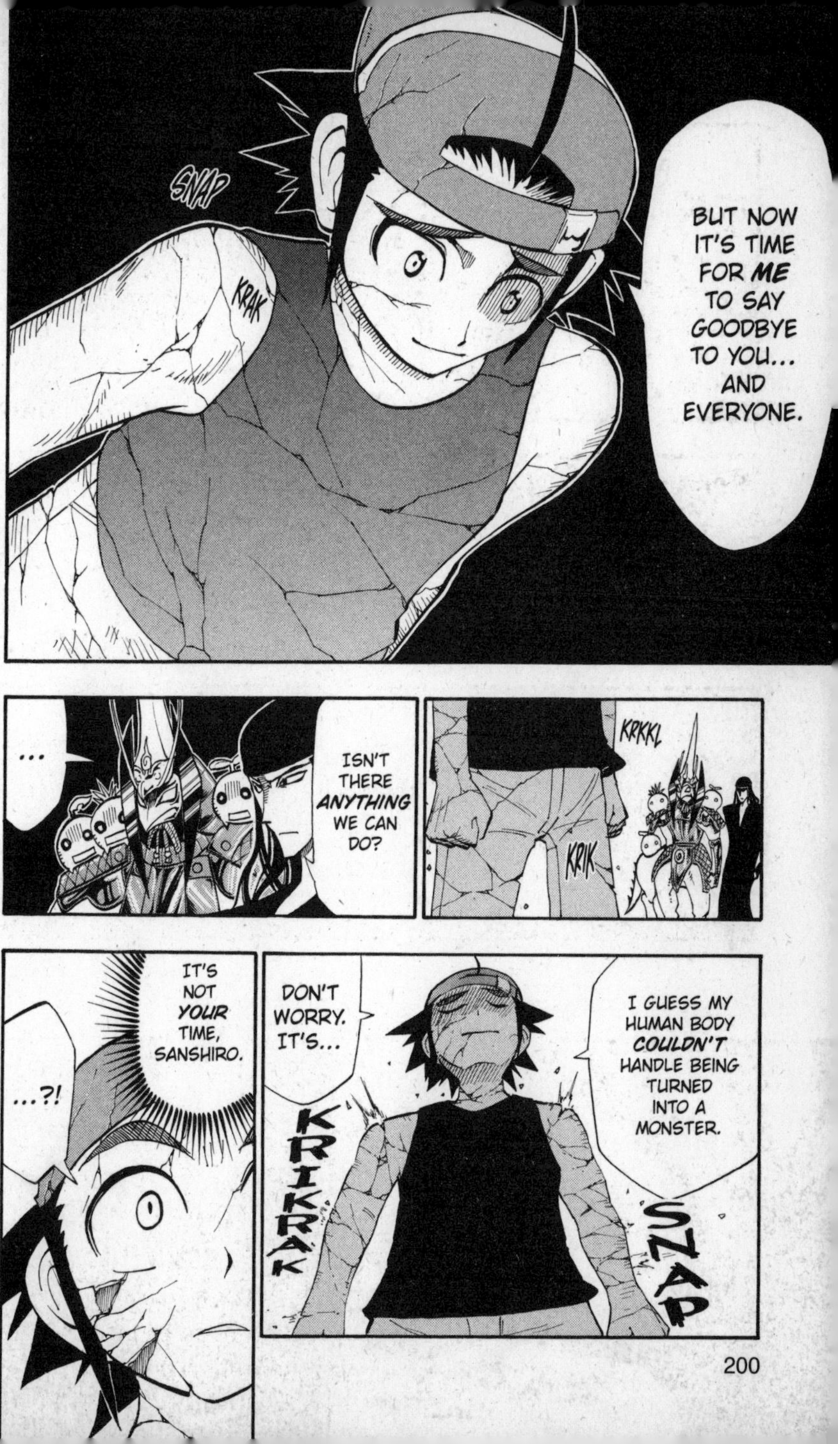
SNAP
KRAK
BUT NOW IT'S TIME FOR *ME* TO SAY GOODBYE TO YOU... AND EVERYONE.
KRKKL
KRIK
ISN'T THERE *ANYTHING* WE CAN DO?
...
I GUESS MY HUMAN BODY *COULDN'T* HANDLE BEING TURNED INTO A MONSTER.
DON'T WORRY. IT'S...
SNAP
KRIKKRAK
IT'S NOT *YOUR* TIME, SANSHIRO.
...?!

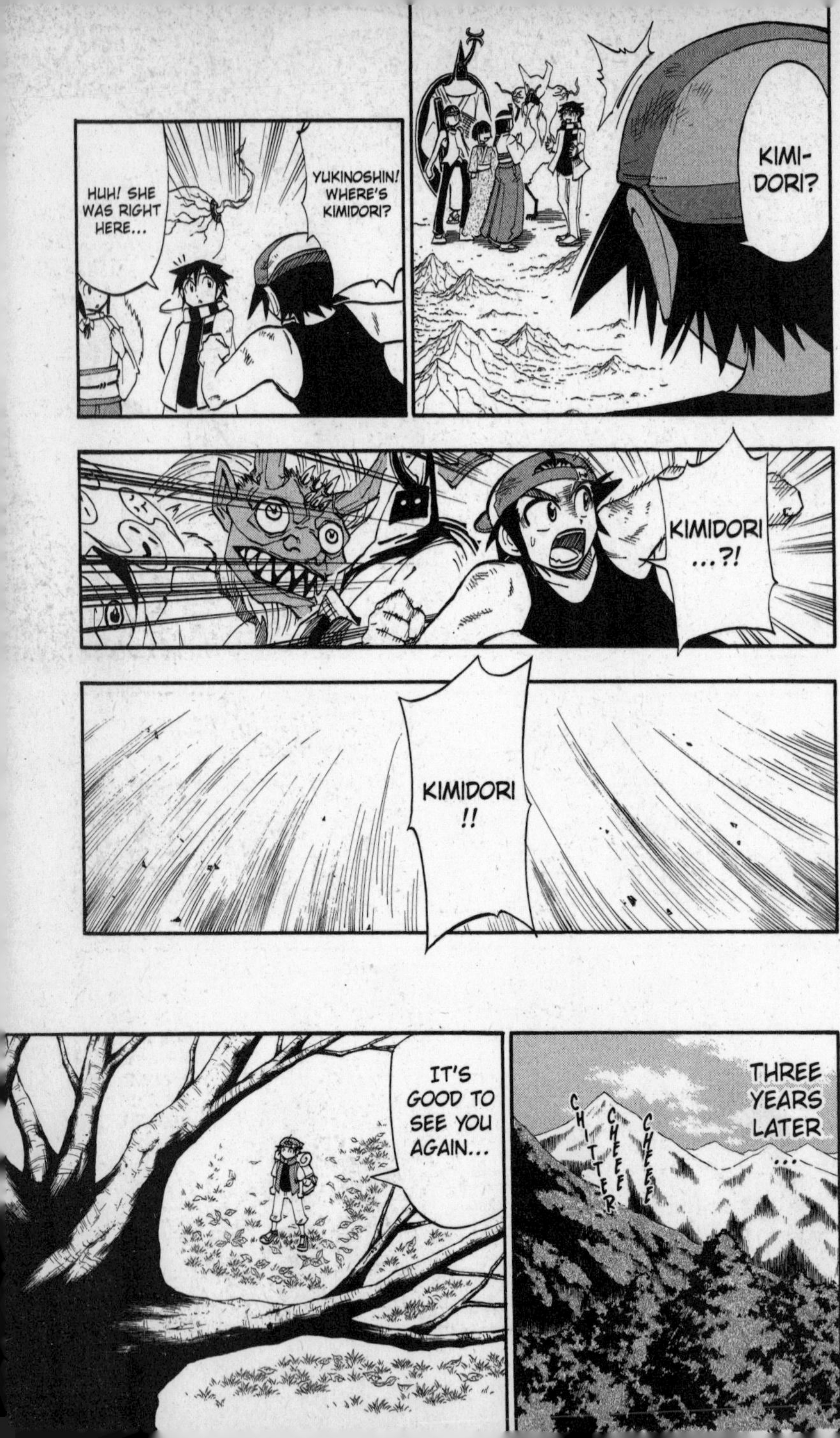
KIMI-
DORI?
YUKINOSHIN!
WHERE'S
KIMIDORI?
HUH! SHE
WAS RIGHT
HERE...
KIMIDORI
...?!
KIMIDORI
!!
THREE
YEARS
LATER
...
CHEEE
CHEEE
CHITTER
IT'S
GOOD TO
SEE YOU
AGAIN...

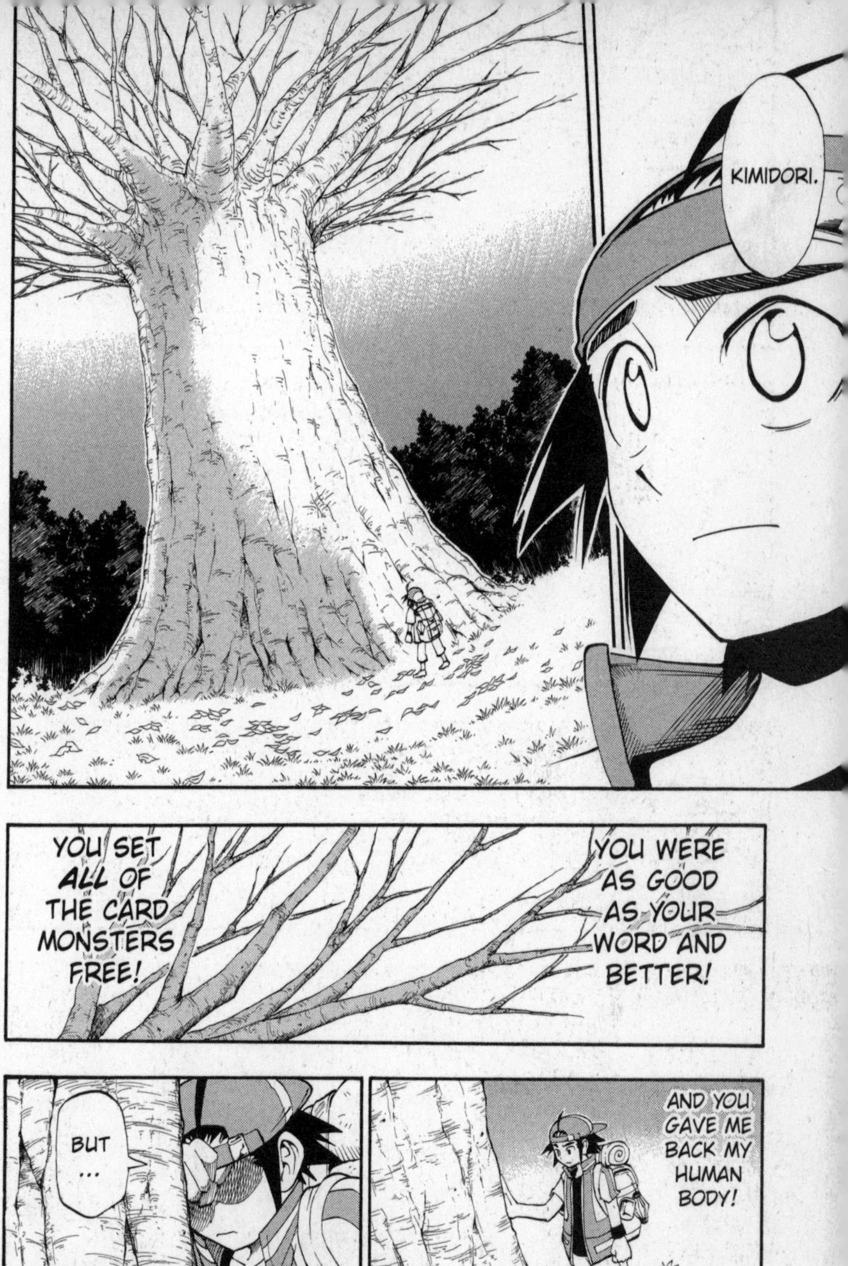
KIMIDORI.
YOU WERE AS GOOD AS YOUR WORD AND BETTER!
YOU SET ALL OF THE CARD MONSTERS FREE!
AND YOU GAVE ME BACK MY HUMAN BODY!
BUT ...

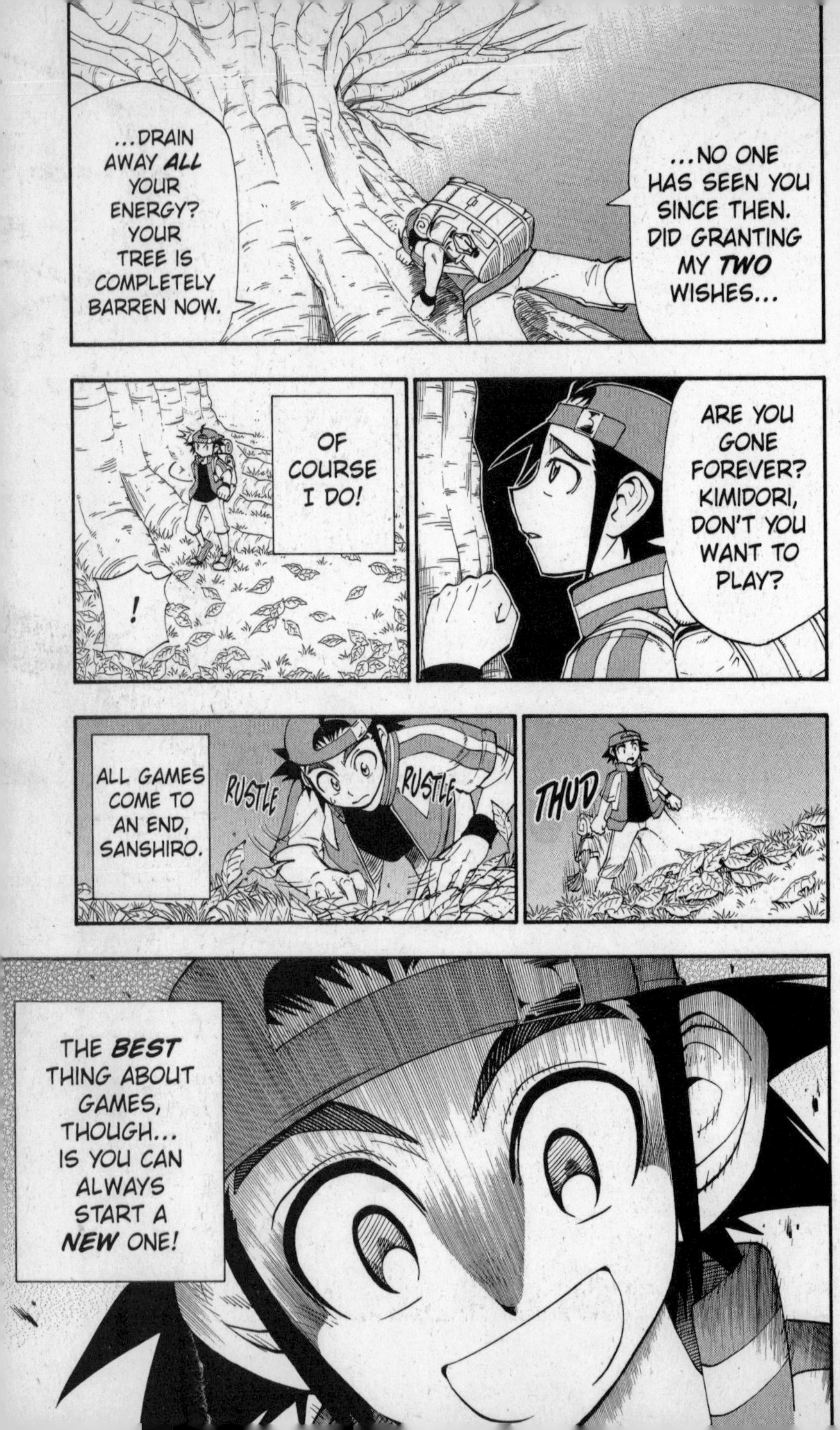
...NO ONE HAS SEEN YOU SINCE THEN. DID GRANTING MY TWO WISHES...
...DRAIN AWAY ALL YOUR ENERGY? YOUR TREE IS COMPLETELY BARREN NOW.
ARE YOU GONE FOREVER? KIMIDORI, DON'T YOU WANT TO PLAY?
OF COURSE I DO!
!
THUD
RUSTLE
RUSTLE
ALL GAMES COME TO AN END, SANSHIRO.
THE BEST THING ABOUT GAMES, THOUGH... IS YOU CAN ALWAYS START A NEW ONE!

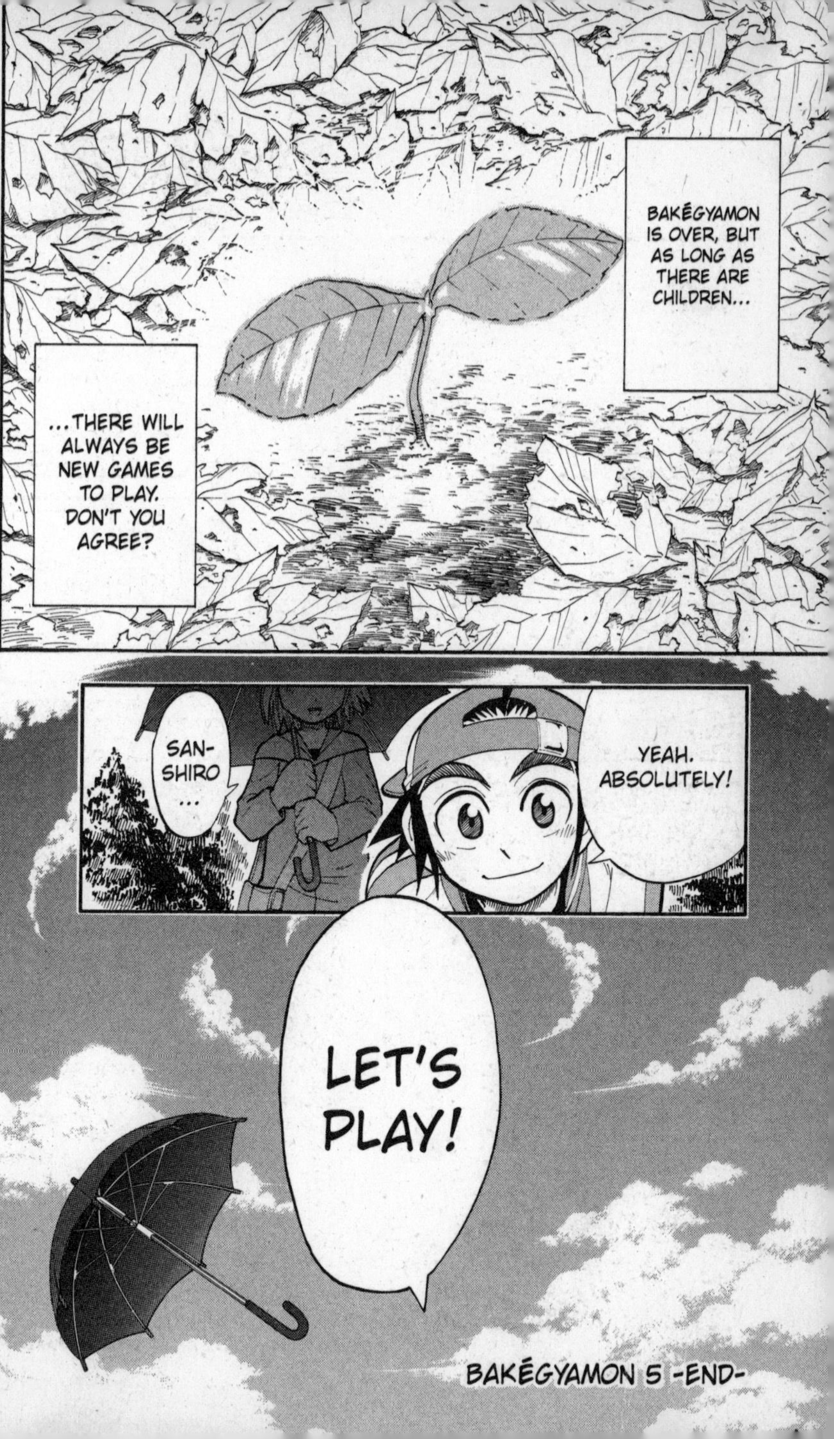
BAKÉGYAMON IS OVER, BUT AS LONG AS THERE ARE CHILDREN...
...THERE WILL ALWAYS BE NEW GAMES TO PLAY. DON'T YOU AGREE?
YEAH. ABSOLUTELY!
SAN-SHIRO ...
LET'S PLAY!
BAKÉGYAMON 5 -END-

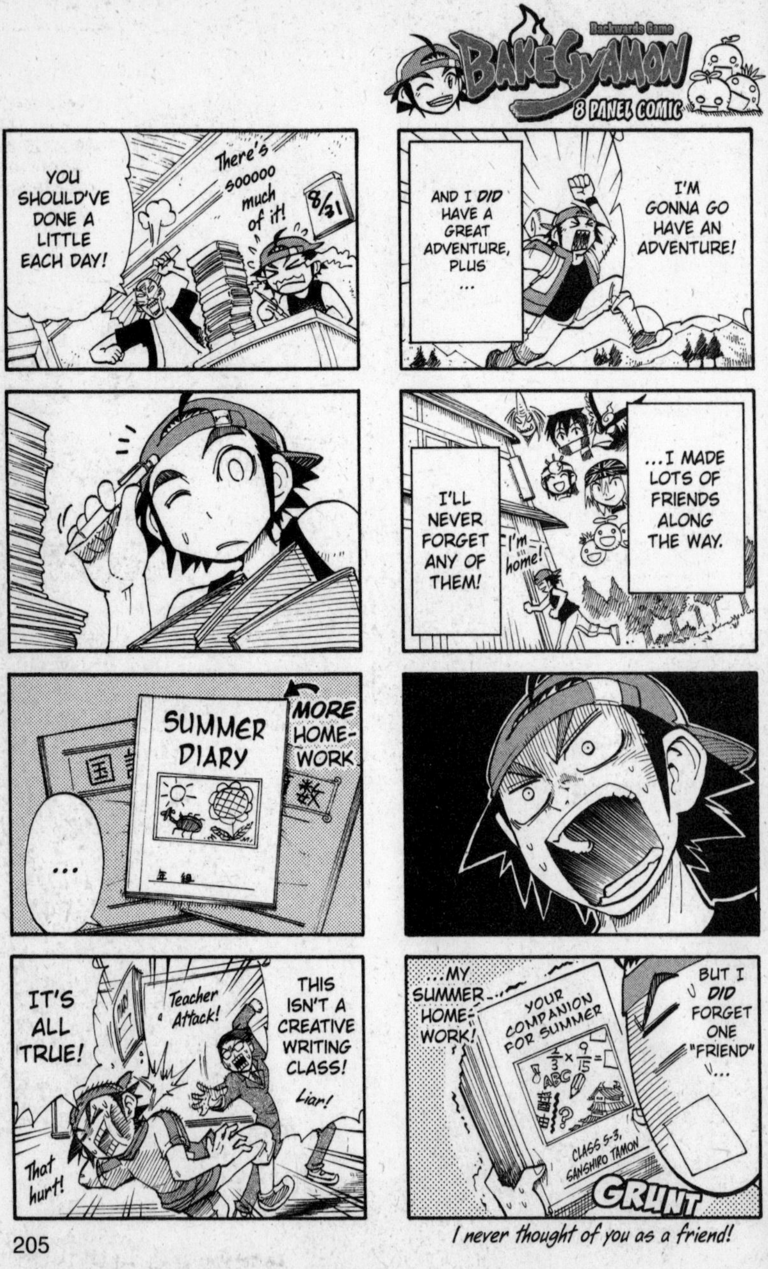
Backwards Game
BAKEGYAMON
8 PANEL COMIC
I'M GONNA GO HAVE AN ADVENTURE!
AND I DID HAVE A GREAT ADVENTURE, PLUS ...
...I MADE LOTS OF FRIENDS ALONG THE WAY.
I'm home!
I'LL NEVER FORGET ANY OF THEM!
BUT I DID FORGET ONE "FRIEND"...
...MY SUMMER HOMEWORK!
YOUR COMPANION FOR SUMMER
CLASS 5-3, SANSHIRO TAMON
GRUNT
There's sooooo much of it!
8/31
YOU SHOULD'VE DONE A LITTLE EACH DAY!
MORE HOME-WORK
SUMMER DIARY
...
THIS ISN'T A CREATIVE WRITING CLASS!
Teacher Attack!
Liar!
IT'S ALL TRUE!
That hurt!

I never thought of you as a friend!

BAKÉGYAMON DIARY 1 DRAWING THE FINAL CHAPTER

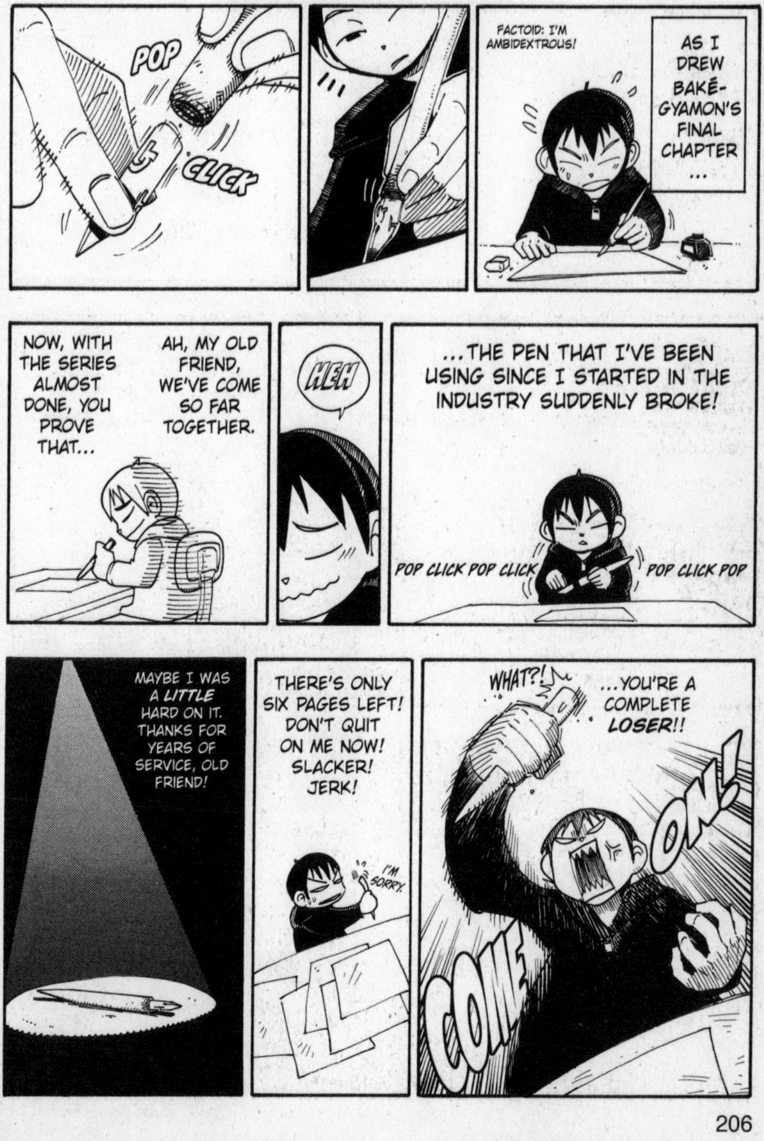
AS I DREW BAKÉ-GYAMON'S FINAL CHAPTER...
FACTOID: I'M AMBIDEXTROUS!
POP
CLICK
...THE PEN THAT I'VE BEEN USING SINCE I STARTED IN THE INDUSTRY SUDDENLY BROKE!
POP CLICK POP
POP CLICK POP CLICK
HEH
AH, MY OLD FRIEND, WE'VE COME SO FAR TOGETHER.
NOW, WITH THE SERIES ALMOST DONE, YOU PROVE THAT...
WHAT?!
...YOU'RE A COMPLETE LOSER!!
COME ON!
THERE'S ONLY SIX PAGES LEFT! DON'T QUIT ON ME NOW! SLACKER! JERK!
I'M SORRY.
MAYBE I WAS A LITTLE HARD ON IT. THANKS FOR YEARS OF SERVICE, OLD FRIEND!

BAKÉGYAMON DIARY 2 POSTSCRIPT

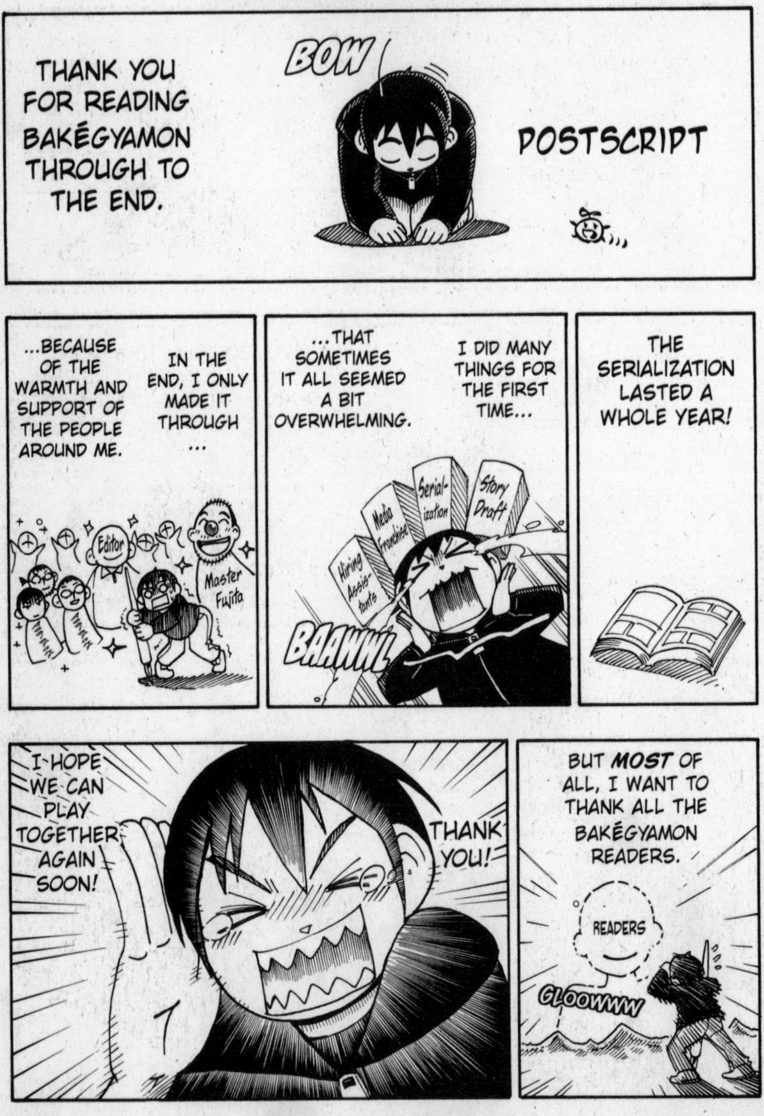
BOW
POSTSCRIPT
THANK YOU FOR READING BAKÉGYAMON THROUGH TO THE END.
THE SERIALIZATION LASTED A WHOLE YEAR!
I DID MANY THINGS FOR THE FIRST TIME...
...THAT SOMETIMES IT ALL SEEMED A BIT OVERWHELMING.
Story Draft
Serial-ization
Media Franchise
Hiring Assis-tants
BAAWWL
IN THE END, I ONLY MADE IT THROUGH ...
...BECAUSE OF THE WARMTH AND SUPPORT OF THE PEOPLE AROUND ME.
Editor
Master Fujita
BUT MOST OF ALL, I WANT TO THANK ALL THE BAKÉGYAMON READERS.
READERS
GLOOWWW
THANK YOU!
I HOPE WE CAN PLAY TOGETHER AGAIN SOON!

Backwards Game
BAKÉGYAMON
SHORT COMIC

ARE YOU GONE FOREVER, KIMIDORI?
OF COURSE NOT!
COULD IT BE...?
SCRABBLE
SCRAPE
!
IS THIS...
...THE NEW...
...KIMI-DORI?!
SPROUT
PWA!
WHAT THE ...?!
DORO-KOZO?!
END

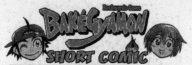

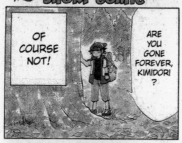

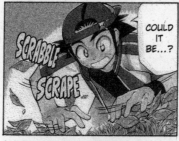

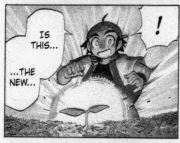

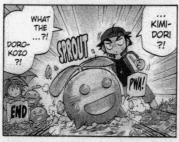

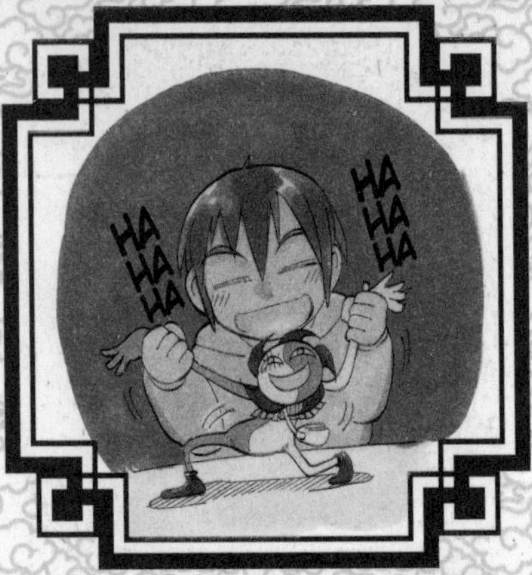
HA HA HA
HA HA HA

Playing games is so much fun! There's no such thing as playing too much! I hope you all had fun with Sanshiro, Kimidori and all the others in this mysterious game BakéGyamon!

-Mitsuhisa Tamura, 2007

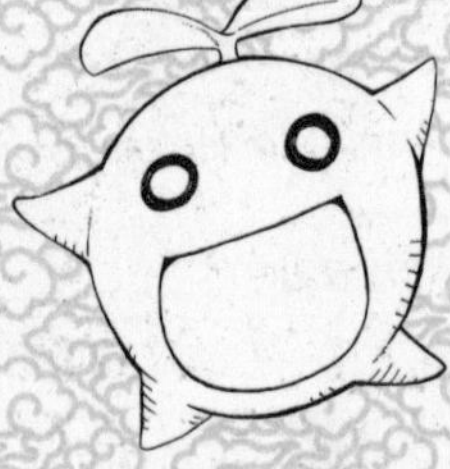

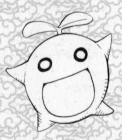

Mitsuhisa Tamura debuted in 2004 with "Comical Magical," a one-shot manga in *Shonen Sunday R*. *BakéGyamon* is his first serialized manga. His favorite foods are cutlet curry and chocolate snacks.

BakéGyamon Vol. 5
Backwards Game

VIZ Kids Edition

STORY AND ART BY MITSUHISA TAMURA
Original Concept by Kazuhiro Fujita

Translation/Labaaman, HC Language Solutions, Inc.
English Adaptation/Stan!
Touch-up Art & Lettering/Primary Graphix
Design/Sean Lee
Editor/Alexis Kirsch

VP, Production/Alvin Lu
VP, Publishing Licensing/Rika Inouye
VP, Sales & Product Marketing/Gonzalo Ferreyra
VP, Creative/Linda Espinosa
Publisher/Hyoe Narita

BAKEGYAMON 5 by Mitsuhisa TAMURA, Kazuhiro FUJITA
© 2007 Mitsuhisa TAMURA, Kazuhiro FUJITA
All rights reserved. Original Japanese edition published in 2007
by Shogakukan Inc., Tokyo.

Printed in the U.S.A.

Published by VIZ Media, LLC
P.O. Box 77010
San Francisco, CA 94107

10 9 8 7 6 5 4 3 2 1
First printing, December 2009

www.viz.com

PARENTAL ADVISORY
BAKÉGYAMON is rated
A and is suitable for
readers of all ages.
ratings.viz.com

www.vizkids.com

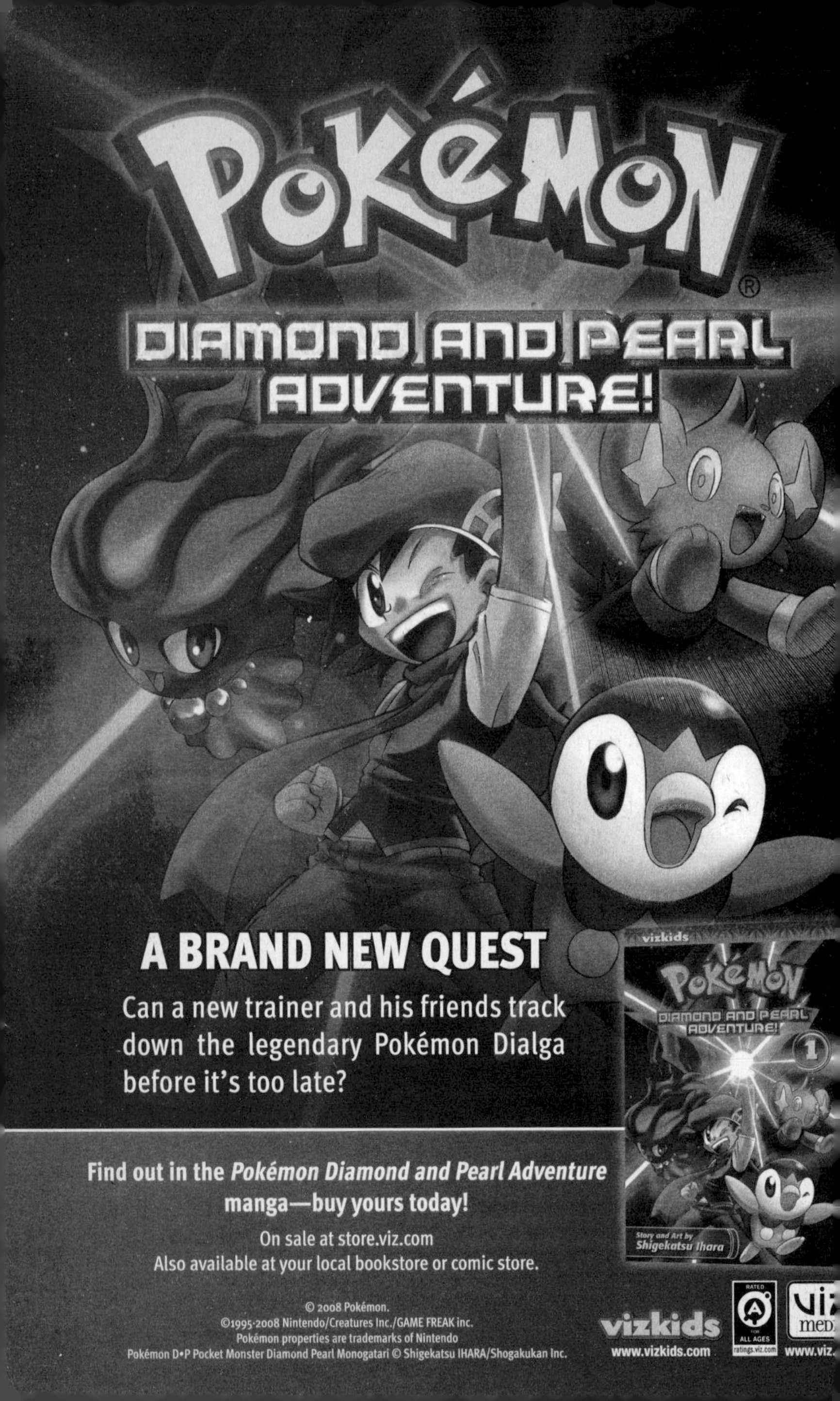
POKÉMON®
DIAMOND AND PEARL ADVENTURE!
A BRAND NEW QUEST
Can a new trainer and his friends track down the legendary Pokémon Dialga before it's too late?
Find out in the Pokémon Diamond and Pearl Adventure manga—buy yours today!
On sale at store.viz.com
Also available at your local bookstore or comic store.
vizkids
POKÉMON
DIAMOND AND PEARL ADVENTURE!
1
Story and Art by
Shigekatsu Ihara
© 2008 Pokémon.
©1995-2008 Nintendo/Creatures Inc./GAME FREAK inc.
Pokémon properties are trademarks of Nintendo
Pokémon D•P Pocket Monster Diamond Pearl Monogatari © Shigekatsu IHARA/Shogakukan Inc.
vizkids
www.vizkids.com
RATED
A
FOR
ALL AGES
ratings.viz.com
www.viz

COWA!

WHO'S GOT THE CURE FOR THE MONSTER FLU?

From **AKIRA TORIYAMA**, creator of
Dragon Ball, *Dr. Slump*, and *Sand Land*

STORY & ART BY **AKIRA TORIYAMA**

MANGA SERIES ON SALE NOW